INIQUITIES

Book 1

The Last Dance

INIQUITIES TRILOGY

Book 1

The Last Dance

Carolyn McCrae

Matador
9 De Montfort Mews
Leicester LE1 7FW, UK
Tel: (+44) 116 255 9311 / 9312
Email: books@troubador.co.uk
Web: www.troubador.co.uk/matador

ISBN
Paperback: 1 905237 73 1
Hardback: 1 905237 93 6

Typeset in 11pt Stempel Garamond by Troubador Publishing Ltd, Leicester, UK
Printed in the UK by The Cromwell Press Ltd, Trowbridge, Wilts, UK

Matador is an imprint of Troubador Publishing Ltd

I would like to acknowledge all the help and encouragement in all things that I have received over the years from my husband Colin.

Thanks are also due to Mrs Jane Martin of Ticehurst and Mrs Dulcie Stevens of Leigh for reading the early drafts of *The Last Dance* and for their comments, criticisms and enthusiasm.

Iniquity

The word has two meanings according to the *Shorter Oxford Dictionary*:

1. Immoral, unrighteous or harmful action or conduct; gross injustice, wickedness, sin.

2. Inequality, inequity, unfairness. (obsolete).

Something by Way of Explanation

In October 1941 Max Fischer made his first English will.

As a junior clerk at Messrs Roberts and Jones Solicitors I was present only to take notes and fetch paperwork, but I did know the contents.

In that first will Major Maximilian Fischer of Millcourt, Hoylake, Cheshire, left all his property to his wife Elizabeth and daughter Veronica, living at the same address; apart from a substantial bequest to his niece, Rebecca Rebmann, current address unknown.

The names meant nothing to me.

It was a very simple will, but I remember thinking how odd it was that he had so much to leave when he had only been in the country such a short time.

It seemed a strange time to have a man like Major Fischer purchase Roberts and Jones from the elderly gentlemen who had founded it before the Great War. Old Mr Jones told us all in his final staff meeting that Major Fischer had come recently from Austria and we were to make him feel welcome and help him in every way. The new owner seemed respectable enough, his completely white hair lending him a look of age and experience although he could only have been in his mid 30s. It was his hands that I noticed particularly when I first saw him, they were very large, more like a farmer's than a lawyer's.

We all knew that change was inevitable with the War and the old boys retiring, but we did not understand how they could sell to such a man. I can't say there weren't bad feelings about him because there were. We knew he had come from Europe but there was talk that he was Jewish, and Jews were not popular at that time. People didn't speak their prejudices - it wasn't done - but they felt them all the same.

We had all seen the newsreels of penniless refugees coming into the country from 'the East' and there was a lot of bad feeling. But this man was not one of those. How he obtained his English legal qualifications or had so much property and money available to him no one in the office ever knew. All through the war, even in the dark days after the Dutch fell, he was never interned nor his movements restricted in any way.

It would have had something to do with the times he was away from the office. He was often absent for weeks at a time – never saying where he was going or when he would be back. We young clerks had a great time imagining all sorts of 'Boys Own' adventures and had decided that he was an agent, spying for us in Germany.

At the time Major Fischer bought the firm I had worked there for five years. I had been a sickly boy and my options of a career were limited so I considered myself lucky to have obtained a position in such a respectable local firm. It was my duty to look after my mother, my father had been gassed in the Great War and eventually succumbed to influenza just after I was born. When the war came I had been pronounced unfit for service so I was able to take advantage and develop my career in the absence of many men senior to me, including Arnold Donaldson, who were called up to the Forces.

On the day 35 years later, when that will of 1941 was finally replaced, I was the Senior Partner of the firm that still retained the name 'Roberts and Jones'.

The value of Max's estate had, unsurprisingly, increased substantially in the intervening years. But there were other differences. In this last will I knew every one of the people he named yet I did no more than raise an eyebrow as I noted the details, had the will drawn up and watched him as he signed the document that reflected the changes in so many lives.

In that second will Sir Max Fischer left no money or property to any family. His wife and daughter were both dead and, as far as I knew, Rebecca Rebmann had never been heard of, no doubt lost in the mists of the war.

Unsurprisingly he left all his books and papers to Carl Witherby. I hoped I would be around to discover what those hand-written journals had to say about Max's life. There were so many secrets and I knew he would never willingly allow them to be read in his lifetime. Carl was an historian who would make best use of them.

Most of his capital was divided between Charles and Monika – enough to keep them both in considerable comfort for the rest of their lives. He did not leave them Sandhey, their home for many years, that went to Charles' sister, Susannah.

The row of terraced houses, where many of the Parry family still lived, he left to Susannah's children. I felt this rather mischievous.

Early in my career I had been told by one of the older clerks 'If you want to know anyone's secrets just look at their will'. It seemed amazing to me then, and it still does now, that documents, matters of public record, can divulge so much about people – all you have to do is know what they own and who they want to have the benefit of it when they are dead. 'Each will has a story to tell.' I was told. But they can also beg many questions and leave many unanswered 'ifs', 'whys' and 'maybes', simplifying to the point of inaccuracy.

And perhaps some of the stories should remain untold, some of the questions raised should be left unanswered. Knowledge may be power but the other cliché 'truth will hurt' is equally valid.

In those years between the writing of his wills Max had become closely involved in the lives of Arnold Donaldson, his wives Alicia and Kathleen and their children who he had always helped in whatever ways possible; even though he was unable to prevent all the great damage caused by their parents.

Charles, Carl and Susannah have had some of the answers to their many questions but they deserve to know the whole story. Their children also need to know why they had to live out their childhood in such an unconventional way. I hope in reading these pages they will understand more of what lies behind those brief and unsatisfactory answers that have been given to them through the years. They all need to understand why such mistakes came about and not judge too harshly the people who made them.

So here is the story of the Donaldson family. The family I know so well, the family I was so close to at times but the family of which, despite everything, I could never be a part.

I accept that my role has not been just the innocent chronicler. Inexcusably, many times, I have crossed the boundary between family solicitor and friend. As their solicitor it should have been my role to show them the unobtrusive deference to requests and the unassuming pleasantness in the face of difficulties I trust I have shown to my firm's other clients and senior staff.

Instead it has been my role to be involved more closely, to listen to their confidences, to know details of their lives as no other did.

But I haven't just listened and observed. I have frequently betrayed their confidence. I have changed the courses of their lives by errors of omission and commission. As I look back over the years there are so many times I should have done or said things I didn't, and other times when I acted or spoke unwisely.

My wish is that these pages will enable them to understand the actions of their parents, but, selfishly, I also need them to understand why I did what I did.

Do not judge us too harshly for things we could not know.

Ted Mottram
Hoylake
1998

Chapter One

Arnold Donaldson was being entirely practical, selfish yes, but entirely practical when he made his decision to marry Alicia at their first meeting in 1941.

He immediately recognised a vulnerable, beautiful woman to whom the electorate would relate and who would win him votes. She was attractive, had a good face, was slight and youthful and would be far more pliable than Kathleen, indeed more than any other woman he had met.

Alicia was young and didn't seem to be exceptionally intelligent. She was frightened, vulnerable and, most importantly, she would be in his debt. He saw also that she was vain and susceptible to flattery. In many ways, therefore, she was perfect.

If she had any spirit left after the effort of regaining the ability to walk he was sure he could soon bend it to his will. She would be happy to receive his view of the world; she would respect him and do as she was told.

He had also seen her ambition to have the things that they both knew his money could buy. For her he was going to be the 'knight in shining armour' who would take her away from her family, give her the things she wanted, and needed, such as good clothes, social standing. Money.

He knew she would put up with a lot for that because he knew where she had come from.

The Tyler family had undoubtedly come down in the world.

Before the Great War Bert, Alicia's father, had had his own engineering company. "I did drains" he said, "I did the best bloody drains in the Empire." He had spent some years in Canada 'doing drains' whose covers bore his name many decades after he had left. They had had a lovely house in Edmonton, Alberta. The three boys were born there, and they had only returned to the home country in 1915 when the war had not been 'over by Christmas'. They exchanged Edmonton, Alberta for Edmonton, North London where Edie and the children lived with Bert's mother, a humourless woman who took every opportunity to make the family aware of how their lives should have been.

1

Bert had joined up and, with his engineering skills, spent much of the war relatively safely behind the lines in northern France. He never spoke about the war, possibly because of his deep resentment at never being commissioned an officer. He knew he should have been, with his knowledge and experience, but nevertheless he ended the war a Corporal. It rankled with him all his life and he took it out on his family when he returned.

It must have been difficult but Edie just got on with looking after the children as best she could. When she found herself pregnant early in the Spring of 1920 she prayed for a girl. Not that any baby could ever replace Margaret who had been just six weeks old when she was found dead in her cot. Granny Tyler had been no help and the doctor had just come and taken her baby away. There was no funeral, no grieving and within hours it was as if Margaret had never existed.

They all knew Bert couldn't have been the father. He hadn't got back from France until three months before the birth.

Alberta Tyler was born in November 1920, "The war got in the way dear" was as far as her mother ever went to explain the gap between Alberta and her elder brothers.

They had her christened "Alberta" but she hated her name, almost as much as she hated her family and she always thought of herself as "Alicia".

There are photographs taken when she must have been about 12 years old. Four children lined up in order of age. Alberta was as tall as her eldest brother. She was bright, alert, slender and delicate with fine, high cheekbones – so different from her shorter thickset brothers.

She thought her brothers to be *thick in body, thick in mind* and she often wondered why she was so different.

"Where did I come from?" "Why can I do all those things that they don't even understand?" she asked God in frustration as she said her prayers every night.

As many children do, she believed she had been collected in error from the hospital nursery. They must have put the wrong label on her toe.

She imagined her real parents as being artistic and refined, famous actors or singers. Her real parents would have encouraged her with her dancing; they would have given her books to read and have played music and sung in the evenings around their grand piano.

She imagined how they would feel about the lump who had passed herself off as their daughter, how that lump would feel. She would have been as unhappy in that family as Alicia was in hers.

But Bert knew why Alberta wasn't like the rest of the family and he took it out on Alberta from her earliest years.

He was the wrong father, they were the wrong brothers.

She left school at 15 and went to work, as girls of her class did, in the local factory. Every day she would do what was required of her but her mind was always on planning her escape. She had no intention of working there any longer than she had to.

When she saw a notice on the wall in Boots' Lending Library and recognised the name of the person to contact, Joyce Price had been her English teacher, she had set about persuading her father to let her go out in the evenings, to join the local amateur dramatic society.

"Alright" he grudgingly gave his permission "the men'll be looking after each other won't they? Not interested in *ladies*" he used the word with heavy sarcasm "are they?"

So for two years Alberta lived for the evenings when Alicia could go to the 'Society'.

Although it was an amateur society the Edmonton Dramatical Society had a semi-professional director who claimed to have worked in the West End several times and 'proper' actors who participated when they were otherwise 'resting'. Every production was professionally presented.

In her third season Alicia was cast as Sarah, the lead role in their ambitious production of Noel Coward's *Bitter Sweet*.

The reviews, though commenting on some problems with the orchestra and noisy scene changes, had gushed about the performance of *undoubtedly a future star of the musical theatre*. Alicia Tyler's *outbursts of passion shone*. Her ability to *meet the challenge of spanning 50 years from charmingly innocent to respectability with a past* was matched only by her *considerable vocal talent*. They were complimentary, too, about the young actor who played Sarah's lover, Carl Linden.

In the group's post-production get-together Joyce sat down with a cup of tea and without preamble changed Alicia's life.

"You can act, you can sing and you've got a real way about you. You could go far with proper training, so we've arranged an audition for a scholarship at RADA." She carried on, ignoring Alicia's attempts to interrupt. "You were born to be on the stage."

So early on the second Monday morning in April 1938 they had taken the train to London and the imposing buildings in Gower Street. She didn't remember much about the day; she was too nervous and excited. She hoped she had done herself justice.

Did her parents notice her excitement that evening, or her increasing tension as she waited to hear the results? If they did they never asked for an explanation and she did not tell them of her audition.

They had all been to see her performances and Edie had been so

3

proud of her daughter, but Bert and the boys had thought it a waste of drinking time. After they had been to watch *Bitter Sweet* they told Alberta that they hadn't seen anything after the first interval. They said they didn't want to stay with Edie to watch a bunch of nancy-boys and tarts prancing about in front of people who'd paid their hard earned money to sit on bloody uncomfortable seats. So they'd gone to the pub.

Alberta was not surprised.

Neither was she surprised at her father's reaction when she told them she would be leaving her job and commuting to London that Autumn. "Don't worry Dad, it'll cost you nothing, I got a scholarship."

"And what are we supposed to do without the money you bring in? That'll cost us." was all her father could say. Her mother simply took her hand and squeezed it, with tears in her eyes. "You'll make your father very proud won't you?"

The time she spent at RADA was the most rewarding time for her; absolutely, she said years later, the best time of her life. "I was really really happy then. I got rid of that *frightful* name and became *me*, Alicia. I could have done anything, gone anywhere, been *me*! I've never been *me*. First I was the dutiful daughter of *dreadful* parents and then it all went wrong and I ended up married and that went wrong, but in between were just a few months when I was *me*!"

A photograph of her taken around that time shows a slim young woman, with long shapely legs striding across an empty street. She is wearing a pale coat, tied at the waist, which is obviously trim. In her left hand she is swinging an empty wicker shopping basket as her right hand holds onto a large brimmed hat which is just staying on a mass of dark hair not primly held in tightly permed waves but irregular, free, loose curls. She is laughing, not just with her mouth – her eyes are alight. There is movement; even in that black and white photograph her vivacity, her love of life and anticipation of the future can be seen.

On the Sunday the war was declared she was at home with all the family gathered, as so many other millions were, around a wireless set with Chamberlain telling them each, personally, that nothing would ever be the same again.

'*You can imagine.... may God bless you all.... the right will prevail...*'

"Well, we couldn't, I'm bloody sure he didn't and I can't for the life of me see how it did for me." was Alicia's bitter response whenever she heard any part of that speech later in her life. She never did see that she was only one of millions whose dreams, hopes and plans were shattered. She only saw her ambitions and expectations unfulfilled, not those of an entire generation.

Years later she would talk for hours about those first two years of the war – about what she could have done and who she could have been. Her eyes would be bright with rare enthusiasm.

She was studying, working long shifts in the local armaments factory and fitting in training as a regular nursing assistant in an ambulance. But she was happy.

It was Bert who hated everything.

He spent most of his time pottering in his greenhouse at the bottom of the garden growing cactuses, eventually joining the Home Guard with the first volunteers in August 1940. But even that didn't make him happy, he was just reminded of his lack of a commission. Not yet 60 he was already an old man, his eyesight was not good, he was hard of hearing and his concentration frequently lapsed.

Alicia was surprised when one morning in early October 1940 he asked her if she wanted a lift into town, she was so surprised that she accepted.

London was not the safest place to be with roads often impassable after the raids.

Perhaps it was that his usual route was blocked and he was concentrating too much on finding his way, perhaps he shouldn't have been driving at all.

He didn't see the car that hit them until the very last seconds when it was far too late to take any avoiding action. Where he had time to brace himself for the impact, Alicia, sitting in the passenger seat, had no warning at all.

She spent the first weeks in hospital with little possibility of ever walking again. She was 19 years old and was likely to be completely dependent on others for the rest of her life.

Her friends soon gave up visiting her even when she was still in the London hospital – they had their lives to get on with. Her friends from school were doing all sorts of things – working on farms with the Land Army, learning to drive lorries with the WRAF, losing their virginity to airmen who had no time at all to live, and so they soon forgot about Ali.

Her parents did not come to visit her either. Her father, perhaps through guilt and embarrassment, her mother because Bert wouldn't like her to and she had no way of getting there without his knowledge.

It was probably a relief to them when, just before her 20th birthday, she was transferred to a nursing home in Buckinghamshire to begin the long fight to health and some sort of mobility. The distance was all the excuse they needed.

Joyce Price was the only person who visited. She had travelled into London two or three times every week in those early days and was able to visit Alicia more often when she was in Buckinghamshire as that was where she was working.

Joyce used her visits to try to pull Alicia out of the slough of self pity she was falling into.

"I'll grow old, a crippled spinster looking after my brothers' ugly children."

"There's no hope now. The theatre was my only escape route. Now what can I do?" she asked Joyce pathetically I'll never be able to go on the stage with sticks."

The doctors and other patients tried to encourage her as she slowly regained some movement in her feet and legs but for long hours she wouldn't even try to do the exercises they had given her.

"I won't even be able to sing." she would complain to Joyce. "I won't ever be able to breathe properly with this chest."

Joyce was very patient with her but must have found her visits a trial.

On one visit the week before Christmas 1940 Joyce didn't visit Alicia alone.

"I've brought someone to meet you"

"Good afternoon, Alberta." The voice was pleasant, with what would be described as rather a 'far back' accent.

"Ali, Alicia, never Alberta." She had meant to sound discouraging, she didn't know why Joyce had brought along this man. She had been looking forward to talking to Joyce and now she would have to be polite.

"Arnold Donaldson at your service" he had said rather theatrically, continuing in a far more normal, but still definitely upper class voice "do call me Arnold, never Arnie." Perhaps he had a sense of humour.

She soon found herself flirting with him in a way she hadn't been able to do for what seemed like months. The 'tall, dark, prematurely balding, rather distinguished looking man in the uniform of army captain with the most wonderful eyes' as Alicia later described him, accompanied Joyce on several of her visits in the following weeks and then began to visit on his own. Joyce still came to see her, but no longer with Arnold. On one of these days Alicia finally asked what the story was.

"Not much of a story really, I met Arnold at a musical recital, he knows Kathleen, you know, that girl I've told you about, and we just got on very well and I told him all about you, and he asked to meet you. That simple."

"Have I spoilt things for you?"

"Oh no. It was never anything serious. I'm a bit old for him really."
Alicia believed there had to be more to it than that.

"He seems quite taken with you, you know. He was talking about
you the other evening. I don't think Kathleen was very pleased."

"He's not really my type. I like them younger, more athletic,
muscular with blond hair and blue eyes. Arnold is so formal and
stuffy."

Although she said these things, and knew that she was not
attracted to him, she was sure he was interested in her. And he had
money. And, perhaps – just perhaps – he might be the way out for her.

Just as Alicia wasn't being entirely honest with Arnold about what
she wanted from him he wasn't being frank with her. Their
relationship began as it continued and ended, based on self-
indulgence and self-interest.

Arnold's background was very different from Alicia's. Notwithstanding
the modesty of their home the Donaldson family was rich. Arnold's
father, George, was a pillar of local society with power and
considerable standing in the town, some time Chairman of the
Council, a benevolent local businessman, provider of charity and
employment for many men and women through his various
enterprises. But it was his mother, Ellen, who made the decisions in
their austere household.

When they had first had money – for George was a self-made man
– she had insisted they buy the bungalow on the last road to be built
before the sand dunes began on the eastern edge of the seaside town
of Hoylake. "Perfectly adequate" was her pronounced judgement "No
need for a big house. People can take us as they find us." She would
not employ staff, undertaking all household tasks herself "I'm perfectly
capable of doing my own cleaning." Her wardrobe was limited, "No
need for anything stylish as long as it's all neat and tidy" though she
did have a fox fur coat which she wore whenever she attended a
function with George, which was not very often.

She had had a very difficult time with Arnold, she had been in
labour for nearly two days, and so, after the long recovery period after
her confinement, she firmly told George that Arnold would be an only
child. This was not a problem for George, as there were a number of
discreet ladies in the town who were happy to oblige him on a regular
basis, in exchange for a house and a regular income arranged through
his legal people.

George enjoyed visiting his ladies, as their houses were larger and
better furnished than his own home, and certainly the welcome was

always warmer. He should not be judged harshly as this was not an uncommon arrangement for well-off men at that time, when their wives had reached "a certain age". It was an arrangement of which Ellen decided to know nothing.

She was adamant from the beginning that her Arnold was not going to 'end up' at the factory. He was going to be important, a lawyer, a politician. That needed a good education – no need for him to be 'down't factory' 'learning the business from t'ground up' as George had wanted. He was going to Cambridge and the Bar and Government. All that would require investment, so, no matter how much money they had, she would not willingly spend it on anything but her son.

Arnold had gone to the best local school – she could not bring herself to send him away to board even though she knew it might give him a better chance in the future if he wore the right tie.

At school he had been an isolated, rather scholarly boy whose only pretensions to popularity occurred during the summer term when he established himself as the reliable, if unremarkable, all-rounder in first his house, and then the school, cricket team. It was the nearest thing to enjoyment he found. Cricket was so civilised, being the only sport where one did not have to have physical contact with other boys and where, despite being a team game, a degree of selfishness could be considered a virtue.

Even when he went up to Cambridge, getting his first taste of independent life, his mother maintained her control over him. Arnold's cousin, Henry, had gone up to Cambridge too and he wrote long letters to his Aunt Ellen, detailing everything that they did, whosoever they met and wheresoever they went. Ellen ensured that Henry, whose father had not been so fortunate as George, never forgot how lucky he was to have her patronage and he felt that writing letters was a small price to pay for not having to worry about his college bills.

Henry did everything his cleverer and better-looking cousin did, but he never did anything as well – even though he always worked harder and took everything more seriously. They both achieved their degrees, and then moved to London to read for the Bar.

It was perfectly natural that Kathleen McNamara, a clever young lady, perfectly presentable and with a well-developed social conscience, would try to make a match of it with Arnold Donaldson.

Kathleen, with her sister Maureen and mother Irene, had first met Arnold and his mother at a church outing in 1930 and had immediately taken to one another. They regularly met Ellen Donaldson at the coffee mornings held for the League of Nations and any one of the myriad of fund raising events held throughout the period leading up to the Second War, and they got on as well as Ellen got on with anyone.

For all the possessive love she had for her son Ellen was a realist. She knew that one day Arnold would have to marry, so she kept an eye out for any contact he might have with the opposite sex. Kathleen and Maureen McNamara weren't the same class as the Donaldsons but Ellen thought there was 'something about them' that meant they were not entirely unacceptable, and she thought that when the time would come, some years in the future, for her Arnold to marry and settle down perhaps the younger girl, Kathleen, would be a suitable daughter-in-law.

So Ellen decided that, although she would never encourage it, if any relationship in that direction developed she would show no opposition. She was a clever woman in some ways. She knew that the best way to hold onto her son was to appear to be happy to let him go. At least Kathleen would be a local girl and wouldn't take Arnold away.

Others of the ladies in the town, those who knew a little more about the McNamaras and guessed even more than they could prove, thought that such a relationship would be 'very interesting'.

Although Ellen had indicated she would have no objections Arnold knew his father would have no truck with the relationship. George's abhorrence of Catholicism was very simple and straightforward. He would not, under any circumstances, have a member of that faith in the family. He did not mind having Catholic women as his mistresses. They knew their place and they understood that there could be never be a formal relationship.

Kathleen understood the reasons when, as they made love for the first time, Arnold told her that he could never marry her. George would never give his consent, and that consent would be required, whatever age he was, if Arnold were to inherit.

Through all his life Arnold had avoided any direct contact with the engineering business that was the source of his family's wealth and influence in the area. But he did like the money.

And since he knew where that came from he was not going to cause a problem with his father.

His future, funded by his father's business, was to be politics and for that he needed a less controversial, more acceptable, vote-winning wife than Kathleen.

But she always knew she would have an informal position, and that suited her very well for she was an independent lady and was going to make her way in the world without having to depend on a man. She was not going to be a kept woman as her mother had been

9

for as long as she could remember.

Kathleen's mother Irene had been intrigued when she realised Arnold' mother was encouraging the relationship. She had rather assumed Ellen was aware of George's mistresses but soon realised that Ellen had no idea she was one of them. Ellen couldn't possibly know that not only had she been George's mistress for many years she had borne him two daughters. She had told Maureen who her father was but Kathleen, several years younger, was not told. Perhaps because the advantages far outweighed any qualms they might have.

When Arnold visited Kathleen, as he did regularly, Maureen and her mother would spend the evening in local pub and sit in the snug with gins and ports discussing whether their lack of concern was immoral.

They felt it was amusing. As long as Kathleen did not fall pregnant.

That would not be fair on the child.

Chapter Two

My first glimpse of Alicia was as she waited in the office reception while her husband dealt with some paperwork. The first thing I noticed was the hat, it was exceptional, but underneath its wide brim she seemed very young and vulnerable. Her clothes were, to my provincial eye, stylish and fashionable though she was sitting awkwardly and obviously pregnant. She was sitting completely still, her long shapely legs tucked under the chair, her hands resting lightly on an ivory handled walking stick.

Arnold was re-writing his will following his unanticipated marriage. Under normal circumstances everything would be left to the wife and any issue of the marriage, but Arnold made his will specifically to exclude Alicia. In the event of his death she was to have only a small allowance, any capital he may have was to be used in a trust fund for the benefit of any of his children, legitimate or illegitimate. "Isn't it a bit of an unusual arrangement?" I dared to ask but probably deserved his uncompromising reply. "None of your damned business."

He was frequently rude to me. He had, after all, been my superior, an Associate Partner, before the war.

As they were leaving I heard Major Fischer asking Alicia if she was looking forward to setting up her new home and asking her if she had found a house yet. She had had no chance to answer before her husband interrupted, saying that she would live with his parents, at least while the war was on. She would need the company and his mother would be a support during the pregnancy.

In the following weeks I visited the Donaldson household several times, accompanying Major Fischer, who was attending to George Donaldson's personal affairs, and there I saw more of Alicia. It was obvious, even on just a few minutes' acquaintance, that she was not happy. She would come into the room that served as the study with the tea tray and pour three small cups, just as if she were the maid, and leave without catching anyone's eye and without saying a word.

She and Arnold had evidently anticipated the wedding ceremony – a circumstance that Ellen Donaldson seemed to take great delight in pointing out on a number of occasions.

"So large it must be twins. Them only five months wed." she would confide in a stage whisper – ensuring that Alicia would hear.

"I kept my figure for much longer when I was carrying my dear Arnold. Why, at five months you hardly could tell I was carrying!"

But even to my bachelor eyes it was obvious she was further gone than that.

She must have been very unhappy and very lonely as well as being in pain and, no doubt, frightened by all her mother-in-law's tales of the birth process. How much pain she felt as a result of the accident I can only guess. The increasing weight of the child must have caused great problems for a damaged back and she still had to use a stick for anything but the shortest of journeys. Unsurprisingly there was not much love lost between the women in that house as they, for differing reasons, awaited the birth of the child.

I asked Major Fischer to raise the subject of the "young Captain" having his own household. This he did, reluctantly, on one of our visits, "George you may wish to invest in another property, that could, perhaps, suit Arnold and his beautiful young bride and the growing family. What do you think eh?"

"No, lad." George had never lost his straightforward Lancashire way of speaking, even when addressing a man in his middle 30s, "No. They'll stop here until we're gone."

Two thoughts occurred to me upon hearing this; one was that it was a mighty small house to have four grown ups and any children living in it and second that George and Ellen being 'gone' was going to be some way in the future as they were both only just 60.

"What about one of your other properties? Could you evict a tenant and let the young couple live in one of them?"

"No. It'll be as I said. They'll wait till we're gone."

And that was the end of the matter.

There was nothing more I could do to try to help her.

Through these early years of the war I would take my mother on a Sunday outing. We would take the bus, which still ran from Birkenhead to West Kirby – the next town along the coast from Hoylake, and spend the afternoon walking along the promenade. Looking at the view across the Dee estuary to the Hilbre Islands and, beyond them, the hills of Wales, it was possible to forget the war and the unhappiness of so many people.

On the last Sunday of May 1942, as we walked past one of the shelters that were set at regular intervals along the promenade I noticed two people sitting close, deep in conversation, their heads close together. One figure was Arnold Donaldson, not in uniform; the other was a woman I also recognised. She was the daughter of one of George Donaldson's 'ladies', Kathleen McNamara. I had thought her doing war work in the south of England. As I failed to catch any of their conversation I was unsure what to think. Everyone had known they were friendly before the war but it had been assumed the friendship had terminated with his marriage.

In the office the next day I was told that Alicia had given birth the previous Thursday to a healthy full term son they had called Charles. The gossips, of whom my mother was one, were also pleased to report that the six month long marriage was, to all intents and purposes, over. They had not shared a bed since their honeymoon.

All this information, and more, had come from the other women in the local cottage hospital who had shared the ward with Alicia as she recovered from the birth. Although it was only gossip I was saddened as I was sure there was more than an element of truth in it.

Over the next few years there were frequent mentions of the Donaldsons in the local newspapers so I was not dependent upon their infrequent visits to the office to pick up titbits of the happenings in their lives.

I knew that George Donaldson was donating larger and larger sums to charities and that he was still very active in the local community – no new fire engine or lifeboat could be brought into service without George Donaldson being photographed with it for the newspapers. He really wanted that knighthood or an MBE at the very least.

I knew that Arnold was elected to the county council and was beginning to cultivate local political parties. A long speech he had made to the League of Nations was printed verbatim, taking up a whole page of the local newspaper in closely printed text.

There were increasingly frequent photographs of him with Alicia, always described as 'his young, beautiful, crippled wife'. He was laying down the groundwork for his post-war political career. Even though she did not appear always to be enjoying it, Alicia was playing her part. She never looked well, she was far too thin and she never seemed relaxed in any photograph – other than the ones connected with her dramatics.

I knew that Alicia had taken up amateur dramatics eventually directing various plays given by the women's organisations in the area. There were pictures of her in the papers, sometimes, though not often, with a growing Charles and frequently her collaborator, Maureen Shelton.

I considered that very interesting as Maureen Shelton's maiden name was McNamara, she was Kathleen McNamara's elder sister who had been married briefly early in the war. I didn't think I was the only one who knew of her mother's relationship with Arnold's father but I wondered whether Alicia knew of the close connection between the families. Maureen certainly did.

Every week I scoured the newspapers for mentions and photographs of Alicia and the Donaldsons because, even if Arnold Donaldson had never fallen in love with his wife, I had.

Chapter Three

I knew of George's death through the office, of course, but I also read the reports in the local newspaper:

> *"The death occurred on June 27th 1944, of Mr George Donaldson of Hoylake."*

After detailing his many public roles, his interest in bowls, his generosity to many good causes they concluded:

> *"He leaves a widow and one son, Captain Arnold Donaldson, a Liverpool Barrister, who is currently serving with H.M. Forces."*

No mention for the "Mrs Arnold Donaldson" who had undoubtedly had to shoulder the entire burden of looking after her father-in-law through his illness.

I saw them often in the weeks that followed. Arnold, on compassionate leave, spent most of his time in his father's old office sifting through papers – trying to ascertain what his father had left him after all the large donations he had made in the previous year. Arnold must have feared he would have nothing left.

He need not have worried. As his father's sole beneficiary he received everything: a business thriving with its wartime contracts and over £250,000 deposited in various bank accounts. In addition there was life insurance, a number of cars and five houses in various locations in Hoylake and West Kirby.

Until the reading of his father's will Arnold had known nothing of the cars or the houses. He was shocked at the evidence of his father's other lives, but he was silenced when he saw that one of the houses that he now owned was the one he visited so regularly, the one where Kathleen lived with her mother. He was not unaware of the implications.

It was left to the 'Mrs Arnold Donaldson' who did not merit a mention in the newspaper article to open all the many letters of condolence addressed to Ellen and to Arnold. They were too upset by their loss to open or reply to them all so it became Alicia's task to read the more important ones to her mother-in-law, who told her what should be written in reply.

After reading one of the many letters Alicia walked into the study and wordlessly placed it on the desk in front of Arnold, who was sitting in his father's chair as if it had always been his. She left through the french windows heading for the bottom of the short garden where Charles was playing in the sandpit. She sat down on the edge and, folding her skirt around her knees, rocked herself backwards and forwards as pieces of various jigsaws fitted together in her mind.

> *My Darling Arnold,*
>
> *Just a few lines to tell you how dreadfully sorry I am to hear of your indescribable loss.*
>
> *I will write more fully in a day or so, as no doubt there are arrangements we must change, but in the meantime I just wanted you to be absolutely certain, for I think you know, that I am always with you in my heart.*
>
> *Yours as always and forever,*
> *Kathleen*

Christmas 1944 was not a merry affair as Ellen had followed her husband to the plot in Trinity Churchyard at the end of November. Arnold had a short leave at Christmas but spent very little time at home with his wife and child.

Alicia had wanted to start clearing out all the furniture, all the detritus of her parents-in-law's lives, and make the bungalow feel more of her own but Arnold forbade her. On the last night before leaving he told her they would be moving. He had asked Max Fischer to find him a home more suited to his position.

Even though he had had no hand in finding it and he would loved to have been able to criticise her choice, Arnold had to admit that Millcourt was the perfect house for the soon-to-be MP and his family.

It was an imposing property, set well back from the road surrounded by substantial and mature gardens with many trees. It had been solidly built a century before with large blocks of grey stone, now covered by a thick wrapping of ivy and Virginia creeper and which gave it the feeling of being a country house.

The accommodation reflected the more leisured era in which it had been built. Upstairs there were several bedrooms and bathrooms with a separate nursery suite, and in the attics plenty of rooms for the staff. Downstairs, in addition to the usual living and dining rooms there was a billiard room, a library, and an airy conservatory looking out over the gardens, which were mainly down to a large area of lawn enclosed by rhododendrons and rose beds. The kitchens and storage rooms were on a lower ground floor, not impinging on the living area, because the house was built on a slope. Arnold knew that it showed the world he was a man to be reckoned with – far more than the bungalow could ever have done.

Alicia was happy. Alone with her son for the first time, her time her own, with no demanding, condemning in-laws she threw herself into the task of completely re-furbishing the house. "It's so dark! So Victorian! I'm going to have *such* fun!" Alicia was determined to completely re-furnish, re-curtain and re-carpet despite the rationing and all the other limitations of wartime.

I am sure Alicia didn't appreciate it when Major Fischer asked me to help wherever I could. It was a request I had no difficulty in accepting. I spent most days in those early months of 1945 at Millcourt obtaining workmen and badgering suppliers, setting up meetings with people who would be able to help her. I was fascinated by her, and happily watched her becoming a more confident and happier person as the house was transformed to her taste. I will always remember those three months in early 1945 in so much detail and with such pleasure.

Years later when I told her how much I had enjoyed helping her when she had been redesigning Millcourt she had said "Were you there? I don't remember."

Arnold, Alicia and Charles moved in in March, well before electioneering began.

Arnold had been adopted as the Conservative candidate in a neighbouring constituency without any difficulty – his father had always been Conservative and Arnold couldn't contemplate doing what many of his brother officers, similarly politically ambitious, had done and join the Labour Party. "The nation will not reject the Old Man, I'll stick with him." He was confident he would begin the post war period with a new career and never have to deal with 'the business', which seemed to tick along quite nicely without him.

During the short campaign Arnold and Alicia worked together for the only time in their lives. Charles was wheeled out to appeal to the women voter "much better to have the candidate's baby being kissed by the electorate than having to kiss all those ghastly children myself!" Arnold would repeatedly joke.

Alicia attended coffee mornings, sat on platforms and shook hands with more people than she hoped ever to meet. As Arnold watched Alicia's active assistance in meeting Ladies' groups, even making short speeches – which she obviously really enjoyed and was very good at – he will have felt completely justified in his choice of wife.

The campaign went well, the canvas returns were excellent and he was confident of success. The night before the election he told his wife his plans for the future.

"You'll make a very good constituency wife, Alicia, while I will occupy myself in London. And then the next election, possibly five years time, will be a good time for you to be pregnant again."

It was only as he stood at the count, watching pieces of paper piling high for his Labour opponent that he began to face the possibility of failure. Men hustled around him looking busy, avoiding his eye, as he watched all his plans disintegrate, his agent stopped briefly muttering "Sorry old man, no one anticipated the depth of the country's need for a new start." How could he be losing? How could he have lost?

Arnold silently drove his wife and child home.

"I'm just going to have a bit of a drive. I've some thinking to do. Tell Cook I'll be back for breakfast."

Kathleen would help him forget his disappointment.

Kathleen would help him come to terms with having to stay and run his father's business.

He had no excuse not to now.

Chapter Four

Some weeks later Arnold had let himself in for his regular Friday evening visit when Kathleen, without warning and before she had even given him his first drink said "I'm expecting your baby, what do you think of that?"

It took only a very short time for him to recover himself sufficiently to ask her how much it would cost.

"What a funny question! A lot I should think."

"Well let me know how much you need. You should go to London. No-one will know."

"What on earth are you talking about Arnold? I'm not moving to London."

"Don't be a fool Kathleen, I'm not talking about moving. You'll go to London to get rid of it. That's what women in your situation do isn't it?"

She could not answer immediately. She had known he was selfish and self-centred and would think only of his own needs. She had hoped this would not be his reaction and nearly failed to control her temper. She had promised herself she would be calm, but when it came to it she found it very difficult. She took several deep breaths and then slowly, deliberately she answered him.

"No Arnold, it is most definitely not what women 'in my situation' as you so euphemistically put it do. Women *have* babies, they *have* children. They do not *'get rid of them'.*"

She knew that tears were welling up in her eyes but she was determined not to let him see how upset he had made her.

Arnold was used to having his own way. He had always had his own way. He was not used to being crossed. But even he could see the depths of the emotion Kathleen was trying to control.

"No, Kathleen, there will be no baby. You must understand that I cannot allow it. And you must know me well enough to know that I am not to be moved by tears."

They were still standing in the narrow hallway of Kathleen's house. The house Arnold had visited so regularly over the years, the house his father had owned. She tried to gain control of the situation by moving into the living room and sitting down. She knew he would follow.

19

"How pompous you are Arnold. It is one of your more annoying traits." After a short awkward pause during which he sat down but said nothing, she continued. "You're the one that doesn't understand, you're the one that doesn't know *me*. I am going to have it."

"Oh no, my girl, you most certainly are not!"

"I'm not going to get into an argument, I'm not the pliant young thing I was before the war. I am a far stronger person. You will not be able to bully me, as you undoubtedly do your little wife."

"You will not have the child."

They sat in silence for a few minutes. She was not going to show him how upset she was and if she tried to speak she would break down. Eventually he continued "How can you possibly have the child?"

Again a silence while Kathleen tried to find the right words, eventually her disappointment turned to anger.

"How can I possibly *not* have the child, Arnold? I cannot 'get rid of it' as you suggest. How little you know me after all this time! It is so stupendously arrogant of you not to care that I am Catholic."

"Religion! Who gives anything for religion these days!

"I do."

They were quiet for a time. Arnold poured them both a drink and handed one to Kathleen.

"You are sure I'm...."

"Don't even think about suggesting you are not responsible Arnold Donaldson. You know as well as I that it couldn't be anyone else's. This, she patted her stomach, was conceived on the night of the election. A future Prime Minister I would say!"

"Not if you bring him up a Catholic."

Her attempt to lighten the atmosphere had fallen flat, so she changed the subject. She had hoped that she wouldn't have to talk about his father, but it looked like she had no alternative.

"Your father didn't like Catholics did he?"

"What the hell has he got to do with it?"

"He didn't did he? He was quite happy to use them, in his business and his private life," Arnold let that pass without comment, so she continued, determined to push the point "but he would never have allowed you to marry me would he? He held your purse strings very tight didn't he? Making sure that you were never independent enough to be able to marry me."

"Had I wanted to."

"Indeed, even if you, *and I*, had wanted to." She paused briefly, he was going to know she had a mind of her own now. "Of course he knew you had visited me in this house, of course he knew why, but he couldn't say anything openly because of his own activities."

"What 'activities' would they be?" Arnold was not going to show her how interested he was in the direction the conversation was heading. He had wondered, since the reading of his father's will, if there was more to the relationship between the McNamaras and the Donaldsons.

"His women of course Arnold, come on, are you saying you didn't know?"

Kathleen was not going to let him guess, she was going to be the one to tell him. "He had his 'needs' as well you know and he wasn't an old man. How old was he when he died 60? 62? That's no age at all."

"It's just idle gossip at your coffee mornings.

"I know a little more than just gossip, Arnold, after all he owned this house didn't he?"

"Are you saying all those houses were occupied by his *mistresses*?"

"Absolutely – his hatred and fear of Catholicism didn't prevent him 'visiting' Catholic women. You might be surprised at how well known your father was around here. And he was far better liked and more discreet than you."

"Did he ever visit you here?" It seemed to have occurred to him that Kathleen may have played both generations.

"Oh Arnold" Kathleen was not going to give him an answer, she needed him to be unsure. "don't be so pathetic."

She had been so disappointed with him for his assumption that she would have a termination she wanted to make him uncertain about something.

"Arnold, there are very grey areas in relationships. Nothing is ever as black and white as you would like it to be. Would it make that much difference if your father had visited here? I'm not saying he did, but would it change anything? "

Another possibility occurred to him. "How long has your mother known my father?"

"Does it matter?" At first she didn't see what he was getting at.

"It might matter if we were brother and sister."

"Do you think that's possible?" Kathleen realised she had sounded surprised, and had lost the initiative again in this conversation. It was something she had considered dispassionately in the past, but she knew her mother or Maureen would have told her – they knew she was 'seeing' Arnold and she knew they wouldn't have allowed that if there were any possibility of that kind of relationship.

He looked at her and raised his eyebrows in silent emphasis.

"Hardly." She said as she finished her drink and walked across the room to pour another. She gestured with her glass towards him, silently asking if he wanted another drink too. He nodded and they moved on.

"To get this conversation back on track what are you going to do for me and your child?" She patted her stomach.

"What do you want me to do for you and your child?"

She didn't like the way he phrased the question, but it was obvious to her that he had accepted something of his responsibilities.

"Firstly, you will guarantee a sum of money to be paid into my personal bank account monthly, you will set up a Trust Fund for the child. If it is a boy you will pay all his school fees and any other education expenses until he is 21, 18 should do if it is a girl. You will sign a document to swear that you will never tell anyone that you are the child's father without my express permission. You will sign this house over to me and, oh yes, I will need a husband."

As he listened he gave no inkling of his thoughts. It was as if he were in court or in a business meeting. He believed that the less the adversary knew of your thoughts the more powerful you were. He hoped to give nothing away, but during the war Kathleen had been in a position to learn something of the subtleties of interrogation.

Arnold left it a few moments before commenting "You have clearly been thinking about this."

"Oh yes, and I have been thinking clearly. I am asking no more than is reasonable. This child will not suffer for its paternity."

"Did you have anyone in mind? For husband that is?" She wouldn't expect him to divorce and marry her, they both knew that that would be impossible.

"Absolutely, it will have to be someone over whom you have some hold, who's not currently emotionally entangled. It will have to be someone who is available and could marry me, say, within the next month – so I will have already met him. He will be financially able to support a wife and the 'honeymoon baby' as he will have to believe that the child is his."

Arnold relaxed somewhat but the smile he gave Kathleen as he caught her eye was completely free from humour. "Perhaps he might work for me, have lost his fiancée and parents in one of the last raids of the war, and by happy coincidence be my cousin, depending on me for practically every decision he has ever made in his life. Is that, by any chance, who you had in mind?"

"It would very conveniently explain any family resemblance."

"Henry. Perfect. Yes, Henry would be perfect. How do we get him to do it?"

Arnold was more relaxed now. Her marriage to Henry would not prejudice their relationship, everything could continue as it always had.

"I don't really care Arnold. That is your responsibility, tell him I'm lonely, tell him you know I have always secretly loved him! I don't care what you tell him as long as he asks me within a month. But I do advise you to get him to think it is his own idea."

Chapter Five

"We're going to the Lakes for Christmas this year" Arnold announced to Alicia at breakfast one morning in late November 1945. "Henry is getting up a party to take over a house in Troutbeck."

Alicia did not like Henry, he was short, weak and rather mean-spirited. He had been a great favourite of her late mother-in-law and had visited the house often with Arnold when they were on leave. Arnold had given him a job in the business at the end of the War, she thought he found him useful, though in what way she could not imagine.

She was pretty certain of one thing, it was not Henry who was getting up the party. "Henry couldn't 'get up' anything, apart from other people's noses."

"I always thought your wit very sharp, my dear, but, be that as it may, we are going."

"What about Charles, and Nanny, will there be other children? Enough room? Has he thought of that? It will have to be a very large house."

"Oh no, my dear, it's quite a small house really, but there will be plenty of room. Charles will be staying here. With Nanny and Cook. They will spoil him completely and he won't even know we aren't there, for God's sake he's only three he won't have a clue what's going on as long as he has a present to open. You will come with me, and act correctly in all ways, as my wife. It is about time we established that. You are my wife and I intend to get some advantage from the expense. It is, after all, about time – unless of course you have found an alternative?"

Stung into a response she snapped "Chance would be a fine thing!"

"You would if you could then? You do remember how? You do remember what's required then?"

There was no point in arguing further so she responded calmly "I suppose I have no choice but to go."

"No. You have no choice."

"Who is in this party which has been *got up*?"

"Me and you, Henry and his wife"

"His *what*?"

24

"His wife."

"That's what I thought you said. When did that happen? I thought he was in love with that young thing who was killed at the end of the war." Her curiosity overcame her normal reluctance to say anything other than what was essential to Arnold.

"He was married a few weeks ago."

"Who to? Why were we not invited?" Surprise and the awareness of a social snub mixed in almost equal shares.

"I did not tell you because they wanted it kept very quiet, that is also the reason you were not invited."

"You say *you* were not invited, the reason *you* were not invited, does that mean you were? You went to your cousin's wedding and you did not breathe one word of it to me. I don't believe this could happen. You can't despise me so much!"

"Do not presume to tell me how much I can despise you. You would be surprised how much that might be."

"Who is she then? This new Mrs Witherby?"

Nothing could have prepared her for the answer.

"Her name is Kathleen."

There was a long pause as this latest blow was assimilated. "Kathleen." She repeated in a very flat voice. "That Kathleen?"

"Yes, *that* Kathleen." He confirmed without any apparent embarrassment.

It took Alicia a few moments before she could find her voice to continue. She changed tack to give herself some time. "Who are the other couple to complete this happy Christmas party?"

"Oh, you won't know them. He's Monty MacFarlane, a chap I knew at Catterick. I don't know much about her."

Very close to tears, she resorted to an unconvincing voice dripping in stage sarcasm "How simply *thrilling* darling, we will all have a simply *dishy* time."

She dabbed her mouth with her napkin, carefully folded and rolled it, threaded it into its silver ring and placed it very precisely on the table in front of her, taking a few moments to straighten it.

"If you will excuse me, I must see Nanny."

He did not need to reply.

She had known about Kathleen and Arnold's relationship since the first week of her marriage. She had understood that it was 'on hold' during the election campaign but by late August, when Maureen had taken her to one side at a Drama Society meeting and explained that, since everyone else knew Alicia might as well too, she had been well aware what was going on. He had hardly tried to hide his movements.

When he was at home, which was increasingly frequently now the war was over, he seemed to be visiting Kathleen two or three nights a week. His car, a dark blue Daimler, was distinctive in itself but his arrogance in parking the car outside her house so frequently and so regularly, with its personalised number plate, was breathtaking.

Maureen had been sympathetic, but pragmatic "Look, my dear girl, as long as he doesn't know that you know you can retain your dignity. You must act with dignity at all costs. Never make a scene, do not shout and scream, do not beg, do not show you care in any way. He really isn't worth it."

"But Maureen I really don't have to make an act. I don't care, I really do not care the tiniest smidgeon what he does. He can do what he likes. Just so long as I never have to meet her. As to sex – I'm more than happy not to have to oblige him on that front."

She added "But I'm curious. What do all these *informed* ladies" she waved her arm in a broad sweep around the room "have to say about how *involved* he is?"

"Do you mean do they think he will leave you? I don't know about them but I'll tell you he won't. He'll not leave you, nor will he let you leave him. He's used to her, she doesn't demand much of him so that will continue in its merry way. And he.."

"Does he keep her?" Alicia interrupted.

"Of course he does! He has for years. She lives in a house that belonged to his father. He also regularly pays her not insubstantial sums of money for clothes. She has some very nice ones and, of course, since she came back from the war she hasn't had to do a day's work. There was talk of her setting up a clothes or flower shop, once rationing is out of the way, but I can't see her needing to do that."

"What about me?"

"He needs the façade of a marriage so he's not about to 'split you asunder' as they say. Divorce isn't easy, it's expensive, socially disastrous and he'll still want to get into Parliament so your marriage is safe."

"How long have you known?"

"That he had re-started the relationship?"

"Yes – I don't care about the earlier time"

"A few weeks."

"That long." Alicia was not surprised that Maureen had kept it from her – she knew Maureen would consider her feelings and be aware of how humiliating it would be for a girl, not yet 25, married less than four years, to find her husband had kept an older woman, his mistress from before their marriage.

"Should I ask you how you know all these things?" she continued after she had made sure her voice showed no emotion.

"Probably not."

Alicia valued her friendship with Maureen, her only friendship with anyone, too much to push her any further, and for her part, Maureen had become quite fond of Alicia and resolved never to tell her the truth behind her relationship with Kathleen. She knew she wouldn't understand.

The house that had been rented that Festive Week was actually just a wing in a larger house on the fell slopes looking down over the village of Grasmere with Rydal Water in the distance. It was a beautiful house in an even more beautiful position. With a maid and a cook supplied with the house, everything was designed for a comfortable and enjoyable stay.

The evening they had all driven up from Cheshire, Kathleen and Arnold went to the station at Windermere to meet the MacFarlanes.

"They failed to show up." Was all Arnold could say when they returned alone.

"No sign of them on the train." Kathleen had added

"*What* a surprise." Was Alicia's only comment

Henry made various telephone calls to try to find out what had happened to them, professing concern and annoyance in turn.

Alicia didn't believe a word of it and she got no reply to her question "They never existed did they?"

As far as she was concerned this whole house party was a pathetic ruse to allow Kathleen and Arnold to spend time together.

When it was clear that there were only to be the four of them Alicia saw an opportunity:

"Arnold, I will move into the Mackintoshes room. They're obviously not coming so I'll get the maid to move my things in there."

"Their name is MacFarlane not Mackintosh."

"Whatever. They aren't coming so I'll take over their room."

"I don't think so. It really wouldn't be appropriate."

"What would 'not be appropriate'?"

"We are here as husband and wife. We share a room."

He turned and left her alone. There was to be no discussion.

Alicia knew why he was trying to give the appearance that they were still happy together. It would keep Henry off the scent. As long as Henry believed that Arnold was in love with her he wouldn't worry about any relationship with Kathleen. Or, she began to think, the paternity of the child.

Christmas Day was a disappointment despite a pleasant enough service in the village church and a decent dinner, the cook having presented turkey with all the trimmings and oranges with the plum pudding – a treat not had since before the war. Alicia drank too much at Christmas Dinner as she did at every opportunity – it was her way of getting through the evenings and allowed her to ignore the fact that Arnold and she were sleeping in the same room.

Throughout the short days Alicia was content to be left to her own devices and to leave the others to theirs. She spent the days reading in the lounge by the log fire when it was raining, walking through the trails in the garden when it wasn't. She was aware that Henry was walking the fells with the housekeeper's two golden retrievers that had taken to him while Kathleen and Arnold played golf – or at least Arnold played golf and Kathleen walked around the course, from a distance giving every appearance of being a happy couple enjoying each other's company.

Most evenings the two couples dined together, Henry fussing about Kathleen, pouring her drinks, making sure she was comfortable. Alicia managed to avoid Arnold's advances by getting drunk as often as possible and retiring early.

So the week passed.

After dinner on New Year's Eve Henry was again plumping the settee cushions for Kathleen and obtaining a stool for her feet, fussing about her. Alicia was a little more drunk than usual and all the attention Henry was paying to Kathleen was annoying her, it emphasised how little attention she was getting, or indeed wanted, from her own husband.

She had watched them all week and Alicia was pretty certain the child was not Henry's. She drank more as she thought back over the past months.

She had not heard of Henry having any relationship since his fiancée had been killed nearly a year before. He had appeared to be completely shattered by that and the death of his parents. Once demobbed Henry had gone to work for Arnold, who had given him a job that didn't really exist in the office. Alicia was sure that if there had been anything going on she would have been told by one of the typists. But there had been no tittle-tattle in that direction.

She looked across at Kathleen, feet up, relaxed and pampered. The pregnancy did seem rather advanced for a September wedding. It was obvious to Alicia that Kathleen must have been pregnant before the ceremony and she was damned if she would believe Henry would have the nerve to take advantage of a woman before he was married. She was irritated, drunk and spoiling for an argument with someone but her voice was apparently gracious as she laid her trap.

"How did you two meet? It is such a romantic story – whirlwind romance and all that," ignoring Arnold's attempts to catch her eye she continued "I didn't even know you knew each other, though it is quite a small town isn't it? Do tell." She knew she was being unnecessarily provocative but was determined to dent their unspeakable smugness.

Kathleen looked to Arnold but he was getting to his feet to pour another drink and was not going to help her.

"Henry, darling, you tell the story."

Dutifully he walked across the room and took his wife's hand. "It's really very simple. We have known each other by sight for years, since before the war, we used to attend the same evening meetings. I didn't know her well, of course, just the occasional Good Evening, you know."

"No I don't know." Alicia was not going to help either. Henry continued, ignoring Alicia, who he realised for some reason seemed to be baiting him.

"Well, we used to see one another, quite often. I think Kathleen knew Joan." His tone dropped as he mentioned his dead fiancée.

"Yes," Kathleen saw a way out "I knew Joan quite well, she was so lovely" she turned to look at Henry, squeezing his hand reassuringly "she used to talk of Henry and how gentle and kind he was, how she worried about him while he was away – I quite fell in love with him just from hearing Joan talk about him."

"This would be before the war would it? You were away a lot weren't you Kathleen? You couldn't have had much chance to know each other during the war could you?"

"Yes, before the war, and during." Kathleen knew she was on tricky ground. Henry would hardly think she had carried a torch for him for all that time.

"So when she.... After a decent interval after.... Well I asked him out – to the theatre – to take him out of his shell, just to be kind to him – he seemed so lonely." She wondered if she had convinced anyone.

"Isn't she wonderful! She would never have said anything to me if Joan hadn't.... Well, once we did meet again one thing led to another and here we are."

"And so happy together." Alicia concluded in her stage sarcasm voice. She had to concede that, although she doubted every word, it was a plausible story – just. Arnold and Kathleen appeared to have been very clever. Well, she would see.

"Do tell me about Joan, Kathleen, I never knew her well."

"Come now – we don't want to talk about sad times – it's nearly the New Year I'll get the champagne." Arnold had at last come to Kathleen's rescue.

So they had one, then two, then three bottles of champagne.

Some while later Alicia, now very sloshed, returned to the subject. "That was all a complete load of tosh you know. You never knew that girl did you Kathleen, *darling*? It's all a put up job. Henry couldn't fuck a knickerless woman in a red hat."

"Go to bed Alicia, you're drunk." Arnold wasn't going to let her continue.

"Sure am. But then so are you. So are we all. Let's all go up – together...."

Arnold grabbed her arm, pinching the skin into a bruise and led her to the door, "Upstairs!"

"The woman's drunk." Arnold said as he and Kathleen settled down to playing cards, taking little notice of Henry. After a few minutes Kathleen looked across at her husband, meeting his eyes but communicating nothing.

Alicia was still quite drunk, and certainly more than half asleep, when she felt a hand push her nightdress aside and force her legs apart. She tried to push the weight off her, but he had already forced himself into her and ejaculated. He didn't say a word as he withdrew, stumbled out through the door fumbling to close it behind him.

That had not been Arnold.

In a state of heightened awareness, almost as if she was not herself but someone looking in on herself, she thought of what had just happened.

Henry had raped her.

She thought quickly, instantly awake and sober. She rushed to the bathroom and washed herself as thoroughly as she could but what if it was not enough, what if she were to be pregnant? Arnold would know it could not be his, they hadn't been together in that way for years. She could not let him have that hold over her, he had already hinted at wanting to think she had other relationships.

She would have to make him think that any baby could be his. But she couldn't allow him to make love to her. That would be too much to bear.

But he must think he did.

Did he know what Henry had just done, had he connived in it? Even suggested it? She did not know. But he must be made to think that any child could be his.

She lay awake waiting for him to come up to bed, dreading the sound of his feet on the stairs, rigid with hatred at the thought of what she knew she was going to have to do.

Henry must have heard what she had said. He had been sitting on the settee looking across at the two playing cards, whispering with each other, in a world of their own that didn't include him. What would he have thought?

Henry had always been Arnold' poor relation, he had always been the hanger-on. She wondered, in rather a detached fashion, whether he hated Arnold. He had good reason to, Arnold had always had more money and had always told him what to do. Henry had loved his aunt Ellen as a mother, he would do anything for her, which was why he had always spent spied on Arnold and her, reporting back all their actions. Yes, he probably hated them both.

Did he love Kathleen? He had probably loved Joan. But he would have been lonely and making a mess of living alone. He would have been susceptible to flattery, Kathleen would have said how lonely they both were and how much she cared for him and how she knew she could never take Joan's place, she would have seduced him. She would have to have been able to persuade him that the child was his.

Just as she now had to be able to persuade Arnold that he could be the father of any child that might result from what Henry had just done.

Arnold was very drunk when he eventually came into the room.

The next morning he woke to find Alicia underneath him in his bed. He felt very sensitive. He could remember nothing.

Alicia stirred as if waking. Even though she was a good actress her horror at him was not entirely feigned. She looked up at him, spat in his face and pushed him away.

For a second time she ran to their bathroom, making it very obvious she was washing her body as if it sickened her. She was washing, scrubbing her hands to remove any trace of him that had lingered after her vigorous handling of him the night before.

"Don't come near me Arnold. Don't. You are disgusting. You, your cousin, her, you are all disgusting."

Very little was said in the Daimler as they drove back to Cheshire later that morning.

Chapter Six

"I am not pregnant. I am not pregnant. I am not pregnant. I cannot be pregnant. I must not be pregnant. I will not be pregnant."

It was a mantra she repeated over and over to herself every day throughout the next month.

Her period did not occur with its customary regularity, she prayed that it was because she was so worried. She checked so often but no show appeared.

By the end of February she was sure that she was, indeed, expecting.

From the first moment she knew she wanted to be rid of it, but she was in no position to do what many in the working classes would have done in her position. She could not find an 'aunty' to stay with for a few months and go home leaving the baby for adoption; she could not find a clinic that would not ask too many questions. She was a married woman, in her early twenties, if not completely healthy she was certainly fit enough to carry a child to term; no doctor would say otherwise. She knew there were back street women who could 'deal with' situations like this but she had no idea of how to get in touch with one. The only person she could turn to was Maureen.

"What do I do? What can I do?"

"It was definitely not Arnold then?"

"Of course not! It was over before I could scream or rip his toady little eyes out. No. It was definitely Henry. The creep! How could he! He's a ridiculous, weak, insignificant toad of a man. How could he have been so disgusting. I can't see him – nor that woman he married. That had to be Arnold's doing too. Henry wouldn't do anything without Arnold thinking of it first."

It was knowledge Maureen kept to herself even when sharing it would have saved people so much pain. She felt it was not her knowledge to give away.

"I will not have this baby, Maureen. I will not."

"I think you're going to have to. In your position you cannot escape. I'm not going to let you get rid of it – abortions are dangerous and you are not strong. You'll have to go through with it."

"What about a proper doctor – couldn't you find one who would help?"

"Absolutely not. It is just too dangerous. You will have to have it."

"Then I'll give it away. It can be adopted. I don't want the bastard."

"Be sensible Alicia, just think. What reason on earth could you give to do that?"

"Then I won't bring it up. I won't look at it after it's born. I won't have anything to do with it. It will live in the nursery and whenever it is out of the nursery I will be out of the house."

"Does Arnold know... that it isn't his?"

"He must know what Henry did, of course he must do, but I slept in his bed that night." The look on Maureen's face made her hurriedly continue "He was completely drunk, he hadn't a clue what I was doing to him, but I was not gentle and he was probably bruised for days. He thought we had 'made love'. What a ridiculous phrase!"

"You may love it. The child, when it's born."

"Never. It should never exist, its life will be hell. I'll never care for it and that's final."

And until the very last days of her life she never did.

Chapter Seven

In the summer of 1946 I had accepted Arnold's obviously reluctant invitation to make up numbers for his village cricket team. "I'm a bit short of numbers Mottram, you won't be doing anything on Saturdays will you? Know anything about cricket?" Most of his pre-war regulars were unavailable for one reason or another – he was starting the team from scratch, and in his efforts to build up the team he had to ask people, like me, who he would not normally accept. I found it interesting watching him in the one environment he appeared to be relaxed. Most of his team worked for him or were neighbours and he was, of course, in charge. It showed something of the way I was advancing my career that I was even considered. He probably never worried about his reasons for asking me, he needed men who were reasonably active and willing to be ordered about and I was available. My motives were very different. I accepted as it meant I could be near Alicia.

In the last weekend of August Alicia was sitting in front of the pavilion scoring. She seemed to quite enjoy this. Arnold could not berate her for neglecting her duties to him as his wife, yet she did not have to talk to him or have any form of communication for the entire afternoon. The one wife she would have no conversation with was Kathleen.

I was umpiring, as a bowler I didn't have to bat for a while and doubled up as umpire when the openers were in. There had just been a polite ripple of applause from the assembled wives as the score reached 50 when we were distracted by urgent calls of "Arnold! Arnold!" One of the wives had the courage to break all conventions and shout out to the centre where Arnold was preparing to face another ball. He was scoring well and was obviously annoyed.

I saw a crowd of women around Alicia and, guessing the situation, told Arnold to go to his wife. I followed him as he walked slowly to the boundary. "Well, what is it?" he asked her as the crowd of anxious women parted.

"'It' as you could possibly guess, is the baby" she replied

"There's no hurry to take you to the Nursing Home. Charles took a very long time. Can't you wait?"

"No, Arnold, I can't. You've got to take me."

Alicia was not looking well but as I picked up the score book that had fallen to the ground I noticed next to the 1s and dots and 4s against Arnold's name in the score book. *Retired. Taking wife to Hospital.*

"I'm not taking you now, there's no hurry and I've just got my eye in. Mottram – you take her and come straight back." I know I should have stood up to him that one time and told him that he should be with Alicia but I was more than happy to oblige. I gave my white overall to one of the other chaps and ran to get the car.

As I drove her towards the nursing home I was so pleased to be able to do something for her. I knew she would never love me. I knew that even if she noticed me she would think I was the wrong class, not good enough for her and I knew that I could never keep her in the style and comfort she accepted as normal and had with Arnold. I knew she was unhappy, I didn't know most of the reasons why until many years later and I knew we would never be together as I dreamed.

For the whole journey, which couldn't have taken longer than 10 minutes, she was crying, lost in her own body's world. She wasn't listening to me as I spoke quietly, soothingly, in the calm voice I used with my mother, trying to soothe her through her pain.

I told her in a voice that could be saying anything that she could never do anything that would stop me loving her and that if I could do nothing else for her I would keep an eye on her and her children, try to make sure that nothing bad ever happened to them, always being there in case they needed someone.

I promised her, though I am sure she didn't hear me, that whatever happened to her I would always see that this baby was kept safe. It was a rash promise, made in a pact with the Gods to make the baby's birth safe.

It was a promise I tried to keep, though I am not sure I kept it as well as I should have done.

I left her at the home, my arm around her helping her up the steps to where the nurses were waiting.

It was the first time I had ever touched her.

There was nothing for me to do but return to the match. When I saw the score book at the end of the day Alicia's comment had been rubbed out and instead Arnold had continued his innings, finally being out caught and bowled for a respectable 74. Kathleen had taken over the scoring.

We were playing the next day as well, and I was surprised to see Arnold changed into his whites hitting balls back to 4 year old Charles who was trying to bowl over-arm to him.

"That's more like it. Keep your arm straight. Don't want you to be a chucker you know."

"What on earth are you doing here Arnold? How's Alicia?"

"Oh she's still at it. I can't do anything there and didn't want to let the side down."

"Are there any – complications? It seems to be taking a very long time" I tried not to sound too concerned.

"It seems the brat is 'breach' or something. Trying to come out backside first apparently. May make it, may not."

Susannah Ellen Donaldson was eventually born, after many hours of labour that nearly killed both herself and her mother, just before midnight on 1st September 1946, four months to the day after Carl Henry Witherby.

There were so many seven-month babies being born at this time that some doctors joked that the human gestation period was being permanently reduced so it had been no surprise that Kathleen and Henry's son Carl was strong and healthy despite being born such a short time after their wedding. He was a bright baby, with a shock of dark hair and strong arms and legs. He appeared to thrive on the clean sea air and there are photographs of him at a very young age pointing excitedly at the gulls as they flew above him and the yachts as they sped past cracking and splashing in the boating lake.

Kathleen appeared at the weekly cricket matches proudly pushing her son in his pram. She would sit back, letting Henry take centre stage as he showed his team mates the photographs of himself with Carl.

Henry was comfortable and secure with his family and loved every moment of being a father. He seemed very happy with his life and his job in the Accounts Department of Arnold's firm. It was equally clear that his wife found the daily round of walking, talking, shopping and housework a difficult routine to take any pleasure from. My mother who, because she mixed with the women of the town, would happily give me such information as I would not otherwise come by, said that Kathleen's only joy was Carl.

"I can't believe what has become of my life, " Kathleen said to Arnold on one of their evenings together. "I know it's dreadful to say but I really do miss the war! I had a good job, responsible and interesting, I was a professional woman, respected and independent. I could have done anything. Now its all gone." She snapped her fingers.

"Just like that."

"Well you wouldn't get rid of it would you?"

"Arnold! Don't even think of saying such things. You know I couldn't, wouldn't ever have got rid of Carl."

"So your predicament is really your own fault."

Sometimes Kathleen saw things in Arnold she really did not like.

"The only thing I have is Carl."

"Probably."

She had looked at him for a few moments, this man she had been with for ten years or more, how well did she really know him?

As the babies grew to toddlers the gossips commented on their similarities. As children connected to one of the most prominent families in the town and with *such interesting* connections they were the subjects of much speculation.

They both had curly dark hair and blue eyes, small noses and ears, delicate hands with long tapering fingers. But differences began to show in their developing personalities. Carl, loved and pampered by Kathleen and Henry, grew confident and open, ready to chuckle at everything, demanding the attention he knew he would get. "Such a happy baby" people said.

Susannah, on the other hand, was quiet, undemanding and quick to tears. She would sit alone for hours playing with her brother's discarded big teddy in the nursery at Millcourt. When she was with people she was desperate for affection, apparently needing their approval, and she would do whatever anyone asked of her so they wouldn't tell her off. At the slightest hint of criticism she would dissolve in tears – an action that simply made her nanny and parents tell her off more.

The ladies of the town who knew them both used to talk about the children with knowing glances.

"So alike to look at those two. They could be brother and sister."

Chapter Eight

In June 1948 I had a letter from Max asking me to meet the train.

He had again been away for several weeks, communicating only by telegram or letter. Since the War he had spent more time out of the office than he had through the whole period of hostilities. Many of the young men who had left the firm in 1939 had returned, of those that did return some left unable to cope with the humdrum nature of their old jobs, but sufficient numbers stayed to relax the burden of work on the rest of us. So Max' absences just meant I did more of his work and passed client issues that I would normally have dealt with down to the returnees – all of whom had been my seniors before they left for war. In many ways it was a difficult period.

Several times I asked Max where he went on his trips – a question one could then reasonably ask as the necessary secrecies of the war receded into memory. He said that some work had only just begun with the ending of the war. He said that this work was the most important work of all. In the harsh winter of 1947 when we all looked back, even to the war years, with fond memories of being warm, he spent many hours in his office with the *Occupied* notice hanging on the door. Whenever we saw him he appeared distracted, angry, frustrated but more than anything he was worried. He told me that living in the peace was far harder than in wartime because in peacetime you felt that things should be *able* to be done and they weren't "At least in wartime there is an excuse for failure" he said.

And then his mood lifted. He became lighter-hearted and even jovial. His visits away became fewer and farther between until, in June 1948, he said he was off on his last trip. I ventured to ask him where he was going. "Austria then France. I will send you instructions. I will need your help Ted." It was one of the first occasions on which he called me Ted.

So it was with a degree of curiosity that I had read his instructions which arrived from France some days later. I followed them to the letter.

I was on the platform as requested, as the train arrived at Lime Street Station, appearing through a fog of steam through the deep cutting. The train was crowded and there was chaos as the travellers dismounted, acquired their luggage and porters and made their way to the taxis lined up along the length of the platform.

I had been told to look out for a young woman who would be carrying a small brown cardboard suitcase. She would have blonde hair, tied tightly off her face and she would be wearing a light grey belted gabardine raincoat. As the crowd cleared she was not difficult to spot even though her hair was covered by a headscarf tied underneath her chin.

"Monika Heller?"

"Oui, Yes, I have sorry." She was flustered and ill at ease, almost frightened. Her eyes, very dark, very opaque, gave nothing away apart from the fact that she, as so many others, had suffered.

"My name is Mottram, Ted Mottram, and I have been asked by Major Fischer to meet you and take you to your lodgings."

I spoke slowly as I had been told her English was not good.

"Where is Major Fischer?" She was looking around her, anxiously.

"He will not be here for some time. You will be well looked after. He has sent enough money to take care of you for a while."

It was many years before I knew anything of how she had spent the years before I met her off that train, and then only when I read Max's papers.

Max had told me something of her background, how she had no family and had come from France as a displaced person under the children's programme. She seemed to me rather too old to be treated as a child but that was not for me to question.

Max had arranged lodgings for her in Birkenhead with Elsie Holt, a widow hardly older than Monika herself but with a young child. Bill Holt had been a merchant seaman lost in the North Atlantic a month after their wedding. Monika would be safe and comfortable there, as well as being company and a help to Elsie, while we established whether she would be able to undertake the work that was being planned for her. Max had told me that Monika was not good with adults and he had it in mind that she should find work as a 'mother's help', 'nanny' would be too grand a name as she was completely un-qualified.

It seemed a good idea. People would be only too pleased to have someone who did what they were told and asked no questions, who neither smoked nor drank alcohol and who would have no designs on the man of the house. She would not be attractive to men, I felt sure about that, her manner was distant and formal, and her eyes would warn any man off before they would even thought of making any advances.

She had told me that she had worked with children during her time in the camp in France and had loved them for their innocence. I felt sure they would love her for her almost childlike qualities.

They would not feel threatened and neither would she.

I saw her once a week when I dropped in the rent envelope and spoke with her for a few minutes each time. Her English certainly did improve as she spent most of every day talking with Elsie and helping her look after young Billy. "She'll do" was Elsie's verdict when I raised with her the idea for Monika's future as a mother's help.

At the beginning of September 1948, when all her paperwork had come through, I drove Monika to meet her new employers.

Chapter Nine

Towards the end of his life Max asked me to write down all that he could remember. We sat in his library with him talking and me writing, for many hours. When Max died I also had access to his papers, written in tight old-fashioned handwriting.

I came across a brown envelope, on which was written a short note addressed to me, asking me to check through the contents and include them only if I saw fit.

I read through the pages, moved, horrified and desperately sad in turn. How could all this have happened and we had not known?

I include a heavily edited version because, if I didn't, the story would somehow not be complete.

I was seconded to the army legal service, attached to humanitarian relief and the displaced persons courts. I, for some reason probably based in misguided romanticism, asked to be attached to the section based in Rennes, in north west France. I was successful in my request and spent much time in the years between 1944 and 1948 in Brittany. I spent my leisure time at a bar in Audierne, a town I had visited in another life, in the mid 1930s when I was a law student in Vienna.

I first noticed her in the early summer of 1947. She was sitting on the wall looking out to sea.

At around the same time the next day she was there again – or was it still? Had she moved at all? Who was she? Where did she live?

I was involved in the work of finding refuge and repatriation where possible for the thousands of "children of the state" that still roamed homeless and rootless in post-war France, so I felt I had some responsibility. I did wonder if she could be the woman I sought but she seemed far too small and too young.

"Who is that young girl" I asked the patron of the café "does her family come from around here?"

41

I spoke in French, my French was good even though I knew my accent was strong, I liked to think the strongest element was English – though I am sure they were suspicious of the German influences.

"No Monsieur, she is a stranger. But she has been here every day now for two weeks, sitting on the sea wall, looking out to sea. She is a clever girl because the time she comes varies with the tides – later and later every day."

"Does she eat here? Drink? Where does she go when she leaves?"

"Why are you interested, monsieur? Do you have an interest in young girls?"

As he spoke he raised his eyes to the ceiling. I could not miss the looks on the faces of the men in the small bar, trying so blatantly not to hear my answer as they hunched over their glasses. I did not rise to his tone of voice, deliberately not taking offence and answered as well as I could.

"Yes, indeed I am. It is my job to get young girls, and young boys, who have no homes and no families, to places of safety. To give them a chance in life that up till now they have not had. There are many children still suffering from the recent hostilities."

"Monsieur, of course I meant nothing other than that. She has been here now for several weeks. I do not know where she eats or sleeps. She just appears here every day and looks out to sea."

I left the bar, conscious of the attention being paid me by the patron and his customers, and walked slowly across to the sea wall.

Standing two arms lengths from her I waited for several minutes to see if she would walk away before I spoke.

"What do you watch so closely, young lady?"

I spoke to her in French, she did not reply. I tried again in a dialect of German that, had she been the person I sought, she would have known.

She did not move away, nor did she turn to look at me. After a while she replied, quietly but clearly "Die unterseeboot."

Several minutes passed and still she did not turn towards me.

It was a perfect description of what she was watching. As the tide receded the sharp lines of the prow of a boat emerged. The boat had obviously been driven ashore some years before and the salt and waves were beginning to break down the structure and it was becoming something of a skeleton. It was not a submarine but it was certainly a boat under the sea.

We sat watching as the tide went lower and lower down the beach. She neither spoke nor moved for some time. I felt a little uncomfortable but was determined to find out more about the child. It was a good hour later, when the boat was again being covered with the waves, that she turned towards me, unsurprised that I was still there;

"It is time to go Monsieur" she said, this time in French.

"Will I see you tomorrow?"

"I shall be here."

The next day I was waiting at the sea wall when I spotted the slight figure walking round the bay. The sea was just beginning to expose the 'unterseeboot' again.

"Good morning Monsieur"

"Good morning Mademoiselle"

"Madam"

"I apologise. Good morning Madam."

That single word shocked me.

She was so young. She was so tiny and vulnerable. She looked no more than 12 years old. I had completely misjudged the situation and felt very foolish. Yet now she was facing me and when I could see her face and into her eyes I realised she was older, but surely still no more than 17.

Over the next few days I met and spoke with Monika, for that was the name she gave, several times. I found her to be polite, answering questions in French and German, equally easily, with as few words as possible but never rudely or brusquely. She gave nothing away about herself at all. I discovered only that she was living in Plouhinec, an hour's walk away from Audierne but came here when she could, to watch the water rising and falling over the shell of the boat.

In the office in Rennes where we were trying to do what we

could for everyone and anyone who came to our centre I raised the subject of the girl.

"What can I do about her George?"

"Absolutely nothing old chap I'm afraid. You can do absolutely nothing about her at all."

"Just because she is older in years, George, just because she is no longer a child?"

"Absolutely old chap, there are rules."

"If you met her you would know that she is still a child in her mind. Her age may be older than 15 but her mind isn't. Believe me." How could I explain this child - as it was as a child I thought of her. "She must have seen so much and been through so much that she has never grown up." If you saw her you would think she was only 12."

"But I haven't and I won't so leave it be."

It was good advice which I should have taken. But I couldn't leave it be.

Two weeks later I was drinking in the café when Monika appeared - as I hoped she would when the tides had worked through their cycle. I walked down to the sea wall.

"Bonjour Madame"

"Bonjour Monsieur"

I asked if she was well, she replied she was and asked if I was well. I replied I was also. The formalities were performed as if we were in a pantomime.

"Do you speak English?" I asked, in English

"A little" she replied - also in English

"Enough to live in England?"

"But that would not be possible Monsieur. I have spoken many times to men from England and have the language a little but I do not think to live in England."

I did not want to think what Englishmen she had met and what language they had taught her. I asked more.

"When did you speak to Englishmen?"

She did not answer with words, simply a shrug of the shoulders.

I understood, but had hoped that that would not have been

the answer.

"Why would they do that Monika, you are so young, almost a child, why would they do that to you?"

"They pay me, monsieur, they have food, I have hunger."

I hoped that it was her lack of english that made her speak in the present tense. Perhaps it was the same now as it was during the war, perhaps nothing had changed that much. This is what happened to all people in war. Even though they did not die their spirits were killed.

"Would you like to leave France?"

"Only if I can have a roof and food. And no need to do things with men."

We spoke now in French. Her French was better than her English. Perhaps she had had to be with more French men. I was sure it was not her native language.

"Where do you come from Monika? Where were you born? What is your real name – it is not Monika is it?"

She did not answer until the tide had turned and the sea was yet again exposing the boat to view.

"I know my real name is not Monika. It is what my mother always called me when we had left the farm. I don't know where I came from, I have been in this country for a long time but we came here from another place. We took many days to pass a big lake. There were mountains and snow. There were boys in brown uniforms."

Her voice tailed off and I realised she was meeting pictures in her mind that she did not want to see and had not seen for many years.

"Boys in brown uniforms," she repeated, very quietly.

Austria, or southern Germany. She must have come from there.

"You are Austrian?" I asked but she had not heard. She was still thinking of the words she had just spoken. In a few moments she turned and walked down the sea wall, away for another day.

"She is Austrian, George, not French. I do have a responsibility. It is up to me to see her safe."

45

"Just because you are also Austrian, Max, does not mean you are responsible for every lost Austrian girl in the entire world."

"What would you have me do then?"

"Leave her be – she has survived, she will survive. She's not your responsibility. Leave her Max."

I had to return to England for some weeks and I decided to leave it to the hand of fate. If she was still in Audierne when I returned I would help her. If she was not I would not try to find her.

I got to the café well before the tide was to turn, and waited anxiously with my coffee and cognac. She did appear, walking slowly along the sea wall, around the bay. I was so very pleased to see her. I drank the glass dry in one and walked down to the wall.

"Good afternoon Monika."

"Good afternoon Monsieur"

She took up our relationship where it had left off, as if I hadn't been away since the summer, it was well into the Autumn as the chill wind coming off the sea sharply reminded me. Monika still wore the cotton dress she had worn at every meeting we had had. I went to take my coat off and put it around her shoulders. She shrugged. "That is not necessary Monsieur, I must become used to the cold."

I decided we could not go on as if time was no object, they said it was going to be a long cold winter. I do believe she would not have survived that winter of 1947 had I had not insisted she allow me to help.

"Monika, I am from Austria. It is a country you may know. It has mountains as you have described, beautiful mountains with snow on them through most of the year, even when it is warm in the valleys. There are many large lakes, beautiful deep blue lakes which reflect the sky and the mountains. The quiet life that existed there, a quiet life led by good people, was disturbed by war and..."

I fought to find the right words to convey the multitude of sins that had befallen my homeland and ended, very lamely,

"bad people."

"Do you remember anything of the mountains?"

46

She looked at me sadly. Said nothing and walked away –
even though the sea had not yet turned to cover up the boat.

She was not there the next day. Nor the next.

I had long since given up trying to explain my interest in the
'young girl' to the patron and his customers. They had accepted
my presence and my conversations on the sea wall. I asked the
patron of the café to find out what he could.

"I have frightened her away George. She has so much fear
and I have frightened her with my questions."

"She will come back, she sees you as a way out. She will
come back when she thinks she has frightened you enough."

I did not want to think that she could be that calculating,
and so I still went down to the café every day for a cognac. I was
getting worried, it was getting colder and I had to go back to
England soon.

After several days when she had still not reappeared the
patron had some news.

"She has gone, Monsieur. Your young lady." Though he
did not say the correct word for 'lady'.

"Do you know where?"

I had spoken out loud not expecting an answer but received
one anyway.

"She is held by the gendarmerie. They have taken her to
Rennes. She is a thief."

You will not need to know the details but I found her in
Rennes, paid off the police and took her under my protection. It
is probably true to say that the gendarmerie believed my interest
to be exactly that that the café's patron had thought it to be those
months before.

She seemed pleased to see me. It was the first time I saw her
smile.

Monika was completely quiet as we drove to the girls' camp.
I made some sort of explanation to the matron and hoped that she
would think Monika no older than 12.

For the time she was in the camp, throughout that
frighteningly cold winter, I visited her when I could. She began
to talk to me, offering me tea in a very formal manner as she

entertained me in the hut that passed for the camp's common room. She said nothing about the boat or anyone she may have known through those months we had been watching the sea do its work. But slowly she confided in me some things of her life.

On one occasion, with great ceremony, she showed me her envelope.

It had been sewn inside her clothes for years. It contained her real papers. I could hardly believe she had kept them through all she had been through.

And they proved me to have been right in my instinct that day on the sea wall and right to have persevered. I knew now I would have to lie for her, do whatever it took to win her confidence and get her to England

At first she not only dwelt on her past, she dwelt in it, always talking as if the events she spoke of were happening now. But gradually her months in the camp helped her. She found children more vulnerable and frightened than she was, she found that she could help others. She made herself useful to the women in charge of the camp, she looked after the young children, she comforted them through their nightmares, she played with them in the snow, she learned to care for children and not be afraid of them, she learned to love their innocence and she found they trusted her. Perhaps, with regular meals and safety and security she was able to experience something of the childhood she had never been able to have.

As she gained weight, and filled out like a woman should, she began to look her age.

I had to get her out of the camp and out of France before it became obvious that she was not a young girl. It was an infuriatingly frustrating wait but eventually, in early summer 1948, news came of a boat going to England carrying 200 children to be adopted by English families. I had to get Monika on it. So I lied, I forged papers, I got her on that evacuation boat.

"Max she is leaving tomorrow with the others."

"Thank you, George. Thank you."

All I had to do was persuade her to go.

What would she think of England? Would it be a better life

for her? She spoke very little English so what could she do? But they were problems for the future, first I had to get her to England and to safety.

It was surprisingly easy to persuade her. She was happy to go where I suggested, I believe she had come to trust me.

Chapter Ten

Alicia had been reaching the end of her tether.

I was becoming increasingly involved in the Donaldson's affairs as Max delegated more and more to me. Four times it had been necessary for me to extract them from contracts they had taken out with Domestic Agencies because a nanny was unsuitable. I only learned later why she was becoming increasingly desperate to find a settled Nanny who would remain in the position for some time, years even.

It was Max who persuaded Alicia to accept someone who hadn't been formally trained, who didn't have the right certificates and wear the correct uniform. He persuaded her to make compromises and take on an untrained nanny, someone who came with a personal recommendation even if they had no formal qualifications. He encouraged them to accept someone who needed the position as much as she needed a nanny for the children.

People said in those two years since Susannah's birth that Alicia had stayed with her unloved and unloving husband for the sake of appearances. Elections had come and gone and she had been the dutiful wife; she had supported Arnold at the company's Christmas dinner dances, smiled prettily while she presented prizes at sports days and made tactful speeches at retirement parties.

But I suspected that the main reason she had stayed was that she had nowhere to go.

It was obvious to anyone who cared for her that she was desperate, with good reason. Everything she had wanted to be she could not be. She couldn't dance because of the accident; she couldn't be involved in the theatre, apart from local amateur dramatics, because of her 'position' as Arnold's wife. She felt the last decade had been one of unremitting loss and failure. Such high hopes she had had when she was 18 had all crumbled. Then she could have done anything, gone anywhere she wanted to. Act, sing – whatever she turned her mind to she had done well. Then came the accident, the war, Arnold and the children.

She had escaped her parents. She had broken free of that drudgery, but she hadn't expected things to get so much worse.

She had no money of her own and had no way of supporting herself. She couldn't return to her parents, they had opposed her marriage in the first place. A reason had to be found to allow her to escape, a reason good enough to ensure Arnold would have to continue to pay for all her needs as she would have no other means of support. It had taken time for her to come up with a foolproof reason with which Arnold could not argue.

She had never been well since the accident and the war munitions work, and then after Susannah's birth she had been very ill. She visited various specialists. Her depression was not taken seriously as such a condition was common in young mothers; but the fact that she was always in pain, that was more difficult to tie down. Recently she had been feeling increasingly poorly. She was always coughing. The family Doctor, concerned that it was something serious, had arranged for more tests.

They decided it could be TB.

She decided it was.

It was arranged for her to spend some time in a sanatorium in Switzerland while her condition was evaluated. She could get all the rest she needed to regain some strength and recover from the past years. She would also get excellent care and treatment of the TB, if indeed that was what ailed her.

But she had no intention of ever returning.

It was with an air of finality that Alicia broke the after dinner silence the day before Susannah's second birthday party.

"I don't think I'll be coming back, after Switzerland."

"No? And why would that be?"

"I think I would be happier not."

She had planned the conversation in her mind. She was going to tell him as little as possible of what she had planned.

"You think you would be happier not." He quoted back to her. "And just how are you going to live – or needn't I ask?"

Determined not to rise to the bait she continued with her script. "You are going to support me. You will pay me a regular allowance and I will stay out of your way."

"And just why would I do that?"

"Because if you don't agree I will tell everyone I know that Carl Witherby is your son."

He had no answer to that. Impropriety such as that would end his

51

political career just as it was beginning to buck up again.

"Pay me a generous allowance indefinitely. I'll stay quiet and out of your way for as long as you like."

She carried on, knowing she held the advantage.

"The new nanny will have to work out, she can do other work around the house as well as look after the children. Max says she's very willing. Cook will help out and if necessary you can always hire someone else. Charles is nearly old enough to go away to school and his sister can go in a couple of years. You can get on with your life. They shouldn't get in your way."

Arnold wasn't going to argue with an arrangement that would suit him equally well.

"I'll talk to Max."

"I have already. He has drawn up some papers and requires you only to fill in the sum and sign."

He nodded at her in acceptance of the *fait accompli*. He would be free to pursue his interests and a young wife in a sanatorium would be good for the sympathy vote.

On the afternoon of her birthday Susannah was joined in the nursery by her mother and father, her brother, Max Fischer's daughter Veronica, the five children of other members of the cricket team, and, of course, Carl with Kathleen and Henry. Alicia watched the children playing their games, organised by Kathleen who dictated to everyone as though she were already the lady of the house.

But it didn't worry Alicia – she had found her way out.

So it was that, two days after the party, I delivered Monika to the Donaldsons. It was the first Monday in September 1948.

It was also the day Alicia left home.

Chapter Eleven

About a week later neither Susannah nor Charles would eat. They both started coughing; a slight, irritating, hacking cough which would not go away. Carl was the same.

"I'm so worried" Kathleen told Arnold on his next evening visit. "He's just not himself, he's not eating and that cough just won't go away."

"I will get the doctor."

"Don't you think I already have? He says it could be something he picked up, possibly a touch of bronchitis, though he did say that was odd for this time of year. Carl isn't like Susannah, though. He doesn't get every illness that's going around. How is she, by the way?"

"Ill, as usual. Probably picked up the same bug. The new woman, hardly more than a girl I'd say, hardly up to her responsibilities, hasn't asked for a doctor yet, as far as I know. I'll make sure she does."

The next day he called Monika to him in his study.

"I hear that Susannah and Charles are not well."

"No, sir, they are quite poorly. They will not eat, Sir."

"Have you called Dr Protheroe?"

"Yes Sir, he came this morning."

"Why was I not told?"

"You told me not to worry you with the nursery, Sir. You said I must not tell you every time the Doctor visited."

He was not, it was true, normally interested in nursery business, but if they had the same as Carl...

"What did he say? Is it anything to worry about?"

Monika had been with the Donaldsons for such a short time. She did not know how out of character this questioning was.

"He will be back tomorrow in the morning. You will want to talk to him?" It was a question.

"Yes. Yes, of course. I will want to talk to him."

Whereas Monika had not known her employer, Arnold Protheroe did. He had been the family doctor for years.

"Why the interest Arnold? You usually couldn't care a dicky bird what went on in the nursery. When Susannah had that nasty do with measles last winter you didn't even visit her, let alone want to talk to me."

Arnold had already thought that this question might be put to him and he had his answer ready, looking away to hide his emotion he said very quietly "But now Alicia is not here."

"Of course, dear boy. How silly of me. Of course it is all down to you with Alicia away. Have you heard from her yet? I know she will get the very best of care, it is a very good establishment."

"No I haven't heard. Now, what about the children?"

"I believe they may have Pertussis, that is the whooping cough. We must get your new nanny, who by the way appears to be very competent for a foreigner, we must get her to keep a good eye on them and let me know if there is any change in the character of the cough."

"Is there anything else she should look out for?"

"Indeed there is, but I am sure she can deal with it – she seems very young but also she seems capable, very capable and the children do seem to like her."

"She is young, Arnold, also inexperienced, not to mention any slight problems there may be over the language. Tell me what you are going to tell her so that I can make sure she understands."

"Vomiting, mucus, that sort of thing. And, of course, the loud 'whoop' at the end of each coughing fit."

"Fit?" Arnold was alarmed

"Coughing fit, Arnold, coughing fit. Not a fit as such. But we must be careful, we must watch for signs of any worsening."

"Such as?"

"Pneumonia, any signs of deafness."

"That bad?"

"Yes Arnold, I would not be playing fair with you if I did not tell you that if it is pertussis it can be very dangerous."

"How dangerous?"

"Indeed, Arnold, in many many cases it is frequently fatal, and I should add not only amongst the poorer in society where the poor mites don't get proper treatment. Young Veronica Fischer is desperately ill with this dreadful illness as we speak. It is a dreadful disease." He paused, he knew there was nothing to help Veronica now and that she would probably not survive the week. "I will go up now. Do you have any other questions?"

"No, but thank you for being so frank."

By the time Dr Protheroe had reached the nursery Arnold was in his car driving to Kathleen and Carl.

"Is he any better?"

"No Arnold, the cough mixture I have been giving him makes no difference, he is coughing much much more, and he has been sick several times now."

"I don't want to worry you, my dear, but it could be very serious. It is very likely to be whooping cough. We must take very great care of him."

Without consulting Henry they arranged to take Charles to Millcourt where they could all stay and Nanny could look after him with her other patients. This was not so unusual, when Susannah had had the measles earlier in the year Carl had stayed at Millcourt for two weeks to make sure he caught it too, to 'get it over with'.

When he heard what had been arranged Henry couldn't thank Arnold enough for all his help at such a difficult time. Kathleen and Henry moved into the spare wing and she spent all day every day with her son. She talked to Dr Protheroe every morning and made sure that Monika knew what to do. It was very hard work for Monika, up throughout the night, night after night, with the demands of three young and frightened children, especially with an over-anxious mother under her feet all the time checking up on her. But she knew the children were very ill, and she knew she had to help them.

After a week Charles was being sick a little less often, his coughing spasms were a little shorter. It was not long before he was up and about helping Monika to look after the younger children. He liked her. She talked to him as if he were a grown up.

But whooping cough has to run its course and it was the end of October before Henry and Kathleen could move back home and another week after that before Susannah was out of her bed.

The 'little infirmary' in Millcourt had been lucky. Max Fischer's daughter Veronica, along with a great many young children that year, did die.

Charles had few memories of his earliest years when he had lived with his mother and grandparents in the tiny bungalow. When the war ended and they moved to the big house he never saw much of his parents. Cook had looked after him, feeding him fresh bread and home made lemonade in the warm kitchen but then Susannah had arrived. There had been a sequence of nannies who he never bothered to get fond of as he knew they'd leave if he did. He had grown up looking, observing, listening and keeping out of the way of adults. He felt unwanted and unloved. From his earliest memories he had no one who cared about him – until Monika.

Although the two younger children had no memories of their illness Charles remembered those weeks for the rest of his life. It was the beginning of a relationship that would last for many years. Charles transferred all his love to his new Nanny. She would smile at him, a big round smile in her round face, when she noticed he was looking at her. He loved the smell of her hair, always carefully tied in a bun behind her neck. She was always warm and he loved it when she gave him hugs to thank him for being a good helpful little boy.

He was nearly seven now. Not so young in many ways.

To him it was simple. His mother didn't love him and Monika did. His mother had left him and he knew his new nanny mustn't leave as the others had.

She must never leave.

Chapter Twelve

I drove Alicia to the station. It was a convenient arrangement as I had been dropping off Monika and I had some papers for her to sign that gave Arnold power of attorney over her affairs and complete control over the children in her absence abroad. There were other papers Max had included which I hadn't had a chance to read through.

She asked me to set up a bank account for the allowance and gave me a contact address. She asked me never to let Arnold have it. Wherever she was, she said, anything sent to that address would always reach her.

The address was Max Fischer's.

She was a much nicer person when she wasn't with Arnold. There were times when I saw her being a real bitch that I wondered why I cared about her so much, but then she had so many reasons for acting so badly. She was always absolutely polite and quite friendly towards me, if more distant than I would have liked, but on this journey she was also quite talkative. Had I ever been to Switzerland? Why did I put up with the way Arnold treated me now I was being promoted in the firm and even talked of as a future partner? How much she was looking forward to being better and having some energy again.

Alicia spent two days in London before taking the train to Paris. She stayed at Claridge's, had lunch with a friend in the River Room at the Savoy. She bought some new clothes at Jaeger and at Fortnum & Mason. She spent some time in Hatchards choosing some books and arranging for them to be shipped to the sanatorium.

I knew all this two days later when the bills arrived at the office, the one from Hatchards with a lovely letter from the manager saying how much he hoped she would enjoy the books and what a pleasure it had been to spend the afternoon with her. I also received a letter from her thanking me for driving her to the station.

She was, indeed, a different person when not with Arnold.

I received several letters from Alicia over the next five years. There was no regular pattern, perhaps she wrote to me when she had no one else to write to. She wrote as if to a friend though there was very little that was personal in any of them.

I have, at last, written to Elizabeth F, she is rather difficult to write to because I really don't know her, and yet one must write at such a time. It must be horrid to lose a child so young.

She hadn't asked about Charles and Susannah.

I have not heard a word from any of my devoted friends.

I think she meant Maureen, though perhaps she included anyone who had been involved with her dramatics.

On Monday I have to register at the gendarmerie as I have been here over three months. If I don't I shall probably be put in jail or something. Registration I might add costs 20 francs. Some racket!

Her sense of humour occasionally showed through the self pity that was the main content of her letters.

At the moment I seem much less at sixes and sevens with myself, and much less agitated. I think I may, at last, have accepted some of my limitations.

I did notice a development in her letters, a development towards a detachment from her life in the Wirral.

Have I been here a year now? I'm not quite certain of the date.

The second half of the century! I frequently wonder where we shall all be in 50 years time, don't you? Shall it be worth living in – this Brave New World of ours?

She had begun to be more philosophical in her outlook.

I have been much interested in the elections – it looks like the old man will return. I hope he does the country justice. Whoever it is has a great responsibility.

I am acquiring a peace of mind which I have been woefully lacking for some considerable time.

She was beginning to look at things beyond herself.

Seven years, seven dreadful years, but only seven. The past is the past and I will have nothing to do with it. I have the future now.

Perhaps she had gained from her experiences.

But she never mentioned her children.

When I asked her some years after why she had written to me she said it was because she felt sorry for me. I had always seemed so lonely.

I think it was, perhaps, that she was keeping her options open, keeping a lifeline to her old life. Just in case.

In early 1952, after I hadn't received a letter for many months, two letters and a postcard arrived at the same time.

I'm writing this right at the top of the Table Mountain. The cable railway is absolutely terrifying but, Ted, the view from the top is wonderful. It was signed 'A'.

All the earlier letters had been addressed to "Edward Mottram Esq" and signed 'Alicia Donaldson'.

'A' wrote again from Mombasa.

"I am looking forward to Aden as I can buy things there quite cheaply. I will have them sent directly to England, let me know if you have to pay any duty or anything."

Two months later, a ship-to-shore telephone call.

"Ted, can I call you that? We're old friends aren't we?" She began. "I've got to be short as *so* many people need to use this wretched contraption. We're arriving in Liverpool on Saturday 4th July. Will you meet me at the dock? Anchor Line from Genoa the times will be in the paper."

Was there any need for me to say I'd be there to meet her? She must have known I would.

"Thank you Ted, you're a brick."

"It'll be a pleasure."

I think I heard her say "I do look forward to seeing you again" before the line went dead.

I had been determined to keep my promise to Alicia, the one I had made her as I drove her to the nursing home nearly seven years earlier. From the day she left I had resolved, with my mother's help, to keep an eye on Charles and Susannah, though what I could have done if anything had 'gone wrong' I don't know.

My mother was a very good source of information as, despite her illness, she kept up her visits to the fund-raising coffee mornings and 'bring and buy' sales that kept her in touch with all the women who would know how the Donaldson family was.

I had good reason to visit Millcourt regularly to check that Monika was settling in and I had an unexpected ally in Max Fischer who, I soon realised, was finding reasons for me to visit Arnold – to deliver and pick up papers, to obtain signatures on more documents than I ever thought could possibly be necessary however complex his private dealings were.

And whenever I was there I kept my ears and eyes open for the children and clues to their well-being. I rarely saw them as they were kept in the nursery on the first floor, well apart from Arnold and any visitors. When I occasionally broached the subject of the children openly with Arnold I would never get a straight answer.

It was easier in the summer; I could see them playing in the garden or they would be at the weekend cricket matches with Kathleen and Carl. I would talk to them, ask them about school, what they enjoyed doing, but I wasn't very good with children, I had no experience, and so I'm not sure they had any idea who I was or why I was speaking to them.

The weeks and months passed as Millcourt had settled into a routine. The nursery became Monika's domain and she ruled it well, with firmness and compassion and Susannah came to love her nearly as much as Charles did. The time Monika spent with her helped Susannah become less withdrawn, responding by becoming a sweeter and less isolated child.

Carl was often dropped off to spend the day at Millcourt, he spent most of his time with Susannah, they were the same age – they played together, had their rests together, listened to the radio programmes together. When the three children were all together at Millcourt Charles was shut out completely. He was so much older they didn't need him. Carl and Susannah left Charles to himself.

When Arnold arranged for them to go the kindergarten together it was probably so he could spend more time with his son but Susannah was happy.

She could spend even more time with Carl.

Chapter Thirteen

It had always been the plan that Charles would go away to school as soon as he was old enough but Arnold hadn't arranged anything until Alicia had been away for nearly four years, and he did so then only because he was forced to.

Arnold summoned 10 year old Charles to his study, a rare event which Charles looked forward to with dread.

Charles remembered the key phrases in his interview.

"You are to go away to boarding school."

"I have had to visit your House Master who is unhappy with your progress."

"We have agreed that you need to get away from the influence of the nursery."

"You are not maturing as you should."

"You are becoming weak and you lack ambition."

Charles had no way to change his father's mind. He wouldn't have dared explain.

As he always did when he was unhappy, he went to Monika.

"He's sending me away!" he cried and burst into tears.

She tried to calm him down but she knew, far better than his father, how difficult it would be for him.

No one had ever come up with an explanation as to why he started to wet the bed every night. The problem had arisen the Christmas night after his Mother had left. That first morning Nanny was kind, saying 'these things happen' and did not make him feel bad. She removed the sheets and bedding and washed them, replacing them with dry ones.

But from then on it was every morning that she had to dry the mattress, covering it with a rubber sheet when she could not.

She had a word with the doctor, asking if it could be because of the whooping cough, but he had said that was unlikely. He would grow out of it, he said, perhaps he's unhappy because of his Mother, but as far as he could see there was nothing physically wrong.

Night after night Charles woke up with the dreaded warm wetness around him in the bed. He hated it. He lay on it hoping that the warmth of his body would dry it out, but that didn't work. It only made him smell more. He knew he smelt. He tried to wash in the morning but he knew that he could not get rid of the smell in the cold water. The boys at school called him 'Stinky' and left him alone.

He hated the wet bed so much he would try to stay awake all night. Lying on the still damp mattress with the sheet gripped in his hands pulled up to his eyes.

"I will not go to sleep. I will not. I will stay awake"

But, of course he couldn't.

He stopped eating and drinking, but that simply made him tired and ill. It was no wonder his school work suffered.

Monika continued to wash and dry sheets, to turn the mattress. She talked calmly to him, trying to reassure him "It is not your fault. Do not worry it will soon stop." But it went on and on. He knew she was the only person in the world who didn't hate him.

"He can't send me away Nanny! He can't! How will I hide it? They'll all hate me! He can't send me away!"

But he did.

Arnold didn't want to drive the 100 odd miles between the school and Hoylake whenever his son had to be driven to and from school, so I offered. I knew it was to free up time for Arnold to visit one of his girlfriends but it meant that I could keep an eye on Charles and, as we spent hours in the car together, perhaps he would open up and I would get to know him better. I first did the trip in November 1952, after he had been at school for six weeks or so, and I suppose I did it seven or eight times in all.

He was tall for his age and slender – like both his parents, but he took after his mother in looks, his brown hair had her unruly curls and his eyes the same haunted look.

It was desperately sad to know how unhappy he was and not be able to do anything about it. I was just so pleased that Monika and Cook looked after him so well when he was at home.

On the first few journeys he would sit in the front seat of my car with his back straight looking straight ahead through the windscreen, lost in his own thoughts. If I asked a question he would answer it politely but would go no further than the briefest of answers. But after a few months he would be more forthcoming. He would make statements about what he had been doing – not really a conversation, but he was trying to be friendly.

"There were lots of golfers out on the links yesterday. They disturb the birds."

"I saw redstart and whimbrel today, they are on their way north from Africa"

These were typical comments, not inviting response or conversation but perhaps trying to be friendly. He didn't comment on the weather or sport in an effort to make conversation but he liked birds and bird watching – it was something he had plenty of opportunity to do living where he did, near one of the most popular bird watching islands in the country. It suited him too, an activity that he could undertake alone, full of patterns but with challenge and variety.

He was never talkative, perhaps he was uncomfortable with me, he did not know me that well and I was an adult. I don't suppose he ever had to get on with many adult men. As far as he was concerned I was just a friend of his father's engaged to drive him to and from school.

Even had I no ulterior motive I would never have minded the drive. I loved the journey through the fields of the Wirral, red sandstone farmhouses standing out against the perfect green fields, then the contrast of the narrow roads with stone walls and the sheep pastures of North Wales. Sometimes I would vary the route and go along the coast, past the steelworks along the Dee and then, after turning the corner westwards, the ever-denser caravan sites around Prestatyn and along the North Wales coast to Rhyl.

After a few journeys he began to open up more and more, telling me a little of how he felt about school, what he had done on his weekends, even what he thought of his father or his mother. He seemed to be relaxing somewhat, less in his own self contained world.

But as he opened up to me it became obvious how desperately unhappy he was.

He told me he was in a dormitory of five boys and the other four paired off together leaving him on his own. He had no friends and as he kept losing them house points they hated him even more.

I only found out years later why he had been so desperate. At the time I knew nothing.

Matron had been forewarned of the 'night problem', but was not sympathetic and did not help, simply telling him, in front of all the other boys, to clear his bed sheets, wash them and hang them out with his mattress in the yard. If they were not dry by teatime, when he had to carry them all inside and make his bed again to the accompanying taunts and jeers of his room mates, he still had to sleep on them.

Every week he was in front of his house master. "Donaldson. You have disgraced us again. Deduct 2 house points."

"But Sir…"

"You are not a child any more. Matron says you are still being a baby. You will lose 2 house points for every night you are a baby and I shall have to punish you, as long as this behaviour goes on."

He pleaded "I don't do it deliberately Sir, I don't know how to stop." But no notice was taken.

Losing house points so regularly he missed exit weekends in further punishment. He had to find a way to be dry.

He took to sleeping in the lavatories. He would stay awake until after the prefects had swept the torch around the dorm to check everyone was there, and then he would slip out of bed and down the corridor. Sitting up as best he could through the night he could sleep very little. Before the bell he would creep back to his bed and pretend he had been asleep all night.

Of course his schoolwork suffered as it had before. Of course he made no friends.

He had never been so alone. He had never been so frightened. His letters home, written dutifully every Saturday afternoon repeated the call "Take me away from here. I hate it. Everybody hates me. Let me come home."

The cry, repeated week after week, fell on deaf ears.

His father did not read his letters, he kept them unopened in a desk drawer where they were found some years later.

He had no love for the boy, he did not even like him, he always compared him unfavourably with Carl, with whom he could now spend a lot of time. He blamed Alicia for giving him such a weak child, all this trouble had to be her fault as Carl was growing up so splendidly.

He was on half term over his 11th birthday. He had said that he was glad he had been born at the end of May as he would be on holiday on his birthday. I suspect there was an element of self-protection in this attitude. If he were at school he would have had to go through the embarrassment of having no friends to share a cake with. Charles had told me of the ritual whereby, on their birthdays, boys sat at high table with two friends of their choice. No-one ever wanted to do this as it meant talking to the masters and being the butt of jokes in the common room afterwards – Charles would have had no friend to join him. So he was very pleased he was on half term and at home.

He was quite talkative on the trip back to school – he seemed less unhappy about returning, which I saw as a good sign. He told me that he had had a lovely weekend. He had had two birthday teas – one with chocolate cake and 11 candles with Monika and Susannah in the nursery, the other with his father in the library. He was given a proper bicycle as a present, he had wanted binoculars but a bicycle was OK, he said.

When we neared the school Charles asked if I would leave him in the town instead of dropping him at the front door of his House. He wanted to buy some stamps and he could easily walk the mile or so back, and he didn't have to be signed in until 7pm. I believed him and I trusted him so I waved cheerily as I drove off, seeing him standing on the pavement with the small brown suitcase at his feet. He didn't normally have a suitcase but, had I thought about it, I probably would have assumed it contained presents.

It took me nearly three hours to drive back to Birkenhead and as it was a lovely evening I drove the inland route, through the mountains and forests of North Wales. As I drove, I thought about the boy and tried to think of something I could do to help. Maybe he was getting over his home-sickness. I hoped so, because I didn't see how he could carry on the way he was going. As I pulled up in front of my house I concluded there was nothing I could do except hold a watching brief. I couldn't write to Alicia, and wouldn't interfere with the way a father dealt with his son. Why did I feel I had any responsibility?

I was very surprised to see the familiar Daimler parked outside the house I shared with my mother. Arnold was inside drinking a cup of tea, sitting uncomfortably at the square oak table in the front room – a room we never normally used.

"Where is he then?"

"Good evening. Where is who?"

"Charles of course, man. He hasn't returned to school."

So that was what he had been up to.

"He was fine when I left him." I couldn't help but sound defensive.

"Where did you leave him, you didn't return him to school did you?"

"Well not quite, he wanted to buy something."

"So you did what exactly?"

"I left him in the town, he said he would walk back to school. He had plenty of time to get back to school before curfew."

"Well he didn't go back. His housemaster called about an hour ago to ask what time he would return. I said he should have been there and I would find out from you what the story is."

"He had some money didn't he?"

"Of course. £10 for the rest of the term."

"Well he can't get far on that. What is the school doing?"

"They have alerted the police and are keeping me informed."

"Do you want me to go back with you?"

"He will turn up somewhere when he realises that he is making a fool of himself."

I should not have been surprised at his attitude. But perhaps it was a little more serious than just missing curfew. Should I say anything or not? I didn't want to get him into trouble, but I didn't want him to get into any trouble on his own.

"He had a suitcase with him."

"What? Why?" Arnold was still angry "Why the hell would he have a suitcase?"

"I supposed it contained his presents."

"He planned this."

"Yes, I rather believe he did."

He got up and went into the hall.

I have frequently thought that only hearing one side of a telephone conversation can be misleading. It is normally very difficult to get the complete gist of the exchange. But what Mother and I were listening to was all the conversation, the person on the other end had little chance to say anything. Detailed instructions were given, only once did he wait for a reply – that was to the question "Are any of his clothes missing?"

He had enough money to buy food, clothes would have been essential as his school uniform would be very conspicuous.

"Blast it!"

It appeared he had taken clothes.

"The weather isn't too bad, but it is getting dark" contributed Mother tentatively.

"He should be alright even if he has to sleep rough tonight."

Arnold had replaced the receiver and lifted it again, he was now talking to the school. In this conversation he spent a little more time listening. He replaced the receiver again and left the house without saying "Good Evening" or "Thank you."

We were all worried in our own ways. Arnold kept making telephone calls to his contacts in the Police force to make sure they were doing all they could; to the school to confirm Charles had not yet returned him.

Then he would telephone me to berate me for not delivering him to the school.

In the days that followed Kathleen spent a lot of time with him at Millcourt because he really couldn't go to work. Henry joined them in the evenings. Susannah and Carl had not been told but they knew something was wrong because Nanny was distracted and absent minded, not listening to what they said and telling them off when they hadn't really done anything wrong.

I got in the car and drove the roads we travelled to and from the school in case he was trying to hitch-hike home.

It was a worrying time.

In the end Charles was missing for ten days.

He turned up back at the school none the worse for wear having, he had told them proudly, walked around the Isle of Anglesey.

I was called upon to go and fetch him immediately.

It was an entirely different Charles that I picked up from his headmaster's study. He was excited, confident and talkative.

"I had an absolutely super time, Uncle Ted, it was worth the telling off. Really it was. I don't care what Father does, I've had a wonderful time."

"I don't think your father is particularly pleased with you, young man. He was very worried you know, and once the worry was over, when he heard you had had turned up safe and well, well he was very, very angry."

"I'm sorry I caused you all worry. I didn't want to do that but I really couldn't go back. They all hate me and I've got no friends – I'm the only one with no friends at all. No one wants to pair with me at games, I'm always the last one to be picked as a partner, no one wants me in their team. They all think I'm horrid. I hate the dorm – they are all horrid snobs and bullies. They call me names and I just hate it."

It all came out in such a rush. Then he slowed up and asked, tentatively, "Did they tell Mummy?"

I couldn't tell him that no one had had any contact with his mother for some time and that his father did not know how to contact her even if he had wanted to. I knew her contact address was only the other side of the golf course from Charles' home, he could see Sandhey from his bedroom, but I had never asked Max Fischer what the connection was.

"No, they didn't think they should worry her, not with the way things are it was not as if she could come home or anything. She couldn't have done anything, just worry, and that would not have helped her health at all would it?"

"I didn't think."

"No, Charles, you didn't."

"Was Nanny worried too?"

"Of course she was, we all were. But you're safe now and that is all that matters to us all."

We drove without saying anything for a few minutes, but it was not an awkward silence. After a while Charles asked "Is he very angry with me?"

"Yes. Very."

"What do you think he will do?"

"I don't think you are going to have an easy time."

"Would it help if I said I was sorry?"

"Of course, it always helps to say you're sorry but you really do have to mean it you know. My mother always used to say "Don't just say 'sorry' say *why* you are sorry. Then you've got a better chance of forgiveness and understanding."

"I didn't want to cause anyone worry. I just couldn't go back."

At the time I couldn't understand why he was so unhappy.

"Why couldn't you go back Charles, are they bullying you? Is that it? If you're being bullied you either put up with it or fight back or, if you really can't do either and it really is that bad, you tell someone."

He was hesitant, he wanted to say something but wouldn't, maybe he couldn't. I hadn't gone to public school, but I knew something of what happened there. He was probably being bullied, possibly even being interfered with, by the older boys. It had to be something very serious to make Charles run away. He wouldn't have done that lightly and it would explain why he wouldn't talk about it.

I decided I would have to have a word with Arnold before I left the two together.

"When we get back you go into the garden. Stay out of our way for a few minutes. I am going to have a word with your father before he sees you. Now. Tell me. What did you get up to on your adventure?"

He relaxed and told me of his week's escape as if he had no cares in the world. He told of walking through the waves on long wide beaches, buying bread and cheese in small grocers shops – he had never had to buy food before – "The smells, Uncle Ted, wonderful smells and everyone was so nice." He had first gone to Beaumaris where he had walked around the castle and watched the ducks and swans on the moat; he'd sat on the sea wall and looked across at the clouds forming and reforming over the mountains of Snowdonia with the sea birds wheeling and turning on the winds above him. He had climbed headlands and cliff paths, he'd seen Puffin Island, he'd run through the surf on wide rounded beaches, he'd lain on the sand drying out in the hot sun, he'd wandered through woods and over heath lands but the thing he seemed most excited about was sitting "for a whole day Uncle Ted, a whole day" at the top of the cliffs on Holy Island looking out at the lighthouse surrounded by so many birds "you couldn't count the different types there were millions and millions of them."

He spent the rest of the journey telling me about that one afternoon. That week's escape undoubtedly changed his life, but I always believed it was that afternoon on Holy Island that was the key-point.

For the first time I felt he knew I was his friend. I think he knew, from then on, that if he needed someone he could count on me. I would not let him or Alicia down again.

"We're nearly there now. Remember go straight out to the garden, stay in the summer house out of sight and don't come near the house."

"Yes, Uncle Ted." The energetic, enthusiastic budding ornithologist had disappeared, replaced by the dutiful, seemingly contrite, young boy about to be severely punished.

I know which Charles I liked best.

"Good evening Arnold"

He ignored my greeting, immediately barking "Where's Charles?"

"Can I have a word?"

"Now?"

"Yes. I would like to see you before you see Charles. I think it important."

"If you insist you'd better come on in."

I followed Arnold into his study.

Ours was not an easy relationship. I had worked for him as his clerk assistant when I first joined the firm in 1936. Then, during the war I had grown in stature in the firm, taken qualifications, now I was a partner, whilst Arnold really didn't progress anywhere and then, since his father died, he had little to do with the firm other than as a client. But I had been in his house so many times, I had visited, carried messages for Max, picked up and dropped off his son, played on his cricket team many Sundays for years but for me, as for several of the others, it was never as if I was playing with him – he was always the employer giving instructions which he assumed would be carried out. We would never be called 'friends'.

But I was now more important in the firm than he had ever been, so he should have had to consider me more of an equal. I had stopped thinking of him as 'Mr Donaldson', I thought of him as 'Arnold' but called him either depending on the circumstances. He still, I am sure, considered me to be his junior and frequently called me 'Mottram'.

Yes, it was an odd relationship and on this occasion was a tricky one. I had decided to address him as "Arnold".

"Sit down Ted." He had accepted the balance of the moment.

I spent the next ten minutes explaining to Arnold that his son had run away because he was scared, worried, but basically because he was lonely. I intimated that he may have problems 'of which he could not speak'. He stood with his back to me looking downwards into the empty fireplace.

I gave Arnold little chance to speak as I told him what an interesting, intelligent son he had and I suggested he needed help not punishment.

"Where is he?"

"In the garden. He is extremely sorry for causing worry but I honestly believe he felt he couldn't do anything else." I changed tack, asking with a confidence I did not feel "Were you ever bullied at school?"

"I really don't know what that has to do with anything."

"You didn't go away to school did you, Arnold?"

"No. I went to school in Birkenhead."

"So you went home every night to be comforted by your parents after any problems of the day?"

Perhaps I had gone too far, but I pressed on. "Arnold, imagine in the darkest days of your school career you could not go home. You had to stay with the people who were tormenting you. Life was never going to get any better. What would you have done? Eh? Would you have had the courage your son had to get away? Could you have planned your escapade over days, weeks perhaps, knowing that you would be completely alone for several days – knowing the trouble you would be in when you got back, as get back you knew you must sometime?"

"You don't think I should punish him then?" He was not giving in, simply observing the other point of view in a dispassionate manner, as a barrister would.

"Don't misunderstand me Arnold, I believe he should be punished. But I also believe the punishment he has already given himself should be taken into account."

"What punishment would that be?"

"He has been imagining the beating he will get. What is it Shakespeare wrote in one of his plays? Something like *"A coward dies a thousand times a brave man only once"*. He has gone through the next few minutes with you many times in his head. He knows it is going to be difficult and he has undoubtedly imagined far worse than it will actually be. He also knows he has to go back to school, where the punishment he will get will not be pretty."

I had probably gone too far already but still I pressed him "Would you consider taking Charles away from school, putting him into a local school, allowing him to live at home?"

He was quiet for quite a while. Arnold was a selfish man whose own interests generally overruled those of any of the members of the household or his business. He was an ambitious man whose political and legal careers had foundered, whose business, a business he had no interest in and was not good at running, was not thriving. He was a father who disliked, and did not know how to deal with, children. He was a husband whose marriage had been an utter failure. But on this occasion he was, I believe, honestly trying to work out how to do the right thing by his son.

"Go and fetch him. I will deal with it now."

Perhaps, as I walked out to the garden, he remembered the loneliness he had suffered at school; how much of a relief it had been for him to get home every evening, to be praised and comforted by his mother, to be able to do the things he wanted, read, walk the dogs along the sea front, be alone in his room. And perhaps he realised how he himself would have dealt with being sent to boarding school.

I left Charles at the door of the library. Before I had been able to close the door and retreat I had heard the opening exchanges.

"Charles"

"Father"

"Uncle Ted had told me many things that I should have known. Are you really unhappy away at school?"

Charles, who had been expecting an entirely different opening to the interview burst into tears.

Arnold was obviously uncomfortable "Charles. Here. Have this handkerchief. Sit down and we will work out what are we going to do with you."

I left them to it and went down to the kitchen and had tea with Monika and Susannah. Such was my position in the house I was both upstairs and downstairs. They had so many questions to ask as, of all the people involved, they were the ones who had most worried about Charles while he was missing.

It was only then that Monika explained the reason why Charles would have been so unhappy.

Later that evening I received a phone call from Arnold.

Could I drive to the school and pick up Charles's trunk. Matron was packing it and it would be ready at lunchtime. Would I be so kind? He was so busy.... So much to sort out.... Telephone calls to make.... Meetings... One last time....

Charles was to start at his father's old school in two weeks time.

He was coming home.

And very soon after so did his Mother.

Chapter Fourteen

She had phoned me from the ship to say she was coming home but had she told Arnold? I doubted it and so I called him. We had been telephoning each other quite a lot regarding Charles and his school problems and so he was expecting me to talk of that.

"Arnold"

"Ted. No problem I hope?"

"No, but it's a little difficult. Could I come round to see you? I could be with you in half an hour and it wouldn't take long."

"Not really convenient. I have to go out."

"It won't take long but, perhaps, I have a little explaining to do so it's a little difficult over the phone. It is important."

"Very well." And he rang off, no doubt giving little thought to my request.

I had been wondering how I was going to explain not only Alicia's imminent return but also how she came to be telling me about it and not her husband and family and in the event I didn't do it very successfully.

"No. Ted. It won't do. She cannot come back as if she's not been away for 5 years. As far as I am concerned as soon as she left the sanatorium she left my protection and I no longer consider her my wife. She has the allowance. You know the agreement, as long as I pay the allowance she stays away. She cannot come back here. Not now. It would be all too much."

"What do you suggest she does? She is arriving on Saturday."

He soon collected himself.

"I neither know nor care. She cannot come here and that is the end of it. You sort it out."

I had no difficulty in recognising her, but she was different. Five years before she had been a child in many ways, now she was sophisticated and confident as she walked through the arrivals hall towards me. I was conscious that I probably had changed not one jot as she walked unhesitatingly towards me, her gloved hand outstretched. "Ted, it is good to see you! Where are you taking me? I can't imagine Arnold would be too happy to see me. I didn't really mean to come to

Liverpool but that's where the ship was headed. So I thought of you. Ted will sort everything out I thought and here you are, sorting everything out for me."

It occurred to me, as I closed the car door after she had folded her long legs without any difficulty into the foot well, that she wouldn't remember the last time I had put her in my car. I had been taking her to the Nursing Home when she was having Susannah. I remembered so clearly, and wondered whether I had adequately kept that promise I had made to her. Did she know how unwelcome her return would be to her husband but how pleased I was to see her again. As I slid into the driver's seat I told her I would explain all over lunch at The Adelphi.

The dining room was crowded, there was a special lunch for Americans who were staying there before crossing the Atlantic. I had forgotten it was their Independence Day.

She started to tell me about her life since she had left.

"I have been around Africa in a wonderful small boat with just five other passengers. Well you know that – I sent you a postcard from Cape Town. Did you get it?" She didn't wait for any reply "I went to America, to New York and across the country on a wonderful train to San Francisco. I have been all around the world." She paused, a trifle dramatically, but I did not interrupt. He voice was lower, calmer as she continued.

"But now I am coming home. I will tell you and you mustn't tell anyone. But I have not been alone!"

I think I was supposed to be surprised by that.

"At the sanatorium I met this wonderful man, Louis. He was French and he was very rich. He was also dying. He said to me that he wanted to spend the last months of his life travelling the world with a beautiful woman! Well what could I say? I went with him. He had a nurse so I didn't have to do any horribly 'personal' things for him. I just had to accompany him in public and sing for him. You see he loved my voice and he just wanted me to sing and I could! After all those years of thinking I would never sing again I could!. I know what you're thinking. Well it wasn't like that. We had separate staterooms and he never expected anything, though I did get to be quite fond of the old chap. But sadly he has just died and I am alone again. You know how much I hate being alone. So I've come home. "

It was obvious to me that she had nowhere to live, nowhere to go and had no idea what to do next. She was not just 'passing through', she needed to establish the groundwork for next stage of her life.

After we had eaten she went across to their table to talk to a loud group of Americans. I watched her as she charmed them, laughing and flirting as she drank more and more champagne. I was embarrassed, but hardly surprised, when I saw her being handed up onto the table where she shook her hair loose from its pins, closed her eyes and sang their national anthem.

I had never heard her sing before.

Her voice was stunning, as good as any professional I had ever heard, possibly with the exception of Kathleen Ferrier whose records my mother was particularly partial to.

I couldn't watch, I hated exhibitionism even when done with such style. I left her to it and went to reception where I booked a suite in the name of the firm, saying a valued client would be unexpectedly staying overnight. This was not unusual other than the fact that the 'valued client' was at that moment standing on a restaurant table. I reassured them that she was thoroughly respectable.

I would have made my excuses but I was sure she had more or less forgotten she was having lunch with me, so I told the manager to send her luggage to her room and explain to her that I had had to return to the office and would call at 10 the next morning.

Back in the familiar surrounding of my office, which years before had been Arnold's, I rang Max.

I needed his help.

"Bring her to me. I will look after her."

"Should I tell Arnold where she is?"

"No need, unless he specifically asks."

"You want me to bring her to you?" I had to be sure that was what he really wanted me to do.

"Yes, Ted. Do it."

The next morning I collected Alicia promptly at 10, surprisingly she was waiting for me in the foyer. For a second time in two days I settled her into the front seat of my Humber.

As we drove through the quiet Sunday morning streets I told her of the arrangements that had been made.

"Max has asked that you be his guest tonight, while things get sorted out."

"I suppose I have been away a long time. Yes, I think that is a very good idea."

I did not know the nature of their relationship – they were obviously good friends though I had assumed it was for business

75

reasons she had given his home as her contact address of 'last resort'.

"How is Elizabeth?" she asked gently, "Has she recovered from Veronica?"

"I don't think she ever will recover, she was almost a recluse before their loss, she was never seen in public, rarely went out of the house at all. Now I understand she rarely leaves her rooms. I think Max will love having you around, you will be company for him."

"I won't be any trouble at all."

As we had entered the Mersey Tunnel no more conversation was possible. A few minutes later, out onto the streets of Birkenhead, the subject had changed.

"It seems a very long time ago that you drove me in the opposite direction Ted, five years and we have a new young queen on the throne. I missed all that excitement."

"It seems that you have managed quite a lot of excitement of your own." I tried not to sound disapproving.

"Of course!" she laughed "and I've told you all I'm going to tell you about it! But what about you? How have the last five years been? You haven't changed a bit!"

Before I replied it occurred to me that the old Alicia would never have thought to ask.

"Everyone's getting back to normal after the war. Houses are springing up all over the place, they're building over the bomb sites. Rationing is all but over now."

"No, Ted. What's happened to you?"

"Well I am getting older." I wasn't used to talking about myself, I wasn't sure how I could describe my life without giving away how much my caring for her and her children had dominated those five years. "I still work at Roberts and Jones, obviously, and still live with my mother, not much has happened really. Five years isn't long in the overall scheme of things you know. My mother needs help, people need my help."

"No girlfriends?"

"No. I'm always busy I suppose."

As I spoke I realised how dull my life sounded.

We were driving down Bidston Hill into the fields of the Wirral when I broached the subject of Arnold.

"Arnold will not be happy that you had returned. He has his life now."

"Kathleen you mean."

I couldn't make a direct reply so I turned the subject. Perhaps I said too much.

"The business, it isn't doing very well at all. I have been sending you your allowance and have paid any bills you send, as was agreed, but the business isn't as profitable as Arnold thought it would be. He inherited a thriving business, of course the war was a very good time, but now he's lost all the military contracts and it's getting harder. He knew he was never a businessman so he should have got a good team around him, but all he did was employ old friends from the army"

"Henry"

"As you say, including Henry"

"No one could ever call *him* a businessman."

"That's true, but the problem is that none of them are."

"But what about the pots and pots of cash stashed in the bank? He wasn't dependent on the business was he?"

"He has been eating into that capital. He loves his cars, he has, well, he has expenses, keeping up his standing in the community."

"Keeping Kathleen you mean."

"That as well."

"How bad is it?"

I realised I had gone too far. It was my job and my responsibility to be discreet – it had been unforgivable of me to breach Arnold's confidences. I had forgotten the lesson I try to teach everyone who joins the firm *Discretion in all things*. I had let my concern for Alicia take me too far.

I tried to backtrack "Oh I have painted a gloomy picture haven't I? It's not 'bad' at all. The Donaldsons are still very comfortable."

"But we were 'rich', Ted, not 'comfortable'. I don't think I would want to be 'comfortable' it sounds very boring."

I remembered that for a very long time and reminded her of it when just to have been 'comfortable' would have been wonderful.

We reached Sandhey and I pulled into the drive. Alicia jumped out of the car almost before I had pulled on the hand brake and ran round the side of the house. I followed her.

The sea formed the backdrop to the scene, the great expanse of blue with wisps of white horses stretched northwards until it merged with the blue sky. It was an idyllic spot, in such a fine position right on the corner of the peninsula. The house had been built on top of the run of low cliffs that overlooked the dunes and the sandstone rocks of the Point. The spectacular views completely compensated for the battering the house took during any gales.

Despite its exposed position the garden itself was sheltered. The large lawn was surrounded by banks of mature shrubs, massed banks of hydrangeas and fuchsias which filled the garden with colour for most of the year, protecting it from the wind that always came from off the water.

Standing on the stone patio at the side of the house Alicia looked across the river to the hills of Wales, they seemed so close on this sunny morning – even nearer were the small outcrops of sandstone that made up the islands of Hilbre. They were only a few hundred yards from the shore and were a magnet for trippers and birdwatchers. She watched a number of small groups of people heading for the shore, just finishing their walk back from the islands, well before the tide came in. She was quite deliberately holding a pose – aware of how beautiful she looked, the wind moulding her thin dress to her figure, her hand raised to prevent her trademark hat from blowing away.

She was well aware that two men were watching her, captivated.

Max emerged from the French windows onto the patio and nodding brief acknowledgement to me addressed Alicia, "Good morning my dear, how lovely to see you so well." Holding her shoulders and kissing her on each cheek in turn in the continental fashion.

"Oh Max how lovely of you to have me to stay in your beautiful house. It is so good to see you again, if only for a few days."

There was something between them, I don't know what, but the understanding between them was almost tangible. From that first moment I saw them together I felt excluded.

I should have seen it coming, really. I knew Max made regular trips to his home country and perhaps the sanatorium hadn't been that far out of his way.

Watching them with their easy familiarity I have to admit jealousy. She was only as nice to me as she would be to any other person from whom she needed favours.

I wondered how easy it would be for the love I felt for her to change to something entirely different. Why she had come back? She knew she would not be allowed back into the marital home. She had no real interest in the children. She had only come back because she had run out of options. I would love to have been part of the solution to her problems but I was a realist.

Now a very reasonable option had presented itself for her in a rich, lonely man. Although Alicia never actually said when they became lovers, she freely admitted to the relationship years later, when it no longer mattered.

78

I knew at that moment that I would only be a part of her life when she had nowhere else to turn.

I do not know the details of that evening's interview between Alicia and Arnold. It was one of the very few things she would not go into when, years later, we had long nights to fill with conversation.

I know it was not a long interview and I was soon made aware of the consequences.

They came to the office the following day. The papers she had signed in my car on the way to Lime Street were destroyed, wills were changed and the terms of the divorce were drawn up. Perhaps they were unduly harsh.

"You deserted your family."

"You were committing adultery, openly."

"Are you saying both Susannah and Charles are mine?"

"I will not answer that. You are beneath contempt!"

That was a surprise to me. If not Arnold, who could Susannah's father be? I had never suspected her of having an affair. Surely not Max even then?

"You cannot, you absolutely cannot put the blame for that on me. I will not have it."

"Ted, could you leave us please. I need to tell my wife some of the facts of life."

I left.

Some 15 minutes later my secretary knocked on the door and took in a tray of tea and biscuits.

"It seems to have quietened down." After she had shut the door behind her. I knocked on the door of my own office and went in. Arnold got up from the chair behind my desk and walked to the window. I made no comment about the presumption – I supposed it was an automatic thing for him to do. I wish he hadn't sat there, I had left the room in such a hurry that I had not closed the file on my desk, the file with all the correspondence from Alicia to the firm over the past five years. I wondered how much he had seen.

"I think we need to try to agree the terms." Bringing everything back to a business footing I hoped no more skeletons would be let out of cupboards. There were certain things I did not think I should know.

Arnold took a piece of paper from his pocket and read:

"The divorce will be on the grounds of my wife's desertion. She will not counter sue on any grounds whatsoever. She is to see Charles and

Susannah for a maximum of two weeks every year. She will see them in an hotel. They will never visit her at her home. She will never be welcome here.

"She is to sign an agreement that she will never," he hesitated for emphasis and repeated "never, communicate with the press or with any other person or in any way use any information she may have, or think she has, to interfere with my social, business or political affairs.

"In return I will undertake to buy a house, for the maximum sum of £2,000 and pay an allowance of £100 per month.

"No! That wasn't what we agreed!" Alicia interrupted, words streaming out "You said you would be fair. You said that you would make sure I was 'generously provided for'. Those were your words. 'Generously provided for'. You cannot, you will not, expect me to live on £100 a month. Arnold, this is ridiculous."

Ignoring her Arnold continued "This allowance will cease when she re-marries as re-marry I have no doubt she will."

He chose to be even more insulting. "Should she choose to live with a man as his wife but not go through any form of marriage ceremony that will also terminate the allowance."

Alicia opened her mouth as if to say something but before she could frame any words that could make sense Arnold had continued.

"The allowance is not a generous one as I have no intention of paying to maintain a lifestyle from which I get no return. I have, as we are all aware, maintained payments throughout the past five years. I did not abandon my wife, where many men would have. I have bought tickets for journeys I would never make, I have bought clothes I would never see, I have bought lingerie for the benefit of other men. I have not questioned this. But it ends here."

"You were rich Arnold, you could afford it. Just because you're going broke you think you can spend what's left on your brat instead of me."

Did she realise what she had said?

Arnold looked at me. I looked away, unable to hold his eyes.

"Why do you say 'were' Alicia? Why do you say I'm going broke? Do you know something more than you should of my affairs?"

I looked up and saw that, although he was addressing Alicia, he was looking at me. There was nothing I could say. He knew that I was the only person who would have told Alicia anything about his business and Alicia had, in that one statement, given evidence of the betrayal of the trust that was essential between a man of business and his solicitor.

We had never been friends, Arnold and I, but I had been able to keep an eye on Charles and Susannah while I had his trust. In that look I realised now I would no longer be able to do that.

Arnold kept his eyes on me as he rose and walked to the door, opening it he said to my secretary "Tell Max I wish to see him."

Alicia looked at me, shrugged her shoulders and followed her husband out of the door.

I sat down.

I put my head in my hands and swore quietly at and to myself.

Chapter Fifteen

"Where do you want to go this summer Charles? Would you like to go to France? Spain? Gibraltar? It's up to you. You know I don't mind where we go."

"Do we have to go anywhere?"

"You know I can't come up to see you, be sensible. Where would you like to go?" She did not mention Susannah.

"What I mean is we don't want to go anywhere with you."

A few moments passed while she collected her thoughts.

"I was wondering when you would say that. Every year I have been waiting for the day when you would finally say you didn't want to see me."

"It's just that there is so much going on. We don't want to do it any more. We don't see the point."

"You don't want to do it any⬛⬛⬛ You don't see the point! I'm your Mother for Pete's sake." She wa⬛⬛⬛g control of her temper.

"You don't really care do you? You don't care what our lives are like do you? You just keep on with these weeks away with us, year after year after year, just to spite Dad. He couldn't care less whether we saw you or not. He probably couldn't care less whether he saw us again. The only person who has ever cared about Susannah and me is Monika. She's stuck it out year after year, putting up with all our problems, even now! If I had to spend a week with anyone I'd want to spend it with her. She's always been our real mother."

It took her a few moments to answer.

"Those are not very nice things to say, Charles."

"I don't bloody care if it sounds 'nice'. Why should I be 'nice' to you? We're not bloody coming."

"Don't swear at me Charles. I won't have it."

The phone went dead.

She stood by the window, the telephone receiver in her hand, looking around her living room.

He had put the receiver down on her.

"Where has all that hatred come from?" she asked herself.

She remembered the last week they had all had together, in a lovely hotel in Devon. It had been snowing and the children had enjoyed sledging and snowballing together with her watching from the terrace like a 'normal' Mother. Except they hadn't really got on had they? Alicia asked herself to face the fact that Susannah and Charles had spent most of the week together, barely being polite to her. She had learnt nothing of their lives, what was important to them, what they thought and believed. They had asked nothing of her life, but then she hadn't asked about their's either.

Charles had always been quiet on their visits, Susannah even quieter, but she had hoped that now they were getting older the children might be a little more interested in her, and a little more interesting. She knew nothing about them really. When did Charles begin to call his father 'Dad' not 'Father' or 'Daddy'? When did he start to swear? Was he right when he said that she had only kept up the trips with them to spite Arnold? Had she ever enjoyed her time with her children? Had she ever enjoyed her children? Had she ever loved them at all?

She sat looking out at the familiar view from her window and made herself think about things she had always avoided.

She was now nearly 38 years old. She would never have another child. Even if she found a man to love her, and to love, she could never have his children. She would only ever have a son, whose conception had led to her marriage to Arnold, and a daughter who was the unwanted result of rape.

Finally putting the receiver down Alicia folded her head in her arms and wept.

Her loneliness was not her only problem.

Arnold had been true to his word, in the beginning anyway. After that meeting in Liverpool he had bought her the little house Maureen Shelton had found for her in Surrey and arranged for an allowance to be paid monthly into her account. It was not a generous allowance but it was something.

Maureen, who had moved down south two years earlier, had been surprised when Alicia had written out of the blue asking her to find her a house quickly as she was moving back to England. She happily renewed their friendship finding a house just a few miles from her own so she could help Alicia put her life together.

It was not an old house but it had some character and although there were neighbours quite close on both sides, the front of the house looked out over open fields and woodland.

She always called it 'the little house' because it was really very small with only a drawing room, dining room and kitchen on the ground floor and three small bedrooms and a tiny bathroom above. She missed the spaciousness she had learned to take for granted. Millcourt was a large house and since she had left she had enjoyed spacious suites in hotels and staterooms on ships. She was not used to being cramped.

Maureen had been practical, making Alicia think about earning her own living.

"£100 a month isn't much you know. £20 odd a week will cover food and essentials but won't buy much in the way of clothes or luxuries."

"I'll get my luxuries."

"Yes I know. But they won't go on forever."

Maureen had soon worked out how these luxuries were obtained.

Once a month Alicia would pack a suitcase and walk to the end of the lane. There she caught the bus to London. She would get off in Northumberland Avenue and walk the short distance up the Strand to The Savoy.

The doormen knew her and always welcomed her as if she were the only guest in the hotel.

She was always shown up to the same suite with a river view. She never tired of looking up the river towards the Houses of Parliament. "At least Arnold will never get in there if I can help it."

Max would have the adjoining suite and they would have dinner in the room together, usually eggs benedict or something light, always with two bottles of champagne. They would talk briefly of politics and world affairs, never would the conversation turn to anything personal. Max did not talk of her children or anything about her ex-husband's life or business.

Afterwards she would soak in the deep bath and envelop herself in the soft, warm towels before slipping between the cool linen sheets and looking out over the Thames, watching the lights reflected in the water. She would sleep well, conscience clear, until tea was brought in the morning.

She would spend the next day shopping, frequently buying books at Hatchard's on Max's account, or, if it was raining, walking around an art gallery or museum.

One month she had gone to a matinee at The Globe to see the latest Noel Coward production but it was too painful to see people she had studied with doing the things she had so wanted to do herself, so she had left at the interval.

She would always return to the hotel in time to change and rest before dining again with Max in his room.

She would again soak in her suite's luxurious bathroom and again watch the dancing lights reflected on the river. She always enjoyed the bath on the second night more than the night before. She was so aware that it would be back to the tiny cold bathroom at the little house the next day.

She never thought that what she was doing was either wrong or reprehensible. It was a perfectly satisfactory arrangement between friends. It suited them both and, as long as Elizabeth did not know, they hurt no-one. They were good friends. They did not love each other, they did not need to. They knew each other well enough to know that their relationship would never be made formal.

On the second morning on those visits they would breakfast together and then he would leave for his office and she would walk back along the Strand to Northumberland Avenue and catch the bus back to Surrey.

On the Wednesdays they did not meet a Harrods or a Fortnum & Mason van would drive along the Pilgrims Way, stop outside the little house and a food hamper, or a hatbox, or a crate of champagne would be delivered to the door. Alicia got to know the delivery men and would often offer them a cup of tea or coffee sitting at the table in the kitchen warmed by the boiler, Montmorency the cat trying to ingratiate herself by winding herself around their legs. Sometimes it was the nearest she had to company for days on end.

It was an unwritten rule between them that Alicia would never ask Max for money nor would he offer any. She tried to save some from her monthly allowance so she could give Charles and Susannah a good time when they had their weeks together, but whatever she did it seemed never to be enough for them.

She did find ways to earn some money. It came in small sums; £10 here for singing at a wedding in the local church, £20 there for a small watercolour for the vicar's wife, £50 for a portrait of the local estate agent for his office, £100 for one of his dog and children.

She hated painting in watercolour but it was what people wanted, and if Alicia had learned anything over the years it was that she could give people what they wanted.

She had tried to get a small class of local children together to teach them dancing, but there was a much larger and more professional outfit in nearby Dorking. She did teach elocution to the children of the more ambitious social climbers in the area but the classes didn't take off. She had never completed her courses at the Academy and she had no formal qualifications.

Occasionally, very occasionally, she would accept payment for the more personal services requested by the fathers of these children.

However much she earned, though, it was never enough. More than once she tried to pay the monthly milk bill with a bottle of champagne that the milkman would reluctantly accept.

The last of the monthly cheques from Roberts and Jones arrived in

March 1958. Her written and telephoned requests had been fobbed off by receptionists.

She couldn't ask Max.

Henry had died in February. He had been drowned as he walked back from Hilbre Island one Sunday afternoon.

What was commented upon at the time was that it was a walk he did regularly. He knew how quickly the tide came in and how treacherous the gullies and channels of the incoming water were. Although the sands appear to stretch evenly and easily to the islands there are actually a maze of dips and hollows where the tide ran, sometimes parallel to the shore, sometimes apparently flowing back to sea as it races in over several miles of sand twice a day. The only way of knowing the exact state of the tides was to read the tide tables. It was impossible to gauge the tide by looking from the mainland or the island as the sea retreated miles across the sands. It was a dangerous place, especially in winter, no one could survive long if they were caught by the tide. Henry would have known that.

There was talk that he had taken his own life.

In the weeks that had followed his death things came to light that made that very likely. An audit of the books was ordered and it was obvious that someone had been embezzling money from his cousin's firm. The likelihood was that it was Henry. He must have felt he had to find the money to look after Kathleen in the manner she was becoming accustomed to as she was spent more and more time with Carl and Arnold at Millcourt. Maybe his wife's relationship with his cousin made him wonder about his whirlwind romance and the cooling of his relations with Kathleen so soon afterwards. Did he guess that Kathleen had been his cousin's mistress all those years. Perhaps he had known all the time but had gone along with the charade to gain the family life he had always wanted.

Did he wonder whether Carl was, indeed, his son?

He had so many reasons why he might have taken his own life but it was entirely possible he had simply forgotten how quickly the tide came in.

His body was found in open water by a local fisherman within a day of his going missing. People said he was lucky to have drowned so cleanly, as he could easily have been caught in quick sands – arguably a far worse death than a simple drowning.

Kathleen showed appropriate regret at the death of her husband but without too much discussion, and without too much concern for what people would, and did, think, she and her son moved permanently into Millcourt at the beginning of April, just over a month after Henry's death.

There were some people who believed that there was nothing between Arnold and Kathleen, not many, but there were some.

When he felt the need to explain his actions to anyone Arnold described the arrangement as a charitable one. Carl could grow up with the other children, they were all, after all, virtually cousins. It would be a great arrangement for all.

Charles, nearly 16, realised exactly what was going on. Arnold had never made much effort to act as if he cared for his elder son and had rarely spent any time with him but with Kathleen and Carl living at Millcourt he made no pretence of caring at all.

Charles withdrew into himself spending any time he wasn't studying or bird watching with Monika.

Over the years their relationship had changed.

After he had returned from boarding school he began to relax and soon his night problem ceased. With that he slowly began to gain some confidence. He liked his new school and, although he didn't make close friends he got on with his classmates well enough. When at home, he spent much time developing his knowledge of ornithology.

He began to call Monika by her name when he was 15, feeling he was far too old to have a 'nanny'. He began to think of her as his friend, she helped him and learned with him.

He had pestered her for years about her life before she had come to Millcourt, but it was only now, as she saw how much Carl's permanent presence in the house excluded him, that she began to tell him something of her childhood and the war.

As he grew older he understood more of what Monika told him about her early years, how her father and brothers had treated her, how the men and boys in the villages she had passed through during the war had used her and the ways in which she had managed to survive after it was over – before she was rescued by Max Fischer and brought to England to look after him and his sister.

Perhaps she told him too much because, despite their age difference, he began to think of her as his responsibility – roles were reversed as she was no longer the adult with responsibility over him.

He knew about his father and Kathleen, he knew enough to see that it was unusual that she and Carl spent so much time at Millcourt. He could see that whenever Henry had been there as well, which had not been very often, he had been shut out just as they shut out everyone.

And he didn't like Carl. He didn't like him because everything came easily to him; and even though he was four years younger he was as tall and as strong as Charles.

And he didn't like the way Susannah was always happier when Carl was around.

Susannah had started at a new school the previous year and still had no friends.

She travelled to school on the bus with lots of other girls but they never talked to her. She couldn't speak about it with anyone except Carl. She'd tried to tell Monika but Monika had no idea what school was like or why she wasn't happy there. She couldn't tell her brother, she didn't think he would understand either, he liked school. And she certainly couldn't tell her father. So she just left the house every morning looking and feeling miserable and every evening, when she got home, she would get on with her homework and not talk about her day at all.

Unless Carl was around.

He understood, he listened as she told him about all the little cruelties of her life at school. With Carl she would escape the household, they would walk along the shore collecting pebbles and grasses, they would play in the garden together. They talked of escape, of leaving home, running away together. They conspired to spend time together doing the things they wanted to do, rather than the things they were told to do. They began a count down to when they were 16 and could leave.

"Only four years to go."

"One thousand, four hundred and sixty days."

"Plus leap years."

"Not long really."

"Then we can get away from this place."

There were always arguments in the house. Whatever the argument was about, whether it was something silly such as when to turn the television on, or something more important like whether Charles should give up his bedroom, the arguments polarised the household: on the one hand Arnold with Kathleen, on the other Charles, knowing that Monika would support him if she could. Carl and Susannah tried to stay quiet or be somewhere else when trouble brewed.

Most of the arguments stemmed from the changes Kathleen made in the household. She started telling Cook what to buy and where to shop. Cook had always had that responsibility even before Alicia left.

And she stopped Charles and Susannah eating their meals in the nursery. The 'nursery' was really a suite of rooms on the first floor where the children had their bedrooms, there was a sitting room and a small kitchen and Monika ruled. It had been the nursery when the children had been small and they had never stopped calling it that even though it now bore no relation to what would be thought of as a 'nursery'. Charles and Susannah had their own rooms decorated as they wanted, with posters of rock and roll stars, the music that played most of the evening on the gramophone was more likely to be Elvis Presley than Beethoven. But since Arnold never ventured onto the nursery floor it hadn't mattered.

Kathleen changed all that.

When they got in from school they were to spend two hours doing their homework or reading. They then changed for dinner, which was now held around the main refectory table with Cook and Monika serving and clearing away. They all would then retire to the drawing room and sit listening to Arnold's choice of music for an hour when they could escape back to the nursery floor.

No one liked the new arrangement apart from Kathleen. Conversation was never free flowing or spontaneous, questions were asked by the adults and responded to, in as few words as possible, by the children who wanted to get back to their own rooms as quickly as possible.

Charles had wanted to tell his mother about it all when she called in May, but when it came to it he hadn't managed to find the words.

She had chosen a difficult time to call. The day before she had called Charles his father had broken the silence at dinner by telling them that Monika was no longer required and would be leaving that week. He told them in the same tone of voice he would have used to say someone or other was coming to dinner the following week.

Charles looked at his father and then to Monika who had just cleared away the plates and must have heard. She half turned round, briefly catching Charles' eye before leaving the room. "What?" he said, rather too loudly.

"Don't say 'what' like that Charles, it is very rude." Kathleen never resisted an opportunity to impose standards on the family.

"I would have thought even you could grasp that Charles," Arnold could be very sarcastic when he chose "There are no longer children in the house who would require a nanny."

"What about Susannah, she's only 11 she needs Monika."

"She has needed a woman in the house, you are absolutely right, but now she has Kathleen." He looked past Charles on his left and Carl and Susannah on his right to Kathleen, sitting at the other end of the table.

"Indeed. I will be a mother to you Susannah. You don't need a Nanny any more do you? You're far too grown up for that."

"Of course Auntie Kathleen." Susannah still liked to do what would please others, all her life she had tried to avoid confrontation.

Carl was no help to him either.

Charles was suddenly frightened. If Monika were to be paid off he would have no one. He had to do something. He could not give in so easily.

"And what do you suggest she does?"

"I don't believe that is my problem."

"Don't we owe her anything? How long has she been with us? I'll answer that, 10 years. She's looked after us and nursed us and loved us when no one else has for 10 years, and you just want to let her go."

"She is not required any more. She will have to go. That is an end to it."

"We may not have a legal responsibility towards her but sure as hell we have a moral one."

"Don't swear at the table. Your father has no such responsibility. She has, no doubt, been well paid for her time here. If your father says she is to go then she will go."

Charles ignored Kathleen.

"If she goes I go."

"Don't be so ridiculous. You're being too emotional. I blame...." Arnold always accused his children of being 'too emotional' if they ever voiced any opposition to him.

"Yes I know. You blame our Mother. If there is anything, ever, that we do right it's because of you or her." He stared at Kathleen. "All the things we do wrong it's because of Mother. It's stupid. I mean it. If Monika goes I go."

Before Arnold could respond to his son's words Kathleen spoke "Melodramatic, you are truly your mother's son." She couldn't keep the dislike out of her voice. "But what a good idea. That way we get rid of both of you troublemakers – absolutely wonderful."

"You're a bitch. You deserve each other."

"Go to your room. You will not speak to Kathleen like that." It wouldn't have occurred to him to take his son's side.

"I'm practically16 now, you can't treat me like a child"

"I can and do when you act like one."

Charles could have gone up to his room, he could have sat down in his window seat, looking out over the golf course calming himself down. But since April he had been watching them and had become more and more certain that Carl was his father's son, his brother, half-brother. He couldn't be 100% certain, but he was pretty sure. His father had chosen Kathleen and Carl over him and Susannah, well he would choose Monika over them all.

90

He could have left the room, but he didn't.

"You just want us out of the way so that you can play happy families with her and Carl."

"You will be quiet young man. Your father has been very kind to Carl and me." Kathleen tried to impose her authority.

"He's only being kind to you because you're..." he hesitated and tried again "because Carl's his...."

Arnold had walked around the table and interrupted him with a sharp slap on the side of his face.

It was the first time his father had struck him for years.

It was the first and only time Charles hit him back.

It wasn't much of a punch and it probably didn't hurt Arnold a bit as it connected weakly with Arnold's cheek. Charles was immensely disappointed at the lack of impact and turned and ran from the room. Susannah and Carl took the opportunity to escape.

"Good God!" Arnold sat down and tried to calm himself down.

She went over and put her hands on his shoulders. "Leave it to me, my dear. I'm going to talk to Monika." Kathleen was not going to let Arnold give in now they had got this far. "I'm going to fire her now. She'll leave immediately and if Charles goes with her then good riddance. How could he say those things!"

Arnold did not argue.

He had let the conversation go this far this evening as he had been distracted. He didn't want to have to tell Kathleen any more than he had to and if he started discussing Charles' future he would have to explain rather more than he wanted to. As Kathleen left the room she noticed he had closed his eyes and covered his face with his hands.

It was as if his life was falling apart.

He must have known then that the business was nearly insolvent. It had been going downhill ever since he had taken it over. He was not a businessman and should never have been made to give up what he would have done well, his mother should have let him be a lawyer. He would have been a good one. But because of the business he had had to spend his life doing something he hated. Henry had stolen so much money from the business but he it hadn't been spotted. He was such a bad businessman that his weak and insignificant cousin could steal all that money from him and he hadn't known.

But it couldn't all be Henry's fault. The war had been good for the business but now times were different, there was little place for small family run firms as new technologies became more and more essential and more and more expensive. Competition from the Far East meant he could not charge what he needed to and so quality was cut and as soon as quality deteriorated he began to lose the customers he had. He knew he had never been a good manager, he knew he was not doing a good job but he also knew he was not capable of doing any better. He found that the people who had been his friends, his brother masons, his political supporters, had all been very nice to him when he had just inherited his father's money; now, as things looked more and more bleak, they were no longer around. He forgot his political ambitions and tried only to stay afloat.

One of the first savings he had made was to stop Alicia's allowance. Kathleen had been urging him to stop these payments but in March he had known he couldn't keep them up anyway.

Other actions were even more blameworthy. He had raided all the trust funds. Arnold had succeeded in raising a lot of money; but not enough.

Chapter Sixteen

It was with mixed emotions when, sitting at my desk early on the last Monday morning in May 1958, I heard her voice. She was speaking loudly and her words were clear despite my office door being quite substantial, and shut.

She was not happy. That much was very obvious.

"I need to see Mr Fischer."

"He is not here today. What did you say your name was?" Judith, the receptionist, had been with us only a short time.

"I am Alicia Tyler." The name meant nothing to the girl.

I had not taken any of Alicia's calls in the preceding weeks. I had had to find excuse after excuse not to take her calls. I knew what she would be ringing about but I wouldn't be able to tell her the truth.

"Mr Fischer is not in today. He will not be in all week."

"Is he at home?"

"I really cannot answer that Madam. Do you want me to tell him you called in? He is telephoning to pick up messages."

Alicia ignored this.

"Is Ted Mottram in or is the office completely staffed by imbecilic young girls?"

"There is no need to be rude, Madam."

"I have come a long way to be here and have had a stressful journey. I did not expect to be disappointed." She didn't sound very sorry for her rudeness.

There was quiet for a few seconds and then, with a softening of the voice, "No I really am sorry, I don't mean to be rude. It really isn't your fault."

One of Alicia's more endearing habits was her ability to change mood almost instantly from an almost pompous arrogance to contrition and charm.

Responding to the changed tone Judith admitted my presence in the office.

"Is he with someone or can I go in?"

"I will ask him, Madam. Do, please take a seat."

Seeing a way out of this difficult start to her working week, Judith pressed the buttons on the intercom and told me what I already knew. "A lady named Alicia Tyler is in reception and would like to see you."

During her visit to the Wirral five years ago I had seen her for a total of, perhaps, three hours, and after that visit I had spent many months trying to live with the humiliation it had caused me. I had spoken to her as a friend, I had told her things I should not have simply because I was fond of her. I had betrayed the confidences of my client, her husband. Max had not been pleased with me, but had understood what had happened, probably better than I, and, despite making life rather difficult for me for a short time, did confirm my promotion that summer – so I knew I was forgiven. The damage had been in my relationship with Arnold. We had not spoken, I had left his cricket team and had lost contact with the children. It was only years afterwards that I spoke with them and with Kathleen and filled in the gaps in my knowledge of their lives. Those five years had been made worse by my knowing that I had broken my promise to Alicia. I could not look after the children, I could not keep an eye on them and keep them safe, even at a time when I knew Kathleen's influence was growing and her ambition for Carl was overruling all the rights of Charles and Susannah.

Before that it had been a further five years since I had seen her. In all we had had two or three meetings in over ten years. But through all that time I had been driven by my feelings for her. I knew so much about her life and, once, we had almost been friends.

She went straight to the point.

"Ted what is going on? I haven't received any money from Arnold for months."

Aware that I had previously told her too much by answering her questions directly, I had to be circumspect.

"Wouldn't it be better if you talked to Arnold?"

"Oh I can't, no I won't talk to that damned man. I can hardly bring myself to hear his name. He has treated me disgracefully. You do not know what I have been through these past five years, Ted. I have had to do such things to get by," she paused, concern on her face, perhaps she was the one to be in danger of giving too much away, "teaching elocution to silly little brats, Ted, no-one deserves that fate!" The change of tone, making a joke of what was obviously hurtful, was the Alicia that I found so appealing.

"I do think that Arnold is the only person who can tell you what is going on."

"Max?"

"Elizabeth is very ill, Max has not been in the office for some time."

"Oh dear, I am sorry to hear that. Has she been ill for long?"

"She never recovered her strength after Veronica, you know. Then she had a breakdown of some sort. She has been in a nursing home for some years now. She had a stroke last week and they think it's now only a matter of days."

"Oh how sad" she said, but then I was shocked at the coldness in her voice as she continued "He'll probably find a widow and re-marry. He would even have another family, he's still young enough to attract someone who could give him the son he wants."

Years later she remembered this conversation. She went over it again and again, in all the meetings with Max in those years he had said nothing. Was she so unimportant to him? She was so hurt that he had never confided in her as a friend.

Seeing her looking so sad I turned the subject. "Arnold doesn't speak to me nor I to him since your last visit."

I hoped she would remember how she had compromised my position, but she seemed to have no thought about that. I looked across at her but she showed no sign of knowing what I was talking about.

I continued "I think you should talk to him. Should I ask Judith to call him and tell him you are in Liverpool and that you would like to meet him?"

"He won't want to see me will he?"

"Even if he does I can't see it doing any good." It was best to be honest. "But I think you have a right to know of certain," I paused to find the right words "developments, but I am not the one to tell you."

I pressed the buttons on the intercom. "Judith. Could you call Mr Arnold Donaldson and ask him if he could make an appointment to meet his ex-wife. It can be here or at some other location of his choosing. Make it clear I will not be present at the meeting. And no, I do not wish to speak to him myself."

So that explained to Judith who this woman in the outrageous hat was.

She knocked on the door. "He was not very happy Sir. His exact words were "I suppose I'd better meet the bitch." Pardon me Madam. He said he would be in the lounge of the Derby Hotel this evening at 5pm. He could not come to Liverpool. He said he could spare her half an hour."

So again I drove Alicia through the tunnel and out over Bidston Hill onto the fields of the Wirral – now becoming more built over with housing estates. This time I dropped her off at the hotel pausing only to make sure they had a room for her for the night. Now was not the time to be troubling Max with a house guest.

In the first ten minutes of their meeting Alicia heard most of what she needed to know.

Henry was dead. "Good riddance" was her response "he was a weak man to allow himself to be so manipulated by you, though you must be so pleased that it fits so well into your overall scheme."

Kathleen and Carl now lived with them at Millcourt, "What a surprise! Not so prissy now then!" but he was selling that house and they were all going to live in her old home. "I haven't told them yet but that is what we will have to do."

She had no easy sarcastic answer to that.

"Why are you selling up?"

"There is no money left."

"None?"

"None. Not one more penny can I give you. That's it. You're on your own."

It was worse than she had imagined, and Max would not be there to help.

She sat back in the comfortable armchair, her saucer held precisely in her left hand, the teacup in her right and reflected. Not so many years ago she had had a position in this community, she had been the admired and respected wife of a rich businessman with realistic political ambitions and the contacts and money to achieve those. She had had a large house with staff, she hadn't had to work or worry about a thing. There were the two children who everyone had thought beautiful, a boy and a girl, just as it should be. She had achieved a good life out of the wreckage of her accident.

She had had all that but still had not been happy, but then perhaps that would have been just too much to ask.

Now she was not only unhappy but also, it seemed, broke.

Her eyes filled with the same pity for herself she had felt two days before after her phone call with Charles.

She did not spare too many thoughts for what this man would be feeling, this man who had been her husband and who a long time ago, and for a very short time, she had thought she loved.

He had what he had always wanted, his sons and Kathleen.

"Why don't you marry her?"

"Why?"

"Do you mean why do I ask or why should you?"

"Why do you ask?"

"It is of importance to my children."

"Since when were your children important to you?"

She couldn't respond immediately, for he had hurt her. She answered with the only weapon she had "You could adopt Carl then, make the relationship legal."

"Don't you dare!" His voice was rather too loud and people in the room began to notice them.

Alicia had wondered why he had chosen the lounge of an hotel just half a mile from his house to meet her, when it was not unlikely that someone might recognise her. Maybe it was to inhibit her, to stop her talking about things that were too personal or to stop her being too argumentative. She wasn't going to be tricked into avoiding the topics she wanted to raise, but she did lower her voice a little.

"Don't you think half the county would be fascinated to know about you and Kathleen. Henry and Kathleen had hardly even met! Such a convenient wedding! Then followed by a 7 month baby, a son who weighed over 8 pounds and was absolutely healthy! He even looks like you! Isn't it about bloody time you made an honest woman of her?"

"No one would believe you. Henry and I were cousins. It's no more than a family resemblance. I have looked after them through family loyalty – that's all."

The last couple having tea in the lounge left, they were alone.

"Oh Arnold, don't be such a fool. Marry her. Get it all over with. Give me a settlement and we can all get on with our lives."

"I've told you. There is no money. There can be no settlement. And anyway I can't marry her."

"Why the hell not – you've practically been married for years – probably since before you met me."

"She is a Catholic. I cannot marry a Catholic."

She knew there had to be more to it than that. What it was she didn't know but she knew there was something.

"I've heard some sorry excuses from men in my time but that has to be the weakest, feeblest reason for not marrying someone I've ever heard."

"It is neither weak nor feeble to me. The arrangement we have is perfectly satisfactory."

"I bet she'd marry you like a shot."

"I am not talking about it any more. It is not a question we should be discussing and I will not have another word spoken about it.

"What about me then Arnold? My allowance?"

"You have the house. No doubt you can find a way of earning a living or of getting someone to keep you, but I can't send you another penny."

"What about all the money in the trust funds?"

He went quiet for a moment, probably debating how honest he needed to be, undoubtedly wishing that she had not raised the subject. "There is no money in the funds."

"There has to be! They are secure! Even you can't have got at them!" She had always assumed there would be some income from those – whatever happened.

"They are gone."

"How? You had no right to touch that money. You had no way of touching that money – your father left it for the children."

"I just used the powers you gave me in those papers you signed before going to Switzerland."

"I didn't see any powers over the trust funds? I wouldn't have signed anything that let you get at that money. I know I wouldn't."

"You obviously didn't read those papers carefully enough. "

Of course she hadn't. She had trusted Max. She had told him what she had wanted and hadn't checked the wording. She found it difficult to believe Max would have betrayed her and the children. Arnold must have got to him somehow.

"You've been milking those funds for years."

"I'm afraid so."

"Do Ted and Max know?"

"I don't see how they could fail to – unless they are completely incompetent which I am sure they are not."

Alicia had felt angry for the weeks since the cheques had dried up, now she felt betrayed. The two men she had placed some trust in, and for whom she had some affection, had lied to her. Neither of them had told her anything of this, neither of them had warned her or given her any idea of the problems that now had to be faced.

"Max didn't tell me. Neither of them told me." Was all she could say. Eventually she continued with an inevitable question "What happened to all that money?"

"I have to think there were people stealing from me."

"Henry? It couldn't have been anybody else."

He did not reply immediately. He did not want to admit to such failure but in the end the need to tell her outweighed his fear of ridicule.

"Probably, he wanted to give his son everything that Charles and Susannah had. Nothing was too good for Kathleen and I can't see him doing it all on his salary."

She burst out in laughter "Wonderful! You! So intelligent, so clever, so gifted and so rich brought down by that ignorant little wimp! Wonderful! Perhaps there is some justice in the world after all!"

Arnold looked at her more closely now. How well did he know this woman, his ex-wife? They hadn't seen each other for nearly five years, their meeting then had been short and antagonistic. They had parted in the offices of Roberts and Jones hating each other. Before those two days in July 1953 they had not met since she had left the week after Susannah's 2nd birthday, nearly five years before that. This was only the third time he had met his ex-wife in 10 years. How different she was from the naïve, sulky, withdrawn, selfish and uncertain woman she had been when she had been his wife. Nearing 40 she had the complexion and figure of a much younger woman. Her clothes were stylish without being too fashionable, her voice was cultured without being affected, her manner confident and refined.

If things had been different he would have found her very attractive.

What had her life been since she had left? He probably imagined one of luxury and well-being, she would not want for anything for long – she was too able to wrap men around her little finger to want for much.

What did she think of him? He was practically 50 with a defeated air about him. He knew that he could not match Alicia's assurance.

"I'd hardly call it any sort of justice I can believe in."

"And you've got nothing left? You had a business, property, half a million quid in cash and you've got nothing left?" Her voice conveyed disbelief.

"All gone. I thought it would go on forever. I bought the things we wanted whenever they wanted them. No one had to wait for Christmas or birthdays for their presents, not even Susannah. I may not have had much time for her or for Charles but I wasn't going to have them seen wanting anything."

"Or Carl."

He ignored her interruption.

"The upkeep of the house is expensive and we have had a certain standard of living to maintain. And the children... the children's education has not been cheap."

"and the most expensive school for Carl...."

He ignored her again, determined to justify his failure.

"It is not my fault. Nothing has gone right, everyone has done well out of me, everyone except me. You've had the house and your allowance – don't forget that, you didn't go cheaply. I've kept you for years and had nothing in return."

"You had my silence, Arnold. That's what you were buying. You were buying off your guilt and making damned sure I didn't tell anyone your precious secrets. And I haven't. All the time you paid me my allowance, hush-money if you want, but all the time you kept your side of the bargain I bloody well kept mine. Now I'm not so sure. I'm coming to realise what a sad, weak man you really are.

She paused, he said nothing, so she continued.

"You've brought it all on yourself, your selfishness, your complete indifference to others, your blindness to your own weaknesses and your absolute inability to recognise anybody else's strengths. These are the reasons you are a failure. You were a failure as a lover and husband, you were a failure as a politician and businessman and you'll always be a failure at anything you do. What have you ever succeeded at? Name me one thing you have done that you can be proud of. Have you ever stood up in front of the world and yelled "I have done this!" No, Of course you haven't. Not one solitary thing have you ever done of which you can be proud. You are despicable Arnold. I don't want to have anything more to do with you."

She had surprised herself.

She gathered her handbag, stood up and walked out of the lounge. She wasn't sure where she was going she just had to walk. She had feared this man. For the best part of 20 years he had been a part of her life and all that time she had considered herself inferior. He had always had the upper hand in their relationship and she was fast realising that he was not worth it. She had hated him for so many years, now she just despised him.

As she walked down the slight hill towards the promenade she took off her hat and scrunched it up, stuffing it into her handbag. He was not worth it. All the anger she had spent on him, all the hours she had wasted thinking of what he had done to her and hating him, all that time and energy had been wasted.

He was just not worth it.

She stood holding onto the railings overlooking the beach and watching the waves break. She took out the pins that were holding her hair in a French roll and shook her hair free, swinging it from side to side in the wind. "I'm free of him." She kicked off her shoes and grabbing them she slid between the railings and jumped the three feet down onto the beach to run over the sand, still warm after the day's sun, wheeling her arms around like windmills. She ran, laughing along the beach towards the sun, one hand swinging her bag, the other her shoes.

She was free.

She had run past where the promenade turned up towards the

town and in amongst the dunes that piled up against the old sea wall she stopped running and slumped down into the protection of a curve in sand. She sat there her legs straight out towards the sun, her eyes closed, enjoying the last warmth from the sun's rays, her fingers digging into the warm sand.

She had neither seen nor heard him as he walked along the sea wall, watching her. She did not notice him at all until she felt her arm pulled sharply, dragging her upright, her eyes opening wide as her body was jerked round to face him. They stood close to each other, face to face in the dunes.

"You loved me once. You cared once."

"I don't think so."

"You did, in the beginning, you believed in me then."

"Not for long."

He grabbed her other arm and pulled her round to face him. He kissed her roughly. "Alicia, Alicia, I loved you once." As he fumbled with her clothing, "I want you now."

Her feeling of freedom had gone but she didn't cower. She was no longer the Alicia who would have been afraid of him or compliant to his wishes. She was far more calculating now.

As he held her, kissing her roughly, she was thinking fast "Could this give me the hold I need over him? Should I pretend I don't want to, but go along with it so that he'll feel guilty?" Yes, she certainly wanted him to feel guilt. But if he raped her, as she knew he had the strength to do, it would hand the power over to him again. She did not want that.

So she went along with the moment.

"Oh Arnold!"

They dropped together down onto the sand dunes and he began pulling at her clothing, and she at his.

Alicia described this years later, with not a little satisfaction.

"He wanted to take the only thing he could have, sexual satisfaction. He put his face into my neck and breathed my smell, as if he was having something he had missed. He kissed my neck, my breasts, my stomach, enjoying the touch and the smell of me. For just a few minutes he was the young lover again.

"But I wasn't.

"This was where I had wanted to get him. In my power. All our lives together he had been the strong one. He had been the one with the power over me, the one with the money, the male with power over the female, the man with education, manners and class over the crippled, working class girl. His power had always been its most fearful in the bedroom where he had so often made me do things that disgusted me.

"But I was more experienced now, I knew how to make him suffer.

"First I made him last, I was not going to let him come until it hurt him. I knew how to make him want me more and more until it was unbearable. I teased and tantalised him. I blessed Max for teaching me the things I really needed to know about how a man and a woman can torture each other as they give themselves and each other pleasure. I worked on him until he had no idea who he was with or what he was doing. Thank you Max, thank you for teaching me the things I knew at this moment to deny this man what he craved. To have the power. To be in charge. I pushed him away just as he ejaculated fiercely into nothingness.

"I sorted out my clothes and stood up, I looked at him with shirt and tie almost immaculate but nothing ordered below his waist, his pants round his knees and his trousers round his ankles. I laughed at his discomfort and I told him never, ever to touch me again. I said I despised him. He had just proved how weak he was. He was always going to be a complete failure, in business, in politics and with women."

He had asked her "Why are you doing this?"

"To prove what a shit you are Arnold. What a complete and utter shit. Oh how proud you were of your prowess in bed! Whoever said you were any good? Kathleen? You were never any good to anyone but yourself. You have always been totally useless in that department. Did no one ever teach you that your job was to give as well as take? To give pleasure not pain? To build up and worship not denigrate and humiliate? Did nobody ever teach you how to make a woman feel so good that you were like a god to her to make her feel that way. No I don't suppose they ever did. You are a fool Arnold. A sad, sad fool."

She turned and walked away with a purpose.

While she had the initiative she would confront them all. She walked the few hundred yards to Millcourt with her head held high feeling more confident than she had for years.

As she rounded the corner of the house she turned to look down on the garden where there were two young people playing, a girl holding a cricket bat and laughing as the boy bowled quite hard and quite fast at her, she whacked the ball which was hotly pursued into the bushes by two barking golden retrievers. They all seemed happy.

She sat on the top step looking down at them wondering why she felt no rush of affection for her daughter. She had wanted to be loved. She wanted Susannah and Charles to need her, but she could never love or need them.

She watched as Cook brought out a tray of lemonade and the children sat down on the grass. They were obviously friends. She couldn't bear that.

She couldn't bear that her daughter was close to Arnold's son.

She didn't wave or try to communicate when Cook glanced up, undoubtedly recognising her old mistress as she walked back with the tray.

Cook went through the French windows into the hall and sat down on the nearest chair to collect her thoughts.

A few moments later Kathleen walked in "What's wrong Cook?"

"Nothing wrong Madam, nothing wrong. Just a bit out of breath."

"What's going on out there? Susannah winning?"

"I don't know, just their usual fun Madam, I'll get to the kitchen now." Remembering herself "Is there anything I can get you Madam?"

The telephone rang so she reached over and lifted the receiver.

"Hoylake 2302 The Donaldson Residence."

Cook answered automatically in her 'telephone voice'.

"Yes Sir."

"Yes Sir. Immediately Sir. No trouble Sir. Yes Sir. Oh dear Sir."

"What on earth is the trouble cook?"

"Its Sir Madam."

"Yes, Cook I realise that." Kathleen replied drily.

"He's had a bit of bother. He says we mustn't let anyone into the house. We mustn't have a guest or anything Madam."

"We weren't expecting any one were we Cook?"

"No Madam. He just said we mustn't allow anyone in. He will be here in a minute."

"It all sounds very mysterious. Do you think it might have anything to do with the woman who is walking in through the conservatory at this very moment?"

With an 'Oh Madam' Cook hurriedly retreated to the safety of her kitchen. She did not think this was going to be a happy reunion.

"Kathleen."

"Alicia."

"I gather you have made this your home now."

"Yes, I rather think I have."

"And Arnold, he is happy with the arrangement?"

"Yes, I rather think he is."

"And the children?"

"Very flexible, children. They do what is easiest for them in the end."

"Indeed." Alicia did not sound like she was agreeing.

"I was so sorry to hear about the death of your husband."

"Were you really?"

Another silence.

"The father of your son."

An almost imperceptible hesitation before she answered "Why do you say that?"

"You know as well as I do that Carl is Arnold's son. Why pretend?"

"Why indeed?" Kathleen hurried on "Why are you here? What do you want from us?"

"I thought you'd like to know that Arnold and I have been renewing our acquaintance in the sand dunes and he rather enjoyed it."

Kathleen was determined to show no feeling or emotion either in her face or her voice. "Did you? Enjoy it I mean?" She was trying to wrest the initiative.

"Not as much as he did." Alicia was happy for Kathleen to hear the emotions in her voice. There was triumph, success and power.

Another silence until Kathleen again tried to outplay Alicia "I repeat, what do you want from us?"

"Absolutely nothing, dear Kathleen, I want nothing from you. I just need to know how happy you are. I think Arnold answered that in the dunes, don't you?" She continued without giving Kathleen a chance to think of an answer "I also wanted to know how the children were. I've been watching them playing in the garden – yes I've been here a while – it was noticeable how close Susannah and Carl are."

"They are very good friends." Not even Kathleen could keep the defensiveness out of her voice.

"But we both know, how dangerous that would be, don't we?" Alicia had no chance to expand on this as Arnold interrupted them.

"What are you doing here? What trouble is she making?" Arnold strode towards the two women and deliberately stood next to Kathleen, his arm around her shoulders. He kissed her briefly on the cheek, making his allegiance clear. Kathleen purposefully turned towards him so their lips almost met. She was going to show Alicia that she was not going to be disturbed by her lies – for lies they must be. She had to believe that Arnold wouldn't have touched Alicia.

"I gather you met earlier?"

"Yes, we had some details to sort out, we had tea at the Derby."

"Tea, Arnold? I rather thought we had a little more than that!"

Arnold looked from Kathleen to Alicia, Alicia caught his look and arched her left eyebrow in a gesture that could mean nothing or absolutely everything.

"Yes, Kathleen," Alicia turned her eyes towards Kathleen, "your, how do I put it, cousin? protector? – do you actually have a name for your relationship? We've been reviving old memories haven't we, Arnold? I remember now very clearly at least one of the reasons I was so happy to leave, and at least one of the reasons I have been so happy to stay away."

They stood there still, despite her sarcasm and her insinuations, arm in arm. They were presenting a united front against her. She hadn't managed to disrupt Kathleen's confidence, she had failed to drive a wedge between them – they went back too far, understood each other too well. Well, let them have each other. It was no skin off her nose.

Looking up to the stairs she noticed a small figure, Charles, who must be over-hearing this conversation.

Still angry with Charles after their telephone conversation and with Susannah for being so close to Carl, she did not care who she hurt.

"Look after your sons Arnold, one day you must tell them both who they really are. Leave Susannah to find out for herself."

Charles knew what he had heard and retreated before his father could see him.

Even though he had to wait until his father and Kathleen had left the hall before he could run down the stairs Charles caught his mother up before she had gone more than a few yards down the road.

"Can I walk you to the station Mother. You will be leaving for Liverpool and the south."

There was so much of his father in him.

"No Charles, I will not. I'll be staying at the Derby. Apparently Max is away."

"He's not there. There's only the housekeeper there and she won't let you in." He had reason to know, he had tried to stay there the previous night.

"Why pay for a hotel, why don't you do what tramps do and sleep on the sand dunes?"

She knew what he meant. "How much did you hear?"

"Enough." The sullenness of a soon-to-be-16-year-old made him sound nearer nine.

"I understand from all that that Carl is definitely my brother."

"Half brother"

"Half brother then. I had wondered. But what did you mean about Susannah? Aren't I allowed to find out anything more about the family?"

"I meant nothing, just a silly attempt at being clever. But yes, you should perhaps know a little more of the family skeletons.

"About Henry?"

"What about Henry?" she hoped Charles didn't know too much. "He's dead isn't he?"

"Why did he bring up Carl? Why did he put up with his wife, you know .... with Dad?"

"You should ask them."

"How can I?"

Alicia decided she should be more communicative. There was little point in being so mean – none of this was Charles' fault.

"You have a point there I suppose. You'll have to listen carefully. Henry was weak, Charles. He didn't know what else to do at the time. He worked for your father as well as being his cousin. He had to do what your father said. Your father was a lot stronger than he was – in personality I mean. Henry had been very unhappy, his parents and a girl he was very fond of had been killed in an air-raid a few months before Kathleen appeared on the scene and people do very odd things when they're unhappy. They do things that they probably wouldn't do if they were content. You'll understand when...."

"Don't say I'll understand when I'm older! That's what they always say when I ask them anything about anything that matters."

"What sort of things?"

"About you? Why did you leave us? Did you find out about her? You must have had a reason. You never said anything about anything important when we visited you. We knew you were only acting when you had us with you. That's why we hated going away with you. Susannah hated being away from Carl and I." He stopped before he could give too much of himself away.

"I think I always knew that neither of you wanted to be with me, even for a few days each year, I knew you had other things to do in your holidays. But I wasn't just being selfish you know."

"Weren't you?"

"No. I wanted you to know that if anything ever went wrong in your lives, if ever you needed someone, I would always be there to pick up the pieces, if ever you needed me I wouldn't be a complete stranger to you."

"But you are."

They walked on for a while, in silence.

"Perhaps I have been wrong in not explaining. I thought you and Susannah were fine, you were young, you were just babies really, not even children, you would grow up thinking that the things around you were normal. When I left to go to Switzerland I was ill, I left England because I would have died if I had stayed. People knew I had been ill and so it was a good reason to leave. I couldn't divorce your father then. It's a bit more normal now, but then it would have been a real stigma – and not just to the parents – you would have found things very difficult at school."

"You left because you didn't love us. I don't believe all that rot about you being ill. I had a horrid time at school anyway." He couldn't explain all the pain to her, not now.

"I'm sorry about that. Why didn't you ever tell me?"

"You never asked." They walked on for a bit. "And you didn't come back when you left Switzerland did you? Monika said that you would come back when you were better but you didn't. It's the only lie Monika has ever told me and you made her do it. Lots of things are bad. Not just school. And now Daddy's making Monika go. He's sacked her. She's got to go at the end of the week."

He suddenly looked very young and vulnerable, as though he was going to burst into tears but she didn't feel she knew him well enough to put her arms around him and give him the hug he obviously needed.

"Perhaps we need to talk a bit. You're right, we never did when you came for those holidays – you wouldn't speak to me other than to tell me what you and Susannah were going to do or had done or what the weather was like, you never wanted to talk about anything that was important."

"You didn't either."

"Didn't I? I should have done. I am sorry. Do you want to walk a little further tonight – not straight back to the hotel? We could talk a bit. I could tell you some things," she corrected herself, "and listen to some things that you want to tell me."

So they walked down to the promenade where she had been only a short time before. The tide had turned now and was racing out into the gathering dusk.

She began to explain.

"Charles, darling, I am a centre sort of person, and so is your father, and we clashed because of that. His way of life was not, and could not be, mine. We made each other very unhappy."

"What about us? Didn't you think about me and Susannah?"

"You will understand – no listen to me – you *will* understand more as you grow older, you will, as you fall in and out of love. Things are never simple between a man and a woman."

"Yes they are. They should be. We are your children. It should be simple shouldn't it? You live with us and look after us. You care about us. Your life *is* us. We are what matters to you. Our lives are what should matter to you. That's what other families are like. The fathers go to work, the mothers look after the children, care for them when they are sick, talk to them when they are worried, play with them. That's what proper mothers do."

"Is that what your friends' mothers do?"

"I haven't got any friends."

"Is that what Kathleen does?"

Charles looked down at his feet. He had seen how Kathleen was with Carl but he would never in a million years admit to being jealous. He didn't want Kathleen for a mother but he had wanted, oh so desperately wanted, a real mother of his own.

"Ideally, Charles, probably you are right. But I am not a perfect mother. No, listen to me. I did love your father, when you were conceived, I did love him. I had had a very unhappy childhood because my Father and Mother were always quarrelling, I don't think your father was happy either. I don't think his parents were very good for each other either, I think they caused your father a lot of problems. Please believe me. I didn't want that for you. I didn't want you to grow up with parents who were always rowing. Your father and I both knew we couldn't live with each other any longer. He and I were so very different, not good for each other, we could give nothing which the other needed."

"Except fucking."

She was surprised to hear her son use words like this, but he was getting older and it seemed pointless to make a fuss especially when it was exactly the right word to use.

"As you say, Charles, except fucking. But you will understand one day that that is not enough. You heard what we were saying earlier? I thought so. Yes, your father and I 'fucked' this afternoon, and I put the word in inverted commas for you. It was not an enjoyable experience for either of us. 'Making love', 'having it off', 'going all the way', 'number 10', whatever you want to call it, should be a thing of beauty between people, but it can become a weapon, a weapon to show power over someone you no longer love. A way of showing that there is nothing left. But it can be a beautiful thing, and I pray that that it will be for you when the time comes."

"I won't ever do it."

"Yes you will, Charles. You will find a girl you love and you will 'do it'."

"Not when it causes so much damage."

He said the words with finality and it was some time before he continued hesitantly "Anyway, I already love someone."

This surprised Alicia, surely Charles was not old enough to go out with girls seriously enough to 'fall in love'.

"You're still very young."

"Stop saying that! I'm old enough to know who I'm going to spend the rest of my life with." He refrained from the 'so there' that sounded like it should have finished the sentence. "You don't know anything about my life or who I love so stop saying "I'll understand when I'm older" I understand now. I will never do what you did. I'll never 'fuck' anyone. I'll never do it. It does nothing but hurt people."

Alicia was surprised at the force and venom in his voice. She was shocked at how adult he sounded, how sure of himself, how certain of his decision.

She waited for him to calm down a bit and asked him "Who do you love?"

He gave no answer, his love for Monika was his secret.

Monika had told him such stories of what people do to each other in the name of 'love' and 'sex' that he knew he would never harm anyone like that. His mother could not know that what she and Arnold had done that afternoon had simply confirmed to Charles something he believed he already knew. Sex was a tool to hurt people and he would never harm anyone like that.

Instead of answering her he talked.

"I'm 16 on Tuesday. All my friends at school are boasting what they get up to. One of the girls in the town is taking them in groups to show them all what to do and they all practise, they all touch each other and find out things I don't want to know. I haven't done anything like that. I couldn't. If anyone touched Susannah like that I would kill them."

"You love your sister?"

"Of course I do. She is the only one I've got, but she's all tied up with Carl, neither of them care about me, Dad doesn't, Kathleen doesn't."

"I care about you Charles, I am your Mother, of course I care about you."

"Then why did you leave us?"

"I did it for the best." She was on the defensive as she knew it was a question she could never answer without exposing her selfishness.

"Was it better for us? Was it? Or was it just better for you? Imagine what it's been like for us. Having everyone at school laugh at us because our father is living with his cousin. Of yes, that's what people say. One day one of the chaps came to school and said that Aunty Kathleen was Dad's sister, but I knew that couldn't be true because Carl was...., as I knew Dad was Carl's dad as well as mine. There's so much mystery Mother. No one talks to us. Everyone assumes we don't care or we're too young to understand or it doesn't matter anyway. But it does."

"I'm sorry you know about Carl, it can't be much fun knowing.

You and he are so very alike to look at now. But you like him don't you? I must be nice having another chap around the house?"

"He's alright." He was not going to tell her how he really felt. "There's nothing wrong with him really. He's Susannah's friend more than mine though."

"Don't you do things together?"

"I'd like to but when we do play together he's going for it all the time – always as if it were some sort of competition to beat me at everything. It's not fair when he is so much younger than me. I just have to let him win, or at least do well, and then everyone thinks I'm no good. I do well at school though, when he's not there."

She was shocked at Charles's lack of self-confidence. She had always thought of him as strong yet he was obviously a lonely and frightened boy clinging to his Nanny, imagining himself in love with her – for it was obvious who Charles wanted to spend the rest of his life with as he hadn't mentioned anyone else but Monika.

Alicia changed the subject.

"Tell me something, Charles, when did Kathleen come to Millcourt?"

"Just after Henry's funeral. They just arrived. Carl had his own room anyway, he often came to stay over when his parents," he corrected himself "when Aunty Kathleen and Uncle Henry were away."

"What did they tell you?"

"That they were staying for a while until they got things sorted out. But she acts like she owns the place. She even wanted me to give up my room to Carl as it was nicer than his. She walks around the house in her dressing gown, she orders Cook and Monika around as if she'd lived here for years. And she's always telling me and Susannah off about the stupidest things. And now she's sacked Monika."

Alicia couldn't ask where she slept. She didn't need to. Charles answered her thoughts for her.

"She's taken over your old room. It's been painted. It's all pink and twirly."

Alicia's room. It had been her haven, decorated in beige and pale blue it had been her sanctuary. Its main door opened onto the landing but it also had double doors opening directly into Arnold's suite. They couldn't be making their relationship more obvious.

"I wish she would leave. I wish Henry hadn't died. I wish Carl and Aunty Kathleen would go away. I don't want them here. They don't belong here. It's not fair. It's all your fault. Everything's your fault!"

She was amazed at how one minute her son was so adult and the next minute talking to him was like having a conversation with a nine

110

year old. One minute he was planning the rest of his life and the next verbally stamping his foot like a child.

"No, Charles, not everything. Lot's of things maybe. But not everything.

"It's not fair!"

She stopped him from walking on by holding gently onto his arm. He reluctantly, truculently, turned to face her. "Charles, if I never say anything to you ever again, and if you never listen to anything I ever say to you hear this. No one ever said life should be fair. Don't expect it to be and you won't be so disappointed. Life *isn't* fair. Life has *never* been fair and life *will never* be fair. It's not what life is for. Life is supposed to be *un*fair. It is unfair so as to test you, to see what you can cope with. Life will give you all the trials and tribulations you can stand. The worse it gets, the stronger you become and the stronger you become the more is heaped on you because you've shown you can cope. Do you understand? Never complain, just decide what you are going to do and do it. Never worry about what others think, what others want you to do, decide what you know is best for you and do it."

He waited a few moments, realising how serious she had become. "Is that what you did?"

"Yes, Charles. I decided that I wasn't good for your father or you, I knew you would be better off without me."

"So you left." He said the words with finality.

"So I left" she confirmed.

"So you won't be coming back?"

"So I won't be coming back." Her turn to be final. Had he really thought she ever would?

They walked further along the promenade. The street lighting had come on, every alternate one was broken. Someone had deliberately thrown stones breaking every other lamp.

But neither Alicia nor Charles was going to say he should go home. It was the longest conversation they had ever had. They were really talking to each other for the first, and as it turned out, for the last time.

"Mother, you never talk about Susannah."

The sun had set and the evening was getting colder. The wind was getting up and the fine May afternoon was turning into a stormy evening and she knew they should be turning for home but somehow she couldn't do it.

"Mother? I said you never talk about Susannah. You were always talking about me. You never include Susannah."

"I heard you Charles. I was trying to find the right way to answer. How could she explain how much she hated the child and what

111

she meant. Charles may appear grown up in some ways and she had told him things he had guessed anyway, but there was no way he could or should bear the burden of that knowledge.

"Susannah was very young when I left. I do not know her. She was always in the nursery." It was a weak excuse but it was all Alicia had. "I never got to know her and I don't suppose I will now you don't want to go on holiday with me."

"That's all over."

"I know that's all over now. When you called last week were you thinking that while everything is changing at home it might as well change everywhere? Get it all over and done with?"

She found it easier to talk to him as if he was a grown man, not her son. Had she ever thought of him as her son? Probably in the very early days, in that wretched bungalow, but certainly not since she went away.

"Probably. I hate Kathleen. She doesn't care about Susannah and me. She wants us out of the way so she and Carl can be a proper family with Dad – no awkward bits of history like us lying around."

"You may be right, Charles, and I know I'm not the answer for you, you would hate it if you came to live with me. Though you mustn't think of yourself as 'an awkward piece of history' you know you were very much loved and wanted when you were born."

"Was I?"

"Of course you were." She convinced neither of them. "Let's get out of this wind."

The road they turned up was Deneshey Road. When they reached the bungalow Alicia stopped and put her arm on Charles' shoulder to stop him too.

"We used to live here, you know?"

"What? Here? It's tiny!" So Arnold had never told him about the days before Millcourt.

"It may be tiny compared with Millcourt but you lived here for the first few years of your life, along with me and your Grandfather and Grandmother."

"Where was Father?"

"It was during the war – he was only here when he was on leave."

"Were you happy here?"

"No, Charles, I was never happy here. Though" she continued quickly in a rare moment of concern at her selfishness "I was happy when we used to play, you and I, in the garden."

"There was a sandpit!"

"You remember! How wonderful! Yes! There was a sandpit, you used to make castles, not very large or elaborate ones but you were very proud of them."

112

"I don't really remember – I think I must have seen a photograph. Why did we leave?"

"Your Grandfather died and left all his money to your Father. He wanted to live in a bigger place, make a bit more of a splash."

"So we've been at Millcourt ever since?"

"Indeed."

"What were my grandparents like?" So as they walked to the end of the road and turned, into the deserted Market Street she told him a very edited, almost fictional version of his grandparents. She only talked about George and Ellen, she didn't mention her own parents and he didn't ask.

"Here comes the rain. We'd better dash or we'll get very wet."

It was raining far too hard for them to get far so they sought refuge in The Lighthouse Keeper. The pub was not crowded and they easily found seats around a table near the fire in the Snug Bar.

"What can I get you?"

As the girl behind the bar disinterestedly asked the required question she did a double take as she saw Alicia. "It's Alicia Donaldson isn't it?"

When Alicia had inclined her head in assent the girl continued in a rush "You won't remember me I'm Brenda. I was in the drama group, you always said I should go into acting but look at me still here. It is good to see you. And this is your boy?"

"Charles. I'm Charles. How do you do?"

"Very well thank you Charles. But before I get you and your Mother a drink I must ask how old you are, we can't have youngsters in the bar."

"I'm 16 on Tuesday." He said proudly.

"Well I'm sure that will be fine then. And many happy returns."

When they had got their drinks they went over to a table by the fire and sat down.

"We've come a long way this evening Charles, you and I, and I don't just mean walking."

"Yes Mother I know."

They sat round the table for an hour or more as they talked. Charles found that he quite liked this woman who was his mother, she was very pretty and the men who came into the bar tipped their hats to her and said 'good evening' very respectfully. He decided she must have had good reasons for doing what she did that afternoon. He was sure she didn't do it all the time. For her part, Alicia decided that she rather liked her son. He was intelligent and spoke eloquently when he started talking about his bird watching. She decided that he would probably turn out all right in the end – as long as he was left to himself. She would not need to worry too much about him as long as he got away from Arnold and Kathleen.

It was after 10 o'clock when Charles got back to Millcourt. He walked into the drawing room, tired, wet and looking rather bedraggled.

"I'm sorry I was away so long Father, Aunty Kathleen. Mother and I went for a walk and were caught in the rain."

"Where is she now?"

"I think she's staying at the Derby overnight."

"You should have let us know you were safe"

"What could possibly have happened to me Aunty Kathleen? We just went for a walk along the Prom and then got caught in the rain so had a drink in the Lighthouse Keeper."

"She took you into a Public House?" Kathleen was more shocked than Arnold.

"Yes, they were OK about it because the weather was so bad, and the girl behind the bar knew Mother from, from before. I only had ginger beer."

"I should bloody well hope so! Now go to bed we have some talking to do in the morning." Arnold knew that he could no longer put off talking to them. In the morning he would have to tell them what was happening and how their lives were about to change. It didn't matter that it was Charles' 16th birthday.

The gathering the next morning was not a happy one. Kathleen marshalled the children into Arnold's study, as mystified as they were as to the reason for the formal meeting. When he had something to tell the children he usually told her first and then they raised it at dinner.

She had got used to living in Millcourt, with Nanny to look after the children, with Cook to run the house – for she was more of a housekeeper than just a cook. Kathleen enjoyed the space, she took pride in watching her son enjoy what she thought of as his birthright. She hadn't really enjoyed those years of living with Henry in their semi-detached. Her regular visits from Arnold meant that she was always reminded of what she was missing.

Henry had been a very boring, insignificant little person, though she did come to care for him as a friend and he obviously cared a great deal for her and Carl. She cared enough about him to hope that he had never guessed the reasons for their hasty courtship and marriage.

Since Henry's death she had picked up life at Millcourt as if she had never lived anywhere else. Being with Arnold every day, seeing him at breakfast and welcoming him back from the office with a glass of whisky and a sympathetic ear had quickly become 'normal' for

Kathleen. Unlike being able to share Arnold's bed as and when he chose, the novelty of running the big house had not worn off after a couple of weeks.

12 year old Carl loved living in the big house. He missed his father of course, he had cried briefly at Henry's funeral, but his sadness was tempered by the excitement of moving. He enjoyed moving all his things into the bedroom he had occupied on a regular basis since he was a young boy at Millcourt. It didn't bother him, as it seemed to bother his mother, that he didn't move into the bigger room that was Charles's. His mother made such a fuss about it "Charles will be leaving home soon, he doesn't need all that space" Carl liked the room he had always had. After he had found a place for everything he had sat on the window seat and stared at the glimpses of the sea over the dunes on the other side of the golf course. He loved to sit there. He would spent many hours watching men pitching up, playing out of the bunkers and putting with varying degrees of skill.

He was very fond of Susannah, he felt sorry for her because she was always on her own. Charles was so much older, he never wanted to play with her. He never minded when Susannah followed him around, when she sat on the floor of his room reading or even perching at the other end of the window seat badgering him to explain the rules of golf. In the summer she would tirelessly play with him in the garden, fielding, bowling or batting as much as he wanted her to.

Moving into the big house permanently gave Carl access to Arnold's library and he loved books. From a very early age he had enjoyed history and reading about the people who lived, ruled and battled years ago. He had spent most of the Easter holiday curled up in one of the brown leather chairs by the fire in the library reading about Napoleon and Wellington, although only 12 years old he didn't tackle the usual fiction of the day, Enid Blyton didn't interest him, the Secret Seven, even Swallows & Amazons wouldn't hold his interest for long, but he ate up books about the Napoleonic Wars.

Charles thought the summons must have something to do with his mother, it wouldn't be to do with it being his birthday. For as long as he could remember birthdays had been ignored in the household. No cards were given, there were never presents to unwrap, except, of course, the small gifts from Monika and Cook. Arnold had always simply told him a sum of money had been deposited in his trust fund. He could not look back to his time at boarding school with anything other than horror, but at least they had made something of birthdays.

He thought that perhaps his father and Kathleen were going to get married. Perhaps they wanted to explain something of the events of yesterday – though what it had to do with everyone else he couldn't guess.

He stood, slightly apart from the others, looking as unconcerned as they appeared worried. He did keep glancing at Susannah though, who stood, as always, close to Carl. He couldn't bear it if anything awful was to happen to her.

Arnold felt awkward. He had to explain to these people, who, to a greater or lesser extent, he cared about, that their lives were to be completely disrupted. He had decided to tell them all at once so he wouldn't have to face their individual problems. This way Kathleen would be too inhibited to voice her anger and disappointment in front of the others, Charles would keep his upper lip very stiff, Carl would accept it with calm acquiescence, as he had accepted everything else that had happened in his life and Susannah, would do what they told her as she always did.

They would have to get rid of Cook as well as Nanny. He was aware that they were, to the children, more important members of the household than he was. Still they had had an easy few years, losing their friends was an unavoidable burden for them to bear.

They would get over it.

When Arnold was not in total control of things he resorted to the language and manner of the pulpit. He had had a grand-father who was a minister and something of that pomposity and grandiloquence had filtered through the generations. He stood with his back to the fire, facing his extended family, with his thumbs under the lapels of his tweed jacket, just as the masters at school put their thumbs under the edges of their gowns, thought Charles.

Arnold fell back on a lifetime of making speeches; speeches in court, on the hustings, in council chambers, to his employees. He had always been a good maker of speeches. He preferred them to conversation. In speeches you just had to communicate facts and your own opinions. You told people what you wanted them to hear, you used language and voice in such a way that they did not interrupt, you did not have to hear anything they had to say.

So he began by making a speech and when Arnold had the floor no one interrupted.

"I have brought you all together this morning to tell you that Millcourt is up for sale and, since there are already people interested in buying it, we will be moving out shortly."

He ignored the gasps and the look on Kathleen's face.

"Shielding you all from the problems that have arisen is a burden I can keep to myself no longer. The business has not been going well, indeed it is folding, all the workers have been laid off with immediate effect."

As he continued he talked less formally; he was not going to break down, but he softened his voice.

"Unlike many in the circumstances in which we find ourselves, we have somewhere to go. A lovely home is ready for us all. We shall be moving into Kathleen's home. We will stay together as a family. This is all for the best."

One voice broke the silence.

"Why?"

"Why Charles? Because there is no money left."

Arnold left the room. He did not want to answer questions, and as he left the doorbell rang.

Those in the study couldn't hear what the voices in the hall were saying. The children and Kathleen stood where they had been standing as Arnold had dropped his bombshell. They all looked through the door to the hall where three men stood apparently arguing with their father.

"We have our orders......."

"No, not today......."

"We must ......"

"No, not today.... it's my son's birthday....."

"I'm sorry for that but ...."

Kathleen walked towards the group.

"What is going on here?"

"We have orders to take away...."

"You have orders? From whom?"

"We have orders to take away goods to the value of three thousand pounds' he hesitated evidently deciding where she stood in the hierarchy of the household. "Madam." He finally concluded.

"I repeat "From whom?""

"From the court."

"They're bailiffs my dear. I have failed...." he hesitated as the word hurt and corrected himself "I have not paid a bill that they now require goods to cover."

"I don't believe this is happening. You must go away. Come another day. Let us get used to this idea before tearing our home from underneath our feet."

"My dear..." Arnold tried to get Kathleen away from the door and back into the library, he wanted the door shut so that she and the children wouldn't witness his humiliation. They had no idea what was happening but they knew it was not good.

"Go away." Kathleen had turned to the spokesman and repeated slowly and clearly "Go away. Say we're not in. Come back tomorrow." She half turned pointing him to the open study door and the three children watching the proceedings with their eyes wide open.

He retreated. "Alright missus, I'll say you weren't in. We'll be back at 10 o'clock tomorrow, mind, you won't get away with this two days running."

The men left, leaving the door open behind them.

"Oh Arnold. What is all this about?" Kathleen walked to the door to shut it. She needed to have her back to Arnold as she fought to hold back the tears of frustration. Just as she had been able to leave that dreadful house she was going to have to return. It was so *humiliating.*

"I will tell you everything later. Take Carl outside and reassure him while I go and talk to the kitchen." Everything was happening far too quickly.

When Kathleen got back to the study only her son was there.

"Where's Charles? The least he can do is offer support to his father."

When Arnold reached the kitchen Susannah was sitting at the table and Cook was pouring some of her homemade lemonade into a glass.

"Where's Nanny?"

"She just left Sir, Charles had come running down the stairs and just grabbed her hand and they left, both went out the back door. Is there anything wrong Sir?

Kathleen had reached the kitchen. "Charles has gone."

"I know."

Arnold went up stairs to the telephone in his, now empty, study. Kathleen following. He asked the operator for the Derby Hotel and after a delay asked to speak to Mrs Donaldson. Obviously it was not a name they knew so he repeated the request for Mrs Tyler. After another delay he was asking what she had said to Charles. Alicia obviously had no idea what he was talking about because he kept repeating the same questions.

The last word Kathleen heard him say as she left the room was 'Police'.

Chapter Seventeen

I got a call from Alicia asking me to help so I set off immediately for the Derby where I was ushered into the Manager's office. There were two policemen, Kathleen standing, holding onto Arnold's arm and Alicia, sitting very upright in the manager's chair. I went to stand next to Alicia, she looked as though she needed some support.

"I know I am his mother and possibly a proper mother would be concerned, but I will not be. He is old enough to know his own mind and to look after himself. For Pete's sake! Fifteen years ago he would be about to fight for his country."

"He has run off with the Nanny!"

"Of course he hasn't. Don't ascribe your own motives to your son. He is protecting her. He knew you'd sacked her. He knew you were going to split everything up and they would be separated. He is protecting her. Don't you see? He is looking after her. He has taken charge for himself."

It was the first time I had spoken with Arnold Donaldson for some years. I had little respect left for the man. He had had an easy life and expected an even easier one. He had failed in every way to support the women and children for whom he had had a responsibility. I did not address him directly, but I sincerely trusted he took in what I said. "Charles is no longer a boy. He is a young man. He is a quiet, intelligent young man who has suffered much from the selfishness of his parents. I agree with Alicia, he has taken his life into his own hands. He has made a decision which I do believe should be honoured."

I had long found that people listened more closely to the words I spoke if I spoke quietly, calmly and slowly. It seemed to work even under these circumstances so I continued.

"He called me at the office this morning. He knew that I would help him, just as I hope I always have. He knows that I have the trust of his mother, and, I hope, at least the ear of his father.

"He asked me to tell you that he has gone to Sandhey. I have spoken with both Max and his housekeeper. Max has given his permission for Charles and Monika to stay at his house until he returns. When he does everything will be reviewed. But in the meantime they have a comfortable roof over their heads, they have a 'chaperone' in Mrs Tennyson and they are safe. I told him that none of you would try to change his mind or visit him or in any way get in touch with him until he returns."

"What's Max got to do with it?" Kathleen asked

"Max brought Monika to this country. Don't you remember? He brought her, God knows how, to this country and found her a place in the Donaldson household. He must feel responsible for her and, also, he has a great fondness for Charles."

"Charles is just an impressionable boy who is being manipulated by that woman." Arnold was having none of this idea that his son had acted in any way as an adult. "He is obsessed with her, he sees injustice everywhere."

"I wonder why?"

"That's not helpful Alicia."

"Charles is still a boy," Arnold repeated "he must be brought home, he makes a habit of running away when things get too much for him."

"What do you mean?" Alicia asked, aware that Arnold was making sure she realised that, even though she was Charles' mother, she knew little about his life.

"He ran away from school. He spent a week on the run."

"When? You never told me. What happened?"

"He ran away from school. We didn't tell you because you were not here. He turned up after a week or so. He was fine."

"Is that why he left boarding school and went to live with you? You never did really explain why."

"He ran away. He came back. What was there to tell?"

"He was my son."

"Yes, Alicia, he was. He is no longer. You have no claim on him and his actions."

"Neither it seems, do you."

The policemen and the hotel manager were bemused. This family bickering was not what they had expected when called to assist with a missing boy, the son of a respected member of the local community.

I did my best.

"I think we're here to find out what is in Charles' best interests. Surely we aren't here to bicker and score points against each other. When he ran away from school he showed that he'd thought it all out, he knew what he was going to do and he did it. We must trust him. I'm sure that now, when he feels he has another person to care for, he has made arrangements, he's done what he thinks he has to do."

I was going to do my best to support Charles. He had been right those years earlier, I believed he was right now.

"You always poke your nose into my family's affairs don't you?" They were the first words Arnold addressed to me directly.

"I've always tried to be here to help."

The police left when they realised that this was not a case of a missing or kidnapped child leaving me with Arnold, Kathleen and Alicia. Alicia and I eventually won the argument. It was agreed that Arnold and Kathleen would not try to take Charles back, they would allow him and Monika to find sanctuary at Sandhey for the indefinite future.

It was a very long time before they left.

Chapter Eighteen

Max was behind many of the changes that now occurred in the lives of the Donaldson's extended family.

He welcomed Charles and Monika into his home and they thrived. He treated Charles as the son he had always wanted, encouraging him in his love of bird-watching by providing him with books and most spectacularly, for his 17th birthday, a pair of German military night binoculars. At the small gathering to celebrate that day no one dared to ask where they came from. Max and Charles would spend hours in each other's company talking or reading quietly together. Max grew to understand and care for the quiet, determined, introspective young man.

After some discussion Charles had agreed to stay on at school for his A levels, but since there was no money for fees from Arnold they were paid by Max. He did well enough in those exams but left school immediately afterwards to begin work in the office at Roberts and Jones. He had a good mind, a clear way of thinking and a clear way of seeing things that would make him very useful in the office, but his heart wasn't in it. He spent most of his leisure time writing pamphlets and magazine articles about the birds of the area.

The secretaries and typists at the office, girls on the train he travelled in on every morning all tried to catch his attention, he was a very good looking and pleasant mannered young man. But he was not interested in them.

He found most enjoyment at the weekends sitting in the garden with Monika, who would be darning or knitting, sitting companionably next to him. Binoculars in hand he would point out birds as they flew passed and write their names along with dates and other details in his notebook. Monika was a willing guinea pig for the talks and guided walks he began to give.

Monika got on well with Max's housekeeper, and they began to share responsibilities. At Millcourt she had always looked after the nursery but she had never known anything of how the household was run, how menus were planned, where and how the food was ordered, which tradesmen had accounts and which required cash. Her job had been to ensure the children ate, slept, did their homework, read widely, didn't spend too much time in front of the television and didn't disturb their father. Now she began to learn how to run a house.

Monika was taught how to keep the house clean, when to clean which rooms, how to clean them without disturbing The Major's bits and pieces. Monika learned to change the curtains in the spring – the week the clocks went forward – and again in the autumn – when they went back. They breathed life into the house, keeping it clean and airy, making it into the home it had rarely been since Elizabeth Fischer had had her breakdown, even redecorating some of the rooms themselves. Monika would take over the role of housekeeper when Mrs Tennyson retired.

Monika had rarely left Millcourt except when she took the children for a walk down to the sands and then she avoided talking to anybody, even if they pleasantly wished her a 'good afternoon'. She had lived in the area for the best part of ten years and had not had any life of her own other than looking after the children. She had never thought about it and certainly never resented it. But now, with Mrs Tennyson as a mother figure and friend, Monika began to meet people, becoming quite well known and liked by shopkeepers and the respectable ladies of the town.

'Mrs Heller' became a regular at the frequent coffee mornings and jumble sales in the town and she blossomed into a relaxed and confident young woman – for she still was a young woman – despite everything that had happened in her life she was not yet 30.

In the New Year 1961, Mrs Tennyson decided Monika was ready to take over the reins and she announced she would retire to join her widowed sister in her cottage in the Cotswolds in the Spring.

Max had a hand in developments between Arnold and Kathleen. Arnold didn't want me to have anything to do with his affairs but, behind the scenes, I was Max's right hand as he helped Arnold through the sale of Millcourt and his formal descent into bankruptcy.

And it was Max who persuaded Arnold that he had to marry Kathleen.

Arnold didn't want to. He hadn't found it necessary in all the years since his divorce and when Kathleen and Carl had moved into Millcourt, he was simply being practical in giving his cousin's widow and son a home. He hadn't cared about the gossip, but he wanted to clear up his vaguely held concerns about the exact nature of their relationship. He had Max check through all his father's papers to see if there were any links between the families that had previously not come to light. Nothing was found, though he had had to confide in Max why he was concerned.

Kathleen enlisted Max's help to ensure that, before they left Millcourt, she would be Mrs Donaldson. She could not bear the humiliation of moving back to her house in Dunedin Avenue otherwise.

Although they had been through so much together, over the years neither Arnold nor Kathleen fooled the other that there was any real love between them any more. They felt loyalty, affection and familiarity but not love, so again it was a marriage of convenience for Kathleen.

After so short a time in the luxury of living in Millcourt she found herself back in her old house, now the mother to two children. She also had to be mother to Arnold as she nursed him through his depressions. She looked back with some longing to the days when she had only seen Arnold twice a week.

She had had a life of her own then.

Max was very aware that there would not be any money in the Donaldson household and he was concerned about how Carl and Susannah would fare.

He knew he could do nothing directly to help them but he was a resourceful man.

In all the papers I had to go through that related to Arnold and his father Max managed to ensure I found one which referred to an investment that Arnold had not managed to get his hands on and that was in the name of Kathleen's mother. He found the deeds to a shop, which, conveniently, had just become empty – the people who had been running it having recently retired. Mrs McNamara had died some years before so the shop was now available to her daughters, Maureen and Kathleen. I didn't make too much of the fact that I had never come across this shop before in all my dealings with old Mr Donaldson's estate and there was no reference to his purchasing it.

But then records may well have been mislaid during the disruption of wartime.

So Max managed to ensure an income for the Donaldsons and a happier Kathleen, both circumstances would ensure a more comfortable life for Susannah and Carl.

In order that we could keep an eye on them Max arranged for me to join the board of Governors of the school they both attended. In that way I was able to follow their progress from a distance.

They both seemed happy growing up together. They spent every moment they could together, loved living in the same house, becoming closer and closer. They met each other after school every afternoon, and went to the local coffee bar along with a group of others.

At home they would always be in and out of each other's rooms, Susannah frequently wearing Carl's jeans and sweaters. They would do their homework together, read together, play records together. They liked the same groups and played pop music hour after hour in their bedrooms.

Arnold and Kathleen were happy that they got along so well and were such trouble free teenagers. So much was heard of the messes that young people got themselves into at that time. But Susannah and Carl didn't get into any trouble, they did well at school and were normally polite to their parents.

At that time it was only their friends who knew the real nature of their relationship. They knew that Carl and Susannah were cousins and stepbrother and sister. Stepbrothers and sisters could go out together, cousins could even marry each other, so it must be OK mustn't it?

With all the changes in his life Max stopped visiting the office in London, sending me in his place. It was only some years later that I knew what this meant to Alicia.

No longer did she have her fortnightly escape to the luxury of the Savoy or her regular deliveries from Harrods and Fortnum and Mason. She found herself in the position of having to earn her living.

Her portrait painting bought in something and Maureen found her a part time job teaching drama in a local school, but she became something of a recluse, not eating well enough and worrying too much.

It was Harry, her next door neighbour, who called the ambulance and went with her to the hospital when she collapsed just before Christmas, six months after her last trip to the north. It was Harry, more or less a complete stranger, who shared the visiting with Maureen as Alicia recovered in hospital from those operations; who looked after the empty house every time she was in hospital and who supported her day after day as she recuperated.

It was Harry who put a vase of marigolds in the dining room window to welcome her home when she came back from hospital, and who went with her every time she had to return.

She never gave him any reason to do all these things other than a smile. She was not well enough to give anything else.

Harry's wife never understood the power she had over him.

I did.

It was the power that only a beautiful, vulnerable woman can have over a lonely man.

Chapter Nineteen

They did not celebrate Monika's birthdays as she wasn't entirely sure what day it was, nor exactly how old she was. Nor did they really celebrate Charles', but just before his 21st she had asked him to take her to the cinema 'to mark the day'.

He later told me that he hadn't wanted to go to see the film in the first place. He didn't like Cliff Richard and *Summer Holiday* was really not going to be his sort of film but Monika had wanted to see it. He had taken her to see *The Young Ones* the year before at the local cinema and she had loved the energy and the songs.

"It will be a good film, Charles, you will enjoy it. You see that you don't"

"Oh no!" he joked. "More tunes to remember, more songs to sing."

"It is good to get out of the house. Good that you take me to the cinema."

They were walking the mile or so from Sandhey to the cinema, along the promenade.

"I like going out with you, you are a good looking boy!"

"I like going out with you, too Monika. But I'm not the boy you always call me! I'm officially an adult next week."

"Even when you earn your own living, look after me, are Max's friend and equal you will always be a boy to me."

"I'm catching up with you, you know. When you first came to our house you were, what, 20?"

"18. No more than 18."

"And I was what? Six?"

"At least six and a quarter."

He laughed.

"You were nearly three times my age. But now, you are, what?"

"Nearly 33."

"And I'm nearly 21 – I've practically caught you up!"

They walked along this road most Sunday mornings but now it seemed different. The tide was in and the waves were gently lapping against the sea wall. He grabbed at her hand and pulled her round to face him. He reached for her other hand and held her at arms length from him. They stood there, to any casual observer, a young man and his girl friend. She looked up at him, as she had to do for several years now.

"I want to say something, properly, formally, and you've got to listen." He had rehearsed what he was going to say for weeks. He had been going to tell her on his birthday but now seemed the right moment.

He looked into her eyes and very slowly said something they both knew.

"I love you, Monika."

"I know."

"But I will never do anything about it."

"I know."

"I will never try to kiss you, I will never try to do anything with you. I will never do anything to hurt you. Just know that I love you and that I will always love you."

"I know."

"I have always loved you. Since the day you came to the house I have known that I would never love any other person as I love you. Everything you have told me about your life before you came here, the war, everything you went through, everything just makes me want to take care of you more. I would never ever want you to have to go through anything like that again. I wouldn't ever want to make you have a baby, I wouldn't ever want to make you suffer that again. I will always, always, be with you. I will never, ever let you down. I will only ever go away if you tell me to."

He stopped with a satisfied pursing of his lips. He had said everything he had wanted to say and she wasn't laughing at him.

She understood why Charles was speaking so formally. She knew how important it was to him to be taken seriously, so she replied in the same formal manner.

"Too much has happened in my life to let me love anyone. But I trust you. That, to me, means more than love. I would like us always to be together but you will meet someone, you will find a young woman who you will want to kiss, who you will want to go to bed with, who will want you too. Then I will step aside and watch as my Charles walks into his life and out of mine."

"Never. It won't happen Monika. How could I meet anyone like you? I don't want to meet anyone else."

They stood for several minutes, then he tucked her hand into the crook of his arm and they walked on. "Come on, we'll miss the beginning of the film."

There was a queue at the cinema, it was half term and it seemed that every young person in the area was celebrating by going to the cinema.

They would have been much nearer the front of the queue if they hadn't stopped to talk on the way. If they hadn't stopped they would have had seats a lot further forward than they did. But they *had* stopped, they *were* late and they were shown to seats near the back of the small cinema, one row in front of the double seats.

Cinemas at the time understood that many young people went to the cinema not to watch the film but to be close together in the dark. The double seats allowed boys to wrap their arms around their girlfriends' shoulders and hold them tight as they kissed them, without the inconvenience of a separating seat arm. These double seats were prized and there was much competition for them, the first in the queue running up the stairs to claim the darkest and most secluded corners. The row in front of the double seats was the last to be filled – in unpopular films it was usually empty.

But Charles and Monika were amongst the last to be shown into the cinema and it was to this row, in front of the double seats, that they were directed. They settled down to watch the film, Monika to enjoy every moment, Charles to try not to listen to the sounds behind him.

Shuffling hands and bodies could be felt as well as heard, as legs and arms entwined and, no doubt, mouths and tongues. Charles knew what other young people did with each other, even if he was not interested in it himself.

He could not concentrate on the film. He couldn't help listening to the pair behind them. He would have been embarrassed whoever it was. It didn't seem to be worrying Monika, who was engrossed in the story of the young people travelling through Europe on a London bus. He kept changing his position. He fidgeted, he could not get comfortable, he felt his insides would never settle down and be right again. He felt he had to get up and walk about. But he couldn't, so he fidgeted, changing from crossing one leg to the other, then back again a few minutes later. Monika 'shushing' him and telling him to sit still. He was consumed by such a mixture of fear and anger that he could not understand.

He had recognised the muffled voices.

The couple behind him were Susannah and Carl.

He hadn't seen them for a long while. He never visited their house nor they his. How old were they now? 17? 18? Old enough to be doing it. Together. With each other. How long had it been going on? Did his father know? Surely not. What about Kathleen? It would be just like her to know what was going on but allow it, even encourage it, as it would tie Arnold even closer to her. What could he do? Should he do anything? How far had it gone? This was 1963, no one waited until they were married to go all the way.

So many thoughts rushed through his head.

As the plot unfolded on the screen he realised he couldn't allow anything between Carl and Susannah to go on. He knew he had to stop it somehow but he had no idea how. It was all he could do not to turn around and hit Carl for taking advantage of a girl who had worshipped him from the nursery. But he knew he wouldn't be able to make any punch hurt in these circumstances. He knew that he would have to sit out the film and do nothing to embarrass either Susannah or Monika. He spent the duration of the film working out different courses of action in his head. He could talk to Max, he could jump in with both feet and go around to Dunedin Avenue and confront his father and stepmother with the facts, he could take Carl to one side and explain what was so very wrong with what he was doing. He could think of pros and cons with each of these ways of tackling the problem which was so obviously developing.

Chapter Twenty

When Charles called me the next day to tell me what he had seen and heard at the cinema I wasn't as worried as Charles thought I ought to be. I knew they were very friendly, but this? "It wasn't just kissing and stuff" Charles had said "he had his hand up her blouse."

"Did you know this was going on?" Charles was angry and accusing.

"Charles, they are young, they will grow out of it."

"But what if they don't?"

"He's her cousin, it's a close relationship, but not too close."

"It's far too close."

"Henry was your father's cousin, Charles, that makes Charles and Susannah second cousins. I know there's been a lot of rumour and tittle tattle but even with your father's marriage to Kathleen they're only step brother and sister. I don't think that is a legal impediment. The relationship isn't close enough to cause any problems."

"But they're not second cousins, not even cousins. I know they aren't. I've known for years that they aren't. Didn't my mother ever tell you? "

"What do you mean?"

"Henry wasn't Carl's father."

I hoped I was wrong, but I thought I knew the answer almost as he spoke, but I had to ask the question anyway. "So, who was?"

"Father. Carl, is my half brother. Susannah is his half sister. What they are doing is immoral, totally and completely wrong."

I should have known, but up to this moment I had had no idea.

"If what you say is true, Charles, what they are doing is more than immoral it's illegal. Are you sure you are right? We can't possibly say anything unless you're absolutely certain of your facts."

"Of course I'm right. I've known since that day before my 16th birthday."

Why hadn't I thought of that possibility? I knew Kathleen and Arnold had been close. Kathleen had married Henry quite unexpectedly, Carl had been born very soon after the wedding. But the thought that Carl was Arnold' son had never occurred to me.

"Are you absolutely certain?"

"Absolutely. Mother told me. She admitted it. She said Carl and I were so alike she wondered how no one else had realised."

"Who else knows? Max?"

"I haven't told anyone but he must know."

All manner of thoughts went through my mind. If what Charles said was true why hadn't Arnold and Kathleen stopped it. They must know what's going on under their noses – or were they so self absorbed, that they didn't care what was happening to their children.

I really hoped they had no idea. I didn't like Arnold and I knew he was completely self-centred, but was he capable of allowing his son and daughter to get so close in such an inappropriate way? I really hoped he was not.

It seemed that the people who knew the secrets of the parentage didn't know the nature of their relationship and the people who knew the way the relationship was going didn't know the problems of their parentage.

That is, until Charles had gone to the cinema the previous evening.

And now it was my problem.

I didn't think I could discuss it over the phone so I drove straight round to see Arnold and Kathleen. Arnold was out, it was Sunday and Arnold always went out on a Sunday afternoon.

Kathleen was distant when she answered the door. The children were out but Arnold was bound to be back soon if I cared to wait.

I hadn't seen them for several years, but it seemed that we only ever met at times of crisis. Kathleen, to her credit, did try to be civilised.

We made polite conversation.

"How are the children? Hardly "children" any more I should think."

"They're fine, but growing up far too fast. It's all this odd music now, Arnold can't bear it."

"I should think it's all boyfriends and girlfriends now."

"They do seem to spend a lot of time in that coffee bar, listening to the juke box and meeting up with some very strange people, not our sort at all. It's impossible to control them any more. Still, they stick together so they'll be looking out for each other, making sure the other one doesn't get into any trouble."

It seemed obvious that she didn't know what was going on.

How could I tell her? How could I explain?

"It's such a blessing, their being so close. They seem interested in the same things, they go everywhere together. I do sometimes wonder if they aren't a bit….." she hesitated a little too much "…too close."

Maybe she was suspicious but was keeping up a brave face.

I decided to take the bull by the horns.

"Kathleen. You know don't you? You know they're brother and sister. If there is anything, anything, beyond just spending a lot of time together you must stop it."

She turned to me with such a great sadness in her eyes. This woman who had loved the wrong man and won him at the wrong time, whose life had never been straightforward or easy, realised that the sins of the parents were now being visited on their children. I wondered how long she had worried about this, how long she had wondered how she could explain to her son the lies that they had always lived. Her life was about to fall even further apart, and she knew that she had no one else to blame.

"Is it so well known then?"

"Not widely, I should think. But people do talk and perhaps some others have drawn their own conclusions about you and Arnold and your children. I didn't know until this morning, maybe I should have guessed – you and Henry got married so quickly, it all happened in a rush and then Carl was born nearer the wedding than perhaps he should have been."

"But it was happening a lot at that time, just at the end of the war, all sorts of people were getting married quickly." She was clutching at straws, and we both knew it.

"But ever since Henry died you and Arnold have been together, as if you didn't care what people thought. My mother tells me what the women in the town say, they remember and you weren't always as discreet as perhaps you might have been. Mind you I didn't put two and two together. But maybe I just don't think that way."

"Who told you?"

"Charles."

She seemed to take that in her stride.

"I suppose Alicia told him. She never did care how much she hurt other people. What's brought all this out now?"

I ignored the dig at Alicia, if it ever came to a contest as to who had used more people, and who had treated their children worse, then I think it might have been close between the two of them, and I believe Alicia had better reasons for her behaviour.

"Charles saw them at the cinema yesterday."

"They said they were going."

"Yes, Kathleen, they were in the back row. Kissing and cuddling, and probably a lot more."

Kathleen had to accept that and all its implications but all she could say was "Oh dear. We're going to have to do something aren't we? We can't hide our heads in the sand any longer."

So they had suspected something was going on but had chosen not to do anything. I believe they would still have backed out of saying anything if they could possibly have got away with it.

"Kathleen you have got to tell them."

"He won't. I've tried to persuade Arnold to tell Carl he's his father but he won't hear of it." She began to explain what I think I already knew. Arnold was too ashamed to tell his son of his behaviour, to tell Carl that he and his mother had had a longstanding affair, that they had arranged for her to marry Henry only because she was pregnant.

His weakness was that he could not bear to lose face with Carl. He needed the respect and admiration of the only son that mattered to him. He had lost so much with the business going down he couldn't bear to lose any respect and love Carl might still feel for him.

"He'd rather they had an illegal relationship."

Kathleen had no answer. She just sat there and shrugged her shoulders helplessly.

When I had first known Kathleen she had been such a strong woman, independent, intelligent and extremely likeable. Then, as Carl had grown older, she had appeared grasping and opportunistic. Now she just appeared broken.

"Do you want me here when you tell them – for tell them you must if Arnold won't?"

"No Ted, I must do it. I *will* do it."

I hoped that the old Kathleen, the woman she had once been, would come to the fore and that she would not let the family down.

Kathleen showed me to the door and I drove away, leaving her to it.

Chapter Twenty-One

Kathleen dreaded the children's return. She had to find some form of words to get through the next few minutes. How does a mother tell her son that the man he had always thought was his father had been the unwitting dupe of his stronger, dominant cousin? How does she tell her son that the girl he was so obviously falling in love with, and who just as obviously loved him, was actually his sister?

How do you destroy so much in so few words?

Kathleen had to do just that.

She sat silently dreading the moment when their lives would all change.

It was an hour or more before the door opened. "Mum! We're back"

"Carl, Susannah, darlings, a word please."

They responded to the tone of voice, neither angry nor bitter. Resigned, sad, old. They went into the lounge, just managing to let go of each other's hands, each realising that Kathleen was serious and wondering what it was that they had done.

The worst telling off they had had was a few months before when they had used Arnold's tape recorder and over-written the only copy of a piano piece he had been working on.

Neither of them could think of anything they had done that would explain Kathleen's voice, or the look on her face. Carl thought maybe Arnold was dead, finally giving up on his ruined life, or maybe it was Susannah's mother.

Susannah walked into the sitting room goose pimples spreading from her chest to her arms, her legs and her face. She was shivering. Something was seriously wrong. She knew it.

"Carl, Susannah. Listen to me. Don't say a word. But what I am about to say is true. I wish to God it could be easier to say."

They realised the seriousness – Kathleen had crossed herself.

"Were you at the cinema last night?" she thought, firstly, she owed it to them to check some facts.

"You know we were, Cliff's latest"

"Did you see anyone there?"

Carl answered, beginning to get suspicious. He had seen Charles and Monika in the seats in front of them. "Why?"

She had decided that the only way to get through these minutes was to be honest.

"You were seen together and I have to warn you. Oh this is so, so difficult, I have to tell you both. Oh I wish to God this were not true or there was an easier way, but Carl, Susannah, you must both be told. Sooner or later, before too much harm is done."

She couldn't get the words out, and as she was so obviously distressed by what she was saying Carl and Susannah looked at each other, she frightened, he concerned – protective.

Whatever it was couldn't be *that* bad, could it?

It was.

Kathleen eventually managed to say the words "Carl, Arnold is your natural father."

Susannah let out a half scream half whimper

"No! No! That's not *fair*."

"I'm so sorry Susannah, Carl is your brother."

Susannah looked despairingly from one face to the other, from Kathleen who she had never grown to love, but who was now pitiful, crying and looking desperately old, back to Carl. Her Carl. His face registering shock his eyes wide as he, in turn, looked from his Mother to the girl he loved more than anyone in the world.

Susannah dragged her eyes from Carl, turned and ran out of the house.

She had to get away.

Carl sat down. His head in his hands.

"I knew it. I really hoped it was not true, but I knew it." He was talking to himself but Kathleen heard and it broke her heart.

Carl had always loved Susannah, since they both had been small children. Now they had grown up she had offered herself to him and he could not say no to the kissing and the cuddling. They had been accepted as a couple by their friends, always 'Susannah and Carl', or 'Carl and Susannah', never one without the other.

As she had grown up Susannah had become more and more beautiful. She had long curly hair that always fell in front of her eyes – she didn't have a fringe cut like every other girl had done as soon as the Beatles had appeared on the scene, she just defiantly tucked her long hair behind her ears. She wanted to be loved and liked but she wasn't going to be the same as everyone else.

She was quite short – she barely reached his shoulders – which was one of the things that made him feel strong and want always to look out for her.

They had grown so close over the years, and he had never doubted they would always be together.

But, there had always been those things Charles had hinted to

135

him years back, he had refused to listen to him, pushed them to the back of his mind, but the fear had always been there, niggling away.

It had held him back from doing all the things Susannah had wanted, when time after time over the last few months he could have. His gentle voice saying "No, Susie, not yet" didn't satisfy her, but he couldn't tell her why not.

He sat on the sofa looking across at his mother, who was gently weeping in her chair by the fire.

He found he couldn't cry, he half expected himself to be crying but this pain was too great. Susie was part of him. She had been part of his life for as long as he could remember. He couldn't bear it if they couldn't be together. He sat there, trying to feel nothing but the physical pain in his chest.

After several minutes of silence he found his voice "Can I ask you something?" and without waiting for an answer he continued "Why have you waited so long to tell me? Why didn't you have the guts to tell me sooner, just after Dad, Henry, died? That would have been the time. I could have dealt with it then. Did you think I would never find out?"

He stood up, filling the small room with his presence.

"It's all so blindingly obvious now. I never felt anything like him. I knew we weren't like father and son. You took me over to Millcourt so often, always when there was a problem we went there. You always ran to Arnold. It's so bloody obvious. Why didn't you tell me before? Why did you let us all come to live here when you knew...."

She tried to speak, to answer even one of the questions he asked, but she couldn't. He was right. She and Arnold had never really thought about the children as people who had their own lives to live. They had never been sufficiently important to them to make them change the way they wanted to live their lives. Why should they do that, 'just for the children'?

"I'm leaving. Now." Carl continued, his voice now cold and distant. "I'll find somewhere to stay but I won't stay here any longer and I won't be coming back."

His pain had changed to anger, the hurt fuelling a resentment so deep that he knew he would never forgive them.

Not waiting for an answer he went upstairs, chucked some books and clothes into a duffle bag and left the house.

He never saw his mother, or his father, again.

And it was too many years before he again held Susie's hand.

Susannah bumped into her father as she ran out of the house.

Ignoring, or not noticing, the look on Kathleen's face and the tears on her face, Arnold sat down and asked "What's up with Susannah?

She didn't seem very happy."

Kathleen had had enough. Couldn't Arnold, just for one minute, notice something of the atmosphere in the house? Couldn't he feel the tension? Had he been playing golf or had he got another girlfriend? When he had been married to Alicia he had visited her on a Sunday afternoon having explained his absence from home as 'golf'. Now, perhaps he was doing the same to her. History *does* repeat itself.

She knew she had lost Carl, she didn't care what Arnold thought now.

"She's not happy. Carl isn't happy. I'm not happy and perhaps, just perhaps, you won't be in a minute."

"What earth shattering event has occurred then, some group not reached Number One in that Hit Parade or he's broken one of her records?" He spoke with the sarcasm of the father of teenage children.

"Carl and Susannah have been 'going out' together."

"So? They're practically the same age, they go around in the same group of friends, of course they go out together."

"No, Arnold 'going out' together I mean *really* going out together. Certainly kissing and cuddling, probably far more. They think they're in love with each other."

Arnold was still acting as though he felt there was no problem at all.

"Women and teenagers! I'm the only sensible person in this house and that's only because I get out of it often enough. You should get out more."

The injustice stung.

Kathleen knew he had been seen around with someone called Judith, who was a lot younger than he was and who undoubtedly flattered him suitably. No doubt Judith listened to his problems and understood completely how awful the last few years had been for him. No doubt she helped him remember, if only for a couple of hours each week, what he could be, what he had been, what he thought he should be. He had probably been with her this afternoon. He obviously didn't feel like sorting out the problems of hysterical women and children.

"Arnold that is unfair! You must listen to this it is important – Carl and Susannah may be lovers!"

"You have obviously got the wrong end of the stick. They have always been inseparable, ever since they were babies they've spent as much time as they can together. They've always played together."

"Ted came round."

"Oh Christ not him! Have you noticed how he's always causing trouble in my family. What did he want?"

"Charles had phoned him, he and Monika had been at the cinema, and had seen Carl and Susannah in the back seats – doing – well – doing what people do in the back seats of cinemas these days."

She began to have his attention.

He looked around the room remembering the scene when she had told him she was expecting. It hadn't changed a great deal.

Then he thought back to the following Christmas when Susannah had been conceived. He knew they had all been drunk on New Year's Night and Alicia had gone to bed early, as usual. He seemed to remember them talking about sex. Had he complained that he didn't have enough sex with Alicia, that they no longer shared a bed? His memories of the conversation were very hazy.

He had gone upstairs determined on having his rights. She was his wife. He could take her when and how he wanted to and the next morning it was obvious that he had had sex though he knew she would never have given in willingly and that he would have had to force her. Alicia's behaviour the next day indicated that he had probably done just that.

He just wished he hadn't had so much to drink so he could remember.

He would have liked to remember.

Could Kathleen have lied, have been seeing someone else and just pinned the blame on him? That was unlikely as the boy *was* very like him. Could Susannah not be his? Who else could be the father? He had kept Alicia on a tight reign and his many spies around the town would have soon told him if she was straying.

"Arnold?" After all these years Kathleen voiced the thought that had occurred to her many times in the intervening years. "Are you thinking about that New Year? Are you thinking that you might not be Susannah's father? We did have a go at Henry. Perhaps he and Alicia..."

She couldn't finish the sentence, but she tried to continue. "Are you thinking that it could be alright for .... after all...? I mean if you weren't..."

"Of course I'm her blasted father" he interrupted, "of course I bloody am. Do you think I'd have kept her all these years if there'd been the slightest question? Do you think I would keep another man's child for 17 years?"

"Henry did." Kathleen started crying again, hopeless tears for things and people lost.

They sat for some time with just the sound of Kathleen's weeping between them.

Could he be sure he was Susannah's father? The girl was so like Alicia it was difficult to spot anything of himself in her.

He tried to dredge up details of that New Year in 1945. Was it possible Alicia and Henry had been up to something? He didn't think so. Henry was too besotted with Kathleen. No he wouldn't have done anything. Or had he been goaded too much? They really had all been very drunk.

Kathleen, wiping her eyes, finally found her voice, "I think we've all managed to make rather a mess of it really."

Arnold was beginning to agree but he was damned if he was going to admit to any wrongdoing. Look what his father had got up to all those years ago and he had never been brought to book.

"What do you want me to do then?" His voice was rising, his anger taking hold. "Do you want me to tell the children that it might be legal after all? That I might not be father to both of them – or even father to either! That their parents were so immoral that they don't actually *know* who their children were? No. We *will not* do that."

Kathleen was stung by the old accusation that Carl was not Arnold's responsibility. She realised how little this man who was her husband really cared for her. She was completely aware, in those few minutes, of how much she had wasted her life on him. Her voice changed, now cold and hard – so like Carl's had been to her a short while earlier.

"So it's OK for my son to know he's a bastard but not for your daughter to know the truth about you? Is that what you're saying?"

Despite all the years they had had together, one way or another, the argument that followed was the worst they had ever had. There were no euphemisms, and no holds barred.

It was bitter and its impact lasted a lifetime.

As is usual in such fundamental arguments words were said that could not be unsaid and Kathleen knew that their relationship would never recover.

Perhaps it was the first time they had really faced the facts of their relationship. How sordid, underhand and downright selfish they had both been all along.

It became clear, as each allegation was met with reproach, each accusation with blame that neither knew who Susannah's father really was and there was only one way to find out.

They would have to contact Alicia. But would she know? What if she had had sex with both Henry and Arnold? If she did know would she tell them? If she gave them an answer would she tell them the truth?

Whatever the risks they would have to ask her.

After tearing the fabric of their lives apart Arnold agreed to call Alicia and explain something of the situation, making it clear that it was for the children's sake – perhaps hinting that things had gone further than they actually appeared to have done.

Kathleen left the room as Arnold made the call.

Only then did she realise how late it was getting. It was dark and neither Susannah nor Carl had come home.

Alicia never adequately explained why she lied in that telephone conversation with Arnold. Perhaps she didn't want to make things easy for Arnold and Kathleen, perhaps she didn't want to help the child she had never wanted in the first place and felt no love or sense of responsibility for. Perhaps she was lonely, ill and self-pitying when she took the call and didn't see why anyone should be happy. Perhaps she remembered how she had felt seeing Susannah and Carl together on the lawn at Millcourt.

When, years later and it was too late, she was asked to explain her actions she said that she had not really lied, she had simply reversed the truth.

When Arnold asked her if anything had happened on all the days she had been alone with Henry she was so surprised she burst out laughing. "My God Arnold – if you think I had the slightest interest in the weak little runt you're even more stupid than I gave you credit for." And then she became angry. How dare he accuse her of infidelity when he had been with Kathleen all those years, and when she lost her temper she didn't really think of the consequences of what she said.

She told Arnold, graphically, that she had only 'handled' Henry. He had come into her room when she was half asleep and she had at first thought it was Arnold. She had pushed him away but he had got rather excited. He was very drunk and was incoherently telling her how much he loved her. She had grabbed hold of him, more in a move to keep him from forcing himself inside her, and he had come very quickly. He was nowhere near being inside her. She said Arnold had raped her a few minutes later. "You're Susannah's father how dare you think otherwise!"

Yes, she simply reversed the truth.

How different all their lives would have been if she hadn't.

It would have been so easy for her not to lie. She hadn't had to look anyone in the face, she was 200 miles away, she could have said "Of course she isn't yours Arnold, of course Henry was her father." After a bit of embarrassing explanation to Carl and Susannah she would be able to clear the air and explain that they could not be related. They would probably never speak to her again, but they could have been together.

But Alicia did lie, and all those lives were changed.

"Of course she's your daughter Arnold. What on earth makes you think she isn't?"

Chapter Twenty-Two

Susannah had dashed out of the house without thinking where she was going or what she was going to do. She just had to walk, and walk, and the longer she walked the less she felt she could go back home.

Her thoughts darted backwards and forwards between Carl, kind, generous, open-hearted, wonderful Carl, Carl – *her brother* – and her father. How could he? She hated him. How could he hurt her like this? How could she hurt him back?

He'd never loved her or Charles, she knew that, he had never spent any time with them – he was always with Carl and 'that woman'. How could he have uprooted them from their lovely house and taken them to live with her? How could he have *married* her? How could he have let her get so close to Carl? He'd known all along and never said anything! She hated them all, Aunty Kathleen, her father, Charles. But not Carl, no, she could never hate Carl. She would always love him.

When this had all settled down they'd go away where no one knew them. They'd go to London, they'd get jobs there, get a flat, no one would need to know they were brother and sister.

But he wouldn't go with her would he? He was too honest and too caring to do that. He would come up with some horrible facts about what happens when parents are too closely related. She knew enough to know that the children of parents who were too closely related were 'not right'.

He wouldn't go away with her like that. She pictured him so clearly, she just knew as if he were standing in front of her, speaking to her. He wouldn't go away with her, he would say 'No' because she was his sister. There was no way she could be with him, even if she wanted to he wouldn't, not now. Had he known? Had he guessed? Was that why he'd never gone all the way?

She was on her own from this moment on.

Walking around the wall of the boating lake, a narrow strip of concrete that separated the enclosed water of the lake from the river estuary, she looked down into the choppy water deciding whether she should throw herself in, but even in the state she was in she realised that it was, at most, 4 feet deep. She wondered for a while, almost academically, how she could make herself drown in 4 feet of water. That would serve them right. They would feel guilty then.

But she didn't only want to make them feel guilty. She wanted not to hurt so much. She would have to go through life without Carl, she loved Carl, she knew he was the only person she could ever love. They had been made for each other, that was what the others said – 'Susannah and Carl', 'Carl and Susannah'. They were so much together. Now what was going to happen? If she were dead he would be free to find someone else, he would be happy in the end. He would always love her, but he would find someone else to marry, never loving that other woman as he did Susannah. She imagined him, in years to come, visiting her grave every Sunday afternoon, laying fresh flowers, never able to forget her.

She knew this mixture of anger and pain was stopping her from thinking straight.

She sat down on the concrete and cried until it hurt and she felt she had cried her heart out.

But there is only so long you can cry and after an hour she began to think properly again.

How had they found out about her and Carl? Who had told them? It had to be Charles and Monika. She had seen them last night.

They were so different – her two brothers. She laughed out loud. Two *brothers*! Charles and Carl, the same name really, it could have been quite funny if it had been happening to anyone else. One she loved and one she hated.

The bottles of wine had been left, opened and almost full, on the sea wall by people who had known no better. She picked them up, held them up to the light, put one to her lips and drank. The tart taste didn't matter, she swigged it down. It made her feel better.

She sat down on the concrete, her legs dangling over the edge, a bottle in each hand, her back to the yachts skimming across the lake in the stiff breeze. She stared across the empty sands at the hills of Wales. They seemed so close.

Looking further and further through the haze to her right, she followed the line of the coast, past the Hilbre islands until she could just see the outline of Sandhey on the headland.

Charles had been all right hadn't he? He'd got out in time. He hadn't gone to live in that stupid house in Dunedin Avenue. He hadn't had to put up with Daddy and Aunty Kathleen playing happy families. He had run away to a lovely large house, far larger than Millcourt, overlooking the sea. He had charmed Uncle Max, he had a wonderful life. How had he managed that?

Anger and fear was giving way to loneliness and jealousy. She took another swig, practically draining the first bottle. She wasn't used to alcohol and it tasted horrid, but it was making her feel better.

She thought about Charles, what hold did he have over the man who owned the place? She knew that older men liked little boys but she didn't think Charles was like that. But he had always been a bit strange since before he had gone away from school, and especially since he had come back. The year he had been away she had been the darling of the nursery. Without Charles around Monika gave all her attention to her.

She had been so stupid not to see it before; Charles was one of those boys who didn't like girls. That's what made it OK for them to live there, they hadn't wanted her because they knew she'd find out and tell.

She took a final swig at the bottle, emptied it and threw it into the lake. Charles had ruined her life. If he hadn't seen her and Carl everything would be OK. They could have been together and it would have been too late to stop them. She'd go to see Charles and ask him what the hell he thought he was doing fucking up her life. If he didn't tell her, she was going to ruin his.

She started on the second bottle, spilling some of the sour red liquid on her blouse.

She was going to go and tell them that if she couldn't live there, with them, she'd tell everyone about Uncle Max and Charles. About Uncle Max and Nanny, Charles and Nanny. Something had to be wrong. All she had to do was tell someone and it'd all be out in the open.

If Charles could live in that lovely house she would as well. She aimed for the house as she walked. Focussing was not easy, the wine was taking its toll. The house couldn't be far, no more than a mile along the beach and across the sand dunes.

She dropped the nearly empty second bottle and set off along the sand.

She was ready for them when she reached the house. She had been going over and over in her mind what she was going to say. About how she knew what she knew, and they weren't going to hide anything from her any more and he was a pervert and if they didn't let her live with them she'd tell everyone. She knew exactly what she was going to say. All the words were there, ready.

But they were out.

The maid who answered the door did not know when Master Charles and the Major would be back. She believed they might have gone to Manchester. Miss could wait in the drawing room, or the garden if she preferred. Would she like some tea? A drink of orange?

The anticlimax of it all was too much for Susannah. They weren't there and all the words she had got in her head had gone. And the world wasn't very straight any more and she wasn't feeling very well. She couldn't wait, possibly for hours.

She turned from the door very deliberately, to avoid falling over, and walked away.

She should have waited, it would only have been a couple of minutes before Max and Charles drove up to the house.

They would have realised why she was so upset and would have looked after her. They would have fed her coffee and listened to her, and allowed her to sober up before sending her home – no harm done.

But she didn't wait.

Instead she decided to walk over to the islands.

Hilbre Island was so beautiful. She had been there many times. She loved sitting out there on the islands looking back at the Wirral, viewed from the middle of the estuary the houses seemed like toys and life didn't seem real.

She had often walked across with the gang, and with Carl. It didn't take long – they normally left from the top end of Marine Lake and walked across to the smallest island in the little group, Little Eye, then across to Little Hilbre, before reaching Hilbre Island proper. They always read the tide tables and set out at the best time of the tide to give them the longest time to laze around on the rocks, listening to their kind of music on the transistor radios that at least one of them would have with them. It usually took about an hour to get there, then they had four hours or more before having to leave to get back before the tide blocked the route back to the mainland. The absolute rule was to leave the island three hours before high tide to make sure they got back in safety.

Those hours on the islands were the times she and Carl had hidden away and she had nearly, so nearly, made him make love to her. He always had an excuse, but she knew he would give in one day. One day they would make love. All the songs said so. He always held out until they had to go back. He must have guessed.

Susannah did not think about the tide. She didn't realise that it was far too late to be setting off across the sands. She couldn't see that the tide had turned; she couldn't see the gullies and channels through which the sea raced, creating a network of impenetrable, fast flowing torrents, invisible until the careless walker was practically on top of them.

These channels were ever changing in depth and breadth, filled by the incoming tide, they trapped the unwary – just as they had trapped Henry three months earlier.

144

This Sunday afternoon she just wanted to get to the sanctuary of the island. She would feel detached from all these people and all this pain if she could only get over there.

The sands stretched out dry and bright in the sun in front of her as she set off.

She had been walking for several minutes when she came to a channel, a steep dip in the sand perhaps as deep as she was tall. She was startled to see brown water frothing and surging up river, fast flowing towards her left. Some part of her realised the tide was a lot higher than was safe. Had she not been running away from Carl, from her father, from home, from disappointment, from fear and loneliness, had she not drunk the best part of two bottles of wine, she would have been thinking more clearly and would have turned back. She was normally a sensible girl who knew the tide was treacherous.

But she was running away and she wasn't thinking straight, and she was more than a little drunk.

She looked across the water and the sands towards Hilbre, the island seemed enticingly close, so she stepped back a few paces to take a running jump over the channel. She cleared it easily, not really stumbling as she landed on the ridges of sand. But she increased her pace.

In a couple of minutes she came across another ditch, this time the water was deeper and running from her left to her right – such was the intricacy and unpredictability of this network of channels. Again she took some steps back to take a running jump and she just got across – the sand she landed on crumbling under her feet and slipping downwards into the surging brown water.

She stopped to catch her breath.

She was beginning to think that she should feel scared.

The island seemed so close, but it was not close enough. There would be other channels – wider and wider until she would eventually reach one she couldn't jump over. Could she swim across them? She knew she would soon meet one that would stop her, but she couldn't go back – the waters she had already crossed were going to be raging torrents by now.

She looked around her to see if there was anyone else out on the sands. She saw no one.

"Shit."

She stood where she was.

There was no point in going forward or back.

How long would it be, she thought with detachment, before the sands beneath her feet would grow sticky and suck her down, how long before the water spilled out of the channels and spread out

145

around her, rising up her legs, her body, as she was held, unable to move, by the sticky, saturated sands.

How long before she would drown.

She looked down the coast to the outline of the Marine Lake and thought of how she had imagined drowning, just a couple of hours before, in such a detached way.

She was now going to know what it felt like.

She had nowhere to go. She could do nothing but wait. She wished she had that bottle still. The warmth of the wine had been comforting, it would be comforting now.

She wondered why she felt no panic. She didn't want to scream for help. It wouldn't do any good. No one would hear her.

She knew she was going to die and she wanted to see the beauty of what she was leaving behind. She watched the birds wheeling in the air currents above her.

She waited. The water was only just covering her knees, but it was rising fast. She wiggled her feet, freed them from the sucking sand, but what good did it do her?

The water was past her waist, she was almost floating now, drifting to left and right, her feet still on the sand.

But now the water was nearly at her neck, she lost contact with the sand and was drifting gently, up and down, gently rising and falling with the swell, the torrents of the channels had merged and now become just sea, the surface deceptively quiet and still.

She was a good swimmer, but she was too far from the island or the mainland, and no match for the currents.

She waited, hypnotised by the rising and falling of the water.

It was very beautiful really. The sky was so blue, with small clouds, white clouds. So beautiful, the white clouds against the blue sky. Birds' heads and wings against the white clouds against the blue sky, free, flying, free of the water.

So beautiful. So gentle – rocking backwards and forwards and backwards and forwards watching the birds against the white clouds against the blue sky.

So this was what it was like, dying, saying goodbye to the world. Was this what it had been like for Henry. Poor Henry, he hadn't been that bad really, had he known Carl wasn't his son? Carl....

Oh Carl.....

"Hold on girl. Just hold on a few moments more. I'm nearly with you. Just hold on a little longer. Don't go under now you stupid bint. Look at me! Here! Who's Carl? I'll be with you in a minute. I'll get you home to Carl. Hold on. Don't go under. I'm nearly there."

Joe kept shouting, saying anything, trying to keep her concentrating on him and the boat, which he was painstakingly manoeuvring against the tide, trying to get close enough to her to drag her out of the water. If she lost sight of him she would go under and he wasn't going to dive in after her.

He was very happy to try to save her from the safety of his boat, but he wasn't going into the water. Like many fishermen he couldn't swim. He worked on the principle that if he could it would only prolong the agony of drowning, if he couldn't keep afloat death would be shorter and less painful. It was always very unlikely that being able to swim would save him in the waters he would be in. He'd either be far too far from land or caught up in unforgiving currents such as this girl was now.

Pity, but there it was, there was only so far he was prepared to go to rescue this girl stupid enough to get caught in the tide.

He reached out for her, risked everything by trying to get his hands under her arms to drag her into the skiff. It was really only big enough for one person but he didn't have much choice.

She heard words but had no understanding of what was being said. She felt his arms, she yelped as he pinched the skin under her armpits, dragging her up the side of the boat, she felt the pain in her chest as he finally pulled her over the edge into the safety of the boat. Then she wasn't sure whether the pain in her chest was more or less than the pain on her face as she felt the flat of his hand against her cheek.

Slowly she realised that someone was shouting at her. Slapping her. She put up her arms to stop him, with her eyes tight shut against the stinging of the salt she flailed her arms like windmill sails in the air, practically knocking the man over the side. He managed to stop her hitting out at him by grabbing her wrists. "No you don't! You'll have us both in the water and then we'll both be drowned."

It took a while, the two of them precariously balanced in the tiny dinghy, the man with one large hand gripping her two wrists together, protecting himself, whilst trying to control the small boat in the current with one oar in his other hand.

Eventually she quietened down and stopped being a danger to them both.

Although her eyes were still screwed quite shut her mind was beginning to recover from the place of safety it had retreated to when she knew she was about to die.

In her mind's eye she still saw the sky, the birds, the island – so near yet so far, the mainland. She felt the acceptance of death, she had not been fighting it.

She knew she would have to open her eyes soon, and when she opened them she would be reborn.

She would have a very different life. She would have to forget Carl, or if not forget him make a life without him. She would have to be with someone, anyone, else.

She said some years later that, as she sat in the dinghy with her eyes tight shut against the stinging salt, she made a decision. She had accepted she was going to die that afternoon so she would accept whatever life was to throw at her afterwards in the same manner. She would be resigned and fatalistic. She would not fight life just as she hadn't fought death. She would start again.

Somewhat melodramatic perhaps but she was her mother's daughter.

When she opened her eyes she saw a man's back.

The shirt was dirty, the hair was long and blond, the shoulders were strong, the arms with shirtsleeves rolled untidily up to the elbows, were taut against straining muscles.

She saw that she was strongly and competently being rowed back to shore.

It didn't take long.

The man ran the dinghy up onto the slipway and turned for the first time, so that she saw his face. It was not good looking like Carl's, but it was pleasant enough. The nose was too large, the nostrils very wide and rather dirty, but the blue eyes seemed considerate, part hidden with long curling eyelashes. Not the same blue as Carl – not the deep almost violet colour she loved – more pale almost grey.

She must stop thinking of Carl. He was history now.

When he spoke she noticed his teeth, how dirty and yellow they were. Almost like an old man's. Though they were even enough.

"That was a bit too close for comfort."

"I suppose I should thank you...?"

"Joe. My name is Joe. You are...?"

"Susannah" Only Carl had ever called her Susie. She would never be Susie again.

"Hello Susannah. Welcome back. I take it you didn't mean to get caught out there."

"Of course not. I just forgot the time and the tide. I do. Thank you I mean."

"Are you OK now? Can I take you somewhere – you have had quite a bit of a shock."

"It's OK, I've got.... friends.... here."

They had come ashore at the Sandhey slipway and the house that she had left barely half an hour before was very close.

Joe rang the bell and it was Max who answered, he weighed up the situation in a glance – the drenched girl, the unkempt boy, both dripping wet.

"Come on in. Both of you. You must both dry out. It's not so warm now and you'll catch your death. Come in, you must get out of those wet clothes, bathe, warm up. I'll get Monika she will take charge."

Monika came running down the stairs holding out her arms to Susannah. "My little girl. What has happened to you?"

Charles, following, thought he knew.

Susannah was taken by Monika to a spare room and put into a bath. "Like old times my dear little girl. Let me look after you. You have had a shock. Get warm and clean and come down to tell us what has happened. Charles will let your family know you are safe."

"Don't call anyone. Please. I need to explain. Just don't call them. Please." There was no trace of the wine, no hint of the belligerent drunkenness she had felt when she had approached the house a little while before.

Charles took Joe up to his room.

"Have a bath, warm up, you are drenched. Use the dressing gown on the door, I'll get your clothes washed and dried. You know, we can't thank you enough. That was obviously a close run thing. We've just got in and I was going to do a bit of bird-watching" he gesticulated towards the binoculars on the window seat "and saw the girl getting further and further from safety. I'd pretty much written her off as drowned. I had no idea it was Susannah, she's my sister, you know. I should have known it was her."

He was shocked at thinking that he had nearly watched her die. His shock made him keep talking.

Joe didn't seem to take much notice of Charles. He was looking around the room trying not to be overwhelmed. He looked at the large bed, the dressing table and the silver hair brushes carefully laid out, his bare feet registered the thickness of the carpets, he stared through the open door to the bathroom and the size of the bath with the hot and cold taps, and he looked at the space that this boy had for his room. This man had his own bathroom. He had more space in his bedroom and bathroom than was in the entire Parry household and there were nine of them. Even though he was nearly 25 years old he had never had a bath in anything other than a tub by the range in the kitchen with people going in and out as he washed.

The Parrys lived in the one remaining end of what had been a terrace of houses. The rest of the houses had fallen apart, damaged by stray bombs in the war and finished off by the elements. He lived with his seven brothers and sisters, and his mother – his father long gone – in less space than this man had for his bedroom.

All eight worked, one way or another, either at the shipyard in Birkenhead or in the local shops and pubs whilst fishing or working the market gardens in the summer. They cycled or walked to work each day, each week they brought back their wage packets for their mum and each week she gave them a little back for their own use.

Jimmy, Joe's eldest brother, owned a boat. He kept this boat immaculate and went fishing night after night. It was the skiff from this boat that Joe had 'borrowed' without his brother's knowledge, to go for a small trip of his own – to get away from the crowds in the house – and it was on that trip that he had spotted Susannah.

He had watched her as she realised she had no escape and had waited, as he knew he must, until the water was deep enough to reduce the impact of the separate channels, then he had rowed as hard as he could to get to her in time. He and his brothers had picked up bodies from the sea most years, from their fishing boat or from the lifeboat – death and drowning did not frighten him – but he hadn't wanted to do that unless he had really had to.

He lay in the bath and scrubbed at the ingrained dirt on his arms and legs. He did the best with his face and hands but he could not remove in one scrub the grime of a hard life. His hair, treated to the luxury of soap and hot water, was almost white in its blondness.

After as long as seemed reasonable he stepped out of the bath, put on the dressing gown and felt the soft towelling dry him far more efficiently than any of the towels he normally used. He walked out into the bedroom and saw Charles sitting at a desk in the bow window looking through binoculars over the estuary. Charles only noticed him when he sat down on the window seat in front of him.

"It doesn't look so lethal from here does it?" Charles said without taking the glasses from his eyes. He was not sure he liked the way this stranger had been eating in every detail of his room.

"It is always beautiful and always dangerous."

"What did you say your name was?"

"Joe, Joe Parry"

"Well Joe Parry. I must thank you for saving my sister's life. I am sure she will herself when we get downstairs."

"She was lucky I was there, I couldn't really leave her could I?"

"Come on. You'd better get dressed. I don't think my clothes will fit you, but you're welcome to try."

The trousers fitted. Joe felt odd, he had never worn anything but jeans since he had first been allowed out of the grey shorts that had been his uniform for the first ten years of his life. These were green cord trousers. He liked the feel of them. But he was too broad and muscular in the chest for any of Charles' shirts. "Here, try this." Charles threw him a cricket sweater, very loose, with the large V at the front exposing most of Joe's chest, tanned even though the summer had hardly started.

Had Charles thought about it he might have wondered what effect Joe's appearance would have on his sister.

He had realised when he had phoned Ted that morning that he was changing his sister's life. He knew she would be very unhappy, and probably that unhappiness would be targeted as anger at him. He had been worrying about her all through the afternoon as he had sat, unable to concentrate, at the match.

But he hadn't imagined that she would try to kill herself.

When he had been watching the unknown girl walk leaping the first donga he had thought she was foolhardy in the extreme. He had followed her movements and what should have been her last minutes through his powerful binoculars. He had not realised it was Susannah. He should have done, but he had seen so little of her in recent years and she had changed. It was five years since he had seen much of her. She was a woman now, 17. He was ashamed that he hadn't recognised her.

He had watched the small boat coming towards her and had decided there was no need to call the lifeboat – either she would be rescued or the man in the boat would pick up the body.

As he looked out of the window, with Joe was in his bathroom, he had wondered how she was going to cope with losing the one person who had ever been able to bring out the best in her, the one person she had ever listened to, the only person who had ever been able to talk her into acting sensibly.

He suspected she would just head off in the opposite direction. Move on, not look back.

It is what their mother would have done.

As Joe followed Charles down to the kitchen where the others had gathered he realised how out of place he was in this grand house but he was confident that he would not be thrown out, whatever he did. The family were class. Whatever he did or said he reckoned they would be polite, grateful and friendly because he had saved the girl's life.

There was not much conversation in the kitchen, the initial freedom from social constraint in the immediate wake of the rescue had gone. Everyone was more self-conscious.

What did the richest man in the area, who owned and was senior partner of the most successful legal firm in the district say to the youngest son of a family of scroungers, a part time fisherman?

What did the brother say to his sister he hadn't seen for five years who had just nearly died in front of his eyes probably because he had discovered her relationship and knew that that relationship was forbidden?

What could Monika say to the girl she had brought up from a baby but who now blamed her for ruining her life.

They drank their tea and had their own thoughts and made their own plans.

Joe looked at Susannah. He had only to watch her for a minute, and he knew she would be his life line. She was wearing a white towelling robe, like the one he had been wearing in Charles' room but shorter, her legs and feet were bare, her hair was drawn up in a white towelling turban. He looked at her and knew what his reward was going to be.

For her part Susannah judged Joe.

There was such a contrast with Carl. Where Carl was still in many ways only a boy, Joe was definitely a man. It seemed to her now that Carl had been skinny and undeveloped when compared with the muscular, hard working and hard worked body that she could see Joe had.

But more than his physical appearance she saw something else. Carl was open and confident, she had never seen him at a loss for words or in a position where he didn't know what to do – whoever he was with or wherever he was. Joe appeared to be out of his depth. He was embarrassed, self-conscious and tongue-tied. At least that is how she interpreted his silence and his quick glances around the room.

She was too genuine a person, too naïve and with too little experience of people other than her small circle of family and friends to recognise that Joe, who had depended on cleverness of a different sort, who had needed a certain selfish cunning to survive in his family, was sizing up the situation to see what he could get out of it.

Joe was weighing up the fact that the girl he had rescued came from a very well off family, that the girl – and her family – would be very grateful to him. He intended to find out just how grateful.

He had a feeling they would be very grateful indeed.

There seemed to be a collective relaxation of tension when the phone rang and Max left the room to answer it, as if he were expecting a call. He returned after only a few moments.

"That was your father, Susannah. He is concerned about you. He says you ran out of the house without saying where you were going."

She didn't reply.

"He wanted to know if we had seen you or Carl."

"What did you say?"

"I told him you were here and he should not worry. I told him you would stay here for a while and we would talk about it when everyone has calmed down. You'll stay here, at least until after Charles' birthday."

"What about Carl?"

"I told him we hadn't seen him."

Joe listened to the undercurrents of family conflict, aware that he did not know the details but equally aware that they gave him an advantage when working on Susannah. He was picking up clues. He knew from experience and not because anyone had taught him, that knowledge was power and the best sort of knowledge was that which people didn't know they were giving you. The more he knew about this family the more he could get from them, but he didn't want to appear too anxious.

"I'll be off. I'll come back with the clothes tomorrow."

"I'll see you out. You'll be wanting to get home." Charles had seen something in Joe's eyes that he didn't like, an ambition, a cunning, a calculating view, a plot being hatched. He wanted him out of the house.

Joe saw himself dismissed but was quite happy to leave things as they were for a day or so. There would be plenty of time. They wouldn't forget what he had done.

He wouldn't let them.

"Can I leave my boat here. I don't want to mess up your nice clothes. Can I come back for it in the morning?" Time now to be deferential, accepting his place. Time enough later to rub their noses in it.

"Of course." Charles was not totally convinced that would be a good idea but what else could he do? "Can I drive you back?" "No, thanks, I'll walk."

As she tried to sleep that night, Susannah found herself engulfed in misery. She missed Carl so much and – how long was it since she had seen him? – five hours?

She lay in bed that night staring out of the window at the moon reflecting on the sea. When would she see Carl again? Where was he? Could he see the moon? Was he looking at the moon now thinking of her? He must know where she had gone. He would call her. They would be together tomorrow.

She spent the next day staring out of the window. How could she fill the time, make the time pass more quickly, until she would see him again? She knew she shouldn't have run away, but how could she have stayed? What will Carl do? Where will he go? How can she find him? She loved him. He loved her. They had to be together. She tried to switch off everything she felt for him but she couldn't.

It was half term so she didn't even have school to keep her mind occupied. Where was Carl? Why didn't he call her? Who was he with? It was hours before there would be anything on the television which would make the time go more quickly. What could she do? She sat, waiting for the phone to ring until Monika, determined to get Susannah out of her mood, tried to give her something to do.

"You can help me clean the house, spring cleaning. That will clear your head, you can't be moping around if you're cleaning."

So Susannah was set to clean the stair carpet. It didn't help as everything she did revolved around Carl. She started at the top, brushing the fluff off the carpet with her fingers, pressing harder and harder until the tips of her fingers seemed singed and her fingerprints were worn flat. 'If I fill my hand with fluff from this step he'll call'. She brushed the beige pile of the carpet to the left and to the right, trying to concentrate on the different colours, one dark, one light. She played noughts and crosses on one step. 'If X wins this one he will call.' 'He will call before I've got to the bottom step.' 'He'll call if I hold my breath while I brush this step.' She managed to make cleaning the thirty steps last all afternoon.

But he still hadn't called.

Monika sat her down at the kitchen table for tea. She had to talk to Susannah, she had been watching her through the afternoon and she knew she had to help her. She knew that Susannah blamed her and Charles for all her problems but she was the only one who could talk to her. So she began by telling Susannah of the times in her life when she had felt alone and that life had seemed too difficult to live. Susannah had listened, perhaps aware for the first time that her problems weren't as enormous as some people's. But she still felt so much pain. She said that the easy way was to let life do to her what it would, and she shouldn't fight it. Monika said that that was what she had done.

There had been a time, at the end of the war, when Monika had decided that the old Monika was dead and that the new Monika was born. She had become a different person, separated from the person she had been. Only then could she look forward. In that conversation Monika told Susannah things about herself she had only ever told Charles before, to try to get Susannah's trust.

She told her how she had ended the war a refugee, she hadn't been able to speak English, she had only one friend in the world, she had spent five years being a piece of driftwood afloat in a troubled sea. But then, through circumstances beyond her control her life had changed, the day before she had one life – the day after a completely different one.

"Now you are feeling alone and adrift. You must make a new life. Now. You mustn't wait until the old life has made you bitter. You must become a new person now. You must learn to depend on yourself. You will never forget Carl but you must learn not to live only for time spent with him, or any other person. Learn to live for yourself, be independent, you must live your own life."

"Like my mother did? As soon as things got difficult she ran off. She probably 'became another person' as soon as she'd walked out on us. Well I can't do that. I love Carl, I want to be with Carl, he wants to be with me."

But as she spoke the words she realised that if he really *did* want to be with her where was he now?

The days seemed very long, spent listening for the telephone every minute of the day, saying 'if I walk from here to there in an even number of steps he will call today' or 'if the third car to come down the road is red Carl will phone today' or 'if the sun stays behind that cloud for ten seconds Carl will call me'. He must know where she was, he would get in touch.

Her 'ifs' became longer term. 'If I get all my A levels it will all end up right in the end.' 'If I'm nice to people and never tell a lie it will work out all right in the end.'

He had to call her.

He had left home, he had been away for five days, and he hadn't been in touch with her once.

She had last seen him on Sunday, by Friday she knew he wouldn't call, yet still she played 'ifs' with the devil.

She was too lonely to enjoy being on her own. She must have someone to spend her time with. She needed a boyfriend, someone whom she could look forward to seeing, who she could see every day, who would be with her whenever she needed him.

By the end of that week she realised that wouldn't be Carl.

Five days can seem like no time at all, they can pass without anything changing, without even being noticed. But those five days were a very long time for Susannah.

They changed her.

By the weekend she had grown up. Yes, she had decided. She would do part of what Monika had said, she wouldn't depend on her family any more. But she knew herself well enough to realise that she wouldn't be able to be alone. She would have to find someone else to depend on.

Ever since she could remember she had concentrated all her

thoughts on Carl, gauged everything she did by what he would think. There would have to be someone else to tell her she was pretty, clever, a good girl, someone else to give her the praise and approval that were essential to her.

It wasn't long before she regretted not having made any attempt to follow Monika's advice.

They hadn't seen Joe when he came back to fetch his boat. By the time the household was up and about on the Monday morning the boat had gone.

He did not return the clothes he had borrowed or pick up his old ones until the following Saturday morning. "Sorry, I've been at work." He explained, he also explained having to take the skiff without seeing them "the tide – I had to get it while the tide was OK and before going on shift."

It all seemed perfectly plausible.

Some time later, when she knew him better, Susannah realised that Joe had been very clever. He had let her recover, not pushed himself forward before she had had a chance to get over whatever it was that had upset her, allow time enough for her to get curious about him.

"We thought you'd forgotten" Susannah had said as he took the tidy pile of clothes from her – his jeans, checked shirt and underpants. Monika darned the pants. She said she had never seen such a holey pair. Have you really got seven brothers and sisters – they were talking about you last night. Does one of your sisters work at the Lighthouse Keeper? My brother Charles, he sometimes goes in there for a drink. He likes it in there."

In her nervousness Susannah kept chatting on, not really about anything and Joe didn't respond. He took the clothes from her and went to walk away.

She could have let him go.

They would have passed each other occasionally in the street, maybe not even acknowledging each other, knowing and caring little about the other. Max would have given the family some money by way of reward, perhaps Joe would have been able to buy his own boat. Susannah's life would have been so different, children would never have been born, the paths of many people's lives would have been altered.

But she didn't let him go.

"Do you fancy me?"

Joe could have ignored this question as coming from an arrogant, spoilt little girl, but she hadn't spoken provocatively, she wasn't flirting with him as the other girls did, she had asked him a direct question.

It even sounded quite innocent.

He had known from when he had been sitting around the kitchen table the previous Sunday that he would get something from the family and he had been more ambitious than getting just a boat. He had been aware then that they wouldn't throw him out because they were beholden to him, but he had quickly decided he was going to be accepted in that family however he behaved. He would get involved with them so closely that they could never throw him out. He wanted to be able to be in that house, in that company, as of right – not because they invited him.

So he played Susannah as he would a troublesome fish and reeled her in gently.

"What do you expect me to say?"

"I just wondered, because you couldn't take your eyes off me in the kitchen last week." She wasn't used to talking to men she didn't know. She had never flirted with anyone. Since she was old enough to go out with boys she had gone out with Carl, he'd been the only boy she was ever interested in. This situation had never arisen before for her.

She had no way of knowing that conversations like this very quickly got out of control.

"What if I do fancy you?"

"We could go for a walk. Talk, get to know each other a little better."

"OK. Let's go."

"Now?"

"Now."

He crammed the carefully ironed bundle of clean clothes into his greasy brown duffle bag and slung it over his shoulder and they walked together down along the coast towards West Kirby.

It was a Saturday morning but the dunes were deserted, it was one of those days when the sea mist hugged the coast. Less than a mile inland it would be sunny and warm – but along the coast it was chilly and misty, not even dog-walking weather. So they had the dunes to themselves.

After walking for a few minutes, not really talking, Joe took her hand and made her stop and sit down, in a small sheltered dip in the sand. He sat down beside her. She thought she knew what was going to happen. She was prepared for him when he turned and kissed her.

She had always enjoyed kissing Carl. He was the only boy who had ever kissed her properly. But this was different. Carl had been gentle and loving. She had never wanted him to stop. She had asked him to go further, but she hadn't known the right words. She had thought it would just happen naturally that one day they would go all the way. But they hadn't.

But with Joe it seemed like she could feel his hunger for her, he was kissing her roughly until she seemed bruised and scraped by the stubble on his chin. When she felt him pushing her down so she was lying on the sand she didn't object and just kissed him back harder. When he pulled up her sweater and t-shirt she felt excited in parts of her that he wasn't even touching. She knew she was getting carried away but she couldn't have stopped him even if she had tried.

And she didn't try.

How different this felt.

With Carl he had always stopped, leaving her feeling lost, bereft, lonely.

Now she knew Joe would go all the way.

She loved the feelings she was having, she never wanted him to stop, it felt so good but far too soon he rolled off her, leaving a trail of sticky moisture on her stomach. He held her wrists down against the ground as her face gradually relaxed and her body lay still.

They lay back in the sand, each thinking their own, very different, thoughts. Joe had made her feel so many things she had never felt before. She knew Carl would have been gentler, less confident and maybe she knew she wouldn't have felt the way she did now. Joe hadn't fumbled as Carl would have done, Joe had known what he was doing and Carl was just as much a virgin as she had been.

She lay back in the sand trying to relax but trying to remember the feeling of that itch she didn't even know she had being scratched, she didn't ever want to lose the memory of that feeling. She hoped she would do this again and again.

"You've done that before."

He laughed "Of course I have. Haven't you?"

"No"

"Shit."

"No don't worry, I'm glad I have now. It's just that I haven't really had the opportunity before."

It hadn't really occurred to him to ask before but he thought he had better now "How old are you?"

"16 How old are you?"

"Well that's all right then" he ignored her question as he kissed her roughly and started working on her again, he wanted it again and so it seems did she.

His immediate needs had been satisfied the first time, so, as he let her do what she wanted, his mind was free. This was the first part of his reward, but the more ambitious plan was working. He was going to marry her, marry all that money, get some of that space and some of those things – a house, a television, a car – that they took for granted, that up to this moment he could only have dreamt of. He had her now, he knew how to get her and to keep her from getting away. But first he had to be nice.

He came again and pushed himself off her, lying next to her in the dunes. "You really have never done that before?"

"Was I alright?" He ignored her rather pathetic question.

"Look, we've been here ages, I'd better get you home."

"Will I see you again?"

"Tomorrow?"

"Tomorrow? Sunday? I don't know we usually.... No. tomorrow. Great."

"When?"

"Oh 7ish"

She had been about to say that the family usually spent Sunday evenings together and she never went out on a Sunday evening, especially with school the next day but that was all in the past now.

"Where?"

"The bandstand."

No one in her group of friends ever went to the bandstand. A group practised there and there was talk of drugs and all sorts. Carl and Susannah, all their friends and anybody respectable had spent their time in the town, at the coffee bar or sometimes even the pub, even though they were too young, but down on the prom? The bandstand? That was an entirely different group of people. That was where people hung out who couldn't afford the coffee, couldn't afford the half pints of shandy and beer. It was risky. It was exciting. It was the new Susannah.

"I'll be there"

"Sure? You know what you are getting yourself into?"

"Sure."

If she couldn't have what she wanted she would explore. She couldn't have Carl, she would have to find someone else. It was fate. She had made a pact with fate as she had been rowed back to shore the week before 'whatever life threw at her' and it appeared 'life' had chosen Joe.

Someone she knew her father would hate.

She got there before he did, and stood feeling very conspicuous, with three or four other girls listening to the band practise. There was a group – a drummer, two guitars and a singer who didn't seem to play anything but just rattled some maracas. They weren't much good but this was the time when groups, even not very good groups, could strike lucky and get a record made. The song she liked most was *Save the Last*

Dance for me. She listened to the words, trying piecing a story together:

You can dance
Every dance with the guy who gives you the eye
Let him hold you tight

That was Joe, dancing with her, holding her close.

You can smile
Every smile for the guy who'd like to treat you right
'neath the pale moonlight

She would spend time with Joe. Joe would treat her right, not leave her wanting more all the time.

But don't forget who's takin' you home
and in whose arms you're gonna be

That will be Carl. Carl will take me home in the end.

Oh, darlin', save the last dance for me

She would be with Carl in the end.

She was only using Joe. She wouldn't, ever, forget Carl.

When Joe turned up that first evening, nearer 7.30 than 7, he said he was sorry to be late and then took her hand and walked away from the others back towards the sand dunes.

This time he had a durex. She had never seen one before and didn't know what to do when he told her to put it on him.

"You won't tell anyone will you?"

"What? Tell them that you and I ...."

"Tell them anything."

"Who would I tell? I don't know any of your friends."

"And I don't know yours."

"And that's the way it should stay."

But, despite that, from then on Susannah met Joe most nights.

She didn't think she liked him very much and they didn't have much in common but she loved the sex. And she knew how much her father would hate him.

She went back to live in Dunedin Avenue at the end of the following week. She could not call it, and said she never thought of it as 'home'. It was so completely different. There was no Carl. The house seemed empty without him.

It had changed in other ways as neither Kathleen nor her father seemed to have any interest in what she did. Kathleen didn't throw her weight about, she didn't tell her off for being late in at night. Her father had never taken much interest in what she was doing but now he took none whatsoever, withdrawing into himself the little time he was in the house. They never asked her what she was doing, where she was going, who she was seeing. Neither Kathleen nor Arnold seemed to have any interest in her or authority over her any more. She lived in their house but she did exactly what she wanted, when she wanted.

Perhaps they knew she wasn't going to tell them anything even if they had asked.

Perhaps they were overwhelmed by their failure which was further emphasised at Charles' 21st birthday dinner. This event had taken place the night before Susannah returned to Dunedin Avenue. The dinner had been awful, no one was comfortable and, although the food and wine were excellent, it is doubtful that anyone enjoyed the evening. Max had told them over coffee that he had made Charles his heir, an announcement that served only to deepen Susannah's resentment against her brother. Charles would have everything and she nothing. It wasn't fair.

Arnold, who had been invited to the evening with Kathleen long before the events of the previous week, could only be made more aware of the differences between their fortunes and those of his elder son now, undoubtedly, a rich man.

Susannah carried on at school – exams were close and she didn't want to fail. She realised, without Carl to look after her, it was more important than ever that she do well and get into university so she could leave home for good. She dropped all her old friends, they only reminded her of Carl and a different life.

So all she did at school was work. She stayed late every day doing her homework in the library so she had no reason to stay in at home.

With no friends and no real family she was as alone as it was possible to be. She heard nothing from Carl or Charles. She was uncontrolled by anyone who might have cared for her.

When she wasn't working she spent her time with Joe, playing on the swings and roundabouts of the kids' playground as the boys played knock-about football on the rec, hanging over the embankment railings watching Joe mess about with his brothers on the boat, hanging around street corners. Then the gang would pair off to go their separate ways and she and Joe would go down to the dunes. Most nights Joe took precautions. He said he didn't want to get her pregnant.

But, of course, that was exactly what he *did* want.

And it took rather longer than he had hoped.

It hadn't been too much of a trial through the summer and autumn after they got together. Things were a little more difficult once winter came, it was a cold winter and they couldn't do it out of doors but there were empty cottages that were easy to break into and he always managed to find somewhere.

And he persevered.

161

He wasn't going to get this far, put up with all the taunts of his mates who couldn't understand what he saw in the stuck up girl they called Sue, just to give up.

Charles should, perhaps, have taken more care about his sister. He should have made the effort to see how she was getting on. But he didn't. She was living with Kathleen and Arnold, surely they would make sure she was OK. She wasn't his responsibility. Nor could he blame himself for the results of their neglect.

Chapter Twenty-Three

The wedding was a small one. Arnold had no money but would have found some had circumstances been different. It was left to Max and Charles who, with Monika, did what they could to make the occasion as enjoyable as possible.

No one was particularly pleased that Susannah and Joe were getting married. So it was just Arnold and Kathleen, Max, Monika and Charles, Alicia and myself who gathered at Sandhey with most members of the Parry family at the end of April 1964.

I had been invited to the reception, despite Arnold's objections, as I was escorting Alicia, who had unexpectedly accepted her invitation. "Curiosity, Ted," she said years later "that's the only reason I went."

I had been happy to accept her invitation as it gave me an opportunity to make my mind up about Joe. Max has asked me to find him a position at Roberts and Jones.

I found myself next to Kathleen who had obviously drunk too much of the champagne. "Of course this is what he has been aiming at since last summer. Nothing but an oversexed gold-digger." She said rather too loudly, ignoring the fact that several of his family were within earshot. "Nice work if you can get it."

Charles joined us, ever the host ensuring a 'situation' didn't arise, and tried to be positive. "Good looking chap though."

"He's so much older." I commented

"Maybe she found someone she could rely on." Charles apparently couldn't resist the pointed remark.

"You're joking – rely on?" Kathleen was uncompromising in her contempt. "What's he going to do for a living? He can't do whatever it is he has been doing, was it fishing or gardening, can he? Not with a wife and child to look after?"

"Kathleen, shut up, Pots and Kettles." Charles had no need to be polite to his step-mother. "Anyway he's probably going to work for Ted."

Kathleen raised her eyebrows in sarcastic surprise as I answered her unvoiced question. "He seems, believe it or not, to be very bright. He's just never had the same chances as you or me. Max would like me to give

Joe a chance – if only for Susannah's sake." and left them to it.

I had liked Kathleen once, she had been an intelligent, gentle and friendly person until she had married Arnold and now she just seemed bitter. I walked back towards Alicia, bottle in hand.

How she had changed since the previous summer.

She put a brave face on it but she looked dreadful. I knew she had not been well, and I knew that she had been in hospital a lot of the previous winter, but until I had met her at the station I had had no idea she was so fragile.

"Drink?"

She put her hand, the lines of bone and sinew clearly visible, across her glass in reply "Isn't it odd how often we end up meeting at definitive moments in the life of the Donaldsons." She was half smiling as she spoke.

"Strange event this isn't it?"

"They seem happy."

I wondered at how many weddings that truism had been spoken when the exact opposite was more likely to be the case, and how frequently those happy weddings ended up on the rocks.

"You never cared for her, did you?" I wasn't sure whether it was a question I should ask.

"No. Not really. I never wanted her. I didn't look after her and I left Arnold when she was still a baby really. She was Nanny's child more than mine. I wouldn't be surprised if she hadn't wanted to get pregnant deliberately so she could have a family that was truly hers."

I think, in that, she was probably right.

"It'll ruin her university career, still we'll help him have a good future. He will do well if he puts his mind to it and is given a chance."

"How are they going to manage?"

"Funnily enough, they are going to live at Sandhey for a time until they find somewhere suitable, then Monika will look after the baby and Susannah will go to University. Strange that isn't it. Max with both your children under his wing."

"Not so strange Ted. He is a very nice man."

"We all thought he would remarry, you know, after Elizabeth died, but he didn't. He came back and took up the reins exactly as before."

"Not quite exactly Ted."

She didn't elaborate.

"Anyway, it looks like it will all work out quite well, considering."

"Yes. Considering."

164

I topped her glass up though it didn't really need it, she had hardly drunk a drop.

She was looking into her glass as if the answers to all problems were there in the bubbles and she didn't want to drink them because then the answers wouldn't be there any more.

We stood together on the veranda, looking back at the small gathering. Susannah was talking to her new mother-in-law, Marina Parry, who was trying very hard not to appear uncomfortable. The brothers and sisters were standing in a group together, not mixing at all. Well I hardly expected them to.

"Have you spoken to Carl?" I had to ask.

She seemed surprised "No. Why would I?"

"Apparently he's got the idea that Arnold might not be Susannah's father."

She looked uncomfortable and tried to avoid an answer.

"I don't see anyone, I've been in hospital, it's been a difficult year."

"He's accepted that Arnold is his father so he hangs onto the idea that he might not be her's."

She didn't ask where he got the idea or dismiss the idea as laughable as I had thought she would. I persevered.

"You have to let him know there's no doubt about Susannah being his sister, then he can get on with his life."

"I can't tell him that, Ted."

"Why not?"

"I can't lie to him again."

I thought I had misunderstood. "What do you mean?"

"I lied"

"What do you mean 'I lied'?"

"Arnold isn't Susannah's father. I lied. When Arnold called me that Sunday I wasn't well, I was upset. I couldn't give him what he wanted. He wanted everything to be all right. Why should it? Why should I let them all off the hook. Of course Arnold isn't Susannah's father, Henry is – was. Of course it was Henry. I suppose you would call it rape – what Henry did that night. It was only a few seconds. Not enough to start a life. But it did. No one wanted her. I didn't. Arnold didn't. Henry never knew. Arnold didn't know. Of course they aren't brother and sister."

I was silenced. So many thoughts, an unwelcome dislike for this woman I had loved for so long. In all the years I had known her this was the first time I couldn't like her. I couldn't believe what she had done and I could see no good reason for her vindictiveness.

Did she know how much pain that lie had cost?

"How could you? How could you lie when you knew how they felt?"

"It wasn't going to be, Ted. It just wasn't going to be. I will not have my daughter, even one I wish wasn't a daughter of mine, married to that man's son. It's very simple. I will not have it. I do not regret the lie – I will never regret the lie. I hesitate to say 'over my dead body' as that is likely to happen sooner rather than later, Ted – you know that – but I *will not* have it. My daughter is never going to marry his son. It was just not going to happen, and now it can't."

Her deception had been deliberate. She was vindictive and that was all that mattered to her – her control over the children and their future. It mattered nothing to her that the children were making such messes of their lives – that things could have been so simple, that two young people could have been so happy. None of that mattered. She had to have her way.

Perhaps she realised my feelings. She looked into the bubbles again. "Oh Ted, what webs we weave."

"I can't believe you would lie about something around which your daughter's happiness revolved so deeply. Why couldn't you have told them the truth? They could have been together after all."

I was so disappointed in her, and in the unfairness of life.

Joe had walked across the patio behind us and stood next to me. Neither Alicia nor I had known he was there.

He was a very different young man from the first time he had been at this house. He was far more confident, his hair was clean and cut neatly, his skin clean though still browner than normal for the time of year, his teeth perfect, the bespoke suit not entirely hiding the strength in his arms. He would do well with the female clients. He did have something about him.

But I could not like him.

"I did wonder."

He was perfectly polite as he spoke. "Sue has told me all about her and Carl, and all about your very odd families. Please don't look down on my family, Alicia, at least we know who our parents are. She still thinks she loves him, she'd leave me if she knew the truth. But even if she ever finds out, and I'm not going to tell her – yet – she will stay with me. Believe me, she will stay with me."

"Of course she will." Perhaps it was Alicia and I that needed reassurance. It wasn't insecurity in his voice, it was an almost threatening determination not to lose what he had achieved.

He was a clever young man and now he knew more than he should. I had to believe that he wouldn't misuse that knowledge but I didn't have much confidence.

He hadn't said a word about making his wife and the child happy.

The marriage lasted longer than many and certainly longer than those who knew Susannah and Joe had thought it would. The child, a girl they named Josie, was born on October 31st. Susannah had been able to put off starting at University until after the birth and had opted for Liverpool, to be close. She had given up any idea of Oxbridge and an academic career but she insisted on trying for a degree, not giving up all ambition and becoming the housewife Joe had wanted.

Susannah had Monika to help most days, even though they had moved out of Sandhey to their own place, a detached house in one of the better roads of the district, heavily subsidised by loans from Charles and a mortgage arranged by the company.

Joe was doing well. His days as a fisherman and wheeler-dealer were long gone. He took to working in an office, wearing suits, commuting by train as if he had not spent the first years of his life crammed with so many others into the ruin of a terraced house built on sand dunes, spending his time fishing and indulging in petty crime. He was rarely home during the week, and at the weekends he was playing golf in the winter or cricket in the summer, developing his contacts, establishing himself as the professional man. He was doing well in the business. Without any prompting he studied at nights for exams he had never had the chance to take before he had had to leave school. He had a good manner with clients, just enough of the 'wide-boy' to tease them – just enough of the servant to flatter them. He acted as a sort of investigator much of the time, checking out the veracity of what people said – he was very good at it.

He was good, too, with his colleagues, having a drink in the pub after work he fitted in with the young men who had always known they would work in an office, have a house and family and do well. Some of them knew his background, but such was his skill and charm with people, that not one, as far as I know, ever threw it in his face.

A son, Jack, was born just after Susannah graduated, 2 days before her 21st birthday, then, since another son, Al, followed under a year later, and since a third, Billy, followed the year after that it had to be assumed that they were happy together.

After she graduated Susannah spent the time keeping house,

shopping, looking after the children and supporting her ambitious husband. We all knew she could have been so much more, but she seemed to be content. The children were growing up secure and well behaved. They were a proper family – to all appearances the close family that Susannah had never had when she was growing up.

I was a frequent visitor to the house and, as well as Sunday lunches with Charles, Monika and Max, I was always invited to birthdays and Christmases. I thought it was only because they felt sorry for me or to make up the numbers and in order for some continuity but it did, of course, help Joe's career to appear to be close to his boss. I later found out it was Charles who always made sure I was invited because he had considered me to be his friend for years – since the days I had driven him to and from his boarding school. I believe he thought me some kind of independent negotiator in the ongoing battle that was his family. I didn't mind, I had no family of my own and, since my mother's death, had lived alone with no idea that it would ever be anything otherwise.

I thought I knew the family rather better than they did themselves.

On these Sunday lunches we would arrive for one o'clock and Joe would give us a drink, opening a bottle of wine well before it was fashionable to do so, while Susannah gave the finishing touches to the roast. There were times when we overheard things that perhaps we shouldn't have done – Joe saying he wouldn't have used that roasting dish – he preferred the glass one, she should have chopped the vegetables more finely, cooked them a little longer; she should have sharpened the knife a little better, strained rather more fat from the gravy; she should have given a smaller – or larger – helping, have crisped the potatoes rather more. They were all silly criticisms, but criticisms all the same. Susannah never seemed to respond though the endless negative comments must have rankled.

Should we, who cared for Susannah, have spotted that things were not as they appeared to be?

I was sure at the time that Joe and Susannah must have had their arguments – as must every married couple. I can see that it cannot have been easy all the time. But it did seem that, despite all the factors against it, it was a marriage that was working. In all the conversations we had over those years, I cannot recall anything that hinted that she wasn't the devoted wife and mother she appeared to be. Always tired, and a little lonely perhaps, always striving for approval and to be considered perfect, but not unhappy.

But what do we know who only see a relationship from the outside and I eventually discovered some of the realities behind the façade.

Susannah later told me that she believed that Joe had deliberately kept her pregnant, year after year, to break down her spirit, to keep her tied to him and to ensure Charles and Max's continued generosity.

I had taken over Max's trips to the London office when he retired in 1966 and so spent two or three days a week in the south. I had been in contact with Alicia and knew how very ill she was. She had talked about Charles, asking whether he was happy, what was his real relationship with Monika? She even hinted that perhaps his relationship with Max was not what it might seem. She never asked about Susannah for reasons I thought I understood.

In December 1967 I went to Sandhey on some flimsy work pretext to talk to Max but what I really wanted to do was get answers to some of Alicia's questions.

"How long can this arrangement continue Max?" I eventually asked as we sat on either side of the fire in his study. He had been reading me an extract from Charles' latest pamphlet, of which he was extremely proud. "Charles isn't a young man anymore, you don't need to protect him. Perhaps he wants a home, a family of his own."

"He has a home, here. This will always be his home."

"But what of marriage?"

"He is not the marrying kind, Ted. He has talked to me you know, about these things and he has told me more than once that he would never marry or have children. He says the institution causes too much pain – a feeling you can understand in his circumstances."

"How long ago did you talk? Could he have changed his mind?"

"Admittedly they were some time ago so, yes, he could have changed his mind, but I very much doubt it. He is not the sort of man who changes."

"But don't you think we should get our information a little more up-to-date?" I knew I was over-stepping the mark, but it was something Alicia had asked me to investigate so I had to persevere.

"Perhaps you're right." So, very reluctantly, he called Charles into his study.

Charles was horrified at the conversation.

"I will not marry. I will not have children. I will look after you and Monika for as long as you need me." A thought seemed to occur to him "Do you want me to leave?"

"Absolutely not, dear boy. Absolutely not. Ted, and I, felt we should

– what was that phrase – 'get our information a little more up-to-date'."

"It sounds like something's happened to change things."

"What I have to have clear in my mind," I tried to explain "is that you are not being held back from having your own home and family."

"Well I'm not. You should know us all better than to even ask that. I will never marry. Why would I want to? No, I'm not queer though I know there are people around who say I am. I am just not interested. I don't mean to be rude but it makes me so angry – I'm surprised you should even think it. Is that all?"

So that was that. Charles had left the room before I had a chance to apologise and I got a lecture from Max, not for the first time with regard to this family, about minding my own business.

Chapter Twenty-Four

It was at Billy's first birthday party, 4th July 1970, that Susannah told me she was pregnant again. By this time she had four young children all under the age of seven and she was still only 23 years old. I could not believe that this was what she wanted to do with her life. She was worth far more than this.

I had been invited, as I always was, but this year I had really not meant to go.

Monika was looking after the children and they were all watching Charles pretending to be a clown. Max had produced presents for all the children so none would feel left out just because it was Billy's birthday – and he was far too young to understand what was going on.

My mind was elsewhere. I had so much to think about that I didn't enjoy watching the children as I usually did so I shepherded Susannah into the kitchen on the pretext of helping her do some clearing up "Have you heard from your mother?" I asked her with some trepidation. "Oh Yes, she sent the usual cheque. I'm not sure how far she thinks £5 is going to go these days – still – if it makes her happy. Funny, it was posted in Liverpool. Have you seen her?"

I ignored the question – now was not the time to get into involved explanations so I simply answered that I was sure she meant well.

Although she said "I'm sure she did." I do not think the words would have convinced anyone.

"She never wanted me did she?" I couldn't see her face. She had her back to me, her hands in the washing up bowl. She stopped urgently trying to clean something and seemed to stare down into the soapy water.

I was a bit surprised at the question. It did not seem to be the right time to discuss matters such as this. "Why do you ask?"

"Because it's becoming more and more important to me. I've got four children of my own now. I wish I could say I loved them all to distraction, but I'm not sure I do – and I just keep thinking of what my life would have been like without them. I keep thinking what I could be doing if they hadn't come along.... if they weren't here. Josie wasn't a mistake. I suppose I needed something that was mine after..." she

171

hesitated, pulled herself up as if to give herself courage to name him, and continued "after Carl. It wasn't so much 'lust' as 'need'. I have tried so often to work out why I got involved with Joe. I suppose it was because he wanted me, he seemed to need me, and that was nice. No one in the family seemed to – apart from Carl." His name came easier this time. "Carl was the only one who seemed to like me. I never knew Mother – those hopeless holidays were a complete waste of time, Dad was always somewhere else, Joe seemed to like me as well as want me and, that seems to have been the reason. I never loved him, Joe I mean. And I'm not sure I ever loved Josie or the boys. It's not loving them as I know I should that makes me think about Mother."

It had all come out in a rush. There was so much bottled up inside.

"I've always been manipulated by Joe. I'm not the liberated woman in control of my life that I've imagined I am, everything I do is dictated by Joe. It has been since the moment he pulled me out from the water. I wish he'd bloody well let me drown!"

What could I say? I really wasn't the person she should be unburdening herself to. She needed a woman, her mother, not an old stick like me, but maybe that was how desperate she was, that she felt she had to unburden herself to me. Maybe I was all she had.

All I could say was "Well. That's a lot to think about."

"The boys, well I just think they came along because he wanted a dynasty. I did everything I could to stop them coming one after the other. It's as though I didn't really have a say in it. I don't even like them very much. I'm just trapped with them, feeding them, cleaning up after them. God knows what I'd do without Monika. He gets out every day, he's not often home in the evenings – he gets back late, usually after having spent a few hours in the pub – I don't know why he comes back sometimes. Sometimes he doesn't – Oh I don't know Uncle Ted. I don't want them. I wish they had never been born. Oh shit! How did I get into this mess?"

She was working herself up into a state.

I sat her down at the kitchen table and got her a glass of wine. I had to let her calm down for a few moments.

"I won't say that you don't mean all those things. I'm sure you do. You're so like your mother sometimes, you've got so much I common with her."

"You mean she resented me? She didn't want me? I was a complete mistake, a disaster and her life would have been so much better if she had never had me?"

"I'm saying that you wouldn't be the intelligent 23 year old young lady you are if you didn't, at times, resent the fact that you have a husband and four children to look after. I'm saying that you wouldn't be normal if you didn't sometimes think 'what might have been'. It's just that both you and your mother both ask what 'might have been' if you hadn't married the man you did and had the children you've had. That's what you have in common. You both keep thinking that 'what might have been' would have been infinitely better."

"You seem to know a lot about my mother."

"I've known her a long time." was all I could say. She didn't need to know any more today.

"She only had the two of you. You've got four, four children are a lot to deal with."

She drank her wine, staring into the glass. "Five"

"Oh no!" The words were spoken before I could stop them. "I mean..."

"Yes another!" she smiled ruefully at my confusion.

"Why Susannah? I'm sure there're ways and means these days. It's easier...."

"You mean the pill? He won't let me. You mean it's easier to get rid of them now? He wouldn't hear of it. It's no easier for me to get rid of this..." she hit her stomach hard with a fist "...than it would have been for mother to get rid of me!"

To that there was no answer.

She looked at me as she had done when she was a small girl. Before she had had Carl's friendship and love, when she had been alone.

"Don't you have anyone who can help you? Anyone you can turn to?"

She and Charles had never been close and although she depended on Monika, she knew she could not help her with this sort of thing. She looked so young as she shook her head.

"Is there anything I can do, Susannah? I know I'm probably not the best person but I'll do anything to help. If I can." I finished lamely.

"Would you? He doesn't know I'm .... you know .... 'up the spout' again. If you could let me have some money – anything, help me find a clinic or whatever, help me sort it out – before he knows – would you? Could you?" She was beginning to cry now .... so, of course, I went to put my arm around her to comfort her.

I was thinking how I could ask my secretary to help – what would she think, would she know what to do? How was I going to sort out this mess? Susannah was sobbing more and more deeply on my shoulder when Joe came into the kitchen.

"I think she is tired Joe, I think she needs a rest."

"No she's just being feeble as usual. Sue, the children are asking for you. You have neglected them too long. It is time to blow out the candle on the cake. You will not want to miss that, will you." It was not a question and I knew she hated being called Sue.

As she left the kitchen and I carefully folded the tea cloth that had been in my hands throughout, Joe took the cloth from me and placed it on the hook by the boiler.

I had no idea how much, if anything, he had overheard. He had overhead my conversation with Alicia in the garden of Sandhey on the afternoon of his wedding – that had been information to his advantage – had he overheard this?

He certainly didn't seem surprised that his wife was crying and that I was trying to comfort her.

"Leave it. Don't interfere. She's fine." He didn't sound like a man talking to his boss.

Susannah did her duty by the children, laughing and playing with them until they were as tired as she was.

As Monika put the children to bed Max and I sat with Charles, Susannah and Joe out on the patio with a bottle of wine. The sun was still warm. I was thinking of a July 4th some years earlier when I had met Alicia off the boat in Liverpool and she had got very drunk with the Americans at the Adelphi. How many years ago? 17 years. It seemed a lifetime.

It was Charles who broke the silence which should have been companionable but wasn't.

"Look I'm giving a lecture next week, there's a series of talks by people with local connections. Would you like to come with me? It would get you out of the house, Monika can look after the kids and I know you'd enjoy it. If you don't want to come to my lecturing on about birds you could always listen to one of the others."

"No I don't think so."

Joe had answered for her. I would have sworn she was going to say "yes".

"And she doesn't need to 'get out of the house' as you put it. She is perfectly happy."

He was talking about her as if she wasn't there.

"I work day and night to get the money to keep her and the children

174

well provided for. I can do no more than I do. All she's got to do is stay at home and keep the house."

There was just the hint of menace in the voice – just the hint that he was annoyed, thinking that we were finding fault with him.

"We're not questioning how you provide for your family Joe, how could we? You have a lovely house here, a lovely garden – Josie goes to a good school – No we cannot, nor would we, question how you are looking after your family."

"Then what are you criticising me for?"

"We aren't."

"Yes you are. You are always checking up on me, keeping tabs on me. Well everything is fine. Absolutely fine."

Without saying a word Susannah got up and went into the house.

"Joe, we just think Susannah looks a little ..."

"downtrodden?" he asked mockingly.

"No. Don't put words in my mouth, a little tired. You have, after all, had your last three children in very quick succession – young children are tiring. Susannah's a very intelligent young woman, she could, perhaps, want to do more with her life than look after babies."

"That, with the greatest respect, is not for you to worry about. It is not your business. Have another drink."

Why do people always say "with the greatest respect" when they mean the exact opposite? Joe was showing how little respect he had for us.

I realised that evening what Susannah must have seen some time ago, Joe was using us all, the firm, the family, all of us.

But we all had another glass of wine and the awkwardness was pushed to the background by gentle conversation about nothing at all.

Susannah phoned me at the office early on the following Tuesday morning, the 7th July.

"Uncle Ted, Can we have a word?"

"Susannah, of course."

"About the party. What I said. It was a mistake."

"What was the mistake Susannah? Your thinking you are pregnant again or your telling me that you are?"

The silence at the end of the line was painful.

"Susannah, are you still there?"

"Yes I'm still here, and I'm still pregnant."

"Do you still want a termination?" I thought I had better bite the bullet. "Because if you do, you know I'm here and will help in any way I can. No one should have to have children they don't want in this day and age."

"Unlike 24 years ago you mean?"

"Susannah for God's sake don't be so hard on yourself! You are you. Take no notice of the past and whatever your parents did or didn't do. You are you. You have your life. Do what you have to do and do it with your chin up."

"I must talk to someone."

"Come in to town for lunch – leave the children with Monika, she'll pick up Josie from school tell her you're going shopping – she will understand. We'll meet at the Adelphi.."

I looked across at Susannah as she held the menu in her hand, I don't think she was reading it. It was the same dining room in which I had eaten with her mother. Susannah was so very like Alicia had been, before the illness that was now eating her away. I felt desperately moved by the thought of the opportunities these two women had missed in their lives, how everything had gone so wrong for both of them.

It was now too late for Alicia, but surely I must be able to do something to help her daughter?

As we sat with menus in hand but taking no interest in choosing our meal, all I could do was listen as she talked.

She told me, in more detail than I wanted about her relationship with Joe. How he had said so often that they liked it at the office when she was pregnant, he said it showed what a family man he was, how respectable he'd become. He'd said that it stopped her straying like her mother had, how 'everyone' knew that her mother was a tart who'd gone with all and sundry, and who left her when she was a baby. She told me how he had explained to her, very clearly, how he was going to make sure she didn't do what her mother had.

"Mother would have got rid of me like a shot. I think that she really really didn't want me and I really really don't want this one."

Her voice was breaking but she carried on, not letting me interrupt.

"He knows that I have always loved Carl, and that he was always second best. He knows I only went with him because I'd lost Carl and he knows that I could never love anyone else. He knows he couldn't hold a candle to Carl, he knows that if Carl turned up I would go away with him just like that," clicking her fingers over her shoulder, dramatically, just like her mother, "even though Carl.." She had great difficulty finishing the sentence, "even though Carl is my brother."

176

She continued with hardly a break "He knows I can't leave the children, though he seems to think that if I had only one or two I would – and the more there are the more I'm tied to him – and so he wants child after child after child – and I just can't do it." Her voice was rising hysterically as she found herself putting barely thought out worries into words.

This was not what I wanted to hear. She had said so much last Saturday but I really hoped that had been the result of the odd wine or two too many. It evidently wasn't. What was I to say? I just sat there and wordlessly handed over a handkerchief for her to blow her nose.

We sat in silence for a few minutes, she looking down at the menu in her hand and the crisp white linen napkin on her lap.

"Do you still want to eat lunch or would you rather go for a walk?"

"Let's go."

I slipped the waiter a note, apologising, saying my friend was not well and we left.

If only we'd stayed just a few minutes longer.

Hindsight is a wonderful thing and we left when it was right for Susannah that lunchtime. But I have wondered over the intervening years what might have happened had we stayed just a little bit longer. It would have saved so much pain. But maybe it wasn't the right thing. Maybe what happened because we didn't stay and meet Charles and Carl that lunchtime was actually better for them all in the end. What was that in Julius Caesar? You can take one route in life and know the consequences but you never know what would have happened if you had taken another? Who knows what would have happened in their lives if Susannah and I had stayed just a little longer in that restaurant.

It would have been only a few minutes after we left that Carl and Charles came through the crowded foyer on their way to the bar.

But Susannah and I did leave.

Maybe we wouldn't have bumped into them anyway.

We walked down to the river. Pier Head was, as always, a good place to clear the head. We stood by the railings overlooking the frighteningly grey river as the tide surged in. The ferries were shuttling backwards and forwards, the seagulls wheeling above, the sounds of the buses and cars all about us, but we were as good as alone.

"I can't have this baby."

"No. I realise that. Do you want to leave it to me? I'm sure something could be arranged. It would be done as soon as possible – probably this week – will you be able to explain it? Why you aren't well I mean? It's probably not going to be easy."

"Monika will help. I don't know what I'd do without Monika."

"Are you absolutely sure about this?"

"Yes."

"The other bits you told me, about Carl, are they true too?"

"Yes. I will always love him – I don't care if he is my brother. You know I tried to get him to go away with me don't you? Go somewhere where we weren't known and we could have lived together – no one would have known or minded and we could have been happy. I really believe we would have been happy. He wouldn't do it, you know, he wouldn't go away with me because it was 'wrong'. He loved me but not enough. He couldn't have loved me enough."

Tears were streaming down her face.

"Perhaps he just didn't want to hurt you."

She wasn't crying, there was no sobbing, no gulped intakes of breath that I associated with someone who is heartbroken crying their eyes out. It was just as if her eyes were leaking independently of herself. She kept talking, not bothering to wipe the salt water from her cheeks.

"I've thought of that. I just think he was frightened, scared, and he didn't love me enough to overcome that. He never got in touch with me. He's never tried to get in touch with me."

What was I to say? I knew it wasn't that he didn't love her enough, he left because he loved her too much.

I couldn't tell her what I knew. I couldn't tell her the true nature of her relationship with Carl, that I had known for some years that they were not brother and sister.

Nor could I begin to tell her the real reason Carl had not contacted her since that Sunday afternoon seven years before. I didn't think she could cope with the knowledge that he loved her that much. How could I upset her so much at this time when she had so much to deal with?

How could I tell her that I knew all her pain had been unnecessary and that one woman's selfishness and pride was the cause of it all.

She was so upset, so close to a breakdown, that I felt I had to keep that information from her until she was more able to deal with it.

At least that was the excuse I made to myself at the time, and so often in the years that passed before I eventually did tell her everything.

I couldn't undo what had been done. Neither could Alicia. Neither would Joe. The only way I could help her was to make practical arrangements and hope to ease some of her burden over the next few days.

"Do you want me to talk to Joe?" I couldn't imagine what I would say to him if she had asked me to, but I had to ask anyway.

"What? Tell him to leave me alone? I don't think that would work."

"No tell him that you need some care and attention yourself, that you are a young woman, he must make you feel important and loved – you don't feel loved do you?"

"No. Whenever he – you know – well he's always saying was I imagining he was Carl. Did I want him to be Carl. Was I imagining it was Carl... you know..... He taunts me with him, all the time. He will never let me forget that I have loved someone else. I thought I did love Joe in the beginning, he made me feel so good. But it's all too late now. He's always saying things like 'if only you knew what I know ...' and 'would you marry me again, if things were the same?' He is always acting as if he knows something that I don't. He's changed. Now I know he's just cruel and manipulating."

She stopped for a moment, looking out across the river. A ferry passed by and it was possible to hear the strains of *Ferry 'cross the Mersey* playing on its loud speaker as it turned against the running tide towards Birkenhead.

As she talked she seemed to be trying to understand what had been going on in her life for the past seven years. It was almost as if she was growing up all at once, realising that she was no longer the 16 year old with everything in front of her, she was now in that future she had thought would never come. The bitterness eventually left her voice leaving her subdued, resigned.

"You know he goes to have tea with his mother every Sunday. He walks down to the old house and spends all afternoon with her. I'm never invited. He doesn't want any of us with him. She never comes to the house and I never go there. It is as if when Joe married me he created a new life that wouldn't change his old one, the new one just superimposed on top of the old. He's changed himself into a different person, one who does all the right things, has his boss to dinner, plays golf. He's absolutely nothing like the fisherman he was at first. He's not him. Can you see what I mean?"

I had to see if there was another side to the story, though after all Susannah had said I hardly sounded convincing – even to myself. "Could it be that his responsibilities, a wife and young family, make him feel he has to work so hard, he has to do all these things to keep you all in the comfort he believes you expect?"

"No."

She sounded very definite about it.

"So you want me to go ahead with contacting the clinic – making an appointment?

"Yes."

I nearly added "or would you like me to talk to your Mother " but managed not to.

That would be one complication too many.

Chapter Twenty-Five

Carl didn't know where he was going to go when he left the house in Dunedin Avenue – he just had to get out.

He wasn't sure where he could go but thought he would try the Forsters. They lived a few minutes away and, although Crispin was sort of a friend at school, they hadn't spent much time together and, most importantly, he didn't know Susie.

In the ten minutes he spent walking to the Forsters Carl tried to think up what he was going to say to them and how he was going to explain his arrival at lunchtime on a Sunday with a rucksack and a request to stay.

They were finishing their lunch, but they sat him down and Mrs Forster put together a full plate of a roast dinner "Sorry there's no crackling left but you look like you need a decent meal" she apologised, "blame Olly and Crisp for guzzling it all" said their young sister. "Eat first, explanations later. Explanations are always easier on a full stomach." their father said firmly.

The contrast between the family meals Carl had been used to and this one could not have been greater. There was friendly banter and teasing here. Carl could remember the tense meals at Millcourt – at Dunedin Avenue they had rarely all sat down to eat together.

The family stayed around the table watching him eat. He hadn't thought he was hungry but he ate, and felt a little better. When asked what the matter was he told them the whole story. He told them how he and Susannah had always been close, how they'd grown to love each other and how, that afternoon, it had all been shattered.

It was perhaps the best thing Carl could have done.

By the time they left the table to all join in with the washing up it was all but settled. He would live with them as long as he needed a home.

The Forsters were something of an unconventional family. The father, Jeffrey, was an internationally respected professor at Liverpool University. All the family called him Jeff and when he was away, which was quite often, the house was a quieter and emptier place. His wife, Pat,

181

always wore long flowery skirts with one of her husband's shirts, her long grey hair tied in a pony-tail at the nape of her neck with black ribbon. She wrote poetry and taught occasionally. At the time Charles joined the family she was working with a group of energetic like-minded people to turn an old chapel into a theatre in Liverpool. It took up a lot of her time, but she seemed always to have had the energy to cook fresh meals, keep the house clean and tidy, badger the boys about their homework and always 'be there' when one or other of the children needed to talk to her about something important.

It was a house full of love, with no shortage of laughs and hugs.

Pat had briefly come across Alicia some years before when she had almost joined the local drama society but she had found the whole thing a little too organised "not much fun arguing with a lot of middle class ladies full of their own importance."

Crispin and Oliver were twins, younger than Charles but in his year and house at school. Despite rarely seeming to work they were always heading the class lists and intended to follow their father into academic life, that was if they didn't get diverted into playing sport professionally – they would both have been capable of it. They had boundless enthusiasm for anything and everything, masses of energy and a confidence born of loving parents and a secure and happy home.

They recognised Carl was different, they saw his unhappiness and they took him under their wing.

Carl had had no idea there were so many interesting things to do after school. He became involved in clubs and playing sports that he never thought he would be interested in. With Susie all he had wanted to do was to dash off to meet her as soon as the school bell had rung to spend hours listening to records, chatting with their friends in the coffee bar and just being together. None of their old friends had thought it cool to be interested in school.

Oliver and Crispin didn't care about what other people thought and were confident enough to do what they wanted and if that was to work hard then it wasn't for others to say they were wrong. It didn't hurt that they were so good at sports, Crispin pipping his brother to be School Captain of Rugby, Oliver had to be content with only Captaining his house.

Perhaps it was because there were the two of them, Carl thought, perhaps having the unquestioning love and loyalty of your family gave you both an edge over the rest of the world – where other people were on their own.

The final member of the Forster family, Linda, cheerfully called herself 'the afterthought'. Being only 9, she was 7 years younger than her brothers who teased her incessantly and treated her exactly as they would have done a younger brother.

They were the most informal and uncritical of people and took Carl into their home as if it were the most natural thing in the world.

On the day after he had arrived Jeff Forster had called the school and arranged that Carl would stay with them until the end of the following year, when he would, he was confident, go up to Cambridge and not need to have any contact with his family.

That evening Oliver went back to Kathleen and Arnold's to pick up the rest of Carl's gear. Carl himself never went near the house or his parents again.

I met the Forsters when Max asked me to draw up 'some sort of document that makes it all a bit official'. Professor Forster was to be *in loco parentis* and Carl was to live with that family until he had completed his full-time education. No money would change hands, Carl would contribute exactly what Crispin and Oliver did to the household as and when they were earning.

It wasn't necessary to get Social Services or any other agencies involved. It was simply an arrangement made by the headmaster between two families that suited both.

I visited the family a few days later, and saw for myself how relaxed Carl was. I hadn't had much to do with him before but found him charming.

He explained, very maturely, that he was genuinely trying not to be a problem for people but he was determined that he could never go back to live with his mother. We talked about the arrangements and I satisfied myself that he would be safe and well looked after.

I didn't mention Susannah – it was Carl turned the conversation towards the family.

"It must be Charles's 21st about now."

I told him there was to be a quiet family dinner, nothing elaborate, and, yes, I had been invited.

"You'll see Susie then."

I told him she was at Sandhey, omitting any reference to the circumstances of her arrival.

"They'll look after her won't they?"

I said I was sure Charles would always look after his sister and that

Max was very fond of her and Monika would always see her as 'her little girl'.

"I'd look after her if I could. But I can't,' he said with finality.

"Well anything, long term would be" I tried to choose my words carefully "difficult."

"Because we're related?"

"Absolutely.

"Not legally. Our birth certificates don't overlap. We could get married when we're 21. There's nothing to stop us. And anyway, who needs to get married these days? There's nothing really to stop us being together."

I told him he was doing the right thing. That not putting them through the deception was absolutely correct. I told him he was being honourable.

"It's got nothing to do with being honourable." He replied "it's got everything to do with it being impossible!"

I couldn't say anything. I thought I understood his reasons. Whatever he said about being brother and sister not mattering he must have known that it did.

"She probably thinks I don't love her, but it's just *because* I love her. We could live together but we could never make it official. She'll want children. I couldn't do that. I can't do that to her. It wouldn't be fair on the children. We could be together but we could never have children and she'll want children. I can't do that to her."

It was hard to listen to his pain especially as by then I was aware that Susannah was getting involved with Joe. I couldn't tell him what she was getting into. At the time I didn't see how bad it was going to get.

When I left I had a great liking for this young man.

He appeared to have fallen on his feet with the Forsters and I wished him luck, telling him that whatever he did, wherever he went, he must be sure to keep in touch with me.

Just in case.

The final contact I had with Arnold regarding his son was a brief note enclosing a sealed letter to be kept on file and sent to Carl on his 25th birthday, 1st May 1971. It seemed like an impossibly long time ahead but was less than 10 years. Neither Arnold nor Kathleen ever tried to contact their son again. It was as if, once the formalities were dealt with, they simply decided to forget he existed. For the first few months after he left home Carl was living less than two miles away from them but they never made any effort to see him so she could explain.

Or apologise.

Kathleen tried to explain their reasons to me several years later when we looked back on the events of that year. She claimed that she had wanted to keep in touch with her son, however much he now hated her, but Arnold's health was so bad, his grip on reality becoming so tenuous, that she had thought it best to get him well first. Then, when his health was improved, he wanted to run away to the Lake District and start a new life. Carl was in university, the time for recovering the relationship had passed.

All I could think of at the time to excuse her was that she must have loved Arnold a very great deal. Why else would she give up all contact with her son? Either she loved Arnold very much and did as he wished, or she loved Carl so much she reluctantly gave him up to a better life.

I have liked to think it was this latter.

That Summer Jeff Forster left Liverpool to work in London and the family, along with Carl, moved to south London.

So Carl wasn't in the area to read the newspaper notices of Susannah's marriage to Joe Parry. He didn't know that Arnold, and some time later his mother, had moved away from the district too, the newspapers noting the termination of the long links the Donaldson family had had with the district and how both George and Arnold had served so well on the Council, how sad for local employment that his business had failed.

In 1965 Arnold had finally accepted that his business was never going to survive and that none of his so-called friends and colleagues was going to help him so he had fallen back on his original degree and got a job teaching in a girls' school in the Lake District to earn a living for the first time. It seemed like an attempt at escape though why he chose the Lake District, which must have held sensitive memories, only Arnold would have known. Kathleen had not joined him until over a year later when she got a job in the office of the school where Arnold taught, having finally sold Dunedin Avenue and her shop. I wondered how much of a marriage it was, they had been apart for over a year.

I received a letter from Carl in 1967, just after his 21st birthday. He was finishing his finals at university, he had been studying history and he hoped to get a First. He was going travelling in Europe for the summer. Would I please let his mother know that he was well. He didn't want her to worry about him.

In the same post I received a letter from Professor Forster, which gave a little more information.

Despite moving schools during his final year of A-levels Carl had done well and had been offered a place at Cambridge but had not taken it up. Instead he had studied at Sussex. He had done exceptionally well. He would undoubtedly get a First and they were very proud of their 'third son'.

Carl was to take a year off before taking up his new position teaching and developing his interest in the Napoleonic Wars. He was to spend the time travelling around Europe.

This letter confirmed that, now Carl was 21, the Forsters had no further responsibilities *'in place of parents'*.

I forwarded a copy of the letter to the last address I had had for Kathleen Donaldson. I hope they were both as proud of their son as the Forsters were. I trust they received my letter before Arnold died, little more than a month later.

It was early in June 1967 that a letter was received in the office informing us of Arnold's illness, and another followed shortly afterwards saying he had died. That set various legal procedures in train but it was not too difficult. Kathleen got everything there was to have – not that they had much that hadn't belonged to her in the first place.

I had attended the funeral, in a lovely quiet church on the edge of the fells.

It is an easy thing to say 'he would have loved it here' and 'what a lovely place to spend eternity' – rather like the platitudes one voices at the weddings of unsuitable people – meaningless clichés that no one believes but which provide people with something to say that fills empty spaces in conversations.

There were a number of Sixth formers and other teachers from the school but otherwise it was not a large gathering. I was the only person who had travelled north from the Wirral. Charles and Susannah had refused to go for their different reasons and both had asked Max not to go either. I couldn't help but contrast Arnold's funeral with that of his father, the newspaper then had taken up several column inches just in naming the mourners.

Kathleen was elegant and reserved, she showed regret rather than grief. I stood with her, having known Arnold far longer than any of the other mourners.

As we stood around the grave I wondered if they had ever actually been in love. They had had, as far as I knew, a relationship for over 30 years – certainly since well before the war. They had both been married to others yet had ended up married to each other. Perhaps that had been expedient, useful to both of them. Certainly Kathleen seemed to have gone along with his wishes but I just don't think Arnold was capable of doing anything that didn't put his own comfort first.

As we walked down the narrow lane back to her house after the funeral she told me how she had worked on ciphers during the war. She had been one of the code-breakers, pushing the bounds of knowledge and logic. While she was doing such interesting and essential work he had been involved in low level legal tasks, standing as 'friend of the accused' in courts martial – mainly defending petty criminals who happened to have been conscripted into the army, or prisoners of war who happened to have been caught making love with a land girl. She was quite bitter as she explained that she was far more intelligent than Arnold, though he was the one who had had all the advantages of education and expectation. And money. "If I'd had the use of all his father's money what could I have done with that!"

Such a story of waste, she told me. Waste of her life, waste of George's money. 'I should have had some of that money'. I didn't then understand quite what she meant.

I had a brief memory of the gossip of the time, Kathleen's mother and Arnold's father, but we had reached the house, other people were there, the conversation moved on and I forgot.

I received a postcard from Charles four months later.

The message was very short.

"Would you be kind enough to tell Susie that I wish her all the best on her 21st birthday. I'm sorry this message is a little late."

The picture on the postcard was of a sunflower, just one large yellow sunflower against a dark blue sky. The stamp was French but the postmark indecipherable.

So he hadn't forgotten her.

But I regret to say that, although I kept the card in the Donaldson's file, I didn't pass the message on.

Why didn't I let Susannah know that her Carl was still thinking of her? Probably because she had just had a child, her second, and I knew that she was feeling rather depressed. She had just completed her degree, where she scraped a third. She should have got a First, but then she had been maintaining a house, looking after a young child and her husband all through her course, and had been heavily pregnant through her finals.

I believe she did very well to get what she did. I could not upset her by raking up old wounds.

She had had a quiet 21st, there had been a small family party to which I was invited but declined. As far as I knew at that time she was happy in her marriage with Joe. Josie was a delightful child and Jack, to all appearances, a welcomed addition.

What would have happened if I had been honest then with Susannah, at that vulnerable time, when she had just had a baby, when she was depressed.

What would have happened if I had told her Carl had been in contact? What would have happened if I had reminded her then of Carl, told her that he still cared for her, still thought of her. Still loved her.

I couldn't do it. I couldn't upset her like that – even though I'd known for some time that they were perfectly free, legally and biologically, to be together. If only she hadn't had a husband already, and the small matter of two young children.

So I said and did nothing.

Because I didn't tell her she stayed in, what I later discovered to have been, a desperately unhappy marriage.

Perhaps I did the right thing. I wish I knew what could have happened had I told her. Was I right? Was I wrong? I stuck to the *status quo*. For better or for worse.

It was only when I spoke with her leaning against the railings at Pier Head three years later that I understood anything of the way she had really felt.

Chapter Twenty-Six

Carl was 21 years old, his final exams were completed, his degree assured. He had money in the bank, at least six months to do what he liked and it was 1967 – a good time to be young.

Photographs taken at the time show that he was tall with a shock of dark hair that reached, in the fashion of the time, well below his shoulders. The black and white photos couldn't entirely do justice to the most striking feature of his looks, the piercing blue of his eyes. Had Arnold Donaldson lived a generation later this was more or less what he would have looked like.

Although Carl had spent all four Christmases since he had left home with the Forsters in Dulwich he had not wanted to take advantage of them so, during all his other vacations he had travelled around the country and worked. He had picked fruit in summer and vegetables in winter. He preferred working outside even though the money was never very good – he could be alone and he could think. In the times he had worked in factories or in bars and restaurants the noise had been far too great to compensate for the money.

He had always found work when he wanted it and so he had managed to save enough money for his year travelling without touching the £21,000 that had appeared in his bank account on his 21st birthday. It was a lot of money and, he felt sure, that it must have come from Max.

He had enjoyed those jobs. He loved to read and to learn different skills. His main hobby was playing his guitar and he had a Spanish acoustic one that a waiter at one of the restaurants he had worked at had sold to him for peanuts.

There was much of his father in him but he had inherited his determination, his sense of enquiry and logical mind from his mother.

It was a very attractive, well-balanced and thoroughly likeable young man who set off to hitch hike around Spain and Portugal to find the battlefields of the Peninsula War.

On the last Sunday in May 1967 Carl sat in an empty carriage waiting for the early morning train to leave Charing Cross station he opened his notebook and began to make a list of all the things he hoped to achieve in the next few weeks. By the time the train was hurtling down through the tunnel under the North Downs and out into the fields and oast houses of Kent he had filled two pages in neat small handwriting – he wanted to keep all his thoughts in this book and he wasn't going to waste space with his usual scrawl. He hoped to learn a bit of Spanish, possibly even Portuguese. He planned to see as many of the places Wellington's armies had marched and fought that he could. He wanted to experience the places that for years he had been seen in his imagination as he had studied them.

At Dover with his bag over one shoulder and his guitar over the other he walked through the town and onto the ferry. He added to his list sitting on the deck looking back as England's white cliffs receded into the haze. *Sleep rough and in posh hotels. Play the guitar better.*

At Calais he found his train for Paris delayed and when he arrived at Gare du Nord he didn't have enough time to get the bus that circulated between the main railway stations of the city so he broke one of his self-imposed rules and spent money on a taxi. "Gare d'Austerlitz s'il vous plait Monsieur" was just about the limit of his spoken French. He read it very well, much of his study had been of French texts, but the spoken language was a different matter. He opened his notebook as the taxi braked sharply, turning right onto the bridge. *"Improve spoken French"*. "Combien? Merci." He would just have time to buy his ticket and get onto the train.

He hadn't planned to spend several hours sitting on his rucksack on the shifting plates in the space between carriages, unable to get any sleep as people pushed past him first one way and then back again. It was the middle of the night when they all had to get down from the French train and cross over the platform to get onto the Spanish train at Portbou. Saying a silent *Thank You* to those military experts long ago who had insisted that Spain had a different railway gauge from France, imposing a train change at the border, Carl sat down in a proper seat for the first time since Paris.

As the train made slow progress down the coast, with dawn lightening the sky over the sea to his left, Carl got his first opportunity of the summer to practise his Spanish on the fellow occupants of the compartment. He found that the French for what he wanted to say came to mind far more easily than the Spanish, but by a combination of sign language and the patience of his companions he gradually began to converse in the correct language.

It would be a few months before he would speak English again.

At Valencia he walked through the city towards the dusty road to Madrid. As the buildings grew fewer and farther between he stood to face the oncoming traffic and stuck out his thumb.

It was a summer of joy for Carl.

He went where he wanted, when he wanted and he gradually ticked things off in the list in his notebook. He saw the battlefields – or what was left of them – and he was able to understand far more of the strategies and genius or stupidities of the generals he had read and written so much about.

He tramped the miles as the armies of Wellington had done. He felt the same heat, crossed the same rivers by the same bridges, marched along the same roads past the same fields and hillsides. He visited many towns and cities that had been besieged, stormed and destroyed in that war 150 years before.

He improved his Spanish and his Portuguese so that, although he couldn't speak those languages without an accent, he could make himself understood – and could understand others – in all regions of the country.

He bought tomatoes, bread and cheese with cheap wine whenever he needed food. When he found himself in the countryside at night he would sleep rough, when in a town he would find a cheap hotel or a room above a bar.

As he had promised himself at the beginning of his trip, on more than one occasion he would use some of his carefully hoarded supply of travellers' cheques to buy some new clothes and treat himself to the luxury of a Parador, the government run luxury hotels springing up around the country at this time.

The receptionists of these establishments would be wary of the dusty unkempt, unshaven, young man but, impressed by his manners and his ability to speak their language, wouldn't turn him away. On those nights he enjoyed the luxury of soaking in a hot bath, anticipating the adventure of getting a table at dinner, enjoying a proper meal and then the prospect of sleeping in a large bed with clean and starched sheets.

On those occasions he would admit to himself that although he didn't need that luxury all the time he did enjoy the finer things in life.

He was equally happy getting into conversation with old men sitting on benches around town squares at the end of hot days, or drinking warm beer and eating tapas leaning against the bar in smoke filled cafes.

Wherever he slept he would always find time to write up his thoughts and impressions of the day in his notebook, filling in the narrative around the diagrams and sketches he had made.

During the long days on the road he came to have a target in mind. To be in San Sebastian on 31st August, 154 years to the day after Wellington and his army had taken the fortress there. He decided that that would be a suitable place to end his summer.

And he made it.

At noon he sat at a pavement bar eating fresh fish and enjoying a carafe of wine in commemoration of the bravery of all the men who had fallen attempting to reach the spot where he was sitting, all those men who had fought so hard to breach the walls, who had died in their hundreds in the few yards which had taken him only a few minutes to stroll along, and the equal bravery of all the men who had died trying to stop them.

He silently raised his glass to the souls of those men, if there were any around, which he felt there were.

31st August, it would be Susie's birthday tomorrow, her 21st.

That afternoon he spent on the beach, bottle of wine to hand, reading though his notebook. He had most of the things he had set out to do, he felt a sense of achievement but he knew something was missing. Although a self-contained, positive thinking young man he succumbed that afternoon to a rare bout of self-pity. It wasn't that some*thing* was missing it was some*one*.

He didn't often allow himself to think about her. But he did now.

It was such a long time ago, she would have her own life, she wouldn't be thinking about him. She will have gone to Cambridge – one of the reasons he had chosen to go to Sussex as he couldn't have borne meeting her at University. She would have done well, independent, loved and ...... He felt the pain he always felt when he thought of Susie.

He decided to send her a message through the solicitors, he wasn't sure they would pass it on but it was the only way he had to get in touch with her.

He sat on the beach imagining a glittering 21st party, probably in the Adelphi. It would be a large gathering of her friends and family, but also the great and the good of the area. Everyone would be in evening dress, Arnold and Kathleen standing in line at the door to the banqueting hall welcoming their guests, putting on a great show even if they were completely broke. Would anyone remember him? There would be a band playing, people dancing. Susie would dance every dance energetically, her long hair spilling over her bare shoulders. Did she dance every dance with the same man? Did she spread her favours around? Did she have a boyfriend? Of course she must have. He would be a very clever – only a First would be good enough – very good looking, rich, soon-to-join-his-father's-firm-in-the-city type.

Or had she managed to break away from her family's expectations.

He had heard nothing of Susie since he had left Hoylake, he wouldn't contact her. He could not be that cruel. He imagined what he did not know. But it was his way to look forward and to resist being maudlin about the past so he began to make plans for the future.

He would go back to the Forster's for a short visit and then his plans for the rest of his year off were to travel to West Germany, north Italy, and Austria. His Spanish and Portuguese were now much improved, if he wanted to be able to read all the texts he would need to read he should address his German.

It was dusk and more and more lights were being reflected on the ever darker water when his thoughts were interrupted.

"You look lonely."

A girl who had been watching him as he sat almost motionless had come and sat down on the sand beside him. She had spoken in English.

"Not really."

"Want some?" as she tried to share her roll-up with him

"No thanks. I don't."

She laughed, "Everyone does."

"Not me."

"Sorry."

Years later he used to tell people that he had been at University in the '60s and not even smoked tobacco let alone anything else that was on offer. After his near misses with Susie in the coffee bar in Hoylake he had kept away from the drug scene and, although he'd had flatmates at university who did, he'd never indulged, thinking drugs a complete waste of time and money.

She didn't go away and after a few minutes repeated her opening shot "You look lonely."

"Not much chance of that."

He hadn't meant to be rude but he did want to be alone and he didn't want to get involved with drugs.

He hadn't had much experience with girls since Susie. He wasn't comfortable with them. He wasn't sure how to speak to them and he felt uncomfortable.

"I'll go if you like."

"No, you stay here, I'll go. I really don't need any company." He went to get up. Putting his hand hard down on the sand to take his weight he accidentally leant on hers.

"Ouch! That hurt."

"Sorry." He regretted his churlishness, he took her hand in his, rubbing it "That better?"

"Yes. Thanks."

He looked at her for the first time seeing a small very tanned face framed in long straggly blond hair.

"Sure you don't want some?" She inhaled deeply and breathed out the aromatic smoke very slowly.

"Absolutely sure thanks."

"Sandie, my name's Sandie." She giggled, picking up a handful of sand and letting it slip through her fingers. She took another long drag.

"Carl"

"That's a nice name. Carl, Yes that's a nice name. Where do you come from Carl?"

"London, well yes London I suppose."

"You don't sound so sure."

"Well I come from near Liverpool but I've been living in London."

"Liverpool! Oh it must be absolutely fab coming from Liverpool – have you seen the Beatles live?" She began to sing *All you need is love, love* as she put her arm around his neck and tried to kiss him.

"Hey! Stop that."

"Cool, that's cool – if you want to we can, otherwise we could just talk. Would you like to talk?" She took another long draw on her roll-up and he began to talk.

When Carl talked about that night some years later, he said it was rather like being on a plane journey. You told the person sitting next to you all the secrets of your life because you knew you would never see them again. No fear that anything you said would ever come back to haunt you.

So Carl had talked about things he had not put into words for years and Sandie had listened.

Carl talked about how he had loved this girl since they'd both been children, how she was everything he ever wanted in a girl, what she looked like, how she laughed. How circumstances had meant he had to leave her and how he hadn't seen her for years but knew she would always be the one for him.

When Sandie had asked what had gone wrong Carl found himself able to tell her about that last weekend – how they had been to the cinema, she laughed when he told her what film it had been – how they kept getting close to going all the way but hadn't – how he had this suspicion that maybe their families weren't as they appeared to be – how his father had died the year before and how his mother hadn't cared – how she had taken them to live with the man who turned out to be his real father – how they had told him that the girl he loved was his sister – how he had run away because he couldn't bear the pain.

"Are you sure the girl is your sister? Just because that man said she was doesn't mean it's true. It sounds like they're all lying through their teeth. I mean, if I were your father, I mean, I'd lie all the way. I wouldn't believe a word I said."

She stood up abruptly, "Gotta go. I bet I'm right. They're all lying. That's what parents do to their children, they lie." There was such bitterness in her voice.

Carl was left feeling a complete idiot. Not only had he not asked anything about her in the hour or more she had been with him, he had just told her things about his life he hadn't even admitted to himself.

Susie and he hadn't kept their relationship that well hidden. They couldn't could they? His mother and Arnold must have seen what was going on and they didn't stop it. They had thrown the two of them together since their earliest years. He thought back to all those visits to Millcourt, of the occasions without number they had spent days and weekends, even before his father – he corrected himself – before Henry had died. They had obviously wanted to spend the time together, it was just unfortunate that it meant he and Susie were thrown into each other's company so much. Or were they just so self centred and wrapped up in their own lives that they didn't care what was happening to their children? They must have noticed something and come up with this brilliant excuse to separate them. And it was a brilliant excuse. It had stopped the relationship in its tracks hadn't it? They couldn't have said 'never see each other again' because a) they lived in the same house and b) they would still have seen each other behind their backs so absolutely, what a brilliant way to bring the relationship to an end. He found he had been scribbling his thoughts on the final page of his notebook, the first entry in English for a long time.

As dawn broke over the mountains behind him Carl had decided what he would do until the Spring.

He would find Susie's mother. He would ask her what was the truth. He would find out whether there was any truth in what they had said, he would find out if there was any real reason why he and Susie couldn't be together. There was absolutely no way he was going to ask Kathleen. He didn't believe she would tell him the truth now anyway.

He walked along the beach, back towards the main town, past a group of people including Sandie who were lying on the sand. All were intertwined as if someone had picked up their bodies and plaited them together. They were all sound asleep as the transistor radio by their side playing *all you need is love, love, love is all you need, love is all you need, love is all you need.*

"Thank you Sandie, if that's really your name." He whispered as he flung his rucksack and his guitar over his shoulder and made for the town.

"I'll do the bank, then the railway station, but first the postcard to the Solicitors." The tune banging away in his head *love love love, love is all you need, all you need.*

Time to go home.

It was the next Monday morning when he left the Forsters. They had been away when he had arrived home, but the neighbours had let him in. On the door to his room was a note.

"This is still your room you know!"

That was nice.

On his desk was a note from Jeff saying when he got home they needed to talk, some postcards sent in early July from Benidorm and a large envelope with forms to complete to formalise his place from next Spring which he completed and put in their self addressed envelope to post.

On the long train journey back through France he had filled up the final space in his notebook with a list of things he knew about Susie's mother, and things he didn't. He hadn't seen her for nearly 10 years. She had watched them playing in the garden – she thought they hadn't seen her but they had. He had seen photos of her, Monika had kept one in the nursery, a young woman in a summer dress feeding a row of black labrador puppies and there were many of her in the scrapbooks that had kept the nursery busy for years. Susie had spoken of her a few times, but had not given much away.

Though there were always Susie's letters and the cards she had sent to him every time she had been away with her mother.

He rummaged in the back of his cupboard and found the small box that contained his memories of Susie. In it he kept all the photographs he had of her, small mementoes and the letters and postcards she had written him when she had been away with Charles visiting their mother. He re-read them all, looking for clues about where Alicia might have lived. But they had never visited her at her house, they had always met on neutral territory.

In one letter Susie wrote *Mother doesn't talk to us, she just talks **at** us, she's always complaining about her house and how small it is.* She didn't say where the house was. He looked through the postcards, there weren't many, and found two that stood out as different – all the others had beaches or blue sea. The odd ones were photographs of rooms in what looked like a large country house. He read the details on the back of the card 'Polesden Lacey, near Great Bookham, in Surrey'. One had the message *Sorry about the postcard, I couldn't get one of where we are in darkest France so this is one Mummy gave me. Yuch!* The second, a year later, *Where does she get these cards from?*

It seemed to be reasonable that she must live close by. He'd try Bookham.

He wrote a short note to Jeff and Pat and a long one to Crispin and Oliver. He said he was sorry to have missed them, he was fine and would see them for Christmas.

He had set himself the deadline. By December 24th he would have talked to Alicia and found out if Susie really was his sister.

He did not think through what he would do with that knowledge once he obtained it but he didn't doubt that he would find Alicia or that when he found her she would tell him the truth.

Chapter Twenty-Seven

The Monday morning train from Waterloo was almost empty. Most people were travelling in the opposite direction – hurrying up to town. He'd bought a single to Bookham. He would find a bed and breakfast for the night as there was no sleeping rough in England in September. He knew he could always go back to London, less than an hour away, but in his mind he had begun his quest for a Holy Grail and he promised himself he wouldn't return to London until he had found it.

It wasn't a long train journey and it was only mid morning by the time he arrived at Bookham Station. He asked the stationmaster where he might find a telephone box and was directed a mile or more to the village.

He found it, complete with directory, and hurriedly leafed through. There was no 'Donaldson, Alicia' in the book.

Would she have reverted to her maiden name? He slid his back down the glass doors of the telephone box and sat on his haunches on the floor. "What was her maiden name?" He racked his brains. He had seen some of her paintings on the wall at Millcourt. Some paintings that she had done before she had married. What had been on them? He couldn't remember. He tried to picture one particular painting in his mind's eye. He could see it, it was in the Lake District, a bridge, over a small stream with a mountain in the background but what was the signature at the bottom?

He decided he must find a library and see if there were any amateur theatricals or arts groups in the area. There were so many pictures in those scrapbooks of Alicia involved in that sort of thing, she wouldn't have given up on those.

On the library notice board in the narrow entrance there were notices about kindergartens and mother and children groups, the local church services, all sorts of things but nothing that mentioned a drama society or art classes. 'Shit'. He stood in front of the notice board, his hands clasped around the back of his head wondering what he could do next.

He ought to go home. There must be another way of finding the truth. That's his trouble, he told himself, he was stubborn. On the one hand he knew it was a stupid idea to try to find her, on the other, he wasn't going to give up on the first day. And he could always try Polesden Lacey.

Then he spotted a notice about a Parish Council Election. The electoral roll. He could sit and look through for someone called Alicia. There wouldn't be many and even if she had changed her surname she would still be Alicia. It wouldn't take long. Yes! He punched the air with his right hand. Why hadn't he thought of that before?

He didn't know whether he had spoken out loud but he did notice an elderly woman who had tried to get past him and who he had practically knocked over.

"I beg your pardon young man!"

"Sorry! I didn't mean to hit anything, anyone! Sorry! Are you all right?"

"I'm fine, thank you." She said looking down at her bag that had been knocked from her hands. Carl leant down to pick it up and handed it to her.

"If you're sure?"

"Absolutely."

He walked quickly out of the door, not noticing the look on the old lady's face.

He walked up the High Street, stopping every so often, seemingly looking into the shops, but really his eyes were focussed only on the wall in Millcourt and that picture. If he could only remember that name it might just give him a better chance.

He shouldn't have expected it to be easy. He hadn't expected it to be easy. She could be in Leatherhead or Guildford or Epsom or any other town in Surrey. Just because she had had a couple of postcards of the village didn't mean she lived there did it? Or she could have moved. Or she could be dead. But he was going to keep looking until he found her or he ran out of time. He was not going to give up.

He looked up at a clock. 12.30. He'd go back to the pub, have a drink, calm down and get everything into perspective. It seemed like it had been a long day and it wasn't yet lunchtime.

Shortly after he had been served and had sat down at a quiet table the woman from the library came into the bar. He picked up his pint and walked up to her.

In the voice he could put on when he was trying to create a good impression, he tried to excuse himself "I'm very sorry for my outburst earlier. You caught me at a bad moment. Can I buy you a drink to make up?"

"Of course you may, the usual please Dave. Come on, let's sit here and you can tell me why a nice young man like you was swearing at notices about Nursery Classes."

He felt as if she was laughing at him.

They talked for a while about nothing in particular, just as strangers do in pubs. He bought her a drink and she returned the favour. When she finally got up to go he knew she was a writer and her name was Maureen Shelton.

The name meant nothing to him.

Why should it?

Maureen had gained a lot more from the conversation.

She had thought she recognised something of Arnold in the boy at the library and had followed his wanderings around the village.

She hadn't seen Carl Witherby for some years but there was so much similarity between him and his father that there was no doubt in her mind who he was.

He may call himself Carl Forster but she knew that this was Kathleen's boy, her nephew. He may spin her some tale about travelling around, perhaps finding some work in the area but she had a fair idea of why he was here and who he was looking for.

As she was about to leave she asked him, almost as an afterthought "Do you need somewhere to stay? My daughter takes in lodgers. If you want I can give you her address."

He was surprised at her kindness but didn't think too hard about why she was giving him her friendship and trust.

"But I haven't got any references or anything and you don't know me from Adam."

"You seem to have a trustworthy face." was all she said, writing an address and phone number on a slip of paper and giving it to him.

"If I can't find anything I may just call her. Thank you."

"Now I must go. It's been very," she hesitated as if trying to find the right word "interesting, meeting you, Carl. Now I must go. Things to do. People to see."

"Well well well" Maureen smiled to herself as she left the pub.

"You aren't going to believe who I met today."

"I'm not in the mood for games Maureen. Of course I won't be able to guess. You'll have to tell me."

Alicia was lying in her hospital room, tubes attached to both arms. She had been in hospital for several weeks now and was tired of it. She wanted to go home. It was weeks since the operation and they still wouldn't dscharge her. Maureen, sitting at her bedside had visited her almost daily, but her patience was wearing thin as all Alicia did was complain.

"A young man you haven't seen for some time."

"Not Charles?" She didn't sound excited by the prospect.

They both knew that Charles lived a very quiet and uninteresting life in Sandhey, he sent her birthday and Christmas cards dutifully signed "With love from us both; Charles and Monika." Occasionally he would include a newspaper cutting or some note from a magazine describing a talk he was giving or a programme he was contributing to. Apparently he was getting quite a name for himself in the world of ornithology. Alicia thought it would be nice to see him again, she hadn't seen him since his sister's wedding and that seemed a lifetime ago though it was only three and a half years or so.

She always thought of Susannah as Charles' sister, never as her daughter.

"No, sorry to disappoint you, but this is slightly more interesting. He calls himself Carl Forster."

"Carl?" She was disappointed "Why's he turned up, he's been missing for years."

"Not really missing. Ted's always known how to get in touch with him if anyone had wanted to bother."

"Oh Ted, he always knows everything doesn't he? Always knows things he shouldn't. The trouble is, people talk to him – they think he's so – inoffensive, so harmless."

"Well he's always had an address where he could reach Carl if anyone had to, so Carl's hardly been 'missing'."

"So what's so great about him turning up here – when we could have reached him anyway if we'd wanted to."

"Alicia. This is not about what you want or what Kathleen or any of the others want. It's about what Carl wants and why he's here."

"What on earth do you mean *why he's here?* in that tone of voice, you speak as if it is some great mystery."

"It could be. I think he's looking for someone, undoubtedly you. Perhaps he's doing that because he wants to know the truth about his family and his parents."

Alicia pressed the buzzer for the nurse and, saying she was tired, asked Maureen to leave her in peace.

Carl hadn't called Maureen's daughter about a room. He found that the Bull really was an Inn in the old sense as it had rooms and so booked in there for the night. Maureen was not like Sandie, he hadn't felt the need to unburden himself to another stranger in the course of a few days – and there was something about the way she looked at him. She seemed to know more about him than she had let on. Why else would she have given him her daughter's address?

He hadn't wanted to ask Dave, the barman, about Maureen, she obviously knew him well and he would know where she lived, but he thought it better not to show too much interest. Instead he had found

Maureen's address easily – she *was* in the telephone directory – and with the help of the map on the wall of the bar he realised she lived in a flat above a shop just opposite the pub.

The next morning was spent sitting in his room waiting for her to leave her flat.

He didn't think following someone would be very difficult – people appeared to manage it in films and on TV without too much aggravation. As long as she didn't go into too many quiet places he felt he would be able to follow her.

She may not lead him to Alicia directly, but he may find out the reason for that 'knowingness'.

It was after 12 o'clock when he was just about to give up his vigil and go down to have a drink when he saw her locking her front door and turning right, down the hill, towards Leatherhead.

For an old lady she walked pretty quickly but he managed to keep her in view. He reckoned they must have walked a couple of miles, when she turned into the driveway of a large Victorian building. It was a hospital.

He hung around outside the gates. Should he follow her in to try to see where she headed? Was she visiting someone or was the appointment for her? He felt awkward and very silly standing there.

Minutes dragged on and he wasn't sure whether to stay or go. He stood by the gates kicking his shoes against the pavement, playing mind games about the moss between the paving stones until, perhaps an hour later, his thoughts were interrupted by Maureen, laughing "Hello. I thought I'd find you here!"

"You knew I was following you?" He was disappointed.

"I'm afraid so. Though I have to say you didn't do too bad a job of it."

"When did you spot me?"

"About when you came out of the pub."

"That's not fair – you couldn't have!"

"There aren't that many tall, good looking, deeply tanned young men in the village you know! And also you must remember that people of my generation went through the war and we weren't all sitting at home knitting socks for prisoners!"

"I never thought that!" He was indignant that she should think he was that patronising.

"My God! You are *so* like your father!" she laughed gently

"You know my father?"

"I do indeed. I recognised you the moment we 'met' in the library. Anyone who knew your father would know you."

"So you'll know why I'm here."

"Not necessarily. There could be any number of reasons but my guess would be that you're trying to find Alicia."

"Do you know where she is?"

"Of course I do. I have just been visiting her. She's very ill you know."

"No I didn't. I haven't had anything to do with the Donaldsons for years."

"Or anyone else from the Wirral as I understand."

"How much more do you know about me?"

Instead of answering directly she said "Come on, let me buy you some tea or something."

They walked in silence back towards the centre of the town, Maureen far more comfortable than Carl who was wondering what it was about this woman, she must have been the best part of 60 but she still seemed very young. She seemed always to be laughing at him.

They walked into the café and Maureen sat down at a window seat. Carl sat opposite her.

"Two teas please."

She had taken control.

"I know you and your family quite well." She spoke matter-of-factly but he recognised the affection behind the voice.

"Even though you call yourself 'Forster' you are Carl Witherby, son of Kathleen and Arnold." It was not a question.

"Yes, but my father...."

"Yes I know, your father was not Henry Witherby, it was Arnold. Very sordid at the time but I believe Kathleen was in love with your father even though he was married to Alicia and these things happen. Arnold had some sort of hold over Henry and it was all arranged. Kathleen wouldn't get rid of you, you know. Obviously she's a good Catholic and wouldn't do that."

He sat stunned by the easy way she had discussed the tragedy that was the beginning of his life.

"Am I supposed to be grateful?"

"Probably not." She continued after a pause "Anyway, you were born and Henry loved you as his son."

"He didn't know?"

"No I'm absolutely certain he didn't know. He was – how do I put this – not a very strong man. He was rather swayed by whatever wind happened to be blowing at the time."

"He was not my father though."

"No. Arnold was definitely your father, though in many ways I do think that Henry was more of a father to you. He certainly loved your mother, they were together for 12 years or more. You must remember that."

"You're sure he wasn't in on it? He didn't know he wasn't my father?"

"No. Everyone who could know is pretty sure he didn't, though maybe he guessed something was wrong – towards the end that is."

"Do you think that's what made him...."

"kill himself" she finished the sentence for him. "No. I think that was money. He had worked for your father for years, he had been under Arnold's thumb for 20 years or more – he wanted something for himself that was not decided for him by Arnold. I think he was embezzling money from the business, I think he was up to his ears in debt. He was afraid that he would be found out. I'm really sorry to say this, but I am afraid he was not a clever man. He was going to be found out."

"So he killed himself."

"Yes. I believe he did."

"How do you know all this about us?"

"I have family in the Wirral, they keep me in touch." Maureen was not going to tell this young man the truth of their relationship.

He was hesitant, but he had to ask "Do you know how Susie is? Is she OK?"

"Susannah Donaldson, yes." She said thoughtfully "*What* an odd girl! Do you really want to know?" She sat stirring her tea for a few moments "If I tell you there is no going back you understand." She paused, suddenly serious. "You must forgive me, Carl, I am an actress and an artist, I see things in a dramatic way. I love words and I love to express myself clearly and unambiguously."

She paused, and it was some time before she continued. "I think this conversation could be a turning point in your life Carl. If I tell you what I know you'll never be the same person again. Does that sound melodramatic? Probably. But sometimes life does have its pivotal points. Whatever you do you'll regret it, you will undoubtedly want to have done the opposite of what you are going to do. If I tell you about Susannah you'll wish you didn't know and if you choose not to know you'll wish you did, as you have imagined worse. Whatever you choose you'll have to live with the consequences for a very long time. It's up to you."

She waited for a few minutes and eventually added in a sad voice "Perhaps you shouldn't have asked the question."

"You make it sound so portentous, all I did was ask about Susie – and whether she was OK."

"No you didn't, Carl, you were asking whether you should re-enter her life. You were asking whether you would be good for her, whether you could love her again – or should I say 'still', whether she could 'still' love you. You were asking a lot more than just how she is."

"You are playing with me."

Carl was aware he was out of his depth. Maureen knew things he didn't, she was holding this power over him and toying with him, as if he were a dog and she had a ball she wasn't sure whether to throw into the distance for him to chase and retrieve.

"No Carl, I am not playing with you, It's just that I make sure that you understand the importance of the question you ask. I will answer it truthfully and completely 'the truth the whole truth and nothing but the truth as far as I know it' but I must know that you can deal with the answer."

He thought for a few minutes, drinking the tea, nibbling at the scone. He decided to change the direction the conversation was taking – perhaps then he could regain the initiative, at least gain some time before making his decision.

"While I'm thinking of that, what of Charles and Monika?"

"As far as I know they are well. They still live at Sandhey, looking after Max."

"Have they married?"

"No, they will not. You know Monika had awful experiences during the war – she will never marry."

"No. I didn't." He thought for a while "Is Charles queer?"

She was not surprised by his question "No I don't think so. He is just" she sought the right words "just sensitive, vulnerable, careful, damaged."

"Aren't we all."

"Some more than others."

The conversation was more on an equal footing now.

"Are you going to stay with Phyl tonight?"

She was going to ignore the question that hung over them. She was going to carry on and let him turn the conversation back if he wanted to. She knew Kathleen well enough to see elements of her in her son now. He was weighing up pros and cons, all the while he was making polite conversation he was thinking.

Kathleen used to say that you could always make any decision by tossing a coin. You didn't necessarily do what the head or tail told you to – it was just that you knew what you wanted the coin to do as it was falling to earth. That was what Charles was doing now. Their conversation was the equivalent of that coin spinning in the air – he was going to know very shortly which way up he wanted it to land.

"I have another night at the pub, perhaps tomorrow?"

"Will you have answered that question in your mind by then?"

"I've answered it now."

"Well."

"Maureen, may I call you that? I have loved Susie since she and I were in the nursery. I have always loved her. I will always love her. I can't do anything about that. If I find anything out about her life I will only interfere if I can make it better. I would never, ever, do anything to hurt her. I'll only do what she wants me to."

"I believe you. But, and I ask this question carefully, how would you know whether you'd hurt her? How could you know whether you'd be good for her?"

"I would know."

"Ah, the confidence of youth."

"I will wait for her to make the first move."

They finished their tea in silence.

"Will you meet me tomorrow – we can answer the questions then. I must give you the day to change your mind, a cooling off period if you like."

"At the pub? At 12.30?"

"Done."

They left the café, and although both should have headed in the same direction, Carl turned the opposite way so they would not be embarrassed. He walked through the town and out into the surrounding woods, imagining Susannah and her life. He had been lucky bumping into Maureen but it was Susie's postcards, that he'd kept despite everything that had led him here. He found he'd walked to the gates of Polesden Lacey.

He'd try to find out the next day how Maureen knew so much about him.

The next morning The Bull was crowded. Carl made his way to the bar and asked for his pint.

"And a gin and tonic Dave, thank you."

She had been waiting for him.

"Come over here, I've saved a table. It always gets crowded here on a Wednesday, never could work out why Wednesday."

"Well..." once they were sitting down and he had drained half the pint in his anxiety.

"What? Here? It seems so – public."

"No one is listening to us."

"How's Alicia?" He thought he would start on safer ground.

"She is very ill, the doctors have done what they can and she may go into remission for anything up to 7 years but they don't hold out a great deal of hope."

"She's so young."

"46. She will be lucky to make her 50th."

"Do they – Charles – Susie – do they know?"

"No, and she won't have them told."

"Sad."

"Yes. Sad."

"Anyway," she continued after a suitable pause "have you decided what you want to know?"

"Yes. I have thought about this." Maureen recognised some of Kathleen's more annoying characteristics in his answer. "If I don't know and can do nothing, I might do harm by inaction. If I do know I can either do something or do nothing, either way I may do harm or I may do good but if I don't *know, really know,* then I don't have the choice. I need the information to be able to make the decision. It's then up to me to make the right one."

"You have thought this through haven't you!"

"Yes. I have."

"Well," and she took a big breath. "Susannah is married. No don't interrupt until I have finished. Susannah is married, she has two children, a girl, 3 years old called Josie, and a boy, Jack who was born last month."

She paused, waiting for the blows to sink in.

"What about her degree? Her career?"

"She did study for a degree but only just got it, not a good one at all, simply a pass. She has no career. She is a wife and a mother."

"Oh. I thought she was going to do more than that."

"So did we all."

They sat for a few moments, Carl wondering how wrong all his other ideas of her life had been. But he had to ask the most important question.

"Is she happy?"

"From all accounts she is. Her husband is doing well in business in Liverpool, she has help with the family."

"Monika?"

"Monika."

"So there really is nothing I can do. If I was in her life I would do nothing to help her?"

"Probably not."

"Nothing?"

"No. It doesn't seem so."

"Ouch."

He had to ask "Who did she marry?"

"You might know him. His name is Joe Parry."

"Not one of the fishing Parrys! I used to go out with Jimmy on his boat, he'd be Joe's eldest brother. His sister worked behind the bar at the Lighthouse Keeper. Jesus Christ! She couldn't have married one of them! Absolutely not! They were..... they were....."

"Awful" she finished the sentence for him flatly.

"I was going to say 'dirty'." There was defeat in his voice.

That evening, as Carl lay on the narrow bed in the pub he allowed himself to think about the Susannah he had known, bright, intelligent, inquisitive, energetic, selfish – yes she had been a bit selfish but that came from her being so unhappy as a child – she grabbed what she could when she could as if she knew it was going to end soon. There was always so much more to her than a spoilt middle class child whose every move in life was pre-planned by her parents and her parents' money.

He thought of her, married with a growing family. He was being selfish himself thinking that she was like him, ambitious, wanting to do something. Maybe she hadn't ever wanted to be anything other than a housewife and mother.

Maybe he was wrong thinking that she couldn't be happy as a mother and housewife. There was nothing wrong with that, even in these days of women's lib and burning bras, the 'swinging 60s'. It was important to have good mothers for children. It wasn't everything to have a career.

He mustn't think that there was anything wrong with 'just' being a wife and mother.

But he found it difficult to cope with knowing she had married one of the Parrys. She had had a choice and she had chosen a Parry.

But, he fought with himself over the answer, had she had a choice? She had a child of three. It must have been conceived so soon after he had left home. What had happened? Had she *had* to get married? How could she have thrown everything away like that? Was it a dreadful mistake?

Maureen and Carl met again the next lunchtime at the Bull. When they were both seated at what he was beginning to think of as 'their usual table' Maureen opened the conversation.

"You still haven't asked me what you really want to know have you?"

"And what would that be?" he asked – knowing that she knew the question as well as he did. Would she give him the correct answer?

"You want to know if Susannah is your sister don't you?"

He was surprised at the question, he had hoped that what Kathleen and Arnold had said that afternoon four years before was not true – but it hadn't occurred to him that others might have wondered.

"They said she is. Why would they lie?"

"Oh, Carl, there are lots of reasons why people lie. Many of those reasons may actually seem good at the time. That's not to say they should lie, or that lying is a good way to run your life, but it does happen and sometimes can be the lesser of two evils."

"Are you saying they lied?" He didn't want to think that they had – but if they had? What then?

"No. I'm saying that what they said may have been the truth as they saw it at the time, but it may not actually have been the truth."

"You're playing with words here, but what I think you're saying is that they said we were brother and sister because that was what they believed at the time but they now know we aren't?"

"No I'm not saying that. I'm saying that the truth is often not really the absolute black or white you young people would like it to be."

"Either Susie is my sister or she isn't. That's pretty damned black and white to me."

"Well it's not to her parents."

"Well who are her bloody parents then?"

He hadn't realised that his voice had risen so high until he noticed two pairs of eyes turned towards them from the bar. He lowered his voice but he was beginning to lose patience.

"I'm sorry. It's just that you are talking in riddles, deliberately leading me on. It may not be important to you but it bloody well is to me."

"Carl, you are an academic, at least I understand you will be soon. You know that there are always more than several sides to every story. Also, you know that you cannot live in the 'what ifs' of life. What if Napoleon had won Waterloo? What if Josephine had had a son by him? What if General what's his name hadn't stormed that bridge at Salamanca."

"Picton. It was General Picton and it was Vitoria, not Salamanca. And how do you know that's my area?"

Not answering his questions she continued "Your father was a pedant too. Anyway, what would you do if it turns out you're not Susannah's brother?"

"Are you saying I'm not?"

"No. I am asking *what would you do if you weren't?*' Think about it."

He did think about it. He thoughtfully drank the rest of his pint, walked up to the bar and bought another round. Returning to their table he sat down and calmly replied:

"I would want to know *how* we aren't. I'm obviously Arnold and

Kathleen's son so I would want to know how Susie isn't Arnold's daughter."

"Good boy, you're thinking now."

"Susie's birthday is the end of August. She would have been conceived at Christmas time. 1945. The end of the war. Was Arnold away? Did he serve away?"

"No. He served – as you so flatteringly describe it – in Yorkshire, at Catterick."

"Would they have spent Christmas together? If they didn't who would she have spent it with. Charles was, what, four years old?"

"Three"

"I was....?"

"about five months gone in your mother's womb."

"Arnold would have wanted to spend Christmas with Kathleen, wouldn't he? She was having his baby – me?"

"Good, you're getting warm."

"So. What have we got? A cosy family Christmas with Arnold and Alicia, with their toddler and the nanny, was Monika with them then? and Kathleen and Henry, Kathleen quite pregnant – with me. Who else?"

"No one else. Though you have one or two details wrong. Charles wasn't with them he was left behind with his nanny, and no, Monika didn't join the family until well after the war."

"So it was just the four of them."

"Yes, Carl."

"No." Realisation of where Maureen was leading him to was dawning. "They didn't do things like that then."

"What makes you think that?"

"You're saying that Alicia and Henry...."

"I am not giving details, Carl, I am simply describing a scenario. Make of it what you will.

"You are telling me, sorry, you are 'describing a scenario', where Henry is Susie's father. That my father – sorry 'the man I always thought of as my father' was Susie's father not mine?"

"I am telling you nothing Carl. I am simply identifying a possibility."

His voice was very quiet, he spoke trying, not altogether successfully, to keep his emotions in check. "What you are saying is that my parents are Kathleen and Arnold, and Susie's parents are Henry and Alicia. We are not related at all."

"If that is what you choose to read from our conversation Carl, go ahead. It is a possible, indeed I would go so far as to say a probable, scenario. It is also, I am afraid, completely impossible to prove one

210

way or the other."

Carl sat over his drink, taking in the implications of what Maureen was saying.

"What were they thinking that day when they told us that we were brother and sister?"

"Ah. You have me there, Carl. They both, of course, knew who your parents are and Alicia is, of course Susannah's mother but as to the father – I do believe at the time they both thought it was Arnold."

"Thought"

"'Thought', 'think' whatever."

"So that's a definite maybe to Susie's parentage." He tried to make a joke of it but her tone of reasonableness was beginning to get on his nerves.

"I think it's a little more than that."

"Please Maureen, what has Alicia told you? What does she know that she will not say? Will she talk to me? Will she tell me the truth?"

"Carl, the problem in all this is that she is very ill. She doesn't need all this history raked up, it will upset her far more than she can cope with at this time."

"I am trying to be bear that in mind but fuck it, this is our lives we are talking about. It is all in her past, but this is our future, mine and Susie's. We must know. She must tell us."

"You are already making decisions, Carl. You are already talking about 'us' and 'our' you've already decided you're part of her life and she's part of yours."

"Of course I have."

"Don't tread on too many dreams. Don't upset too many people, my boy. Wrong upon wrong, lie upon lie, they don't cancel each other out. If you do anything do it openly, do it without subterfuge, without causing any more pain."

"I've got to see her, talk to her, sort this mess out."

"Think carefully, you and she are not the only two involved in this. There's the husband, the children...."

"....who exist because of the lies that have been told."

"But they can't be proved to be lies. You can't prove any of this."

They sat for a few minutes, Carl trying to find an answer.

"Blood tests. We could have a paternity test done. We could check that way. Arnold and Susie can do blood tests – we would know then if they were related or not..."

"Unfortunately no, there is one thing I haven't told you."

"I don't think I'm going to like this am I?"

"I don't think you are. Arnold is dead. He died last June."

She went up to the bar for another drink while she let that

information sink in, but Carl had felt absolutely no emotion at being told his father was dead.

He had never felt Arnold's son, the years they all lived at Dunedin Avenue had been when he was growing up – his interests were Susie and his friends – not his family – and his mother had been so tied up with Arnold and the failure that he was coping with. The impact of his father's death was a practical not a sentimental one.

Maureen put the glasses down on the table and looked at Carl. He was very clear as he looked back at her.

"That's it then. No paternity test. No confirmation. No proof."

"No."

"Shit."

"I did warn you that answers to questions more often than not throw up more problems than they solve..."

"I know. But still shit."

"You could always forget her. Get on with your life."

He had to clear something up that had been niggling in the back of his mind.

"Will you tell me something, Maureen? How do you know so much about me, the family, the Peninsula thing? Just coming from the Wirral isn't enough." She sipped at her drink while deciding how to answer.

"You won't remember a man in your father's old office – not the factory, the lawyers in Liverpool – there is a man called Ted. He used to work for your father and he always had a special interest in the family. I never did understand exactly why, as he had many clients and there were other partners in the firm. I think it was probably that Arnold used to get him to do things that he should have done himself."

"Was he the one who used to drive Charles to school – the one who lost him in Anglesey that time?"

"Well he didn't exactly lose him – Charles gave him the slip – but yes that's the chap."

"He always used to turn up at odd times – tall, rather stuffy, big nose, nice face."

"That's him. Well he keeps in touch with me. I think he cares very much for Alicia. Sad really. He tells me what's going on with the people she used to care about and I, well I tell her the things I think she should know, the things that won't hurt her. She really has been very ill for a long time you know."

"Will you tell her about me?"

He waited a few moments for her answer. "Well, will you?"

"Do you want me to?"

Carl stayed at Phyl's that night. He was beginning to know so many important things, but he felt there was still so much more to learn.

On her next visit to Alicia Maureen decided to jump in with both feet.

"I've been seeing quite a lot of Carl these last few days."

"Kathleen's boy?"

"Yes, Arnold and Kathleen's boy."

"You said you had seen him. I'm not completely ga-ga you know. I do remember some things. But why should I care whether you've seen him or not?"

People moved around the ward, Maureen sat knitting by the bedside, waiting for Alicia's curiosity to force her to show an interest.

Eventually Alicia broke the silence "He must be quite grown up now. A man really."

"Indeed, and a very good looking one too. Clever, he got a First and is now going to do post grad at Cambridge."

"Don't tell me. History – the Tudors? Just like his father."

Maureen nodded her head "But not the Tudors, Wellington. But you're right when you see him you don't really need to guess at his paternity."

"I don't suppose many people did, it was so bloody obvious."

"Well, he seems to be a very nice boy – man."

"Does he look very like Arnold?"

She couldn't answer directly. "You can tell they're father and son, but he is somehow softer than Arnold. His long hair and dark tan make him different, but he has the eyes."

"Is there anything of Kathleen?"

"Probably not to look at, but definitely in the mind. He is a very intelligent boy, but also somehow far more clever than Arnold ever was – more practical. I think there really is a lot of her in him. He certainly inherited his conscience from her."

"Did she bring him up by her faith?"

"He hasn't said. I don't know. He certainly ran a mile when you dropped that bombshell on him about Susannah being his sister. He seems to want to do the right thing."

"Whatever that might be."

Alicia lay back on her pillows and wondered why people were always so desperate to 'do the right thing'. It didn't occur to her then to worry about how much her *not* 'doing the right thing' had affected that young man's life. Susannah had 'done the right thing' by marrying that boy and that had always looked like a disaster waiting to happen.

Maureen told her snippets of information about her family though how she knew Alicia had no idea. She told her that she was a grandmother and that Joe was doing well at work and Susannah seemed to be satisfied with her life as housewife and mother.

Alicia didn't believe a word of it.

She could not see how any child of hers would be happy with being a housewife – especially with that awful boy as a husband. She had seen neither Josie nor Jack Parry. She knew that Charles and Monika visited them, Monika looking after the children as she had done their mother. She knew that Arnold had recently died.

Other than the bare bones of 'hatches, matches and despatches' she had little knowledge of the goings on in her immediate family. She didn't really care. They hadn't been a family for the best part of twenty years.

"Do you want to meet him?"

The question surprised her "Why on earth would I want to do that?"

"He is an interesting young man and he wants to see you."

"What does he want to see me for?"

"I think he wants to find out a bit more about you, a bit more about himself. He knows he is living dangerously."

"I should coco! Oh hell, bring him along. What have I got to lose?"

Carl went to see Alicia the next day, he had been briefed by Maureen that he would find a very sick, very frail woman, she had warned him to be very careful.

It was unfortunate that as soon as he saw Alicia he saw Susie. He saw Susannah's face, he saw her vulnerability and he saw her smile. He had not seen his Susannah for over four years but he now saw her lying in the bed in front of him – this woman was Susannah, just a lot older.

Where Carl saw Susannah in Alicia, Alicia saw much of what had attracted her to Arnold all those years ago.

It occurred to her that she had also been in a hospital bed when she had first met Arnold. Maureen had been right. It was the eyes.

As Maureen watched the two beginning to get to know each other she was not at all sure she should have introduced them.

"When do you get out of here?"

"Soon, I hope."

"What are you going to do then?"

"I don't know."

"Who is going to look after you?"

"I don't know"

"You know very well, my dear" interrupted Maureen rather impatiently, "You are going home in a week or so and then Harry, Phyl and I will be looking after you, as we always do after your operations."

"I am always so grateful to you all but I really shouldn't put on you as much as I do?"

Alicia was very experienced at manipulating people's sympathy.

"Have there been many operations?" Carl knew nothing of this woman's life other than what he had overheard from his mother and Arnold where words such as 'lazy', 'bitch', 'never done a day's work in her life' 'good-for-nothing sponger" were the ones he remembered. He had never heard 'ill' 'cancer' 'operations'. Perhaps they had chosen not to know or, at least, if they had known they had chosen that no one else would.

"Yes, dear." Alicia had decided this young man was going to like her. "Yes, this is the seventh in seven years. I seem always to be in the hospital."

"Oh Alicia, don't be so dramatic." Maureen interrupted again. "It's true she's had seven operations, but several of them were quite minor, and she has usually been home in a week or so."

"Still that's a lot isn't it?"

"Now, that's enough about Alicia – tell her about you and what you are doing."

So the conversation went onto safer ground.

Carl told Alicia something about his life, the Forsters, the university, his summer in Spain. Alicia listened, observing closely the eyes, listening to the nuances of the voice, hypnotised by his youth and enthusiasm.

At the end of the hour Maureen and Carl got up to leave

"You will visit me again won't you?"

"You will be out of here very soon" Maureen replied before Carl could answer.

"Then you will visit me at home won't you – I would so love to hear more about your trip to Spain."

So throughout September Carl stayed with Maureen's daughter Phyl and visited Alicia, first at the hospital and then, after she had been discharged, at her home on Pilgrims Way.

When Phyl and Maureen drove the five miles up to the little house twice a day they did not take Carl, so it was quite a trip for him. He had to take two buses and what with the walks to and from the bus-stops it took him the best part of two hours. He didn't mind and he made the trip two or three times each week.

He enjoyed the time he spent with Alicia.

He was getting to know Susannah's mother, he was getting to be part of the family that had once almost been his.

Talking to Alicia he found himself remembering things about his stays at Millcourt, and found himself building up something of the history of his life – a life he had never had any previous inclination to remember. She was quite happy to tell him about those people and those places because it kept him with her – and she was beginning to want not to lose him.

The times he wasn't with her he spent in the library, reading – reminding himself of his real life.

It was a very comfortable few weeks but it was only a matter of time before Alicia asked him to stay overnight. It would save him the trip – he spent so much time with her anyway he might as well stay overnight especially as the evenings were getting shorter and the spare bedroom was always made up. It would be no trouble for her as he could help with food and drinks, and help her downstairs to the television.

On the first Saturday in November, he finally took his suitcase from Phyl's and paid her all he owed.

"Are you sure about this? We have loved having you here." Maureen had talked to her daughter about her concerns that Alicia and Carl were getting too close.

"Absolutely, I spend much of the time at Alicia's anyway – and she has invited me – it would be odd not to accept."

Alicia was getting better, able to get up every day, able to walk along the lane to the village shop and cook her staple diet of macaroni cheese. They came to an arrangement whereby Carl shopped and cooked every other day.

On Wednesday 29th November Carl took Alicia to London to celebrate her birthday.

He had asked here where she would like to go as a special treat 'money no object'. It was a target date for her to feel better by. She said "The Savoy" without really thinking about the cost or the history. It was certainly special and he had seemed to like the idea. Carl hired a car and drove up to town – they didn't want to worry about buses and trains. He chose something comfortable and luxurious.

It was nearly 10 years since she had been a regular visitor at The Savoy and she was happy to see that it hadn't changed. She imagined the concierge recognised her. She knew that she was older, gaunter, but she had always imagined her voice was unforgettable.

As she had been driven up those same roads she had travelled so many times on the bus it would have been difficult for her not to think of her trips to meet Max. She wondered how he was, what he would have thought of her today. She realised she hadn't thought of him for a very long time and would probably never see him again.

She wondered whether this trip would be so very different.

And there were distinct similarities. Carl had booked adjoining rooms, overlooking the river. It didn't occur to her to wonder how he could afford this as she took advantage of the wonderful bathroom and, sitting alone in one of the armchairs wrapped in the luxurious towelling robe, drank the champagne she had ordered from room service and looked out of the window at the lights glimmering on the Thames.

She took more care dressing than she had taken for a very long time.

She wore a dress that, although ten years old, at least two sizes too large and completely unfashionable, managed to convey a style which was timeless. She wore the long pearl drop earrings that she knew made her neck look like a giraffe's. She knew she looked good. She stood looking at her reflection in the full length mirror. "Not bad for 47 old girl".

They met, as arranged, in the American Bar. She got there a few minutes late to ensure her entrance was sufficiently dramatic. He had somehow organised a very stylish dinner jacket.

Alicia thoroughly approved of this young man. He had, she tried to think of the right words, presence, class, panache. Although his tan had faded he was striking enough to draw the admiring glances of most of the women – and some of the men – in the bar. She felt they made a fine couple.

Carl was an attentive host as he bought her cocktails and escorted her to the River Restaurant for dinner. As they sat down at a window table he voiced the question that had also been going through her head.

"What do you think people are thinking?"

"About us?"

"Of course."

"They are thinking how lucky I am to have such a handsome escort. Actually, they probably think you're my gigolo!"

"Even if they are they'll be thinking I struck lucky to be escorting such an attractive woman. Happy Birthday, Alicia. Many Happy Returns."

"Unlikely" was her rueful answer. She continued in lighter vein "One night I was staying here, some years ago, and I couldn't sleep, so I crept down to this room, and sat – just over there – and looked out over the river. It must have been 3 or 4 o'clock in the morning. I'd just slipped a shirt on and was woefully underdressed, barely decent really. So I sat there, in the quiet, and wondered about my life and what I was doing and whether what I was doing was right – you don't need to know the details. And in came a waiter, completely dressed as he would have been for dinner hours earlier, a white napkin over his forearm. He asked if I was a guest with them and I replied that I was. He asked if there was anything he could do for me. I said a jug of orange juice would be wonderful and so he brought me one – a full jug of freshly squeezed orange juice, a bowl of ice, a glass, a long silver spoon – all on a silver salver and asked if I wanted him to pour or whether to leave it. He never asked me for my room number or name or anything. It was wonderful. Just perfect."

After their comfortable and companionable dinner they went upstairs to her suite.

They sat looking out over London, finishing the champagne, sipping the coffee in silence as they each thought about the evening, enjoying the feeling of having eaten and drunk very well, not too much – just very well.

She stood up and looked out of the window at the lights playing on the river.

"Do you know *Bitter Sweet*?" she asked, rather wistfully.

"A film?"

"No, silly, the musical play."

"I've heard of it, of course. I don't know anything about it. Why?"

"It meant a lot to me years ago. Without it my life would have been very different. "

Alicia then began to softly sing Noel Coward's words,

I'll see you again,
whenever Spring breaks through again,
Time may lie heavy between
but what has been, is past forgetting

She stopped singing and held out her arms to him "Will you dance with me?"

He stood up and held her lightly around the waist, her hand resting on his shoulder. She began to sing again quietly.

This sweet memory
Across the years will come to me
Tho' my world may go awry
In my heart will ever lie
Just the echo of a sigh
Goodbye

"I sang that song on the stage, many years ago."

He hardly heard her ask "Would you like to take me to bed?" as she turned away from him to pour the last of the champagne into his glass. He didn't have time to answer as she continued as if she had said nothing.

"I was Sarah and I sang it with my husband whose name was Carl. Sarah and Carl were made for each other but they didn't spend much time together before tragedy intervened. That's quite ironic isn't it?"

She could be very persuasive.

So he did as she asked.

As he rang for the butler to bring them early morning tea she started to laugh quietly.

He didn't want to ask her what was so funny as he didn't want to appear as unsure of himself as he felt. He had been in this "morning after" situation before, but that not many times – and certainly not with someone he knew he really shouldn't have slept with.

Perhaps he should have thought more about this trip – he had just wanted to give her a memorable birthday.

"What's so funny?"

"Oh darling, not you, not you."

She had not called him 'darling' before and he didn't like it. It was too equal in a condescending sort of way.

"What then?"

"You know what yesterday was don't you?"

"Your birthday of course."

"No it is also my wedding anniversary. It would have been 26 years. That makes me feel very old."

"It makes me feel very young."

"I'll take this with me and have a bit of a soak darling." Alicia excused herself, picked up her teacup and walked through to the bathroom. As she closed the door firmly behind her Carl thought that they had both come to the same conclusion.

There would never be a repeat of last night.

On the drive back Carl said he had to leave. He had to get back to the Forsters, he had not seen them since before he went to Spain and then only for a short time. He really had been very rude, he said, and he must make up for it before the house became chaos for Christmas.

He had wanted to give her a wonderful birthday present, one that she would always remember him by, but he really had to move on. She was so much better now, she could manage much better on her own. There was no need for him to stay, invading her space.

"Of course, darling. You must go back to your home."

He wished she would not keep calling him 'darling'. It wasn't just that the night had been a mistake and that he had serious regrets about it – it was that he hated the word. He found the word offensive, it was so false – as if someone couldn't really be bothered to find a more personal term of endearment. It reminded him of his mother, calling Arnold – he still couldn't think of Arnold as his father – 'darling'. It hadn't seemed like she meant it as a sign of love either.

As they drove through the woods on top of the Downs, nearing the end of the journey, Alicia finally asked the question she had been wanting to ask since Carl had first visited her at the hospital, nearly three months earlier.

"Now that you're going I do need to know something. Why did you want to meet me? I mean, in the first place. Why did you go to all that trouble to find me? There must have been a reason."

"Of course there was. But I didn't realise you were so ill. You needed looking after."

"and you got to like me too I hope."

"Of course I did. Do." He corrected himself quickly – but she had noticed.

"Well, are you going to ask me the vital question or not?"

"What makes you think there is a 'vital question'?"

"Stop beating around the bush Carl. I think we both know what it is don't we? Let me do it for you."

She continued, sounding so much harder than she had the previous night "You are still, have always been, in love with my daughter. You were devastated when you found out she was your sister and you have been completely lost ever since. You have worked hard and studied well but emotionally you are lost. She is your soul mate – or so you firmly believe – and so you have come to me to beg me to say that she is not your sister. Am I right?"

"Not exactly." He stopped the car in the lay-by. He did not want to drive when such things were being spoken of – and perhaps he would be able to live more comfortably with the events of the previous night if he had some answers. "Not exactly." He repeated. "Part of what you say is absolutely right but I have not come to beg you to say something that isn't true. I came to ask you if there is any way Arnold is not her father. I mean, I know he was your husband and everything." He was beginning to get flustered as he realised the enormity of the accusation he was about to make.

"Yes, Carl, he was my husband."

Having led him into the situation where he had to ask her intrusive, and probably offensive, questions she was not going to make it easy for him.

He drew breath. He had come so far he just had to do it now. "I know he was your husband but is there any chance he would not be Susannah's father? I mean..."

"I know what you mean Carl." She admired his bravery. Not many young men would have the courage to ask what he was asking." She was not going to let him off lightly "Especially in these circumstances."

She tried to catch his eye, but he was avoiding her.

"You are asking me if I was unfaithful to my husband, whether I had an affair, that someone else – an unknown man – could be Susannah's father. Well the simple answer is that I was never unfaithful to my husband. I never had affairs whilst I was living with him. Certainly not until several years after Susannah was born."

"Oh. I had always....." his voice tailed off, his disappointment palpable.

"You had always hoped that I was as faithless and disloyal to him as my husband had been to me? He had affairs, I know, and your mother was certainly not his only mistress. Oh yes, for that was what she was, his mistress – for many, many years – certainly since before the war. No. Don't interrupt. Your mother, Kathleen, had been kept by your father as his mistress for several years before she married Henry. Arnold's father had kept Kathleen's mother so it kept it all in the family. Interesting don't you think?" She said this as if it had only just occurred to her.

"They wouldn't have cared if you were sleeping with Susannah, if you were sleeping with your sister, they'd been sleeping with each other for years. Incest was perfectly normal for them.

"It never made the slightest jot of difference to either of them. As soon as they both got back from the war they were at it again. They had no shame, they had no consideration of my feelings. They couldn't care less what anyone thought – and then she was pregnant. God knows how they got Henry to marry her, she didn't care a fig for him and he probably knew it. Anyway marry him she did."

She paused slightly, she had the opportunity to stop there, but she was watching his face – there was no judgement in it, simply shock and pain.

If she went on she would tell him everything and he would have to live with that for the rest of his life.

She continued.

She was enjoying the power that knowledge gave her and the pain it was causing. She wanted to shock this young man who sat next to her in the car in the lay-by in front of the church. She wanted to make him hurt as she had been hurt by her lost opportunities, her lost talents, the battle she was now losing against her body.

But she knew herself well enough to know that this wasn't about Carl, the last few weeks, and especially last night. This was about Arnold. She wanted to hurt Arnold one last time now it was too late. She wanted to hurt the man who had ruined her life, the man who this young man was so like in so many ways.

She had made love the night before to the Arnold she had hoped Arnold would have been.

Once he was committed and his objections had been overruled Carl had been gentle, sensitive and thoughtful in his love-making. She knew she would never make love ever again as her body's weaknesses increasingly defeated her.

She felt that the last time a person made love was as important as the first.

Arnold could have been like this she had thought over and over as his son had made love to her.

It was only months later that she was able to justify her actions to herself in these terms. At the time she didn't think of the implications or of the effects her words would have on the lives of others. At that time she had just wanted him to hurt as much as she did.

"We went away for Christmas that year just the four of us. It was engineered completely so that Kathleen and Arnold could be together. Henry and I were observers only."

He thought he knew where this was leading, it was somewhere he had been with Maureen. Maureen had been right.

"So Henry was Susannah's father."

"Yes. Henry was Susannah's father."

She was not going to let him off without knowing the whole truth.

"He raped me. Henry came to my room and raped me. It took only a few seconds. Not enough time to create a life, but it did. Susannah is the child of rape. Unloved and unwanted from the moment she was conceived. Born with the very few good features of her father and the very many bad ones of her mother she never had a chance."

She then proceeded to tell Carl exactly what had happened that night, exactly why she had not shared a bed with her husband for years.

"It's ironic isn't it, darling" she continued as Carl tried to find some response – any response "you were born effectively a bastard, your parents were brother and sister though you were conceived in what I suppose must have been love of a sort. And then your Susannah was born in wedlock but out of hatred and malice, unwanted, unloved by her mother, unknown to her father, despised by everyone, except you. I suppose that makes you a couple worthy of each other."

"Fuck you," was all he could say when she eventually stopped.

"Very apt," she said dryly.

"This is not a fucking joke." He had snapped. He wanted to hit her. Hard. He really wanted to slap her across the face. He had never been violent, never ever wanted to hurt anyone but he wanted to hurt this woman now. Why was she telling him all this stuff if she didn't want to hurt him too.

Carl, who had been experiencing so many emotions – pain, sorrow, regret, embarrassment – as Alicia had told her story, had reached anger. It was not an emotion he was familiar with. He had never learned to deal with it. He so rarely lost his temper. He couldn't remember when he last shouted at anyone.

But now he was very angry.

He spoke slowly at first, deliberately spacing his words, making sure he found the right ones. As he spoke his anger rose and he just said whatever came into his head.

"You all fucking knew. When you separated Susannah and me you all fucking knew. Why? Why did you do it? What did you hope to gain? You are all so fucking selfish. You were only concerned with yourselves. You've only ever cared about yourselves. The children – us – your children – Charles and Susie and me – we just happened to be there. That was just so fucking unfortunate for you all wasn't it? You couldn't carry on with your stupid fucking little mind games. You had no fucking responsibility for us. You handed us over to other people because we all got in your fucking way. You are all shits, fucking shits – I can't think of words bad enough for what I think about you. Anything I called you would be too bland. You all *knew* all of this and you couldn't fucking well bring yourselves to ease anyone else's pain and hurt because it would mean you would all have to admit what utter shits you've been all your lives. You probably didn't care how much you hurt anyone as long as you were OK. You and your precious fucking lives. What about us? What about *our* lives? I don't care *why* you did it. You *did* it."

She slapped him as hard as she could across the face.

"Stop it. Carl. Stop it. You're acting and talking like a little boy."

"A little boy! You have just told me that my life, Susie's life, they're all built on absolutely fucking nothing! You tell me my parents were brother and sister! You tell me that your utter god-awful selfishness and your fucking lies are fine because you were *all* doing it. You were *all* lying. You have all always lied. And *you* call *me* a 'little boy!'"

He grabbed the car keys from the ignition and, slamming the car door behind him, practically ran into the churchyard, sitting down on a tomb as soon as he was out of sight of the car.

He had not thought that knowing Susie was not his sister could possibly cause him so much agony. The joy of knowing that they could have been, could be, together was completely lost in the knowledge that, because of this woman's lies it was all too late.

He couldn't marry Susie.

He couldn't marry anyone.

He could never have children of his own.

His parents were brother and sister.

He sat there trying not to think what might have been, if only that bitch hadn't lied.

And he had slept with her!

He not only hated his mother, his father, Henry and that woman, he hated himself.

It took a while, but he did eventually pull himself together. He did get himself back under control and went back to the car, where she was still waiting.

He drove her back to her house, he packed his things and put them in the back of the car. He was leaving and he would never see her again. If she said something like 'don't think too badly of me' he probably would have hit her so it was lucky she didn't say a word as he piled his things into a case and a rucksack and left – not even 'goodbye' or 'thank you'.

He took the car back to the garage, walked to the station and caught the first train to London.

As he sat in the empty carriage, going home, he cried for everything he had lost.

He was embarrassed by his emotional response. He wished he hadn't said some of the things he had said. She was right, he had been childish, he realised his vocabulary had been limited – what a pity there weren't enough words for 'fuck' when you were angry. She was absolutely right he had reacted badly.

But he knew he had had every right to.

He went back to the Forsters and over the next few days spent many hours in his room, reading, trying to study, trying to take control of his life again. Pat and Jeff didn't press him for explanations, they didn't ask any difficult questions.

They just let him find himself again. They knew he would start being Carl again when he was ready.

He kept thinking how much he wished she had not told him. But he had wanted to know. It was just that truth didn't stop where he had wanted it to and he now had all sorts of knowledge that he really didn't want. He could have gone through life never knowing, possibly eventually marrying and having children.

Maureen had known. She must have known. She had hinted that the truth would be too much. They had both asked him whether he really wanted to know.

He had always understood knowledge to be a good thing, the only bad thing about knowledge was not having it. He now knew that that was not always the case.

Not only had he lost Susannah, he had lost his future. He couldn't marry now. He couldn't have children. He would be the *no issue* on the family tree. His genes wouldn't go on down through the generations to come.

He was the end of the line.

Chapter Twenty-Eight

Maureen rang me on Remembrance Sunday, after the Cenotaph ceremony had finished on the television. It was unusual for her to call.

"Ted, I'm worried. That woman is predatory. She has absolutely no scruples. She will do exactly what she wants regardless of how many people she hurts."

"What are you afraid of?"

"They don't seem to have a.." she fought for the right words and ended lamely "mother-son relationship."

"You're not suggesting they're sleeping together?" It should have been a completely unnecessary question, but the more I thought about it the more it seemed a very real threat.

"That's exactly what I *am* suggesting." Maureen was firm "and I'm very much regretting ever having put the two together. Think about it Ted, she's vulnerable he's caring; she's so like Susannah – the girl he believes is the love of his life; and he's very like the nicer bits of Arnold, not to mention very good looking, young and probably very virile."

"But she's nearly 50 and he's what.... just 21?"

"She's 46. And this is 1967. Stranger things happen – just read your newspapers."

"What do you want me to do? Is there anything I can do?"

"God knows Ted. I haven't a clue. Do we have to do anything? Even if they are" she hesitated before speaking the words as if speaking them made the fact more likely "sleeping together or whatever the current euphemism is. Is that so very wrong? I really don't know. Sometimes I think it is the worst thing that could possibly happen and then I think 'why ever not?' If he was 46 and she was 21 no one would bat an eyelid."

"It's not just the age gap though, is it? They're practically family."

"But they aren't family are they? They're absolutely no relation to each other whatsoever. They have not lived in the same house together – she's not his step-mother or anything, they've probably only met twice – if that – before last month. There is no reason to object. No real reason."

"Of course there's a reason. There must be hundreds of reasons."

"Name three"

"Sorry, Maureen, put like that I can't. But both you and I have the gut feeling that it is completely unacceptable. We can't both be wrong."

"Let's hope that if there is anything between them it's only sex. They'd soon get that out of their systems."

I tried not to be shocked. Or jealous.

"Keep an eye on it Maureen, if you think there is anything I can do I will come down – of course I will. But you know you can always call me – just to talk if you need to. We both care for Alicia too much to let her make a complete fool of herself."

"Yes, Ted, we both do don't we."

In early December I had another letter from Maureen.

Alicia had told her what turned out to be a very edited version of her birthday trip, but did admit to telling Carl his and Susannah's true parentage and worse, something of the circumstances.

Maureen wrote in no uncertain terms that she thought Carl was a loose cannon – she didn't know him well enough to be able to guess what his reactions might be. She couldn't contact the Forsters but she knew I could.

Someone had to make sure the boy was all right despite the revelations that had been sprung on him.

I would have to get involved.

And so on the next of my monthly trips to London I visited the Forsters in Dulwich.

They made me very welcome. We had a lovely informal meal with Pat and Jeff reminding me of our brief meeting four years or so earlier, when I had worried about the arrangements after Carl's precipitous departure from his parents' home. We all decided it had worked out well. They asked about the circumstances of Arnold's death and I briefly described the quiet funeral and Kathleen's quiet life. "Carl will always be welcome here, you must tell his mother that he always has a home with us."

But the whole meal was not taken up with sadness, much of the conversation around that table was light hearted and Carl seemed completely at ease. I understood in that one evening how much better Carl was as a person because of his time with the Forsters than if he had been exposed to the politics and darkness of life with Kathleen and Arnold. This Carl was adult, relaxed and polite, showing no sign of the trauma or imminent breakdown I had feared.

After dinner the Forsters left us alone to talk and I soon realised, when we turned to the subject of Alicia and Susannah, that he was under control.

It was a talk where we had slightly different agendas.

He wanted to know if what Alicia had said about Susie's father was actually true or whether it had all been a rather dramatic figment of her imagination. I had to confirm that it was, as far as I could tell him, indeed true.

I had to agree that all four parents in this imbroglio had behaved very badly. I had to agree I had known since Susannah's wedding, though of course, by then, it was too late to do anything.

It upset him to hear the words, but once spoken he wanted to know all about it and about Joe and the children. I needed to know if there was any way he felt the need to tell Susannah what he had found out. I told him I hoped he would do nothing rash.

It was obvious he still cared for her a great deal. I knew that values were changing, that many young people are fickle and change their allegiances and loves like changing clothes but in those few minutes with Carl I realised he was different.

He was one of those rather old-fashioned, rare, possibly unlucky, people who once they give their hearts to someone never, ever, take them away.

It was a characteristic I recognised.

He mentioned nothing about any relationship between his mother and his father. If he had done I would not have been able to confirm or deny anything other than the fact that Arnold's father knew Kathleen's mother and that some people thought it a distinct possibility. Nothing, of course, could ever be proved.

I felt I needed to tell him something I did know to be true that he didn't know, to clear the air completely, so I told him about Maureen.

I told him how Maureen and I had written to each other over the years, because she had been a good friend of Alicia's when they had both lived in the Wirral. That she had an interest in what the family was up to. I told him that I had never broken confidences, merely sending her copies of newspapers and short notes to keep her informed. When he asked me why she would be so interested in them I had to tell him. She had taken such an interest in him because she was Kathleen's eldest sister.

She was his aunt.

I think of all the things I said that evening that was the one that made him feel most betrayed.

He was quiet for a short time, peering into the fire that was beginning to die down in the grate. "Why did she play such a game? Why didn't she say? She did seem to know a lot about us. She seemed so nice. Why didn't she say?"

"That I cannot answer, I believe she wanted to keep that up her sleeve, you see Alicia has never known that her best friend over the years is the sister of the woman she most dislikes, her husband's mistress and second wife. How do you think she would you feel if she knew that?"

He sat there staring at the dying flames. He seemed so sad I wondered whether I should have told him.

"I still love her you know." He said, almost to himself. "I can't change that. I need to know she's happy. I can't just forget her. I need to look after her, know she's OK, even if I can't do anything about it."

I thought he was going to say more but he didn't.

I was just about to leave, we were all in their large hall saying "goodbye" and "thank you" and "lovely to meet you again after all these years" when the phone rang.

It was Maureen, Alicia had been rushed to hospital haemorrhaging. They were transferring her to a hospital in London as it was very serious, could we go to her there. She was very ill, time may be very short.

I said there was no need for Carl to go, though he didn't appear to want to anyway.

And so I became more closely involved in Alicia's life.

She was in hospital for some time and I visited her on my monthly trips to London. After she was discharged I arranged for her to have a full time nurse living in with her so she could go back to her 'little house'. I visited her there many times, month after month.

I had always known her to be a fascinating woman; but now I got to know the true depths of her vulnerability, intelligence and wit. She seemed to want to talk about old times, she told me many things I didn't know and some I didn't particularly want to know.

Our talks answered many of the questions I had had from seeing the Donaldson and the Witherby families from the outside. I was able to tell her some things she didn't know – about Charles' escapade when I had been taking him back to school. She was able to tell me about her history, her family, why she had married Arnold in the first place and how the convoluted parenting had really happened.

I had, and still have, no reason to believe she told me anything but the truth.

I don't think she knew that my visits were the highlight of my life. They were days I looked forward to all the time I was away, and how much I loved heading off into Surrey those Thursday afternoons each month.

Initially it was the nurse who made the tea and set everything out for my visits, Alicia was far too ill. Then she was up and about – I suspected especially for my visits – in the early days of the spring of 1968. Then we would sit out in the garden, the nurse enjoyed gardening and kept the small area neat and tidy.

As the months passed I kept her up to date with family events, another grandson, Al, born on 8th June 1968. "Do you think they called him after me?" she had asked rather wistfully. I said "yes", though I didn't think for a minute that they had. Joe had had an uncle Alfred who, I think, had died during the war.

On July 4th 1969 news of another grandson – Bill. I had not told Alicia of Susannah's pregnancy, aware that she would think it was far too soon, but I had to tell her after the boy was born. She didn't dwell on it, simply changing the subject to current affairs. Another topic we covered over the long hours of our conversations.

On one visit, June 4th 1970, she met me at the door and completely without preamble told me the news I had been dreading. "The doctors have finally decided they can't do anything. They've given me six months at most." I had dreaded the words, but it wasn't that much of a surprise, anyone who saw her could see she was losing the battle with the cancers inside her.

"Are they sure?"

"I'm afraid so. It's all moved from those bits to those bits." She waved her arms vaguely across her body.

I had known what I would do when the time came.

"Right then, we have to sort out the rest of your life."

"I knew you would be practical. No one else would be able to help."

"I'm always here at your service." I tried to sound light hearted and chivalrous – I fear I just sounded flippant.

"I know, Ted, you have always been a good friend to me – God knows my only real friend."

"What do you want to do with this time that you know you've been given?" I leant forward and put her hands between mine. I don't think I had touched her in this personal way before.

"I don't want to be alone, Ted, I've never been very good at being alone."

I squeezed her hand "You told me that once before, you won't remember, when you got back from Switzerland. I promise you you'll only be alone when and if you want to be. Anything else?"

She thought for a while.

"I would like to see Charles. I want to know how he's turned out. Whether there is anything of me heading off into the hereafter. It's the only 'life after death' I can believe in."

"What of your daughter, your grand-children?"

"No. No need to see them. There's nothing of me in Susannah."

So later that month I packed Alicia into my car, specially driven down for the day. I couldn't help remembering driving her to the hospital when she was having Susannah, and the other times I had ferried her between Hoylake and Liverpool. I knew her so much better now.

She didn't bring much luggage.

She sat almost silent in the passenger seat next to me as I settled in to drive the 200 odd miles back to the Wirral.

I had loved this woman who sat to my left, looking out of the window as we drove, for so long. She had prevented me from loving any other woman, and yet she had no idea what she had done to me and my life.

She simply had no idea.

The traffic was light – there was a general election. Polling Station signs littered the towns and villages as they passed. We talked of politics, how in the old days she would have been so involved – what Arnold would have thought of the unfolding events.

We had decided that, for as long as she could, Alicia was going to stay with me. I had a large flat, plenty of room – she would have her own bathroom and sitting room.

I wondered what she would say when she saw my new arrangements.

She had never asked where I lived now my mother was dead, she had never asked and I had never told her. As we drove northwards I couldn't find the words to warn her and so left the words unsaid. She would find out soon enough.

There were motorways open now, there was no need to follow the A1 up through Dunstable and Atherstone, past Birmingham and along the wonderful long straight road built by the Romans up through the forest until the right turn to Brownhills and Newport.

But I drove the old road anyway.

231

This would be Alicia's last drive through the heartland of England. She would never see these fields, these towns and villages again. She had made the trip north many times as new wife and reluctant mother, now she was making it for the last time. We both knew it but, of course, neither of us said anything.

As we approached home, driving northwards up the Wirral, through the sandstone cutting of Thurstaston and down past the cricket pitch and the open fields towards West Kirby.

"Shit."

"Pardon?"

"Sorry, I was just remembering those long summer afternoons, watching the cricket, scoring matches at that ground. It all seems so very long ago."

"So you did have good times?"

"Yes. However much I would love to say 'no' I must admit there were good times. It couldn't have been all bad could it?"

"No. There are always good things to be remembered."

As we drove we reminded each other of cricket matches and the other times we had been together. Our lives had overlapped for so many years.

As we came into West Kirby, she asked me to stop the car at the top of Grange Hill.

"I love that view. The view over the Dee and Hilbre to Wales, I gave birth looking at that view – Susannah it would have been. I can't remember having Charles. Perhaps I ought to see her. None of it was her fault really, was it? None of it was any of their faults, not Susannah nor Charles nor Carl. It was us wasn't it?"

I didn't, I couldn't, answer.

I drove on, down the hill, past the station – all the places she had been familiar with and which were now bringing so many memories back to her. I turned into the drive.

"What the hell are we doing here?" She sounded surprised

We were pulling up outside Millcourt.

"They divided it into flats a couple of years back – I'm afraid I couldn't resist it. My rooms are on the second floor – where the nursery used to be. I have a lovely view out over the golf course. I'm sorry I hadn't told you. I thought you might find it a little – well – morbid."

"Oh Ted! It's absolutely wonderful. Perfect! Oh how fantastic! I'm going to die here at Millcourt!"

She actually seemed amused by it all.

She walked through the door – the same front door as had been her own – and she tried to see the house as it had been. The partitions made it almost unrecognisable. I helped her up the stairs – surely not the old staircase – until there was another door – the entrance to my flat.

This had been the nursery suite.

She tried to work out the rooms as they would have been when she left, when Charles and Susannah had been so ill, where had Nanny slept? Where had the cots and the beds been? As we walked though what was now a well proportioned and spacious three-bedroomed flat she knew exactly what the rooms had been.

In another life.

She sat down in the window seat of what was now the lounge, which had been the old playroom, and looked out over the garden to the golf course and the dunes beyond.

So many things had changed. So many things had stayed the same. So many things looked the same from the outside but on the inside had changed utterly and completely.

She soon settled into a routine, sleeping late, the nurse I had engaged getting her up just before lunchtime, eating, resting and getting dressed ready for my return from the office at around 6pm.

We would have drinks in the small sitting room, immediately above Arnold's old library, and eat supper, either on trays or in the small dining room, which had been Monika's room adjacent to the kitchen.

"Very different from the old days?" I ventured after Alicia had been there a week.

"Indeed."

"How are you, my dear? Settling in?" We were very comfortable together.

"You are very kind. I feel well looked after."

"I will be going out on Saturday."

She didn't say anything so I continued. "You aren't asking me where I am going?"

"That is none of my business."

"But it is. It is your youngest grandson's first birthday party."

"Oh." That seemed to shock her. "You're invited?"

"I am, I am often a guest in Susannah's house, I normally get invited to the children's birthdays – I think Joe thinks it is a way of tying himself into the future of the firm and I try to go when I can to keep an eye on them."

"Of course, he works for you doesn't he?"

"Yes. And he sees me as an integral connection with the Donaldson family."

"Is he that cold blooded?"

"Yes. I'm afraid he is. He's clever, don't get me wrong, he's taken and passed all the relevant exams with flying colours and has established himself in the office as an extremely useful voice of what people are really like. You can imagine that we were rather staffed with the 'old school' well Joe is definitely 'new school' he sees the way people think in far clearer perspective than we old fogies do. He is making himself quite indispensable."

"You sound bitter."

"I don't mean to. In many ways he is a very useful young man, working and trying hard. I just can't trust him. Sometimes he's just a bit too good to be true."

"Is Susannah happy?"

"As far as I know, yes. She's always very supportive of him"

"And he of her?"

"Not so obviously."

"Tell me about it all when you get back. They don't know I am up here do they?"

"No. I haven't told them. We need to wait until you are well enough to visit on your terms."

So I went to Bill's first birthday party.

Two days later I took Susannah to lunch.

Two days after that Susannah had her termination.

What was I to say to Alicia? What could I say?

I said nothing.

Chapter Twenty-Nine

Charles' surprisingly successful booklets about the bird life of the estuary had given him a career. He had sighted some rare species and had hopes of others. He had a recorded spotting of a Great Snipe in October 1957 and it was that that had sparked his interest in birds. He really wanted to see a gull-billed tern, an ambition finally fulfilled one hot August day 19 years later. His bird reports had a good following and he got a spot in the local newspapers. He was becoming quite well known and in early 1968 he had been asked to record a programme for the BBC. His gentleness and complete lack of ostentation made him an instant hit with listeners and by 1970 he was a regular contributor to many BBC nature programmes – on radio and television.

One of the regional newspapers had arranged a day of seminars to be held early in July 1970 to be given by local academics – not just people from the university but people who had links with the area from a wide variety of backgrounds and covering a wide variety of fields. Amongst those invited to give talks at the Liverpool Philharmonic Hall were two young men both making their reputations on radio and television, Charles Donaldson, local ornithologist and Carl Witherby, originally from the Wirral but now an increasingly popular national television historian.

By lunchtime on July 7th Charles had given his talk and was waiting for a taxi in the foyer. Carl, sitting next to him, was deciding whether to go straight back down south or spend some time with the Forsters, who were now living back in the Wirral. The two men were both reading The Guardian and had cast no more than a casual glance at each other.

They hadn't recognised each other. Why would they? It had been a long time.

"Carl, are you OK? Do you need anything?" Amanda, a secretary at the paper was making sure one of the guests assigned to her was comfortable. She noticed the man sitting next to him "Ah Charles. Have you two met? Carl this is Charles Donaldson, the ornithologist. He's been giving one of his wonderful talks on the recent rare bird sightings on Hilbre Island. Charles – this is Carl Witherby, you know the budding young historian, he's ..."

Carl interrupted her "Hello Charles"

"Carl. 'Long time no see' as they say."

"You *know* each other – how marvellous!"

"Not necessarily. Is it marvellous Charles? How long's it been?"

"The Winter Gardens, May 1963"

"Saturday May 18th 1963 at about 10 o'clock in the evening to be precise."

Amanda was beginning to realise there were some serious undertones to this conversation and she was out of her depth. It was not just a fortuitous meeting between old friends.

"I don't suppose you are going to forget that."

"No I don't suppose I ever will."

"Come on you two" Amanda tried to ease the tension "whatever it was it was a long time ago – you must both have been children then – come on let's all go for a drink. It's still early but I think you both need a drink – I know I do!"

"Yes, why don't we Carl – we've a lot of catching up to do."

There was quiet reluctance in Carl's voice as he agreed. "I suppose we have to start somewhere."

So Amanda shepherded the two to the pub over the road and bought the first round of drinks.

By the second round the older man had relaxed. He was confident in his life, 'content' as Max would say, but unused to beer at lunchtime.

"You won't believe this," he turned to Amanda

"No, Charles." There was warning in Carl's tone but Charles continued regardless.

"Carl and I are brothers."

Amanda showed shock and delight all in one movement.

"How *fantastic*! That's absolutely *fab*!"

"Half brothers. We aren't brothers – only half brothers – we share – if that's the right word – a father." Carl tried to correct things.

"So it's *complicated*." Amanda said slowly, "*Wonderful*! What a *fab* story!"

"No!" they both shouted at the same moment. That probably broke the ice between them. They had a mutual cause now, they were on the same side against Amanda.

She looked from one to the other. Charles the older was traditionally dressed in suit and paisley tie whereas Carl wore jeans with a black polo neck sweater and a leather jacket. Charles' hair was cut short, a traditional short back and sides where Carl's long hair was tied back in a pony tail. But there was a real similarity between them. Their hair was the same dark brown, their eyes the same deep blue.

She decided to leave them to it.

"Don't go." Charles put his hand out as Carl got up to leave with Amanda. "Stay. Let's talk."

It took a few moments to confirm after Amanda had gone, but they both knew Carl would stay.

"You still live in Hoylake?"

"Yes I do, still, funnily enough, still at Sandhey. And you?"

"Cambridge, just outside actually. It's not so easy a drive. I'm staying at the Adelphi. Should we go back there, have something to eat? I think perhaps we need to talk. Maybe we've met like this for a reason."

Carl wanted to find out about Susannah, he needed to know how she was as he hadn't heard any news for a couple of years, since his autumn in Bookham. Charles's motives were rather less clear. Perhaps he was just curious, perhaps he wanted to try to sort things out, perhaps he felt responsible.

As they got back to the hotel Charles saw a young woman leaving the hotel with a man he recognised. He didn't say anything. He couldn't think of any good reason why she would be in Liverpool on a Tuesday lunchtime.

After they had ordered their meals Charles opened the conversation.

"Did you marry?"

"No. Far too young yet."

"What you mean is no one came close to Susannah."

"No one came close to Susannah." He agreed flatly. "How is she?" No point in hedging around the subject.

"Difficult to say." No point in being dishonest.

"When did you last see her?"

"The day before yesterday actually, it was her youngest's first birthday. They had a small party."

"Her youngest? How many children has she got?"

"Four."

"Shit."

Charles deliberately misunderstood "Yes, that's what we all think actually. He *is* a bit of a shit."

"That's not what I meant and you know it. But is he?"

"Absolutely. Did you hear how they got together?"

"No – just that they did, and it must have been bloody soon after I had – gone"

As they ate their meal Charles told Carl details that he had not known. It hurt, but he had imagined things far worse.

"How are they? I mean are they happy?"

"No. Sorry, I'd love to say they are but it's pretty obvious they aren't – at least Susannah isn't – Joe's as happy as a sand boy. He's got absolutely everything he could want – a wife, children, a home and a job – none of which he could possibly have had if he hadn't got Susannah pregnant. No he's fine and dandy, it's Susannah we're all worried about."

"Worried about?"

Charles told him about the birthday party and the tensions and something of Susannah's obvious pain and loneliness.

"Why haven't you done anything about it? Why haven't you got her away from him? Why have you all just sat there and make her put up with it? I can't believe you've just left her to it!"

"We didn't do anything because, until last Saturday, we had no idea how bad it was. She has always, always, put on a brave face."

"For Christ's sake Charles, couldn't you stop him or something? Four children and she's not 24 yet!"

"It was her decision."

"No. It was not. It was her family's. It was yours and mine and Arnold's and Kathleen's, and yes, and Alicia's – the only person who has had no say in it at all is her. Christ what was she when she married? 16? 17? They all – you all – we all should have known better."

People were looking at them.

Charles tried to calm him down so he changed the subject by asking Carl what he had been 'up to' in the intervening years and was rewarded by a brief summary of life with the Forsters, his degree years in Sussex, his lecturing at Cambridge. Carl ended up thoughtfully. "Funny that – us both writing books and being on the radio."

"Perhaps there's more to this 'inheritance over environment' stuff than meets the eye!"

They relaxed again as the coffee was poured.

"I met your mother you know." Carl decided to stray onto dangerous territory.

"Oh yes? When? What was she up to?"

He didn't answer directly "In Leatherhead, I went travelling after finals, to Spain, and when I got back I decided I would find her to check that Susie really was my sister. Silly really. Anyway I did find her eventually.

"And...."

"And she told me that Susie and I don't share one parent, let alone two. After all that shit and bollocks we aren't related at all."

"What?" Charles was clearly stunned.

"You don't know?"

"Absolutely not! She must be your sister – you're definitely my brother, Arnold's son, aren't you?"

"In a nutshell then – my parents are Kathleen and Arnold. Susannah's parents are Alicia and Henry."

That was greeted by the shocked silence Carl had hoped for when he had dreamed of telling someone in the family the truths he had known since that dreadful trip to London on Alicia's birthday nearly three years earlier.

"How the hell?"

"To cut a long, and not very pretty, story short Henry raped Alicia when his wife, Kathleen, was carrying Arnold's child – me."

He fleshed out some of the details – he had forgotten nothing that Alicia had said to him but he was definitely not going to tell Charles everything. The restaurant was emptying – they were alone.

"God almighty! I knew they were all a bunch of selfish shits but I didn't realise..."

"Anyway – the day after you saw Susie and me in that bloody cinema Kathleen and Arnold rang Alicia. I don't think they knew who Susie's father really was – I think they thought she had sex with both of them."

"Good God!"

"Anyway they phoned Alicia. Who lied. She said Arnold was Susannah's father. She lied quite deliberately."

"And because of that lie Susannah married Joe, you went off to god-knows-where and nobody lived happily ever after."

"Pretty much."

"Shit."

"Yes, she was wasn't she?" It was Carl's turn to deliberately misunderstand.

"Well what are we going to do about it?"

"Nothing. Absolutely fucking nothing. We can do absolutely fucking nothing to put past wrongs right."

"I suppose she needs to know but it can't help her now."

"Well, Arnold is dead. Alicia's very ill – probably not got long." He was matter of fact though it was his brother's mother he was talking about. "Henry's dead and Kathleen has probably made her own life – nothing's been heard of her since Arnold's funeral."

"So if anything's going to be done it has to be...."

"....while we've still got Alicia with us." Carl finished for him.

"If we don't have one of them to tell the truth – sign an affidavit or something in front of a solicitor – then nothing can be proved. Where is she?"

"I don't know – I used to but I know she's moved – but we both know a man who will."

"Ted! Of course! Funny how he always gets involved in this family. And I know where to find him."

"Do you go alone or do we go together?"

"A united front I think. Do you have to get back to Cambridge now or could you stay up a day or so?"

"I don't have to be anywhere for a few weeks actually. I'm on vacation – supposed to be heading off to Italy in a few days but nothing is cast in concrete. I can stay up – of course I can – this is far too important – for Susie."

The two men drained their cups. "Yes. Let's." And they walked quickly together out of the bar, through the foyer, practically knocking over a young girl as they pushed through the crowd "I beg your pardon."

"Wow! That's real polite." A sarcastic American voice was lost on them as they had already pushed through the revolving doors to run down the steps and grabbed the pale green taxi that was just about to leave from the bottom of the steps.

As they settled back Charles said with uncharacteristic mischief "You really will never guess where he's living!"

Chapter Thirty

When the doorbell to the flat rang I was not well pleased.

I had had a harrowing day, lunchtime with Susannah had been followed by various unusual telephone calls from my office. I had managed to arrange for Susannah to go into a clinic in Liverpool the next day. I wasn't happy about my part in this at all but she was very grateful and she had no one else.

She had given her lies to Joe about meeting an old friend from university and having lunch – Monika would look after the children. It was all arranged but I was exhausted even though I had left the office early.

When I got back to Alicia at Millcourt I was completely in two minds as to whether to tell her about it or not. I decided not, and the lying just made matters worse. All I wanted to do was have something to drink and sit watching mindless television.

And then the doorbell rang.

Almost the last thing I expected was the sight of Carl and Charles in the hallway.

"Good God – come on in – both of you. Good God!"

"Who is it?" The unmistakable voice of Alicia from the lounge meant that my two young visitors were as shocked as I had been a moment before.

It wasn't just the two young men on my doorstep who had some explaining to do.

Charles hadn't visited me since I had moved into the flat in their old house. He had had no reason to.

She had been very ill for a long time but her voice retained many of its old qualities. There was no mistaking who she was.

"Mother?" Charles looked at me for an explanation.

"Alicia. Oh shit!" Carl was obviously not prepared for this.

"Yes, it's Alicia and she is not very well at all. She has forgotten much and forgiven that which she remembers."

I was talking to them both, and hoped they would both be reassured. I ushered them into the drawing room. Alicia was lying in the window seat, her legs covered by an eiderdown. She had had a reasonably good day and, to me, looked relatively strong, but the boys hadn't seen her for years and their shock was palpable.

Alicia was tired and she had taken her evening drugs. Her hair, once dark and wavy was now thin and grey, and it was obvious even with the eiderdown and her dressing gown that her figure had completely gone to skin and bone.

Her voice sounded unnaturally strong "How wonderful to see you, both of you." I recognised it as the voice she used when she was not taking anything in, she was simply acting the part of Alicia.

Neither said anything. Alicia continued as if she understood what she was saying "All we need is Susannah and we're all together. A very long time." But I knew she wouldn't remember this in the morning.

I took matters in hand.

"Now, Charles, your mother is very tired – she will be better in the morning. Can Carl stay with you go at Sandhey? Can I come round tomorrow? After breakfast? We have much to talk about. Good." Charles had assented with a nod of his head. "Now off you go. I'll see you about 9 tomorrow morning. Alicia must rest. She is shocked. You really should have telephoned first."

It was pointless of them to remind me that they had not known she was here.

The mood I was in and the things going through my mind meant that I was unreasonably short with them.

The next morning I waited until the nurse had arrived and left Alicia at the normal time, as if I was going to the office but instead I walked across the golf course to Sandhey.

There were already quite a few people on the course as it was a lovely day, and I enjoyed the quiet walk across the dry springy grass and sandy paths to another world.

I sat down at the kitchen table with Max, Charles and Carl as Monika handed round mugs of coffee. Conversation was somewhat strained as we tried to find out what we were really there to talk about.

Carl and Charles explained how they had met and the coincidences in the way their careers were progressing were quite striking. Seeing them together it amazed me that anyone could think they *weren't* brothers though the difference in their ages seemed far more than the four years it actually was.

I watched Max looking at them as they were talking. The one man who had lived in his house for so many years and who was a son to him, and his brother who he had hardly known. I wondered what he was thinking.

We listened as Carl explained what Alicia had told him about Susannah and the happenings in the Lakes that New Year. Some of us knew some of the facts, but to hear the circumstances was shocking.

As the facts presented themselves we found we were trying to decide whether or not to tell Susannah the truth, whether it would be better simply to get Alicia to confirm the details 'just in case circumstances change'. There were arguments for and against both courses of action.

I had to explain how, over the past years, I had been visiting Alicia and how, now she was nearing the end, I had taken it upon myself to look after her as there was no one else. I couldn't resist looking at Max to see how he took this. He gave little away.

I told them I didn't think it would be easy getting Alicia to swear to anything.

Carl didn't mention his mother and I rather assumed that he had no interest in that side of his family – all he cared about was making sure Susannah would have the correct details of her parentage. He told us that he knew it was too late for it to make any difference to his life but he knew how important it would be one day for Susannah to know the real truth.

As we sat around the table for most of the morning, I kept thinking of the poor girl, who we all cared about, who would be worrying about getting the train to Liverpool; she would be picturing the walk up the hill to the clinic and imagining what she would have to go through in a few hours.

It was Monika who brought our conversation to an end.

Perhaps we hadn't realised she was there as we talked across each other, adding details to one or other's generalities.

"Susannah must be told all that you have said and it is *she* who must decide what she wants her mother to do. Susannah must decide whether *she* wants to do anything. It is not up to *you* to decide for her. You *men*. Why do you think that just because you are men you have the right to decide for her? You don't. You are all trying to do the right thing for her but you haven't once mentioned asking *her*. She is not a child to be manipulated for her own good any more. She is the one who must decide. Only she can."

It was probably the longest speech any of us, with the exception of Charles, had heard from Monika. She was also absolutely right and I for one felt ashamed that I had presumed to know what the right answer for Susannah would be.

"Quite right, my dear." Max spoke for all of us.

"I'm looking after the children this afternoon so she can visit a friend, I will go around now and talk to her before she leaves. I will tell her. all that I have heard you discuss today. She must know the truth so she can decide what she wants to do."

Max nodded in agreement as Charles looked at Monika and smiled. "Yes, you're absolutely right."

After all the years of lies and part truths I felt I owed it to them all to speak the truth, for once not to hide.

"Don't worry her now. Please. Talk to her another time, she has enough worries on her plate at present. You saw her on Saturday – she's nearing the end of her tether."

They all looked at me. We all knew something of the life she led with him, but it was to me that Susannah had confided the detail of how he controlled her. It was me she had told of her unhappiness and fear.

Perhaps they thought it wasn't for me to say. Perhaps they felt they should have realised she couldn't cope with much more and were disappointed in themselves not to have thought of it. Perhaps they realised there was more to it. "She's not visiting friends in Liverpool, she's seeing a doctor."

"Do you know why?" Max asked the question, but they all knew the answer.

I decided there was only one way to tell them. "She's having an abortion."

Carl broke the silence that followed.

"How do you know this?"

"I organised it."

They must have wondered why she had asked me but none of them said anything.

Carl looked unbelievably hurt.

"Why?"

"She hates him." Monika answered Carl's question. "She has hated him for a long time. He forces her. Just like you said happened to make her." She sounded very defeated and there was nothing we could say.

"What were your arrangements?" Max was the first one to be practical.

"I'm to be there by 12 and stay with the children until their father gets back from work or until Susannah returns."

"If she's having an abortion she won't be well."

"Will she be able to hide that from him?"

"We mustn't leave her or the children alone with him."

"He's suspicious of her already, look how he didn't want her to go to my lecture. He must realise that there is something going on. Joe mustn't find out the real reason." Charles had realised the danger she would be in if he did.

Carl asked the question we who knew Joe answered in our minds as he asked it. "What will he do if he does?"

"He mustn't."

"She will be in no fit state to argue with him."

"She will need our help."

"He must not find out."

"What *will* he do if he does?"

The answer was left unspoken.

Chapter Thirty-One

Monika was getting the children's tea when Joe got back from work. Josie, nearly 7 years old, helped her. Jack, Al and Bill were sitting in high chairs around the kitchen table. The radio was on, playing a lively tune about the *weather being hot* and it being *summertime* and someone having *women on their mind*.

Monika remembered that clearly for years to come.

"Is that woman not back yet? It's 5 o'clock."

"No, Susannah is not back yet."

"I came home early especially, I wanted to hear all about her afternoon with her old friend from university." It was obvious from his voice that he had not believed a word of her excuse.

"She is not back yet." Monika repeated as she continued to feed the children their tea.

Joe had frequently told Susannah that when he wanted to enjoy a bit of fun with another woman he had to do it away from home. He would tell her how he would like to bring one of the women from the pub back and have sex in their bed. He had taunted her by saying that that was exactly what he would do the moment he was ever left alone in the house long enough – even if the children were at home.

Another of the visions he had taunted his wife with was his curiosity about his having sex with Monika. He would talk about it when they were in bed together. Susannah put it down to his wanting to humiliate her, wanting to arouse himself as he went through the motions of sex with her.

There was enough reality in the threats to have tied Susannah to the house when there was any chance he would be there. She had had to make sure that neither the children nor Monika were left alone with him. Under normal circumstances.

But she had had to leave them this afternoon, she could not have another baby, she had to get rid of it. Perhaps Joe would be late back from work, she would get home and he wouldn't know anything was wrong.

It must have seemed like a golden opportunity to Joe. An opportunity

246

that wouldn't occur again in a hurry. He hadn't believed the story about an old university friend and he wasn't sure what it was she was up to, but this was too good an opportunity to miss.

"Josie, take your brothers out into the garden."

"But Daddy...."

"No 'buts'. Do as you're told. Now. And don't come back inside until you're told to. I'll call you when you can bring them in."

Monika lifted the boys out of their high chairs and went to carry them out to the garden, holding her hand out for Josie to hang on to as they went. What could Joe have in mind? The children hadn't finished their tea.

"Not you, Monika. I want a word with you."

She put the boys down. She knew better than to cross him.

"Now Monika, its my turn."

"What do you mean?"

"It's my turn. With you. You don't belong to Charles and the German, it's my turn now."

It took a few moments for Monika to realise what he was saying but then the look in his eyes reminded her of the past.

"That's not true!" She tried to think of a way out of this. She had to keep him talking. She must not let him do what she knew he was going to try to do. She tried to make sure the kitchen table was between them.

"Of course it is. Everyone knows what you and those two perverts get up to. Now I want some of it." All the middle class façade he had wrapped around himself for the past 8 years was gone.

He was too quick for her, darting round the table he grabbed both her wrists with one of his hands and with the other reached under her skirt. She remembered thinking that he seemed very skilled at practically undressing her with only one hand. He was very strong. She struggled to free her arms from his grip. He was unzipping his trousers when she managed to free one of her hands – she reached back behind her, desperately trying to find something to hit him with – she had to distract him – there had to be something....

She had been raped too often during the war, she had been forced too many times, to let it happen again – after all those years of peace and happiness she would not, could not, let it happen.

Her hand found the handle of the bread knife.

She swung her arm round in a wide arc the blade facing forwards. His shirt offered no resistance and the blade slid into his side. It jarred in her hand as it glanced off a rib and dug even further into his body. She let go of the knife as his grip weakened. He let her go.

He had cut himself many times, on the boat. Fishing hooks,

blades and thick canvass needles had stuck in his legs, arms and hands. He knew that it was essential to do these things without thinking of the pain. You just did it. You worried about the pain later. He reached round and gripped the knife and pulled it out of his body. The pain in his side and in the palm of his hand took his concentration for just long enough for Monika to squeeze past him. She headed towards the door, reaching down to pull up her pants as she tried to run.

But even with the pain, perhaps even because of it, Joe was quicker. He pushed her out of the way swearing at her. 'Vicious fucking bitch' was all she could make out as he headed through the door and into the garden.

"Oh my Christ – the children!"

She ran after him – she must save the children from him – God knows what he would do to them.

He still had the bloody knife in his hand.

By the time she reached the garden he had the three babies in a bear hug in his arms, Josie was struggling and had got away from her father. The young girl was staring at the red stain spreading rapidly across his shirt and the knife still held in one of his hands. "Aunty Monika?" Josie, frightened and confused, started to cry.

"Is everything all right there?" a voice came from the neighbour's garden, the thick hedge preventing him from seeing what was going on.

"Absolutely. No problem – just the children playing up a bit while they wait for their mummy to get home." Joe sounded almost normal.

"Good, good, try to keep the noise down old chap – it's such a lovely evening out in the garden."

"Shut the fuck up." He did not shout, he did not want the neighbour to hear – but he said it with sufficient menace to silence Monika and Josie.

He was walking quickly out of the side gate clutching the three young children in his arms. They saw him turn right, towards the sea.

Josie bent down and picked up the knife her father had dropped. "No!" screamed Monika as she grabbed it out of Josie's hand and ran inside to the phone.

"Come quick! Come quick! He has taken the children. He has gone mad!"

"What do you mean 'he has taken the children'?"

"He's taken them to the sea."

Max had answered the phone and immediately decided to divide resources. There was no time for explanations – he realised the gravity of the situation.

It was a good thing he had answered the phone, time would have been wasted if Charles had done so as Monika had spoken in German – a language she had not used since she had come to England 22 years before.

"Charles, go to the quay. Joe has taken the children."

"I am going to the house – Monika is hurt. No Charles, you go to the boat, take Carl with you – stop Joe from taking the children on the boat. Run!"

The brothers had quite a way to go – the quay was far nearer Joe and Susannah's house than it was to Sandhey – there was no way they could get there first. But they had to try. It would be quicker to run along the beach than to drive.

They ran.

When Max reached the house Monika was standing by the kitchen table. Josie was standing behind her, holding onto the hem of her skirt with her thumb in her mouth, as she had done when she was a young child.

Taking in the bloodied knife on the table in front of Monika and the tears in her dress, Max did not take long to read the situation pretty accurately.

"Oh my dear girl! He didn't try to..."

She nodded, her eyes dull, her face as lifeless as it had been when they had looked out over the *unterseeboot* 25 years earlier.

"Did he..."

She shook her head, lifting up the bloodied knife.

"Is he badly hurt? My dear child we need to know. If he has gone on a boat with the children and he is wounded.... it will be dangerous."

She shook her head, then nodded, then shook it again then cried out "I don't know! I don't know! He mustn't harm the children! Oh the poor children!"

"What about the 'poor children' where are they? What is happening?"

Susannah had arrived home.

Carl and Charles reached the quay to see the children crammed into the skiff with their father who was rowing out to the fishing boat. He was not making a very good job of it as he was obviously hurt. He was favouring one side, the boat was not travelling in a straight line.

They watched with the dawning realisation that the boat was not making headway and had been caught in the current of a channel in the incoming tide.

It was not making any progress, it was being swept along – Joe had no control over it – he was fighting the oars so hard he was not even trying to hold onto the children.

Charles yelled at a man in a boat completely unaware of what was going on "Help us! We've got to get out there!.

"No way. Tide's running. They're gone"

"Jimmy, for fucks sake it's your brother!" Carl had recognised the fisherman.

"No room." With no redundant words Jimmy pushed Carl away from his boat and pushed off into the water.

Charles and Carl watched Jimmy rowing strongly, swiftly catching his wounded brother. They saw him trying to lift the young boys to safety from the tiny skiff, yelling at Joe to stop trying to row. He was taking no notice. Jimmy said afterwards that it seemed like Joe just had to get away. He was trying to row with his right hand – his left arm was useless now the full impact of the knife wound was making itself felt. Jimmy had had to lean on the skiff to grab the children, then it just careered over, throwing Joe into the sea.

He had grown up within spitting distance of the sea, he had been a fisherman, made a living from the treacherous waters; but he could not swim. His survival instinct made him try to do some kind of doggy paddle to keep afloat but he was hurt. His left arm would not work properly, his head went under. His brother tried to reach him but watched helplessly as he was swept out of reach.

He hadn't stood much of a chance once he was in the water.

Chapter Thirty-Two

They all sat around the fire, specially lit even though it was July.

Susannah's thoughts she spoke out loud. "Do you think he remembered when he saved me? Do you think he thought about me as he was swept away? Do you think he remembered saving me?"

"Did he ever think of anyone but himself?"

The police were gentle when they interviewed Susannah but she couldn't help their investigations. She had been out all day.

It was Monika they were hard on.

Monika had been looking after the children as she frequently did. The deceased had come home early. No, she didn't know why. No, there was nothing 'going on' between her the deceased. Monika would not allow such a thing. Had the deceased come home knowing his wife would be out in order to have an assignation with her? Why would he try to assault Monika? Did Monika encourage him? Had Monika led him on? Why had she stabbed him? Was it a lovers' quarrel? He loved his children he would not harm them, would he?

Monika tearfully made her statement, haltingly, with Max standing with her trying to help her. She seemed to have forgotten all her English. She spoke in an almost unintelligable mixture of languages, part French, part German and an Austrian dialect she would have sworn she had entirely forgotten.

Max, increasingly concerned, translated for her. He would have been better making her speak in English as the policemen had already made up their mind that 'the foreign bit' had murdered her lover after a quarrel sparked by his refusing to leave his young family and set up home with her.

Monika's mind had had enough and as the questioning continued she could only cry, looking from person to person in the room, not taking anything in.

It was left to Max to try to sort the police out. He told them they were wrong. There had been no relationship, Monika was simply looking after the children. She was an old friend of the family and had been the young widow's nanny. The deceased had attacked her for no reason and, when she had wounded him defending herself and the children, he had run to the sea.

Was there any way they could not believe one of the most eminent men in the district?

Even though he, too, was foreign.

The ladies at their coffee mornings and the newspapers had a field day.

"It must have been the wife. She was mad with jealousy because she had found out he was having an affair."

"It was the wife but she was depressed, who wouldn't be after having three children in as many years."

"He was trying to murder the children and the nanny saved them."

"It was the nanny, she wanted him for herself."

"It was self defence, he was trying to rape her."

The two local papers were divided, one decided that Monika, the mysterious foreigner, had wormed her way into their life and was definitely not the innocent victim she made herself out to be. The other paper decided that Susannah was the guilty one, driving her hard working husband to despair.

It was a difficult time for everyone.

Max tried to keep Monika's and Charles's spirits up but it was difficult in the face of the hostility they met. No one who knew them personally believed that there was anything untoward between the occupants of Sandhey, but the great majority who didn't were sure there was something 'odd' about the household.

Monika's history was raked over, everyone in the office was interviewed about how she came to be in this country and what her relationship with the Donaldsons had been. Her papers were investigated for irregularities. The policeman who conducted the interviews made it clear he didn't like foreigners. "Bloody foreigners. Should have stayed where they were. We don't want them here." "Anyone who speaks German must be German," he was heard to say "and I spent six years of my life fighting them. I'm hanged if I'm going to be nice to them now." "I don't know why we're wasting all our valuable time, it's obvious they killed that poor bloke. We don't know why but we'll find out."

The police had a particular interest in Max's relationship with Monika especially when they found that he had sponsored her arrival in England after the war.

They felt there had to be more to it when their enquiries about Max met official silence and the Chief Constable became involved.

Monika was looking after the Parry children at their house, so when the Inspector called at Sandhey to explain their conclusions he was shown through to Max, who received him in his study. Although quite elderly he was still an impressive figure behind his leather-topped desk. He did not stand when the policeman was admitted. He did not ask him to sit.

Eventually the Inspector spoke. "We will not be pressing any charges. "He did not want to say "Sir".

"Miss Monika ..."

"Mrs" corrected Max.

"*Mrs* Monika ..." he looked down at his notes very obviously even though he had interviewed her several times and was undoubtedly very familiar with her name "Heller. *Mrs* Heller need have no concerns about any charges relating to the death of Mr Joe Parry."

"You accept then that it was self defence?"

"We will not be pressing any charges." The policeman hesitated rather too long for politeness. "Sir."

"And Susannah?"

"She is not your responsibility. Sir. We will let her know our decision in person."

"I beg your pardon, Inspector." The uplift in his voice seemed to question the rank of the officer with whom he was dealing. "I beg your pardon, but Mrs Parry is very much my responsibility. You should know that her father gave her into my guardianship before he died. Both Mrs Parry and her brother, Charles, are very much my responsibility."

"Oh yes," the policeman said not really bothering to keep the smirk from his voice "Oh yes, of course, Mr Charles Donaldson is also your 'responsibility' isn't he?"

It was difficult to see how much more rude he could have been.

Max realised that the policeman wanted him to lose his temper. He had been in this position many times before – it was a normal way of getting people in an interview, or interrogation, to reverse their roles. The weaker gets the stronger to lose his temper.

Max stood up. He spoke very quietly.

"Am I to understand from what you say that you have listened to rumour and innuendo and that you have allowed that rumour and innuendo to cloud your judgement as a police officer? Is that what all this investigation into my ward's husband's death is all about?"

"I expect you to know my standing in this community." Max continued with just a hint of veiled threat in his voice "I expect you to treat me with respect due to that standing. I do not expect to have to remind you that not all bachelors are queer, and that not all people who care for their fellow human beings have an ulterior motive. You have put this household through a very difficult time simply because of your prejudices. I could have gone to your superiors as soon as the incident occurred and ensured that there was no proper investigation if I, or anyone in my household, had had anything to hide. But I did not. I have a great belief in the British Justice system that even your grubby behaviour does not shake. I have said enough. Please now go."

Max realised that he had said too much, he had not lost his temper but he had said too much. He knew what people said about him and had been saying for years, but the strain of seeing people he cared for being put through so much anguish and uncertainty because of prejudice was too much for him.

It was one of the reasons he had left Austria 40 years earlier.

Carl, not being able to resist listening in on this interview between Max and the Inspector, found answers to some of his questions and gained something of an understanding of what Charles felt for this strange old man.

Chapter Thirty-Three

Susannah was very ill after the events of that dreadful day. The delay over an inquest and the uncertainty over police action did not help her state of mind so she came to stay with her mother and me at Millcourt.

She did not want to see her children. She didn't want to talk of the events of that day.

Susannah and Alicia were surprisingly generous to each other. Perhaps they both realised the other's vulnerability.

I had worried that Susannah would blame her mother, blame all her misfortunes on Alicia's abandonment of her family.

But she didn't.

I thought perhaps Alicia wouldn't recognise how disturbed her daughter was.

But she did.

Alicia had one last chance to be a mother to her daughter – and she did try, increasing her drug dose to what I considered to be dangerous levels to help give her sufficient strength to support her daughter. They had some catching up to do.

So they listened to each other's problems and answered some of the other's questions. I believed that she had forgotten the visitors at Millcourt the night before the incident but I prayed anyway that Alicia would not mention or disclose the identity of the friend Charles had been with when they had tried to save Joe and the children.

This was not the time for Carl and Susannah to meet again.

I would sit reading, listening to music and smoking whilst they talked or rested together. I couldn't help but reflect that these were the same rooms where Susannah had had whooping cough and Alicia had not been here to nurse her – having left for Switzerland the week before. These were the rooms where Monika had held sway. It hadn't been that many years ago. 22 years. A lifetime in some ways but in others, especially to someone nearing 60, it seemed like no time at all.

The children stayed at their home, looked after by Monika. It was thought that they would feel less disrupted in their own bedrooms. Monika was not happy to be in the house but felt that Josie and the boys needed her, so she had reluctantly agreed.

Carl had to stay in the area, the police had said they needed him until their enquiries were completed, even though his role had been entirely peripheral. Max had insisted he stay at Sandhey and made his library available. It was unspoken by all that Carl would keep to the background, rarely go into the town and certainly not visit Millcourt.

By the end of July it was all over. Police investigations were completed, the inquest was formally adjourned and funeral held. It was the only time that Susannah left the flat that month.

As the small group stood around the grave she did not see the tall young man standing under the trees observing them. He had no intention of upsetting Susannah even more by making an appearance in her life now.

He would be patient, but he had had to see her.

"I want a birthday party." Jack had told Monika a few days after the funeral. He was going to be four years old and wanted to have a party. "Bill had a party. I want one." Monika did her best to put him off the idea, no one needed a party just now. "But you are a big boy now, you don't have a birthday party every year."

"I don't care that Daddy's gone away." They had told them, but it was not really clear how much they had understood. "I don't care that he's not here. I want a party! I want Mummy! Mummy's never here!"

"Oh Jack, you must be a good little boy. I'll see what can be done."

So a party was planned for 1st August. Jack's 4th birthday. Susannah agreed as long as it was not held at the house that had been her home. Charles and Max offered to have it at Sandhey, Carl agreed only to make an appearance if it seemed appropriate.

There had to be a time when Carl and Susannah would meet again. Perhaps a children's party – when there was so much going on and attention would be on the children – perhaps when they would have to behave in the face of such company – perhaps a children's party was going to be a good time. Susannah still had not been told he was so close, she had not asked where he was. Why would she?

Food was prepared and decorations hung in the dining room at Sandhey. Lots of games were to be out in the garden. Children from

Jack's kindergarten were invited – with their parents. It is highly likely that a number of them only accepted out of curiosity, after all, the Sandhey household had been the subject of much speculation over the past weeks. In the social scene it was a prized invitation for the parents, the children were less pleased to go – Jack and Josie were not very popular.

Monika arrived with the children in good time, they were cleaned and dressed in their best party clothes. "They look wonderful!" Charles was so pleased to see Monika with the children. "They are easier to manage than you and Max." was her response, but in truth she was ready to come home.

The guests began to arrive, unusually almost exactly at the appointed time. The garden filled with the happy cries and excited shouts of the young things. The parents were kept happy with tea, cakes and the odd glass of something to keep them comfortable.

They had told Susannah to arrive a little late – when all the guests were there.

I drove Susannah and her mother down the road towards Sandhey, turning into the driveway as I had so many times before. But this time I had such a feeling of dread. Susannah was only just strong enough for company of any sort. Alicia had taken so many pain killers to get through the day that she seemed almost unnaturally alert and talkative. And Carl was here. I couldn't help but think that this party was a monumentally dreadful idea.

Alicia held Susannah's hand. "Chin up old girl. They're only children!"

"I can't do this. I can't go in. I don't want to see them."

"You must child. You must go in, be strong, show all those gossips and ghouls you have nothing to be ashamed of. You must go in and show them how much you love your children. You are my daughter, Susannah, be as much of an actor as I have been through the years. You must do this. If you don't the rumourmongers will go even harder at you. More people than do already will think you connived with Monika to murder your husband."

"Is that what they think?"

"Unfortunately, many do. We have shielded you from the worst things that have been said, Ted has dealt with their lawyers...."

"Whose lawyers? What's going on? What's going on that you haven't been telling me?"

"Now isn't the time to go into all that – just believe me when I say you must put on a good act for all these mothers – the only reason they're here is to get inside information on you to report back to their friends about how you are."

"So I've got to look like I love them all and am the grieving widow, the doting mother with nothing on my mind other than the good of the children?"

"Exactly."

Susannah hadn't seen her children since she had left for Liverpool two months before and they were shy when they saw her. Monika was carrying two of them – one on each hip, the other two were holding onto her skirt, thumbs in mouth, half hiding behind her. She had gathered them up from the lawn to take them to their mother.

Josie was the first to speak, resentfully. "Where've you been?"

"Oh, darlings, I've not been well. You must forgive Mummy when she is ill. She doesn't mean to be. It just happens."

How could she know that that was the speech, almost word for word, Alicia had given her when she was young. "You've been all right with Monika haven't you?"

"Oh yes," said a very grown up Josie "but she's not our Mummy."

"No she isn't darlings. We'll all get back together soon."

Fully aware that all the mothers were closely observing the reunion – though their children still rushed around oblivious – Susannah reached out to take the children from Monika with all the appearance of the loving Mother.

At that moment, doing what she had to do for the many curious eyes around her, she was truly her mother's daughter.

He watched them from the window for an hour as they played musical bumps and pass the parcel, and musical chairs. He watched them all eat their ice cream and jelly and he still didn't go outside.

He watched Susannah. She looked so different, yet so much the same. Her hair was different, her figure fuller, but she was undoubtedly his Susie and he loved her still. "I love you so much but how could you ever love me enough?" He longed to go out and talk to her, start up again where they had left off.

But he couldn't.

He looked at her with her brood of children. She looked so happy to see them. He had held back for the past weeks, he had to give her time.

He knew as he looked out at her that if he stayed much longer he would have to talk to her, he couldn't keep away from her much longer.

She still had not seen him.

She was hugging her children, and seemed completely happy. However much he needed her it seemed obvious that she did not need him.

As he watched her silently through the glass he hated what his mother and his father had done to him more than he had ever thought possible.

He could get away and no one would notice.

At the end of the party, all guests and their parents finally gone, the family sat around in the drawing room, the children with glasses of home-made lemonade and bottles of pop, the adults with something stronger. Charles asked Max "Where's Carl?"

"I don't know – I haven't seen him all afternoon."

"He was in the dining room earlier? Have you seen Carl?"

Monika had spoken the words before she realised it was Susannah she was asking.

"Carl?"

They ignored the question for a few minutes, making comments about how well the party had gone and how well behaved Josie and the boys had been, trying to cover up.

"You haven't answered me. Carl?" There was desperation in her voice.

"Max, you're hiding something. So are you, Charles, Monika? What's going on?" She looked from one person to another in the room – increasingly fearful of the answer she knew was coming. "Alicia?"

"Don't ask me darling."

"I know you think I am, but I'm not completely stupid. You're all hiding something – someone – from me aren't you?"

No one responded. More drinks were poured into cups, more wine into glasses, more straws put into lemonade bottles.

"It's Carl isn't it. He's been here." There was no questioning in her voice. It was complete certainty. "Where is he? I want to see him."

It was Monika who eventually spoke "He appears to have gone. Yes, it was Carl, he has been here and he has now, apparently, gone."

"Carl was here? Today? Here at Sandhey? What's he doing here? How long's he been here?" Her voice, originally hysterically high pitched was now flat, cold.

"A few weeks."

A gasp of disbelief from Susannah.

"He has been here since the day of the...., the day of the accident."

Susannah looked around the room. Charles, Max, Monika – the people she most trusted in the world. Her mother who she was just beginning to think she could love. Her children, sitting unaware of what was going on watching the mute television in the corner.

"You all knew didn't you? You all knew he was here and you didn't tell me." She spoke slowly, as if each word hurt. She had raised her arms – as if in supplication towards them but let them drop to her sides.

She was completely defeated.

Her legs bent and she crumpled down to the ground, sitting cross-legged, childlike, and she began to sob. She sobbed as she hadn't been able to throughout all the pain and anguish of the past few weeks.

"He....was.....here.....and .....you.....didn't......tell.......me."

Alicia and I took her daughter back to Millcourt. We put her to bed, and all she did was cry. She appeared to have so much pain inside her it was best to let her get it all out of her system.

The shock of the events of the past few weeks had been almost impossible for her to deal with. The whole afternoon had been a strain – putting on an act *Putting on a face to meet the faces that she meets* as Alicia frequently misquoted.

She didn't want to see her children, she didn't want to see anyone. It was heartbreaking that Alicia wanted to care for Susannah so much but she just didn't have the strength.

I only found out afterwards what Max had done about the children. It was obvious that Susannah could not cope with them and probably would not be able to for some time. Monika had been an angel – but enough was enough.

In the autumn of 1970 Max had bought a small terrace of houses at the bottom of Fore Street. The houses were immediately opposite the cinema that could be said to have started the whole thing. He arranged for Joe's mother and the remaining Parrys to live in part of the terrace and for Josie, Jack, Al and Bill to live in the other part with a live in Nanny.

It was, I suppose, a buy off. With Susannah in the state she was it was entirely likely that Joe's brothers would have tried to obtain custody of the children, and they could possibly have won. They had even talked of having her committed as 'incompetent' if they'd not been given access and it could all have got very nasty. They would not hear that there was another side to the story until Max bought them the houses.

Perhaps it was for the best. Perhaps they were all as mercenary and money-grabbing as Joe had been, as nothing more was heard about litigation and committals after they had moved into Fore Street.

Chapter Thirty-Four

And so we all rubbed along, some licking our wounds having lost, some learning to live with their gains from those appalling events.

I must admit being one of the ones that could be seen to have gained. I had Alicia and Susannah.

As Susannah recovered her physical and mental strength so Alicia became weaker and weaker. Her cancer was spreading, inoperable and victorious. She was taking more and more painkillers. Day by day she weighed herself, marking any slight gain triumphantly in a diary. But it was never Alicia who was gaining the weight – it was the cancer.

Susannah would sit in the window seat reading aloud as Alicia listened, her eyes either shut or gazing out, unseeing, over the golf course. On her better days Alicia would read and record those poems, those sections of Dickens and Shakespeare that had meant so much to her over the years, Susannah carefully marking up each tape with the contents and duration.

Their favourite was Sir Henry Newbolt.

There's a breathless hush in the close tonight
Ten to make and the match to win
A bumping pitch and a blinding light,
An hour to play, and the last man in.

Alicia told Susannah of the day she had been born. Of the cricket match, the people, the sunshine. "You mustn't think it was all bad."

And it's not for the sake of a ribboned coat.
Or the selfish hope of a season's fame,
But his captain's hand on his shoulder smote
"Play up! Play up! And play the game!"

She must have recorded and re-recorded that poem ten times to get it right, to get it the way she wanted to be remembered.

She was preparing to die with dignity.

It was heartbreaking.

We had heard nothing from Carl for several months when I got a phone call at the office.

"Ted, it's Carl." He sounded nervous, tense.

"Hello Carl, are you well?" I tried to sound unsurprised at his call.

Ignoring my pleasantries he continued,

"I understood that there would be some money coming to me on my 25th. That's on 1ˢᵗ May. Was that true or is it just one more fiction?" I wondered why he sounded so bitter.

"No, it was not a story – there was a trust fund." I was surprised, I hadn't thought Carl had any interest in money.

"Was?"

"I have a letter here for you. It was written and left here by your father to be sent to you on your 25th birthday. I haven't known where to send it. Since you walked out of the party last summer we have had all our letters returned 'gone away' we haven't known how to contact you."

"I moved." He wasn't going to explain why he had left so suddenly. He wasn't going to ask any questions about Susannah and the children.

Carl gave me his address, he had moved from Cambridge to Oxford, and the call ended abruptly.

I forwarded the letter unopened. I had no idea what the contents were and I had no copy.

On the following Monday I took another phone call.

With little preamble Carl began to read from the letter and, although I felt I had to interrupt at times he continued over my protests.

My Son,
You are now 25 years old.
Many Happy Returns.

If you do not know by now I must tell you the truths behind some of the skeletons in our family cupboard. I will be brief as you will probably have guessed or been told much of it. I do, however, find it necessary to write it down.

Both Charles and you are my sons – the elder with Alicia, conceived before we married in what I can only describe as "circumstances brought about by the war" and you, during a long love affair with your mother. I am grateful to Henry for having given you a home and having been such a good father figure to you. As far as I know he never knew your true parentage.

I have to tell you that I discovered the day you left home that Kathleen is my father's daughter. For years her family kept the truth from her and from me.

Do not judge us too harshly for things we could not know.

Be assured that from that day on we are not Man and Wife.

Susannah, on the other hand, is not my child. You would have been free to pursue her and for the pain it has caused you I regret that. She has made her own way and I neither know nor care what she will do with her life.

To other matters.

You will, no doubt, remember that there was a trust fund set up by your grandfather to ensure there was something for all my children, also your mother insisted I set up a fund for you alone.

These Trust Funds were the first things I used to try to clear my debts when it became obvious the business was in trouble. Max had left loopholes when he set them up, loopholes of which I was aware and of which I took advantage.

So there is nothing for you, for either of you.

Even if there had been I am not sure inheritance is wise. The substantial sum I received from my father has done me no good. I have inflicted enough on you I will not add the "burden of wealth". You must make your own way.

Ever, your father
Arnold Donaldson.

"How long have you known the contents of this letter?" His voice was accusing, harsh, cold so my response was defensive.

I did not try to hide my shock.

"I did not open the letter, I have no copy. I did not know what the letter said until you just read it to me. I had no idea."

"You must have known about the money." Still accusing. He was concentrating on the Trust Funds. He must have known the other things before, but it was his father's relationship to Kathleen that was making me think.

I should have realised.

"I knew nothing about the Trust Funds until Charles' 25th. I didn't draw it up – Max did – I was just a junior in the office when your grandfather died. I had no knowledge that you would have been included in it so I had no knowledge that you had lost out. I am sorry, Carl but there is nothing else I can tell you."

I could say nothing that could justify the actions of others. It was not for me to apologise for them.

"Max must have known he had connived in cheating Charles and me out of our grandfather's inheritance."

"I wouldn't go that far, Carl, but I am sure he felt he had some responsibility."

Absolutely. This answered so many of the questions that had remained unanswered over the years. I had always wondered why Max had been so generous to the children of the Donaldsons. This was an explanation. Though from a lawyer's point of view not a very good one.

"I thought it was because he was in love with Alicia."

Now that was something I had not thought of.

In all our talks Alicia had only mentioned Max briefly, a few meetings in London, some assistance when she was really low – but a 'love affair'. I didn't think so. I hoped not, though I did remember the electricity of their meeting when she had returned from Switzerland.

There was a pause on the line. I thought perhaps he had hung up.

After a while in a completely different voice, softer, gentler, "How are they?"

I did not need to ask which 'they' he meant.

I told him how Susannah had been very ill for some while after the events of last July and especially after the party, how she had been distraught that he had been there and not wanted to see her, how she still could not face her children, how she now lived with her mother and me at Millcourt. I told him how she was slowly coming to terms with events. How unhappy she was. How lonely. How guilty she felt at not being able to look after her children. How guilty she felt about bringing them into this world in the first place. How day after day we all tried to comfort her and keep her from walking out over the sands.

"Yes, Carl, it really is that bad."

"I didn't know."

"No, of course you didn't. How could you?"

"She looked so happy at the birthday party. She had her arms around all of them and was laughing. She didn't seem to need anything, anyone, else. Certainly not me."

"That's the first time I've ever thought you to be selfish Carl. She was acting. It was so very difficult for her. She was being her mother's daughter. It was so very difficult for her and you didn't see. But now I know why you couldn't go to her. You knew, didn't you, but believe me I had no idea. No idea at all."

I continued swiftly, to cover our embarrassment. "She was just being very brave. But all that has taken it's toll. She had her breakdown very soon after that. The Parrys threatened her with all sorts of legalities.

They wanted all Joe's money. Wanted to leave her with nothing. Wanted her committed. They kept opening up wounds, trying to get the police to re-open the case, to charge Monika and Susannah with murder – manslaughter at the very least. They were very vindictive until Max persuaded them to come to that agreement."

"Is it all settled now?"

"Oh yes. Now they have property and income they are quite happy. The children are well looked after and Monika and Charles keep a very close eye on them."

"Goodbye then. Ted, I don't mean to be so difficult. Thank you for forwarding the letter and for all the information." He hesitated as if unsure whether to continue. "I could come up you know. I could come and see them. Nothing heavy. Just to show I care."

He seemed to want me to ask him up. He seemed to want me to make his decision for him but it was not my decision to take.

"I don't think that would be a good idea at the moment. Susannah is far from pulling herself together. A shock like meeting you again might not be the best thing."

He was quiet for a while, then asked "Will you say I have been in touch?"

"Do you want me to?"

"Probably best if you don't."

"Probably."

And so another opportunity to bring Carl back into the family was lost.

Although I now understood more about the complexities of his situation I couldn't help feeling I had, yet again, done the wrong thing.

Chapter Thirty-Five

Towards the end of that year I had a phone call from her solicitors in Keswick. Kathleen Donaldson had died. She had left our address as a point of contact for her next of kin, her only son Carl and her sister Maureen Shelton.

She had lived the four years since Arnold's death in virtual isolation in a cottage in the Lake District. She had given up the job at the school, she had given up practically all contact with anyone.

I now believed I understood why.

I told the Keswick solicitor that I would get back to him as soon as I had made contact with the son and phoned Carl to tell him the news. He showed no sign of emotion at all. He asked if he needed to do anything, anything he needed to sign. He asked when the funeral was and whether he should go.

"Carl, there is no funeral organised. There is no one to organise it. Only you and Maureen, and Maureen is getting on you know. You must go up to the Lake District and sort it out – there is only you who can do that. You are her son, her only child. Just because you are estranged doesn't mean that you have no responsibilities."

"I can't just drop everything here."

"You must, and you will." I sounded more certain than I felt and he was silent for a while.

"OK then. Would you meet me there? Would you help me sort it out?"

"Of course."

I got home that night and at dinner looked at the two women who lived in my flat and who were now so much a part of my life. What would the news mean to them?

I sat in my chair by the fire, whisky in hand, not watching the inane comedy on the television – but as long as the voices and canned laughter filled the room my thoughts were my own and I didn't have to make conversation. What they would feel if they knew the latest news, I had to tell them – but how? Alicia would probably be glad to hear of the end of Kathleen, the woman her husband had always been in love with since well before they had even met.

Perhaps Kathleen was the woman Arnold should have married in the first place. Had she, even then, known that they couldn't marry? Less attractive than Alicia, less vibrant and less dynamic – probably more intelligent, more steadfast and certainly healthier – yet she had died first. Just. What would Alicia think?

And Susannah? What of her thoughts of her step-mother, the mother of the boy she loved – she did not know the man, but she still loved the boy. Did she hate Kathleen for what she had done to their lives? Did she despise her? Resent her? What would she feel that Kathleen was dead?

I had to tell them and face the consequences, but, as ever, I tried to avoid the issue.

Susannah and I would join Alicia in her room at the end of each evening, she was now too ill to get out of her bed which had been moved so she could always see out of the window. We would sit companionably and drink cocoa – or at least there would be cups of cocoa to be drunk – Alicia never touched hers.

That night I interrupted the quiet. "I have to go to the Lake District tomorrow. I will be away for a few days. Will you both be alright while I am away?"

"Of course. We'll be fine." Susannah now spoke for them both.

"Business or pleasure?" asked Alicia.

"Business."

"It's Kathleen isn't it?" Susannah somehow had understood my feelings of not wanting to tell them any more than I had to. "She's dead isn't she?"

"What? Who's dead?" Alicia had missed threads of the conversation.

Susannah continued "Kathleen is dead isn't she? There's absolutely no other reason for you to go to the Lakes. She is the only contact you have there. She is the only one you would feel you had to up sticks and go to. Perhaps she's not dead yet and you've got to go and see her. But it's Kathleen isn't it?"

"I'm not sure...."

"It is Kathleen isn't it" she was going to persevere.

"Yes, it's Kathleen. I heard today that she has died. I have to go to sort some things out, arrange the funeral, that sort of thing. There is no one else."

"Do you have to?" Alicia asked. "Please don't."

Perhaps she knew that her time was drawing to a close. Perhaps she thought it was disloyal of me to go to Kathleen when she, Alicia, needed me so much. I was thinking of that rather than what I said next.

"I have to go, I'm afraid. I am meeting them there, Carl and "

I stopped, realising what I had said and looking at Susannah who was staring at me open eyed. "You know where he is? You've been in touch with him? Why do you always keep him away from me?" Her voice rose with every question, she was getting increasingly hysterical.

"I'm coming with you. I'm coming to meet him. I've got to see him. You've got to take me with you. I must see him. He'll need me."

"Susie." Her mother tried to be calming but using the name that Carl always called her only made things more difficult. Susannah stood up, as if ready to leave that very moment.

Alicia's voice was thin and tired, "Please, I need you here."

But Susannah had gone.

I was so angry with myself. A momentary lapse had ruined all the care and attention of the past months. I regret so much what happened then and I will for the rest of my life.

"Now that's not the real reason is it Alicia? Is it you think she'll be hurt? Or do you think they'll get together again or you are jealous and want her hanging onto you every minute of the day?"

"That's unfair."

"Yes, Alicia, I know. But this has all gone on long enough. You know that I will be with you every moment I can. But you cannot demand that of Susannah. She has her own life to lead. Good God look at the time she's had of it! Haven't all your talks proved to you how much she loves the boy? Don't you think she deserves some happiness?"

"And she'll get that from him? You think she'll find happiness with *their* son?" She asked the question hesitatingly but with venom.

I was firm in my reply. "She won't be happy without him."

She changed tack "Do you hate me that much?"

"Stop that now. Do not try one of those making everyone feel sorry for you. Do not try to make me feel guilty. Whatever I do for Carl is not *for* Kathleen or *against* you. It isn't a competition. Can't you see that?"

"No."

"Well I'm going to help Carl. I will leave after breakfast and be back late."

"You hate me." She was crying, looking at me with her overlarge eyes – the illness having removed any softness from her face.

"You know I could never hate you and you won't get round me like this."

"You want to help her, you don't care what happens to me." She was childlike in her attempt at emotional blackmail but very much the old Alicia in her attempts at manipulation.

I'm afraid I had had enough.

"Do you want to know what I really think Alicia? Are you interested?"

I carried on without waiting for an answer.

"You have always known I could never hate you. I have loved you so very very much, you have always known that since the earliest days. It is something you have taken for granted. But the fact that I love you, and will always love you, doesn't mean to say I always have to *like* you. And now I don't like you very much. Think of Susannah. Don't think of yourself. Think of Susannah's life, Susannah's future – not yours. Your daughter has always loved Carl. They were probably, as far as anyone ever is, "made for each other". She has made her mistakes; he, no doubt, has made his. Sure as hell their parents did."

I wondered if she had taken any of this lecture to heart. She had, and I had made her cry and I felt dreadful.

I had to be conciliatory.

"If you are ever to make recompense for your lies and deceits then now is the time. They have a chance to get together. They have a chance at least to find out if they have a future together; you, we, must not take that away from them."

We were quiet for a few moments. She changed the subject. Perhaps she had not really been listening to anything I had said.

Later I had reason to hope she hadn't.

"You said you were meeting 'them'. You never said who the other one was."

"I meant Carl and Maureen."

"Maureen? Who's Maureen?"

"Maureen Shelton"

"Why would Maureen go, she didn't know Kathleen."

I knew it would be a blow. I knew it would hurt her.

"She did. She was her sister."

Perhaps I was too cruel.

She had never known how close her best friend was to the woman she had considered her enemy for much of her life.

She was absolutely silent for some minutes.

"Go then Ted, I don't think I can cope with anything else. No more surprises."

I couldn't tell her. I had to leave her knowing she was crushed, wishing I hadn't said anything – but I was tired of lying for this family. All I can say is that I always tried to do what was right – or what seemed to be right – at the time. Had I always known? I say No. I can only say in my defence that I had always tried not to get in position where I should have to talk about Kathleen and Maureen's true relationship to Arnold. I had been so angry with Alicia's selfishness and so sad knowing I was going to lose her soon but at least I hadn't been *that* angry.

I went along the corridor to Susannah's room. I knocked and a small voice said I could go in.

She was not lying on her bed, head down as I supposed she would be. She was standing looking out of her window across the golf course towards Sandhey.

"You know, Uncle Ted, this room was part of the old nursery when this was one house. I used to sit here with the boys and nag and nag them to tell me all the ins and outs of the rules of golf. On other days, when they didn't want a girl hanging round, I used to look out of this window and watch them playing with the dogs on the lawn. Now Charles is living over there" she nodded her head in the direction of Sandhey "and God knows what his life is like. He writes, I know and he's doing so well at that and I am so pleased for him. Monika looks after him, I know. Is he gay? I wonder." She carried on, not waiting for answers to any of her questions "If he is, he doesn't seem to do anything about it. He seems happy though, so does Monika. Max is good to them and seems to like having them around. But they never come to see us do they Uncle Ted? It's as if we aren't family to them. Charles doesn't seem to care that his mother is dying. There can't be much more time. But Charles doesn't seem to care – if he does he doesn't show it. He is so wrapped up in himself. Do you think he hurts that much?"

"I think you have got it in one there Susannah. I think he hurts a great deal. He's never learnt how to get on with other people – he inherited that from his father – Arnold never knew how to get on with people – Arnold never gave anyone credit for being anything other than supporting actors in his life story." I hadn't meant to sound so bitter. I was still upset with myself for arguing with Alicia..

"Is that how you think he saw you?"

I didn't answer immediately, I simply walked closer to her and took her right hand in both mine, kissed it and gave it back to her. We stood close together looking out over the darkness of the golf course towards the lights of Sandhey and the other houses stringing out along the road to Red Rocks.

We stood there for a while before I answered.

"Yes. Yes Susannah, that is what I believe I have been – a sort of walk on part in the lives of your entire family. But don't let that make you think I'm bitter, I care for you all in an odd sort of way and I will always be here to pick up the pieces and help you if ever you need it. You must know that."

"That's what mother used to say – *I'll always be there to pick up the pieces'* as though she didn't trust us to manage on our own. We haven't really though have we? But she hasn't been there either."

We stood there for some while, before she plucked up the courage to ask me the question she had had in mind for some time.

"How is he?" There was such sadness in her voice. "I know he's my brother and I can't do anything about that, but I do love him. I have always loved him, and I do need to know that he is alright and happy."

Alicia had not told her.

She had lied, again. In all their talks and discussions she had not told Susannah the truth. Of all the people who knew of the events of that Christmas 1945 no one had ever seen fit to tell Susannah. We had got so close that morning of Joe's death but we had never told her.

What was I to do?

Either I lied and continued this web of deceit that had started that so long ago or I told her the truth, telling her that the people she loved had lied to her for years. She would never trust any of us again even if she would know the truth. But I had just told a truth to Alicia and that had gained nothing other than hurt. Why had I said all those things? I had achieved nothing.

I remembered what Maureen had said about her conversation with Carl, when he had argued that at least if he knew the truth he would know what he was going to do with it. Now finding myself in that same position I found I couldn't lie any longer. I was getting too old.

"Yes, Susannah. He is doing very well. He is an academic; Oxford now, History."

"Just like Father."

"Just like your father."

Susannah didn't pick up on the ambiguity in my words so I repeated myself with different emphasis "Just like *your* father."

Did I want her to know the truth? Yes. Did I want to be the one to tell her? No. I wanted her to guess. I didn't want to lie any more – but neither did I have the courage to tell the truth and go against what Alicia had asked – *"Over my dead body"* she had said on Susannah's wedding day. It wasn't going to be many weeks, days perhaps. I wanted Susannah to guess, before it was too late, I wanted her to talk to Alicia, to find out what had really happened from her Mother, she was, after all, the only one who could really tell her.

But she didn't pick up on it and my courage failed.

"How is he?"

Her mind was too much on Carl. She needed to know about him. She was not really listening to anything else.

"He's fine, as I said, doing well. He has published quite a bit and he's getting quite a reputation – he'll probably break into film soon – he is such a good communicator and he loves his subject. "I wondered if I was painting too bright a picture.

"Is he married?"

"No. He hasn't married – nor," I continued swiftly, "do I believe him to be living with anyone. I think he is 'unattached'."

Susannah said nothing, after a few minutes of gazing across the darkness towards the lights of Sandhey I left her to her thoughts.

"Kathleen really is dead. It's here in the paper." Susannah saw the notice in the newspaper at breakfast the next morning.

"Donaldson, Kathleen, (nee McNamara, previously Witherby) from West Kirby, Wirral, Cheshire," she paused for effect, then continued but Alicia was not listening, she had half turned towards the window: *"later moved to Grasmere, Cumberland, passed away peacefully at home on 14th December 1971 aged 56.*

A tired, small voice "I didn't realise she was so much older. I hate her so much, I've always hated her. I am so glad she is dead. She should have died years ago and then there wouldn't have been all this trouble."

Susannah had missed the defeat in Alicia's voice "Don't be a bitch mother beloved sister of Maureen, who's she? We never knew her did we?

"I knew her. I was her friend. She was my friend, at least I thought she was. How could she have been my friend when she was that woman's sister?"

Susannah didn't hear and continued reading.

"widow of Henry and wife of the late Arnold, mother to Carl" No flowers but enquiries via….."

Susannah stopped reading out loud. I remembered the wording of the funeral notice. I had written it with Carl over the phone. I remembered it gave an address – a local solicitor in Grasmere. We had deliberately not used Roberts and Jones.

I saw the look on Susannah's face – one of dawning recognition, hope, determination.

"I know where he is." She whispered.

Alicia saw the look in her daughter's face and just said, as if to herself, "Don't go to that boy."

I don't think Susannah even heard her as she was already out of the room.

She certainly didn't hear her mother's quiet last words to her "Please. Don't go. I need you here. I love you."

I didn't go to the Lakes that day. I had to stay at home.

Alicia was dead.

As Susannah drove off I turned round to Alicia. She was sitting up in her bed looking out of the window. "This made such a lovely nursery."

And she just died.

I sat with her for a few minutes, thinking of so many things and yet focussing on nothing. Our last real words together had been angry. I had only really told her how much I cared for her the previous night, and in anger, but she must have known. She had not told me how she felt about me, and she hadn't told Susannah – oh so many things she had not told her daughter.

I sat holding her hand looking at her dear face.

She was so much loved and yet it had never been enough, she had had so much talent and had used none of it, she had suffered so much pain.

And now she was gone.

I had to call Sandhey, Charles and Max needed to know, but first I called Grasmere, but I held out little hope that the young solicitor was going to be able to keep Carl and Susannah apart until I could get there. I would have to talk to Carl.

Carl, Maureen and I were supposed to be meeting for lunch at a local hotel. He had travelled up the previous day and I was driving up this Monday morning. We were then going to sort out all the myriad of things that can be sorted out after a death, papers needed signing, certificates to be obtained, there was so much running around – I had always had the idea that it was no bad thing, keeping, as it did, the bereaved's minds from their loss. Now it was just going to be a nightmare of logistics.

And it had started to snow.

I called the hotel and spoke briefly to Carl. I told him what had happened to Alicia and that Susannah was on her way to the Lakes, the weather was dreadful but there was no way I could stop her. She did not know that her mother had died.

I was surprised at how easily the words could be spoken.

"Carl, you will have to sort out your mother's affairs, Gordon at the solicitors will be able to do everything I could do for you. I'm sorry. I can't come up."

He seemed to take that in his stride.

"What radio station does she listen to in the car?"

"What on earth sort of question is that?"

"What radio station? I'll call them and get them to broadcast one of those emergency messages – you know the sort of thing, *dangerously ill, daughter must return home, believed to be driving north through Lancashire.* She might hear it and get back to you. You know that if she comes here I will have to see her and I really don't want to do that, not yet. It's not the right time to do that."

He was talking sense but I had to admit I hadn't a clue what radio station she might be listening to.

"I'll try the BBC anyway – they'll help."

In the end it was the weather that stopped her. I got a call from a phone box just south of Preston.

"Ted what should I do? It's snowing and the roads are dreadful. I think I'm stuck. She was crying with frustration and anger, but was able to give details of where she was.

"I'll get someone to come and get you. There's a chap from the office who lives not far away – he'll find you and get you into the safe and warm." I wasn't going to tell her then, when she was cold and alone.

So it was amongst concerned and sympathetic strangers that she heard the BBC announcement. She called me immediately and I told her it was too late – her mother was dead.

"I didn't tell you when you were on the road as I didn't want you to be worried and frightened – I wanted you to be with friends."

"I know Uncle Ted, thank you." I think the fact that she had called me Uncle again told more about how vulnerable she was feeling than anything else she could have said.

When she got back home and the doctor had been and Alicia taken away we sat at the table where only that morning we had all been reading the paper at breakfast.

I sat her down with a glass of brandy and began to talk about Carl.

I told her that I knew where he was, that if she really wanted I could put them in touch with each other, I told her how concerned he had been that morning when we had spoken, how he had tried to get news to her over the radio.

"But if he really wanted to see me he could, couldn't he?"

What answer could I give?

"Of course he could have been in touch with you at any time but he didn't when he thought you were happy without him.

"But he knew that wasn't true. And he was here when Joe – when Joe died."

"Perhaps he wants to wait until you are well again."

She argued that she was well, but the tears running effortlessly down her face showed that she was not.

"Susannah, my dear, you have been through so very much in the last few months. You have had so very much to deal with and been hurt and troubled so very deeply. Carl has had the good sense to stay away from you – he feels, and I believe quite rightly, that to come back into your life at this time would harm you far more than it would help."

"So I've got to pull myself together."

"No one's saying that, my dear. We are saying that you need some time to come to terms with everything. For a start," I tried to turn the conversation to more practical things, "you cannot stay here. You must go and stay at Sandhey. Max believes that would be the best thing. Monika can look after you until you are better able to set up your own house again, with your children."

Chapter Thirty-Six

Perhaps that is what life is like, years of routine punctuated by *events* that disrupt everything for short periods of time, changing people's directions, but not lasting long. And after the *events* of 1971 the next few years seemed to be a quiet time in the lives of the Donaldsons.

Susannah went back to live at Sandhey immediately after her mother's funeral, and she began to be more peaceful. Perhaps it was hearing Carl on the radio, seeing him and listening to the enthusiasm behind those programmes that led to her decision to go back to University. She was going to earn that good degree she had failed to get five years earlier. She had changed subjects – to History – and was going to study like she should have done before. Circumstances were not going to get in her way this time. For some reason she had determined on Sussex and, as soon as her application was accepted in April 1972 she spent all her time in Brighton.

Meanwhile her children grew older without her. She had not seen them since the birthday party in 1970, she didn't so much avoid them as make sure she was never in a situation where she would see them. They lived with a succession of mother's helps in the houses next to the Parrys. They had frequent visits from Monika and Charles. The Parrys didn't interfere – having made their point about the children being 'Parry Children' they seemed to be content as long as someone else paid.

Meanwhile, after Alicia's funeral, I got my life back together at the flat in Millcourt and concentrated on the business.

I had tried to avoid Carl's programmes when Alicia and Susannah were with me but now I made the effort to follow his career, watching his successful television series based on the battles of the Peninsula, listening to his participation in various quizzes on the Radio. He was doing well, juggling his development as popular communicator on television with his growing reputation in the academic world. He was also publishing fiction, historical novels which captured even more of the public to his enthusiasm for those times. They were going to film these, a well known actor was to star. Everything was going well for him.

I knew so much of what he was doing but direct contact was limited to Christmas and Birthday cards.

When, in July 1976, Susannah graduated Max wanted to mark the occasion. A party was held in the garden at Sandhey.

I stood in the brilliant sunshine of that long hot summer on the lawn of Sandhey that had seen so many family gatherings. Watching Susannah standing with champagne glass in hand, just as Alicia had stood on the afternoon of her daughter's wedding, I was struck by how much she was like her mother and how little there was left of the young girl who had made that disastrous marriage twelve years earlier.

The thought occurred to me that it could have been exactly the same glass.

She caught me looking at her and walked over.

"Am I like her?"

"Very"

"Is that a good thing?"

"Very"

She laughed. The years of study had changed her, she had lost the defeated, vulnerable, child-like quality that had hung around her throughout her marriage. She was no longer a victim.

"Ted, I haven't asked this for years – you know as well as I do why not – but how are the children?"

I laughed out loud, I knew she was going to ask me that so I had been to see them just the day before. Monika and Charles weren't the only people who had kept up the contact with them.

"What are you laughing at?" she was bewildered

"I just knew you would want to see them now."

"I didn't say that! I just asked how they were."

"But you do want to see them don't you?"

"I am just wondering how they are."

"Yes, of course you were 'just wondering'."

"Stop messing with me! I'm serious." She was laughing, a relaxed, confident laugh such as I had never heard from her.

I stopped joking.

"Yes, Susannah – it's about time you were serious about those children. They have not had a mother for 6 years. They have been brought up by nannies and they don't know what or who they are."

"You make it sound like it was my fault."

"Fault doesn't come into it. We're not talking 'fault' we're talking about what is best for those children of yours. Josie is nearly a teenager now – she's old enough to know she's been abandoned."

"She hasn't been abandoned! She's had the best possible care!"

"And if Charles and Monika hadn't visited them every week, if they hadn't given them birthday and Christmas presents every year – if they hadn't taken them away for holidays what do you think they would have been?"

"They haven't done all that?"

"Of course they have. Didn't you have any idea?"

"No."

"You are so like your mother, so like the worst bits of your mother!"

"What do you mean?"

"Your mother was the most beautiful woman I ever knew. No don't interrupt. She was beautiful, but she was also the most selfish and self-centred woman. Nothing existed if it wasn't in her life, if she hadn't a starring role in it. Just like you. You have had your eyes completely shut to everything and everyone since you started this course. You have been 'focussed' – that's the modern term for it isn't it? – focussed. Focussed to such an extent that the rest of the world can just take a running jump. Well we haven't all been idle while you have been somewhere else in your mind. We've been looking after your children, your brother, you. We've been making sure everything went well for you because sooner or later we knew you would grow up. Well, we're still waiting!"

I had said far too much – but yet still nothing like enough. I watched the shock on her face, hating myself for spoiling her big day, the day she had worked so hard for.

So yet again I left, hoping things would sort themselves out – a failing of mine that seemed always to cause more problems than it solved but which I couldn't correct.

I got a phone call from Max the next day.

Susannah had asked for a serious talk with him, and she then found out all the extended family had done for the children, all she owed him and Charles and Monika. She talked to them long and hard around that wretched kitchen table at Sandhey that had seen so much of the family history. She had learned of the childhood illnesses, the traumas, the broken bones, the Christmas presents, the way Josie acted as a little mother to the boys, how they always asked how their mummy was, "is she better?" "When is she coming to take them home?"

She then sat in the garden with Max and Monika, finding out all the little details of the family that she thought she had no feelings for looking through album after album of photographs that Monika had kept, for when she might need them. She went inside and asked to talk to Charles on his own, he told her how they knew she would pull through someday – that they all understood how awful it had all been, how Monika had always told them that one day 'Mummy' would be better.

"You've kept them together."

"Yes, we have. We've kept them together for you."

"Ouch! Have I really been that selfish?"

"Yes. Don't expect me not to tell the truth now you're strong enough to take it."

"That's a compliment isn't it?"

"Probably."

"Will you go and talk to Monika?" Charles knew there was much Monika wanted to tell this new Susannah.

"Let me tell you something you don't know." Monika was sitting with Susannah on the sea wall at the bottom of the garden, mugs of iced tea in hand. Two hours later they were sitting on that wall with their arms around each other, both crying.

It must be a difficult thing, at such an age, to realise that there are people whose feelings and thoughts matter as much as your own. In those two hours Susannah learned that she had more to look forward to than many, that she had more to be thankful for than most and that she had a wonderful future ahead – if only she would face it.

"I'm so sorry."

"No need to be sorry Susannah, just understand. Just understand through all your book-learning – that there are people who love with no return, who love where there is no reason, who love through thick and thin, who care for other people simply because they are other people with feelings and who are hurt."

After the phone call from Max I called Carl. I had been calling him regularly every month to keep him up to date with Susannah's progress and the children. We spoke frequently enough for him not to think too much of it, but this time he knew exactly what the call was about.

"She did it didn't she?"

"Yes, Carl, she did. She did what she should have done years ago. She got her First. They've offered her a job doing research."

"I'm so pleased for her. She deserves something to go right for her."

"She still wants you, Carl. She hasn't ever forgotten. She won't ever forget."

"Did anyone ever tell her?"

"No. No one ever did."

"I won't marry her, Ted. You know that. I can't have children. It wouldn't be fair."

"I think she has enough children Carl, I don't think that's a problem."

"Is she back with them?"

"Practically."

"I'm glad."

"Are you ever going to do anything with your life, Carl? Other than work I mean. Are you ever going to do anything if you can't have Susannah?"

"Nope. Her or nobody – always has been, always will be. But sometimes I almost give up hope that she will need me as much as I need her. She's got to need me – not because of desperation or pain or that she had no one else – but simply because she's on top of her life and thinks I would make it even better. Do you see what I mean?"

"I believe I do."

Susannah came to see me at Millcourt that evening. She told me what had happened, she asked how much I had known – I had shrugged – and I listened as she asked question after question.

We sat into the night, talking, sitting on the same window seat that she had played on as a child with brother Charles and Carl.

Now was the time. I could put it off no longer – nor did I need to.

"Susannah, when do you think things all started to go wrong with your life?" I had changed the subject hesitantly but she answered immediately and with force. "That Sunday, when they told me Carl was my brother. That was the day I met Joe, that was the day my life headed off at a tangent from the route it should have taken."

"Did you mean to kill yourself that afternoon?"

"No. I don't think so. I wanted to hurt Daddy. I wanted him to feel pain like I was feeling – the loss of someone I loved. I wanted him to feel that. I hated what he had done to our lives. He had moved Carl and I about like we were pawns in a chess game...."

"Rather like you've done with your children....."

"Shit. Yes. Probably. But no, I didn't want to die."

"What went wrong next?"

"Getting pregnant I suppose. It was pretty much downhill from then on."

"So the children were always the problem? Without them you would still be free? The children tied you into a life you didn't want? Is that what you're saying?"

"Probably. Maybe that's why I didn't want to be part of their lives."

"Now if I were to say that is exactly how your mother felt what would you think?"

"What do you mean?"

"If I were to say that your mother felt as trapped by you and Charles as you do with Josie, Bill, Al and Jack would that make you think about her – and them – differently?"

"But how could it – how could she feel as trapped by us? She had all the money, the husband and everything."

"Susannah do look at the facts. Your mother was several months pregnant when she married Arnold." I didn't say "your father".

"Charles was born when they had only been married for 6 months. They married on her 21st birthday because her father refused to give consent. You can say this for Arnold – he accepted your choice of Joe without demur – despite all the problems that he foresaw."

"So they had to get married – so what? That was happening all the time during the war. I was born well after that wasn't I? You're not saying that Daddy forced himself on Mummy as Joe forced himself on me are you?" That was the first time I believe she had spoken objectively of the difficulties in her marriage.

"When Joe forced himself on you why didn't you ask for help? Charles, Max, me – we would all have helped you. You know that we would have done. If you'd asked."

"It isn't rape when you're married – you've got to do it haven't you? The man has the right doesn't he?"

"Legally perhaps, but I don't believe morally. But we digress. Your mother married Arnold because she wanted to escape her parents – that is a story for another day but believe me it is true – she married Arnold to escape her father and because Charles was on the way, probably Charles was on the way *because* she wanted to escape her father."

"I can understand that."

I nodded in recognition of her interruption.

"She learned very soon after her marriage that it had been a dreadful mistake. Arnold was not right for her. They had some dreadful times together. His mother was clinging in the extreme and, of course, he had been having a long standing affair and was probably in love with someone else."

"Kathleen?"

"Exactly. Kathleen. He continued his affair with her, right under your mother's nose – placing her in more and more embarrassing and humiliating positions – the whole town knew what he was up to. Your Mother was very brave. Then Kathleen got pregnant."

"Carl."

"Yes, Carl. He was the child of Kathleen and Arnold." Still I would not say "your father".

"What they didn't know at the time, and no one knew for certain until after he'd died was that Kathleen and Arnold were brother and sister."

"Shit."

"Arnold's father, George, had kept a number of local women – many said his wife was frigid and refused to let him touch her after the conception of Arnold. Anyway – one of these kept women was Kathleen's mother. She could easily have been having other affairs – she was an attractive woman and I don't think George was particularly strict with his women – but she believed George was Kathleen's father but didn't tell her until it was too late."

I waited for the family tree to form in her mind.

"So …. Carl's parent's were brother and sister. Oh poor Carl! How long has he known? He must hurt so much!"

"He's known for about five years."

She looked so concerned, so hurt for him.

"Who's helped him through it? I mean it must have been such a shock. It must make him feel so… oh I can't think. He must seem so worthless. No I don't mean worthless but.. Oh poor Carl." she finished, unable to find the right words.

"I think it has made him feel very lonely. Indeed. He says he will remain unmarried as he feels he must never have children."

"So what happened?" She wanted to know everything now.

"Arnold arranged for Kathleen to marry his cousin Henry, a pleasant but weak man who had lost his fiancée and parents at the end of the war. Henry, I truly believe, never doubted that Carl was his son."

I continued, thinking there was no way out now – it had all to come out.

"Can you imagine what your mother felt? Her husband's mistress was having a child? He spent no less time with her, continuing his affair after she was married and the four of them went away, at Arnold's instigation, for Christmas 1945.

"Henry and a pregnant Kathleen, Arnold and your mother."

"Christmas 1945 – that must have been about the time I was conceived."

"It was New Year's Night. Your mother went to bed early leaving the others drinking downstairs. She was raped by Henry." I ignored Susannah's face and continued "Henry and Arnold had been so drunk they couldn't remember what had happened. But Alicia knew. Henry is your father, Susannah – not Arnold."

The room was quiet for a few minutes as we both sipped our drinks.

"So I'm the child of rape, just like my little ones."

"Your mother never wanted you, I'm afraid to say, but she wouldn't have an abortion. She left the house as soon after you were born as she could."

"History does repeat itself."

"I'm very afraid it does."

"It wasn't their fault, was it? Just as it wasn't mine?"

"No Susannah, it is not your fault and it was not theirs."

"Can I have another drink?"

I got two more large brandies and sat down beside her on that window seat looking out over the golf links.

"I know what you're going to ask now." I said

"Why did she say we were brother and sister?"

"She was trapped by the lie, once told she could not rescind it. The longer it went on, the less she felt able to tell the truth. I came close several times but never had the courage."

"Once a lie starts it isn't easy to kill is it?" After a few moments pause she continued, "You loved her very much didn't you?"

There was no answer to that. In any case it hadn't really been a question.

"I don't think she ever wanted to tell you because that would mean you would be with Carl. Remember she hated Kathleen, she was humiliated by her and by your father – how could she bear your being happy with the child of that union?"

Another rhetorical question neither of us tried to answer.

We drank our brandies – the lights shining across the golf course reminded me of other nights we had talked like this.

"I have always loved him, you know."

"Have you loved him or the idea of him?"

She left the question in the air but I persevered.

"Do you even know him?"

"I see him on the television, I read all his books and his articles. I know what he was like."

"13 years ago"

"Why did no one tell me?" There was no anger in her voice, no self-pity or recrimination – simply curiosity.

"At first, of course, we didn't know. But when we did we didn't say anything as we believed you to be happy. You had a lovely house, lovely children. Charles and I, because it was really only the two of us who could tell you, truly thought you were happy. We couldn't upset your marriage in that way. And then, when we discovered how desperately unhappy you were we couldn't see that Carl would be right for you. You were so ..."

"unstable." She found the word I couldn't.

"Unfortunately so, my dear, you were very unhappy for a long time. Carl would not, could not, have helped you. How could we risk your being rejected by him, we didn't know how supportive he would be, we could not know whether or not he loved you..."

"enough to take me on in the state I was in."

"Indeed. It wasn't until your mother died that we realised how strong he is and how much he still loves you but by then we knew why he felt he could never be a real husband to anyone."

"That still leaves five years!"

"Five years isn't so long a time really, Susannah, when you love someone. You will wait. You will wait forever if that is what is required. You just wait until the moment comes and is right. Carl knew how much you wanted to prove yourself. He knew you needed to get this degree, he knew you had to do it, if he had come into your life you wouldn't and you would have resented him. He was not going to interfere with your studies, he wanted you to find your own self. I don't think he knows how to cope with loving you and the problems he faces because of his parents. He doesn't want to hurt you. He never has, he has tried to protect you from more hurt."

I wondered if she remembered the times we had come close to talking like this in the past, and whether she understood why I had always backed away.

"You're going to have to make the first move, Susannah. I think you really are strong enough now to give him the help he needs. He needs you to want to get to know him the way he is now. He's been the strong one for years – he needs to know you want him as he is now not as he was years ago when you were both very different people."

As I said it I realised the truth in what I was saying.

I had always assumed Carl was the strong one and he would save Susannah, but it was the other way around. Carl needed Susannah's strength.

"Do you really want to meet him again or are you happy just having known him in the past? Do you want to risk being disillusioned or do you want to move on?"

"I want to meet him *and* move on."

It seemed like the right answer.

"If you're sure I'll see what I can do."

"I am."

I called Carl the next morning. He was surprised to hear from me so soon after our last conversation so I explained that, after all these years and after all the procrastination and weakness, I had finally told Susannah everything she needed to know.

"Everything?"

"Everything."

"Even about my parents?"

"Absolutely everything."

"She's OK?" He seemed so tentative and so vulnerable.

"She seemed to take it all in her stride. I believe your Susannah may finally have got rid of her demons and may actually be able to help you get rid of some of yours.

"Should I..?"

"Yes"

"I'll be there in four hours."

And he was.

Finale

It was over 22 years since Carl had driven from Cambridge to get together, at last, with his Susie.

22 years isn't so long as you grow older. You look at a pair of shoes, a shirt, a tie and think "I bought that 22 years ago" or you meet someone in the street and explain to your companion "I first met them over 22 years ago."

22 years is not that long at all.

November 29th 1998 we were all gathered again in the study of Sandhey.

It would have been Alicia's 78th birthday, her 57th wedding anniversary.

It was the day we all gathered to hear the reading of Max's will.

The house hadn't changed much in the intervening years. There was no building around, none of the new roads came anywhere near the old house. The sand dunes and rocks were protected, the golf course inviolable – nothing could ever happen to Sandhey or to Hilbre.

But we had all changed.

All the members of the old family were present. Charles, now 56 years old, stood with his hand resting on the back of Monika's chair, still protective of her. Monika, nearly 70 years old now, looked the archetypical *hausfrau*, grey hair tied tightly in a bun behind her round head, apron wrapped around her now ample frame.

Carl, 6 years younger than his half brother, was just as tall and distinguished, his grey hair was longer, thicker and tied in a pony-tail at the nape of his tanned neck, his eyes were darker but there was a definite resemblance between them. Carl stood with his arm resting around the shoulders of Susannah, his collaborator and life long love – practically the same age, she still had her own dark wavy hair but her figure was filling out; 'matronly' was how I could best describe it.

They were very comfortable with each other and I believed that bringing them together was perhaps the best thing I had ever had a hand in. Their colleagues at the university and at the filming companies had given up asking them why they never married – they were obviously so happy with each other it didn't matter. All the gossip columnists assumed they were.

Susannah's children were there also. Josie, nearly 35; Jack, 31; Al, 30 and Bill, the youngest, 29.

There were also the men and women who had joined this family over the intervening years.

I began reading the codicil, explaining that the main reading would follow immediately after. It was dated just two months earlier.

I, Max Fischer, being of as much sound mind as I have been at any time in my life wish to make the following clear, to you all, you who have been a part of my life for so long.

I begin with a quotation Exodus chapter 34 Verse 7

Keeping mercy for thousands, forgiving iniquity and transgression and sin – and that will by no means clear the guilty – visiting the iniquity of the fathers upon the children, and upon the children's children, unto the third and to the fourth generation."

I can see you all now, pondering that quotation.

Well Charles, Carl, Susannah you are the second generation. Arnold and Alicia, Maureen and Kathleen, they were the first to suffer from the actions of their parents.

Susannah, your children are the third generation. I know you and Carl have given them all the love they could possibly need to end the sequence. If God wills it the pain will end now.

For you all I would say 'Do not judge them too harshly for things they could not know'. Much of this is not your responsibility. Do not blame yourselves.

I paused, looking around at all the serious faces. How many of them remembered Arnold, or Alicia. How many knew where Kathleen and Maureen fitted into their family's history? Some of them would have had no idea what Max was talking about. I continued.

"The first and most important bequest for you all is this book of Ted's. Read it carefully, learn from it. Learn to forgive your elders their mistakes for they make them either unwittingly or through weakness.

My second bequest is an explanation.

When Monika came into our lives it was not by accident, luck, chance, fate, whatever you want to call it but it was not an accident. I had spent a long time trying to find her.

When I was a student in Vienna, before the war, I occasionally visited my sister and brother-in-law on their farm. I loved my sister dearly but had little affection for the man she had married and felt sorry for their children. They had two sons and a daughter. The sons were considerably older than Rebecca and she had a lonely childhood.

On one occasion we were all having lunch around the big table by a roaring log fire. My brother-in-law and the boys were complaining about the land and how stony and steep it was and how dark it was throughout the winter when the sun never rose above the mountain on the other side of the valley.

So I had told them about a land that had no steep mountains or lakes, a land where they spoke a soft and gentle language, where people were free, where they got their food from the sea and the animals grazed the lush grass rather than being used to plough the land. This place was always sunny and the people were always happy. Rebecca had wanted me to draw a picture so I had drawn an outline of Brittany on the only piece of paper I could find in the kitchen of that farmhouse, an envelope, and had written some place names on it – "Brittany", "Audierne".

That envelope was used by my sister to hold Rebecca's papers when they had escaped to France. She had kept it by her as they moved from place to place as the war took its course. On the day she died she called her daughter to her and gave it to her, telling her daughter never, ever, to lose it. As her mother lay dead beside her Monika spent hours sewing the envelope into the hem of her dress.

In the years she was alone, as the war drew to a close, she had survived; her movements unrecorded, her actions unnoticed by anyone in the world. She was as near to invisible as she could be – a homeless, stateless individual in a chaotic world.

When she was particularly lonely and frightened she would remember her mother's envelope and take comfort that it was still sewn inside her dress. It was a ritual for her that whenever she obtained new clothes she would cut the crumpled and dirty envelope out of the old and sew it into the new. Every time she would look at the familiar lines and squiggles, they always made her feel safe even though she had no idea what they represented.

In the spring of 1947 she had fallen in with an English soldier. He gave her a new dress. As she was transferring her envelope to the new hem he tried to take it from her but she wouldn't let him see it. When he eventually persuaded her to show it to him he stared at the faded and barely visible shapes, holding the envelope one way then another. He was a kind man, with daughters her age of his own back in Newcastle. He told her he was not going to steal her envelope, and asked if she wanted to know what the markings meant.

*"It's a map." He told her. "I can just make it out. It's a map of Brittany –
that's a part of France about a hundred miles from here. There's a town marked on
it. It looks like 'Audierne'."*

So he had taken her there.

*I had always wished that I, instead of her Father, had been the one responsible for
her safety. I like to flatter myself that I would have made a better job of it – but I
could not have improved on the person she became.*

*Monika, I have loved you as a father might for all your life. Your real name is
Rebecca Rebmann. Your mother was my sister. You are my dear niece – but I could
never tell you for all the memories I knew it would bring up to mention it. As we grew
older together I knew your knowing our relationship could not make us any fonder of
each other. So I let it be.*

*You mother's grandfather, our father's father, was a jew. It was a close enough
relationship in those times for it to be too dangerous to stay in Austria. Your father
hated the connection, your brothers hated you because of it that is why they treated you
as they did. They left for the army the day you and your mother left Austria as
refugees.*

*So you see, you are the one person who has broken the sequence. You were the
second generation and you did not pass the evil of hatred on to a third. You have no
sin to pass on. Your love for every one of the people in this room has gone beyond
family, gone beyond what 'should be' to what 'can be'. Monika, we have all learned
from you.*

*Now, my dear children, Ted will read the formal part of my Will and the
disposition of my assets.*

*I hope you will each understand why I have done what I have done. To help you
understand read the words I have asked him to write.*

They will explain everything.

This is the first chapter of

Walking Alone

Book 2 of the Iniquities Trilogy, which
will be published shortly.

The three figures presented a clear illustration of the downside of
international travel.

They must have been very tired as the middle-aged woman,
although somewhat dishevelled, looked far too smart to be used to
sitting on kerbstones with her feet in the gutter. She yawned as she
ran her fingers through her hair.

"When I do that I get told off," her daughter complained,
continuing in a voice mimicking her mother "*You should always
put your hand in front of your mouth when you yawn.*" She was
only silenced by a look from her father.

It was lunchtime but Speke Airport had a middle-of-the-
night feel about it as no more flights were expected to arrive or
leave for some hours. They had had every opportunity to know
this as they had had only the arrivals and departures screen to
entertain them as they had waited for their bags to arrive on the
carousel. What other passengers there had been on the flight up
from Heathrow had had only hand luggage and had all passed
through the hall before any luggage had appeared.

Their 'middle-of-the-night' feeling was emphasised when
they finally wheeled their luggage trolleys outside to be met by an
empty road with no sign of a cab waiting for a fare.

They had stood for a while by the Taxi sign before deciding
it was to be a long wait and making themselves a bit more
comfortable. Holly perched herself on top of the cases on the

trolley, Mary sat on the kerb, her legs stretched out in front of her and Matt tried to put as much of his weight on the handle of the trolley as he could without tipping it, and Holly, onto the pavement.

"At home there'd be hundreds of cabs." The young girl wound her long hair around her fingers and sucked on it.

"Don't do that! How many times do I have to tell you?"

"A cab will be along soon just hang on in there a few minutes more. We're on the last leg." Matt tried to sound encouraging but there was no sign of any vehicle let alone a taxi cab.

"At least it's not raining." Mary had been expecting it always to be raining in England, even in July, but the sun was shining and it was pleasantly warm.

"What time is it?" asked Holly "I'm ready for a shower, though I bet they don't have such things as showers over here."

"Of course they'll have showers." Matt sounded rather more confident than he felt. Most of the hotels he had stayed at in Europe hadn't had showers. He hoped that the hotel he had been assured was the best in Liverpool would live up to its reputation. "You'll be very comfortable here, Sir," the reservations clerk had said "we have lots of Americans staying here. We're used to your special requirements." *Whatever that means* Matt had thought at the time. Still a shower shouldn't be too much to ask.

Holly was not only tired, she was sulking because she didn't want to be in England.

She hadn't wanted to leave her friends and her school to come to England for God knows how long – a few weeks, a few months, years, forever? Especially Paul. She hadn't wanted to leave him when she'd only just managed to get him to notice her. She did wonder if it was her leaving for England that had got him interested in the end. She was determined to write him every week, as she had promised. She was pretty sure he would write to her.

"I bet they only have bathtubs. I hate them. Why did we have to come?"

"You'll be OK tomorrow, right now you're just tired. You always act way below your age when you're tired." Her father had a way of putting her down that she could never argue against.

There was no way either of her parents would have answered Holly's question and explain why Matt had uprooted his family.

The simple answer was that her mother had been persuaded

to leave her job in Boston to take up a visiting lecturing job at Liverpool University in their Department of Statistics and Computational Maths. But it was more complicated than that. It had all been Matt's idea and Mary felt he had never really explained why he had wanted to uproot the family and move to England.

It took over half an hour before a cab finally appeared. It was small and an undistinguished shade of pale green but at least they could finally be on their way into the city. The driver got out speaking loudly and quickly in what sounded to them all like a foreign language.

"I think he's telling us not to worry – he'll fit us and all our luggage in the cab." translated Matthew. "I'm not so sure."

As they drove towards the city the driver kept saying something what was probably an apology but none of the occupants understood what he was saying.

"Can you speak slow?" Matthew had decided we must try to communicate with the driver.

"Sorry wack! Keep forgerring you don' speak English you know warr I mean like you being yanks an all you know warr I mean like!"

"Is that English? I'll never understand anyone." Holly moaned and slouched against the door.

Matthew and Mary settled back as best they could amongst the bags on the back seat.

"He's driving so fast."

Mary was used to more gentle speeds and the way they were being driven was almost the last straw. She felt like she would soon break down and cry. "Oh Matt are we doing the right thing?"

"It'll be fine Mary, it'll all work out OK you'll see."

"Sure, it'll all be OK." She didn't sound convinced.

A few minutes later she spoke again, hoping that Holly couldn't hear her with the noise of the car and the driver who was still talking to no one in particular. "I'd thought that England would just be like home only wetter and, just, somehow, greyer. I thought the people would be just like us, and the language just the same. But it's all so different."

Holly had regained some of her energy when they arrived at the hotel.

She ran up the steps, turned round and looked out at the

crowded city streets, her tiredness and bad mood forgotten. "Wow. Liverpool. This is so neat!"

"Tomorrow, Holly, you can explore tomorrow. Meanwhile take this and stay with the bags and wait while I check in." Matt, having got his family across the Atlantic, had just about had enough. He was ready for a shower and bed.

As they walked across the foyer Holly walked straight into a good-looking young man.

She noticed him because he was exactly as he had hoped English men would be, with long dark brown hair tied in a pony tail and wearing a black polo necked sweater with a brown leather jacket and denim jeans.

"I beg your pardon."

"Oh no, Holly got in *your* way – it's not your fault at all." Mary knew she was in England when people apologised for things that were not their fault.

"Mom! He walked into me. It wasn't my fault. But he was kinda smart don't you think?"

The young man didn't hear her as he continued talking animatedly to his older companion, engrossed in their own business as they left through the revolving door.

As Matt had a bath Mary unpacked, bemoaning the lack of drawer and cupboard space. She sat down on the side of the bed, hit by the realisation that there was no going back, for a year at least they were stuck here, in Liverpool. She repeated to herself the question her daughter had asked earlier "Did we *have* to come?"